KRISTINE SMITH

CODE OF CONDUCT

AVON BOOKS, INC.
1350 Avenue of the Americas
New York, New York 10019

Copyright © 1999 by Kristine C. Smith
Cover art by Jean Pierre Targete
Inside cover author photo by Barbara Keisman Photography
Published by arrangement with the author
Library of Congress Catalog Card Number: 99-94994
ISBN: 0-380-80783-1
www.avonbooks.com/eos

First Avon Eos Printing: November 1999

AVON EOS TRADEMARK REG. U.S. PAT. OFF. AND IN OTHER COUNTRIES, MARCA REGISTRADA, HECHO EN U.S.A.

Printed in the U.S.A.

WCD   10 9 8 7 6 5 4 3 2 1

CODE OF CONDUCT

Jani looked up just as Lucien Pascal, dressed in full Service winter camouflage, leaned over the log. "You have a lot of nerve, coming here," she said as she sat up, rocks clasped in still-buried hands. She jerked her head toward the house. "You know you've been seen."

"Depends who's watching." Lucien's breath fogged the clear humidifier mask. He smiled, which wasn't necessarily a good sign, and reached a mottled-white arm out to her. "Could you come with me, please?"

"I'd rather not."

Lucien's arm hung in midair. What did his eyes, obscured by darkened goggles, look like now? Jani knew she'd see more warmth in the rocks she held.

"I wish I could say you had a choice," he said, his voice muffled by the mask. "But you don't."

Acknowledgments

A first book is usually the most difficult to write, firstly, because you're still trying to find your sea legs, and secondly, because you've no assurance whatsoever that what you've spent years producing will go anywhere other than a box in the cellar.

I've been lucky enough to have had help from many people in assisting me through the difficulties. In particular, I'd like to thank Katharine Eliska Kimbriel, who helped keep me on track, and my parents, Gordon and Charlotte Smith, whose love and support helped keep me going.

The visible aspects of the condition, it is believed, first manifested themselves during a stressful period in the patient's life. Therefore, the mild agitation that commonly precedes the acute phase, although evident, was easily ascribable to the patient's augmentation or other, more mundane, causes.

—Internal Communication, Neoclona/Seattle, Shroud, J., Parini, V., concerning Patient S-1

CHAPTER 1

The frigid morning dampness seeped through Jani's weatherall as she hurried out of the charge lot. She jammed the notes from her crack-of-dawn meeting into the side pocket of her duffel; as she did, she quickly surveyed the scene behind her. Rain-slick skimmers hovered beside boxy charge stations. Trickle-charge lights glimmered like distant stars. A single streetlight bathed everything in a cold blue sheen. No movement in the ice-light. No sound.

Jani took a step. Stopped. She could feel eyes follow her, could sense their probing like a skin-crawl across her shoulders. She turned.

A few meters away, a feral cat regarded her from its perch atop a discarded shipping crate. It stared at her for a few moments, then poured to the ground and vanished into an alley. Seconds later, Jani heard the scatter of garbage, followed by a strangled squeak.

Sounds familiar. The poor mouse. It probably never knew what hit it. Jani could sympathize. Her meeting had gone much the same way.

It's like everyone's forgotten Whalen's Planet exists, girly. Commercial traffic at the docks is down sixty percent in the last two weeks. That's six-oh.

She trotted down a side street that led to the main thoroughfare. Her right knee locked as she turned the corner, and she stumbled against a pair of mutually supportive inebriates who had emerged from one of NorthPort's many bars.

One of the drunks shouted as Jani disentangled herself and

3

hurried away. Something about how her limp made her ass wiggle. She looked over her shoulder, caught glimpses of brightly colored ship patches and a slack-jawed leer. She felt the heat creep up her neck and kept moving.

She entered the lobby of a hostel that catered to merchant-fleet officers, tossing a wave to the desk clerk as she hurried to the holoVee alcove. Several employees already sat on the floor in front of the display screen, their positions carefully gauged to allow them a clear view of the front desk.

On the lookout for the manager. Jani kept quiet until she entered within range of the holoVee's soundshielding. She knew an unauthorized break when she saw one. "Is this it?"

One of the cleaners nodded. "Hi, Cory," she said without looking up. "It's the CapNet broadcast. It's just getting started."

Jani did a quick mental roll call of the small group, counting faces, uniforms. She didn't know their names—she tried to avoid the complication of names whenever possible. "Where's the garage guy?"

"He's still out sick," the cleaner said. "Should be back tomorrow. He'll be mad he missed this." The young woman grinned. "I'll tell him you asked about him. He thinks you jam."

Jani responded with her "Cory" smile. Quiet. Closed. A smile whose owner would blush and keep walking. She leaned against a planter and surveyed with satisfaction the lack of fuss that greeted her arrival. Yes, Cory Sato, documents technician, had settled quite nicely in NorthPort over the last six months. Jani Kilian had never seemed farther away.

Until her morning meeting.

Business has dropped over the side these past two weeks, girly. NUVA-SCAN annex won't answer our calls. Even the Haárin are complaining. But you wouldn't know anything about that, would you?

An overwrought voice interrupted Jani's troubled meditation. "A great honor is being paid the Commonwealth," the CapNet reporter gushed, "opening a new and exciting chapter in human-idomeni relations!"

Spoken like someone who has no idea what she's talking

about, Jani thought as she watched members of the Commonwealth Cabinet walk out onto the sheltered stage that had been erected in front of the Prime Minister's palatial Main House. Steam puffed from their mouths. A few of the coatless ministers shivered in their formal, color-coded uniforms. Chicago in winter looked even less hospitable than NorthPort, if that was possible.

Treasury Minister Abascal, ever-flushed face glowing in lurid contrast to his gold tunic, trundled to the podium "to say a few words."

"Where's the ambassador?" someone grumbled.

"He doesn't come out till later—you want the poor old bastard to freeze to death?"

"Never get to see him at this rate." One of the day-shift waiters checked his timepiece. "All fourteen ministers gonna talk—it'll be hours."

"Not all fourteen," said the restaurant hostess. "Van Reuter's not there."

Really? Jani studied the rows of faces, looking for the one she knew. Had known. Long ago "Too bad," she said. "He's the best speaker of the bunch."

"You like him?" The waiter glanced at Jani over his shoulder and sneered. "He's a Family boy nance."

"He knows the idomeni," Jani replied. "That's more than you can say for the rest of them."

"You don't see him much since his wife died," the hostess said. "Poor man."

"You hear about him, though," the waiter muttered. "Nance."

On-screen, Abascal finished to scattered applause and gave way to Commerce Minister al-Muhammed. Jani leaned forward, straining to hear the commentary over the buzz of multiple conversations. Commerce controlled trade and transport schedules—maybe something al-Muhammed said would shed light on the slowdown around Whalen.

"Is al-Muhammed the 'A' in NUVA or the 'A' in SCAN?" someone piped, drowning out the minister's voice.

Oh blow! Jani shouldered her bag and walked through the middle of the huddle. "Al-Muhammed's the 'A' in SCAN," she said, bumping the speaker in the back of his head with her knee.

"He's another nance," griped the waiter.

"Cory, I thought you wanted to see this," someone called after her. "You'll miss the ambassador."

"I have to go. I'll catch it somewhere else." Somewhere quieter. She should have known better than to try to watch the program with others. Some things needed to be studied in private. Pondered. Mulled.

We've officially reopened relations with the idomeni. Jani rubbed her stomach, which had begun to ache. *Wonderful.* She walked past buildings of black-and-yellow thermal scanbrick toward NorthPort's Government Hall. The elegant twelve-story edifice loomed over all like a stern but forgiving patriarch, offering numerous types of guidance to his wayward children. Audit assistance from External Revenue Outreach. Documents counseling from the Commerce and Treasury Ministry annexes. By all appearances, family relations appeared very close.

Appearances, as the old saying went, could be deceiving.

Why you always hang about with the nances at Guv Hall, girly? What goes on there so interesting you need to see it every day?

She increased her pace as she headed out of the business district, monitoring her stride in shop windows and mirrorglazed brick. She had only become aware of the hitch in her walk over the past couple of months, and had attributed it to a combination of the NorthPort weather and a cheap mattress.

Among other things. Jani took a step. *Right foot down.* Another. *Left foot . . . down.* She had to assume that. She hadn't much sensation in her left leg. Or her left arm. The lack of feeling sometimes made quick movement an adventure, but she maneuvered pretty well for a half-animandroid patch job. *And my ass does not wiggle*—she glanced at her reflection—*not much, anyway.*

Block after block fell behind as she tried to walk off her growing apprehension. She passed warehouses, long-term skimmer charge lots, then a three-hundred-meter stretch of sand and scrub before coming to the houses.

The facades of the one- and two-story polystone homes

would have appeared familiar to most humans, but a careful observer would have noticed the subtle alterations. Smaller, fewer windows. No doors opening out to the street. Blank walls facing the human side of town. *For humanish ways are strange ways, and godly idomeni avert their eyes.*

The low clouds opened. Cold rain splattered down. Jani yanked the hood of her weatherall up over her head, but not before looking around to see if she was being observed. She wouldn't be welcomed here. The made-sect Haárin, like their more disciplined born-sect counterparts, preferred that their humanish neighbors keep their distance.

Except when it comes to business. The Haárin were non-violent criminals and other idomeni social anomalies, their manufactured sect the pit into which the born-sects dumped their misfits. Even though Jani understood the Haárin better than most, she still couldn't be sure whether they settled on human worlds because they enjoyed aggravating their governing Council or because they actually liked the neighborhood. They definitely enjoyed learning concepts like float-rebound accounting. They liked dealing, and possessed a disrespect for Commonwealth rules and regs that was almost colonial in its fervor.

They're probably all at the gathering hall, waiting for Tse-cha's speech. The reopening of formal diplomatic relations between the Commonwealth and the Shèrá worldskein, and the subsequent reevaluation of trade and taxation laws, concerned them as much as it did Jani's bosses in the Merchants' Association.

I foresee busy times ahead for documents technicians. Jani squinted as the rain pelted harder and thick fog wended around homes and down the empty street. Then a shadowed movement in the murky distance caught her eye; her stomach clenched as it always did when she saw a NorthPort Haárin. Their born-sect forebears had been Vynshàrau and Pathen, and the strains had remained undiluted. The approaching Haárin was rope-muscled, slender, and two meters tall. His yellow-orange skin, which screamed *jaundice* to humans, in idomeni reality marked the races that originated in Shèrá's desert regions.

It's only Genta. Jani's anxiety subsided. The shuttle dealer walked toward her with long, loose-limbed strides. His dark green overrobe clung wetly to his matching belted shirt and trousers, the hem catching on the fasteners of his knee-high boots. Clothing drenched, fine brown hair plastered to his scalp, the Haárin appeared completely at ease. With his narrow shoulders, age-grooved jowls, and wide-spaced yellow eyes, he bore more than a passing resemblance to a bored cheetah.

"Nìa Chaw-ree." Genta crossed an arm over his chest in greeting. His right arm, palm facing inward. A sign of regard, if not respect. "You ar-re noth ath a holoVee, watching speeches? That is wher-re all idomeni ar-re, watching speeches." The English words tumbled from barely moving lips, all trilled r's and fuzzed hard consonants. "Insthead, you ar-re her-re in the rain."

"Yes, ní Genta—I don't like speeches," Jani replied as she returned Genta's greeting gesture. *And I have some nerves to walk off.* But a Haárin wouldn't know a nerve if it reared up and bit him in the ass, so no use mentioning that. "Why aren't you in the gathering hall? Tsecha's born Vynshàrau—they've always been friends of Haárin. You might like what he has to say."

Genta held a spindle-fingered hand to his face and brushed water from his hairless cheeks. His stare pierced Jani. She, of all people, should have been used to it by now, but the direct gaze of idomeni eyes, dark irises surrounded by more lightly colored sclera, could still disconcert. Looking strangers in the eye was taboo for all born-sect idomeni, but the NorthPort Haárin were adopting the custom as a matter of good business. The fact that it rattled the hell out of most humans had nothing to do with it. Of course not.

"I did not wait for Vynshàrau to tell me to live with humanish," Genta said, "and I do not need what Vynshàrau says now to work with humanish." Like all his fellow worldmen, he became much more intelligible when he had a point to make. "NìRau Tsecha is not for Haárin. He is not for Vynshàrau, or even for idomeni. He is for something *here*"—he thumped the middle of his stomach, where most idomeni believed the soul resided— "and to fight for such does not extend GateWay rights or alter contract law." With a distracted gesture of departure, he started back down the street.

"It will be bad for business," he continued, his rumbling voice deadened by the fog. "Bad, as it was before. Even now it starts—where are all the ships these past weeks? No good can come from this. No good." With that, Genta disappeared into the swallowing mist, leaving Jani alone in the rain.

Eventually, she returned to the human side of town. She wandered from storefront to storefront, finally joining a small crowd that had gathered in front of a communications shop. Every holoVee screen in the window contained the image of Prime Minister Cao.

"And now, fellow ministers, distinguished guests, ladies and gentlemen," Cao paused, drawing out the moment, "it is my honor and my privilege to introduce His Excellency, ambassador of the Shèrá worldskein, of the Vynshàrau and of all idomeni peoples—"

"Sects," Jani muttered.

"—Ègri nìRau Tsecha." Cao looked off to the side and extended her arm. "Excellency!"

Jani sensed the tension around her as, on the screen, a familiar face came into view. Familiar not because of the Genta-like skin tone, the same gold eyes and long, straight nose, but because of something deeper, something older. She felt wet cold wind brush her face and imagined it drier, hotter. Instead of damp mingled with the acid bitterness of skimmer cells, the sweet odor of lamptree blooms filled the air. The crowd surrounding her towered above her, wore flowing overrobes, and spoke in lilting rises and falls.

Eighteen years ago, in the godly capital of Rauta Shèràa, when we both were known by the names we'd been born with—

"Dear-rest fr-riends—"

—I almost got you killed, didn't I, nìRau?

"—it has been too long."

The recorded audience exploded into applause as the ambassador raised his right hand above his head in a subservient greeting. The red stone in his ring of station flashed reflected daylight like a small warning light. As the clapping died, Tsecha bowed his head and continued his speech in High Vyn-shàrau.

Jani positioned herself so that the crowd blocked the subtitles. She watched Tsecha's posture and gestures, the sweep and flourish of the highly choreographed language, and intuited meaning the way a musician discerned note, tone, and tempo. It had taken her seven years to develop the skill; pride and respect for the language prevented her from playing ignorant and covering it up. The Haárin had noticed her ability soon after she'd arrived in NorthPort. Whenever their trade council experienced a communications breakdown with the Whalen's Planet Merchants' Association, they always contacted Cory Sato to help resolve it, a fact that only helped worsen her relationship with her bosses.

Jani flinched as the woman next to her pointed to the newsscreen. "It's so beautiful! That language. Those gestures. Like a kind of dancing!"

A man in a dockworker's coverall shook his head firmly. "Don't trust them. None of them, not even the ones we got here." He gestured in the direction of the Haárin enclave. "Sneaky bastards. Don't see none of 'em here, do you? No, they gotta shut themselves away all private."

"Tsecha's the Pathen Haárin's religious as well as secular leader," the woman said. "They're required to gather together in their meeting hall to listen to him. Then afterwards, they'll pray."

Jani nodded in agreement. Genta had, in fact, committed a serious breach of order by not attending the program. But even the most humanish-behaving idomeni felt that acting one way while believing another was disorderly; Genta's cultural conditioning prevented him from hiding his displeasure with his ambassador. Likewise, his council's action against him would be very public, and very swift. *If his delivery contracts are canceled, the MA will explode.* And she would be dragged in to ladle oil over the whitecaps, sure as hell—

"Them and their prayers." The dockworker glared at Tsecha's image. "Everything's a damned prayer. Even their damned meals. Say it's their religion, but whoever heard of a religion where it's a sin to eat in public? With friends. Like normal."

The woman frowned at him. "Eating's different for them. They store food very carefully and keep records of where it comes from. They call their meals *sacraments* and their cooks *priests*. They eat by themselves and pray the whole time. Very ceremonial. Very precise." She nodded knowingly. "That's how they honor their gods."

"The Haárin honor money more than gods," another man said. "You can buy some of their blessed sacrament if you really want it." He grimaced. "Don't know why you would, though. They season their food like to blow the top of your head off. Even the sweet stuff."

"Sacraments." The dockworker snorted. "Bunch of creeps. Talk like they got marbles in their mouths, look at you like you're dirt." He walked away, his expression stony. "Didn't need any damned ambassadors for almost twenty years. Why now?"

Interesting question, sir—I've pondered it myself the past few weeks. Jani cast a last look toward the screen, taking note of the ministers sharing the stage with Tsecha. Every face wore a broad smile. Well, those expressions would be wiped out soon enough when they realized what they'd let themselves in for. At least this time she'd be far enough away to avoid shrapnel. For once in her screwed-up life, she'd stationed herself, as her mainline Service buddies used to say, well back of the front.

The rain had turned to mist. Time to head back to the Association tracking station she called home. Jani hurried in the direction of the lot where her skimmer sat charging, picking up her pace even though her back had begun to ache. Her bosses would soon be screaming for the official morning docking numbers. She couldn't afford to piss them off any more.

A shout sounded from behind. The pound of running feet. Jani's heart raced. Her breath caught in her throat. Then chill calm washed over her, like an old friend resting a hand on her shoulder. She reached into the inner pocket of her duffel. Her hand closed around the grip of her old Service shooter. She turned, only to see the desk clerk from the hostel racing toward her.

"Jeez, Cory, wake up!" The young man slowed to a gasping halt. "I need—to talk to you."

Jani withdrew her empty hand from the duffel and tried to smile.

"Boy, you look wrecked." The clerk's voice dropped to a whisper. "You get those old farts you work for through that audit ok?"

"As always," Jani replied.

"You know"—he leaned closer—"there's a doe here from SouthPort Consolidated. Jammin' blonde. She's looking for doc techs. Pass her exam, she's offering Registry-level jobs."

"So?"

The clerk rolled his eyes. "*You*, dummy! You're the talk of the Merchants', my manager says. All the paper you vet is so clean, it squeaks. Six months on the job, not one observation from Guv Hall. My manager calls it a miracle."

My bosses call it something else. Jani's smile faded. The word "verifier" hadn't been said aloud at this morning's meeting, but the mute accusation had hung heavy in the air. *Government spy. They think I'm a government spy.*

If they only knew.

Jani glanced down the street, where the crowd still gathered in front of the communications shop. "I'll think about it."

The clerk sighed. "Yeah, well, don't think too long. She's checking out tonight." He shook his head. "Registry-level jobs. Just think. Exterior Ministry on Amsun. Maybe even Earth!" He punched Jani's arm. "Registry—that's the top of the tree!"

I know all about the Registry, child—my name resides in a very prominent place in that epic tome. "Thanks for the word," Jani said. "I'll give it all due consideration." She left the clerk to argue with her retreating back and ducked into the alley she always used to reach the charge lot. Then her stomach grumbled, and she tried to recall what waited at home in her cooler. *Cold air—damn, I need to buy food.* And all the decent shops were in the opposite direction.

Jani hurried out of the alley, slid to a stop, and scurried back into the shelter of a doorway. The desk clerk was talking to an attractive blonde. His new contact from SouthPort Consolidated, Jani assumed. Try as she might, she couldn't recall ever seeing that company name on any shipping logs that had passed through her hands.

Jani studied the woman's neat hair and stylish clothes, both several GateWays removed from the best SouthPort had to offer. She watched as the desk clerk nodded, then pointed in the direction of the alley.

She backed down the passageway, her sore back protesting every stride. When she reached the other end, she looked up and down the street, ducking into the shadows as a passenger skimmer drifted by. She listened, until she heard only faraway street sounds and knew for certain that she was alone. Then she ran.

CHAPTER 2

Scrub and sand blurred past as Jani concentrated on the approaching tracking station. The squat building sat like an overturned bowl in the middle of the plain, its safety beacon shining gamely through the fog.

The steadying hand on her shoulder returned as the calmness reasserted itself. A survival checklist formed in her mind. What she had to do, how quickly, and how thoroughly. She hadn't always been that organized. The Service had literally drilled it into her head. Augmentation. The implants in her brain that had, at least officially, made her a soldier. Jani resented augie when she didn't need it, but gripped it like a life preserver now. As she neared the station, it kept her focused, compelled her to watch the shallow recesses in the dome, the dark shadows where someone could hide.

She circled the small dome twice before she edged the skimmer into its charge slot. Shooter at the ready, she carded through the station's two sets of doors and scanned the cell-like single room. Finding nothing out of place, she set the weapon on standby and tucked it into the belt of her coverall. Working with speed born of habit and dispassion born of chemistry, she packed her few clothes into her small duffel. Then she stripped the bed and bath area, feeding the flimsy sheets and towels into the trashzap. The volume of material overwhelmed the unit's filter; the odor of burnt cloth filled the room.

Jani rummaged through one of the side compartments of her duffel and carefully withdrew the small Naxin bomb. After the protein digester did its work, no trace of her presence, no hair, skin cell, or fingerprint, would remain. A second bomb nestled in her bag. She would use it on the skimmer after she reached the shuttleport.

Jani checked her timepiece. Shuttles to the NorthPort docks departed every half hour, but with the slowdown, there was no guarantee they'd follow their normal schedule. She sat on the narrow bed, bomb in hand. If this all turned out to be nothing, there would be hell to pay. Naxin lingered like bad memories—the station would require a thorough decontamination. Expensive decontamination. *In other words, kiss this job good-bye.*

But who knew? Maybe the desk clerk's friend with the Registry job would come to her aid. Jani smiled sadly. Who could guess the offer of a Registry job would hold enough attraction to make her drop her carefully maintained guard?

Someone who knew her well.

And who knows you that well, Captain Kilian?

She broke the seal on the protein bomb, set it on the mattress, and hurried toward the door. Within seconds, the device's outer housing would split, releasing a steady yellow stream of digestive mist.

Just as the door swept open, the station's proximity alarm activated. "Skimmer approaching from north-northwest," the tinny voice entoned. "Speed sixty-five kilometers per hour. Single occupant. Estimated time of arrival two minutes."

Jani looked back at the bed. The protein bomb emitted a sound like cracking ice, releasing the first puffs of corrosive fog. Too late to hurl it out the door. A few good pulls of Naxin would turn her lungs to soup.

She let the station's inner door close behind her, backed against the narrow entryway wall, and forced the outer door to remain closed by pushing with her left foot against its raised metal frame. Then she reached up and shattered the casing of the overhead light with the grip of her shooter, plunging the small space into darkness. In the meantime, the barest whiff of Naxin had worked its way through the gaps in the inner door seal. Jani closed her eyes against the stinging mist and stifled a cough.

The alarm spoke again. "Approach is made."

She activated her shooter. After her visitor made a few attempts to force the door, she'd pull her foot away. Allow the door to open. Then wait for that first tentative step forward into the dark.

Oblique line of fire—aim for the head.

Jani heard the crunch of footsteps, a plastic click as someone inserted a card into the reader, silence as the jammed door forced the reader to deny access. Again, the click of the card. Once more, nothing.

"Damn her!"

That voice. Jani tensed as the outer door shook under the force of banging knocks.

"Jani! It's Evan! Please let me in!" A pause. "I'm alone." Softer. "Please."

Her calm cracked like the bomb housing. *Oh God! Not him!* She tightened her grip on her weapon. *They wouldn't let him come here alone.* Evan. Van Reuter. The Commonwealth Interior Minister. No security officer worth a damn would have allowed him to wander unescorted on any colony. His face had been plastered on the cover of every newssheet for weeks—even the most info-starved transport jockey would recognize him.

"Jani? Jani?" The banging resumed, louder, more insistent. The air in the tiny space shook with the noise. *"I know you're in there! Talk to me!"*

More Naxin had seeped into the enclosure, choking Jani's breath away as she tried to inhale. Her eyes burned. The skin of her face felt hot. She pulled her foot away from the door. It slid open, but she remained back in the shadows, letting the cold air pour over her.

At first, nothing. Then Evan van Reuter stepped forward. Almost twenty years had passed since Jani had seen that tall, slim form, that tilt of the head. Not as much of a stomach-clench as with the Haárin. Not quite. "Should I curtsy, Excellency?" she asked as she stepped out of the doorway, forcing him to backpedal.

"Jani?" He stared at her, broad brow furrowed in confusion. "Is that you?" Then his gaze fell on her shooter. Thin lips tensed in a tight line. Dark, hooded eyes narrowed. Jani could hear his thoughts as though he spoke them out loud.

After so long, he was unsure of her. She almost felt flattered.

"It's really me, Evan." She disengaged the power pack and shoved her inactivated weapon into her duffel.

Evan thrust his hands into the pockets of his Interior field coat. The hem of the heavy black garment flapped around his knees as the wind howled. "I need to talk to you. It's important. But it's freezing out here! Can't we go inside?"

Jani shook her head. She felt the augmentation leach away, leaving vague edginess in its place. She held up her right hand and watched it shake. "Can't. Bombed it."

"Well, at least we can get out of this damned wind!" Evan grabbed her arm and pulled her after him behind the small building. There, a sleek black sedan hovered shadowlike beside her battered single-seater.

He yanked open the sedan's gullwing and pushed Jani into the passenger seat. The heavy door closed over her with a solid *thunk*. Black trueleather cushions, soft as butter, sensed her chill and grew warm.

Evan got in beside her and pulled his door closed. "God, how can you live here!" He dug under his seat, came up first with a large thermoflask, then two polished metal cups.

He thrust one of the cups into Jani's hand and filled it. The weighty aromas of chocolate and fresh coffee flooded the cabin. Despite her nerves, her mouth watered—she hadn't tasted truebean in years. She drained her cup with childlike greed.

"Jani? For cry—you want more?" Evan held out the thermoflask, then hesitated. "What's wrong with your face? It's all red."

She felt her cheek. Despite exposure to cold wind and rain, the skin felt dry and hot. "Naxin exposure. It's like sunburn. I'll be fine."

"I have to get you to a doctor—"

"I'll be *fine*."

Evan retreated slowly. "And to think I thought this would be the easy part, after what I went through to find you." He set his cup in a niche in the dash and dug through his coat pockets. "I had nothing to go on. Your file's been buried. All I had was your canceled lieutenant's ID, the one you gave me after your promotion to captain. I had copies made, sent out to my people.''

"Like your blonde from SouthPort Consolidated?" Jani slumped in her seat and felt the ergoworks vibrate in their efforts to support her properly. "Why that hostel? Why the hell did I have to run into *that* hostel?"

"I had people all over NorthPort," Evan said as he searched. "SouthPort, too. The docks. I had no intention of letting you slip away." He pulled a tiny slipcase from the inside pocket of his coat. "My blonde came back and told me they had found a likely suspect. You, of course. Only problem was, you didn't look like the holo. But she did say the Haárin liked you, you were damned good at your job, and the people you worked for couldn't figure you out. That sounded familiar." He removed a card from the slipcase and handed it to Jani. "The crash changed things, I guess."

Jani avoided looking at the ID at first, then grim fascination got the better of her. She took the card from Evan and stared at the image that smirked back.

Her hair had been longer then. A stick-straight, collar-grazing pageboy, rather than the scalp-hugging cap of waves she now bore, framed a rounder, less angular face. Fringed bangs accentuated thicker eyebrows, an upward-curving nose.

Jani ran a finger along her current arched bridge. Her coloring hadn't changed, though. Hair thick and black, then as now. Skin still light brown. Eyes . . . still green.

Well, they are—I just don't show them to company. The black color filming she'd applied the previous day felt scratchy in the dry air of the skimmer cabin. She restrained the urge to rub her eyes and refocused on her image. Yellow lieutenant's bars imprinted with tiny silver *D*s shone from the sides of her steel blue banded collar. Sideline yellow. Sideline Service. Not the real thing, her mainline buddies had stressed to her repeatedly. Real lieutenants, *mainline* lieutenants, had red bars. She was a documents examiner. Ineligible for command school. Banned from combat training. Not a real soldier.

Let us sing a song of real soldiers. Jani tossed the ID back in Evan's lap. "Too little-girly, don't you think?"

Evan grabbed the card before it slid to the floor, polishing the places where his fingers had smudged the surface. "I always liked it," he muttered defensively as he tucked it gently back into the slipcase and returned it to his pocket.

A few fidgety moments passed. Jani toyed with her empty cup. "I didn't see you on the welcoming committee." She shrugged at Evan's puzzled frown. "That thing for Tsecha. They broadcast the holoVee show here today, but it happened over six weeks ago. Takes about that long to get here from Earth."

"Jani—"

"Even sooner, when you can clear the nav paths by invoking ministerial privilege. What are you doing here?"

Evan tapped a thumb against the skimmer's steering wheel. He'd worked off his coat, revealing the dress-down Interior uniform of loose-fitting black tunic tucked into dark grey trousers. His profile, backlit by the skimmer cabin's subdued lighting, now resembled his late father's in a way Jani would never have thought possible years before. *From Acton to Evan—the van Reuter hawk lives.* Closely clipped dark brown hair accentuated his cheekbone, the curve of his long jaw, the line of his neck. *What I used to do to that neck.*

Correction, what the girl in the ID used to do to that neck.

Evan sipped his coffee. "The reason I didn't attend the welcoming ceremony for the ambassador," he said quietly, "is because the PM requested I stay away."

"That makes no sense. You knew Tsecha when we were stationed in Rauta Shèràa. You're the only minister who can claim that. Doesn't Cao realize how valuable that experience is?"

Evan smiled grimly. "Thanks for the vote of confidence. I'll add you to my list of supporters. There's plenty of room— it's shrinking as we speak." He watched the storm rage outside. "How much have you heard out here about my wife's death?"

"We heard what we were told," Jani said. Every aspect picked over in sickening detail. Tsecha's welcoming was the first program she had watched in the four months since. "Lyssa died at the spa on Chira."

"An accident?"

"With mitigating circumstances. Hints she'd been ill." Jani

hesitated. "Later, there were rumors she'd been drinking, doping. She tried to hop the road skimmer she was driving over a narrow gorge. Road skimmers don't hop. She lost control, flipped into a rock formation." She remembered the OC-Net cut-in, the crumpled skimmer, and the reporter running his hands over the rocks in question with the bright-eyed wonder of someone who had never seen a person die.

"Any—" Evan's voice cracked. He pulled the thermoflask from beneath the seat and refilled both their cups. "Any speculation that I could have been involved?"

Jani studied the side of Evan's face. Only the way his jaw muscle worked indicated the tension he otherwise managed to hide. "No. Why would there be?"

"There have been rumors, damning enough for the Cabinet to initiate a Court of Inquiry. That's why Cao asked me to stay away. Because things are so touchy. Our relations with the idomeni. Earth's relations with the colonies. Our colonies butting heads with the idomeni colonies. Does the term 'vicious circle' mean anything to you?" Evan's hand moved to his throat. "Cao's trying to use it like a noose around my neck. She and her old school friend, Exterior Minister Ulanova. I don't agree with the way they do business. They want me gone."

"You once told me the occasional purge is a fact of political life."

"I don't possess the edge I used to, Jan. My wife is dead. Our children died years ago. I stink of death. It drives people away. People I thought I could count on." The rain had intensified, sluicing down the windows as though they sat beneath a waterfall. "The knives are out for me this time. I can't fight alone."

Jani watched the rain. The statement that Evan was only forty-two, that he'd live to fight another day, remarry and father his own Cabinet if he so desired, didn't seem appropriate. Death altered that scenario. It raised imposing questions. Questions of coping, closure, setting the record straight. *And I know all about that, don't I?*

She heard Evan stir beside her.

"I believe Lyssa was murdered, too, you see," he said. "I think since we're on speaking terms with the idomeni again, someone wants me out of the picture. That's why I need a friend." He reached out to her, his hand hovering above hers without touching. "A friend who can find out what happened."

"You want to take me back to Earth with you?"

"I need your help, Jan. I need a friend who knows me, knows the idomeni, and knows where the bones are buried."

I buried some of those bones, Jani thought as she watched Evan's hand. It shook. Very slightly. Did she make him that nervous? Or was he in that much trouble?

"I know what we had didn't end well," he said as he let his hand rest on the seat near her knee. "Do you hold a grudge?"

"No."

"I didn't think so. You're not the type. You follow your own rules, your own code. You're tough, but you're fair."

"You haven't known me for a long time. I may have changed."

Evan continued as though she hadn't spoken. "For my part, I'd show how much I trust you by placing my career in your hands. All I ask is that, as events warrant, you proceed with caution."

"That would be a first for me, don't you think?" Jani studied her distorted reflection in her cup's polished surface. "You really want to take me back to Earth?"

"You have to go somewhere. My blonde mentioned I blew your situation here."

" 'Blew' doesn't begin to describe it. The Merchants' Association blames me for your traffic slowdown. They think *I'm* a verifier. I'm probably being watched. If I returned to NorthPort after being seen with you, I'd be dead by nightfall."

"So, you need to get out of here." Evan's voice sounded stronger, surer. That made sense. He was negotiating now. "Ok, I'll get you out of here. Where do you want to go?"

"I don't know."

"Then what's wrong with Earth?" He counted on his fingers. "Look, we pass through four GateWays on the way. Amsun, Padishah, Felix, and Mars. If you change your mind

on the way, I'll give you whatever you need and let you go.''
He leaned toward her, his voice coldly eager.

"But if you had a chance to work at a job that utilized
your training, realized you could live a different life, wouldn't
it make sense to stick with me? Look around you, Jan.'' He
gestured toward the storm-whipped scenery. "You don't belong here. You deserve a second chance. Officially, sure, the
Service is still looking for you, but unofficially?'' He shook
his head. "They think you're dead. You can reinvent yourself
any way you want, and I'm offering you the opportunity to
do just that."

"If I work for you?''

"If you find out what happened to Lyssa. Call it working
for me if you want. Call it anything.''

"You could be the bait in a Service trap. Why should I
trust you?''

"Well, if what you told me about your popularity in
NorthPort is true, you'd better trust me at least as far as Amsun.'' He raised his cup to her in a toast. "What choice do
you have?''

What choice, indeed? Jani stared into her cup. Then she
drained it and handed it back to him. "You know, some old
Service officer once said that if you fall back far enough,
you'll just wind up at the front again.'' She pulled the second
Naxin bomb from her duffel and punched a fingernail through
the sealant coating. Popping up her door, she darted into the
rain, pulled open the door of the single-seater, tossed the
bomb inside, slammed the door, and closed herself back in
the sedan before the first wisps of Naxin appeared in her old
skimmer's windows.

Evan stared at her. "That was quick.''

"The Service taught me things like that, remember?''

"Remind me never to pull up next to you.'' He glanced
down at the floor near her feet. His smile flickered back to
life. "Still carrying your bag of tricks, I see.'' He punched
the sedan's charge-through. The vehicle activated with a low
hum. "I'll send some people over to mop up. It'll be like you
were never even here.''

"They're going to need HazMat gear.''

"People always need HazMat gear when they clean up after you. It's one of the constants of life." His eyes glistened with suppressed merriment. He reversed the skimmer out of its slot, then eased it forward. "Is there anyone you want to message before we leave? Anyone you need to notify?"

"No," Jani said. That was the advantage with avoiding names—it always made bugging out easier. She reached beneath Evan's seat for the thermoflask. "I didn't watch the entire welcome program. Were you the only minister Cao took exception to?"

Evan steered the skimmer into a wide, banking turn. "No, there were more. Gisela Detmers-Neumann, the Communications Minister. Fitzhugh and Ebben, the deputies from Commerce. Unser from Education."

Coffee sloshed into Jani's lap, running down her weatherall and spilling to the skimmer floor. "Why them?" she asked.

Evan looked at her, then at the beading puddle on the carpet. "Now, Jani, you of all people should know the answer to that." He reached into the glove box, pulled out a dispo, and handed it to her. "Don't get too nervous. This visit doesn't have to be all business. Who knows, you might run into Tsecha. You were his pet at the Academy. I'm sure he'd enjoy seeing you again."

"At this point," Jani said as she dabbed at the spilled coffee, "I think any running I'd do with regard to him would be in the opposite direction."

The faint glow of the shuttle pad glimmered in the distance. Evan pressed the accelerator. "By the way," he asked, "who was that old Service officer? You always used to mention him in Rauta Shèràa, too."

"Wasn't a 'him.' Was a 'her.' " Jani sighed. "It was me."

CHAPTER 3

Amsun Primary's VIP wing exuded the chilly luxury of a Family mausoleum. Jani hitched her duffel, eyed the sculptures lining the station's carpeted gangway, and kept pace a few meters behind Evan, who was busy dictating orders to a quartet of Amsun annex staffers. Each underling took their position at his shoulder, then backed off and let another take their place, just like lead changes during skimbike races. It had been that way since they'd left Whalen two days ago. Every time Jani tried to question Evan about Lyssa, an advisor would turn up to drag him off.

Maybe I need a uniform and a title to get his attention. A possibility, but not one she wanted to consider. Even in her current circumstances, she wouldn't have traded places with Evan or any member of his escort. Voices snapped. No one smiled.

We're in Exterior country, my friends. Unlike every other Ministry, which located its main headquarters in Chicago and scattered its annexes throughout the colonies, Exterior had moved its Main House to the Outer Circle planet of Amsun and maintained only a token presence on Earth. That hadn't seemed wise when the late David Scriabin, Lyssa van Reuter's father, had set the transfer wheels in motion fifteen years before.

Smacks of genius now. Exterior burgundy formed the basis for every aspect of interior decoration in Amsun Primary, a constant reminder to all parties wearing Treasury gold, Commerce green, Interior black, and every other Cabinet hue in exactly whose sandbox they played.

Jani passed the portrait of a severe, dark-haired woman wearing a high-necked tunic in the ubiquitous *colour du monde*. Everyone thought Exterior Minister Anais Ulanova should have stood for Prime during the last election. When she didn't, the Earthbound news services professed shock. The colonial reaction, in contrast, had been blasé. *Why fight to be shepherd when you already own the sheep?*

As she came upon yet another holosilk study in red and orange, Jani rolled her eyes. It was partly artistic opinion, partly aggravation. Red was the color of blood and warning lights to her augie, the chromatic equivalent of a scream in the night. Unfortunately, the action caused an eyefilm to shift. She tried to blink it back into place, and it hung up on her eyelid. Tears brimmed, then spilled as the film edge curled and split. She cupped a hand over the damage and searched in vain for a sign indicating a restroom.

"Ms. Tyi?"

Tyi? Tyi? That was her name now. Risa Tyi. Josephan. Bad choice. She couldn't speak Josephani.

"Ms. Tyi!" Evan had pulled up short and stared back at her. "Is everything all right?" The look in Jani's visible eye must have set off alarms. "Folks, I'll get back with you." He left his puzzled entourage behind and hurried to her side. "I knew you shouldn't have flown so soon after the surgery." He gripped Jani by the elbow and pulled her toward the elevator bank. "I hope the incision glue held."

One of the underlings called out, "Your Excellency, if a physician is required—"

"No, no," Evan said as he pushed Jani ahead of him into the first open car. "We'll meet you at the *Arapaho* gate in a few minutes." The door hissed shut. "What happened!"

Jani sagged against the wall. "Film broke."

"Can you fix it?"

"Yeah." She shivered as the odor of berries filled the elevator. Her mouth watered. What the overdose of red started, the stress of the moment intensified. She breathed through her mouth in an effort to block out the smell of fruit.

"Are you all right? I know red used to get to you sometimes.'' Evan leaned close and blanched. "Oh shit." As the door opened, he held her back and looked up and down the hall. "Still red—cover up."

Jani pressed her hands over her eyes as she was herded, dragged, and prodded. Another door opened, then whispered closed. "Evan? What color are the walls now?"

"They're a very calming shade of blue."

Jani lowered her hands. The walls were indeed quite relaxing, but some of the fixtures appeared unusual. "Evan, we're in a men's toilet."

"It was the closest door to the elevator, ok? People were coming." He activated the lock. "There. That lights up the 'being cleaned—come back in ten minutes' sign."

"If the hall monitoring picked us up—"

"This is the *private* section. Anais does any scanning here, I'll have her ass." Evan's voice grew hushed. "That look you had in the eye I could see scared the hell out of me—like you were staring up from the bottom of a pit. Was that some kind of seizure?"

Jani walked to the mirror above the row of sinks. "No." A few fissures had formed along the film's black-and-white surface. "A combination of the stress and the environment. The nervousness of the moment. The augmentation kicked in."

"Augmentation." Evan gave each syllable a twist of disgust. "You were sideline Service, not mainline. How could you let them do that to you?"

"I was still Service, Ev. When they tell you to peel and bend over, you drop your drawers and think of the Commonwealth." Jani dug into her duffel. "Guess they thought we all needed it, with the way the Laumrau-Vynshà situation was heating up." She shrugged. "I have mixed feelings about it. It helps me think more clearly in emergencies—almost like a permanent tranquilizer implant. If I get hurt while it's active, it kicks on adrenal and thyroid boosters, and helps the wounds heal faster." She checked her clear face in the mirror. The peeling skin and rash caused by her brief exposure to the Naxin had healed in two days, instead of two weeks. "Dulls pain."

"Helped you survive the crash," Evan added with an encouraging smile.

"That's why I have mixed feelings." Jani freed the bottles of film former from the depths of her bag, then blended the memory film with its activator. "Sometimes I think justice would have been better served if I'd died with everyone else. Or if I'd died, and they'd lived." She looked up to find Evan's reflection staring at her in shocked surprise. "Don't worry. I won't go suicidal on you. Just a little objective over-analysis on my part."

"Really?" He studied her skeptically. "I know some people back home you could talk to about it."

"PTs?" Jani peeled the ruptured film from her eye. The tear-swollen black-and-white fragments smacked wetly into the sink. "Ev, if the psychotherapeuticians ever got me, they'd never let go." She activated the faucet, cupped tepid water in her hand, rinsed away the last specks of old film, and washed them down the drain. She didn't notice Evan's approach until he stood beside her.

"Jesus!"

Jani stared into the mirror at her eye. The iris was still the dark jade of her childhood. But the sclera, instead of white, shone a lighter, glassy green that took on a bluish cast in the harsh bathroom lighting. *Corroded copper coins—built-in pennies on my eyes.* At least the pupil hadn't changed in shape or size. And her sight had never seemed any better or worse than other people's.

Evan drew closer. "How the hell did that happen?"

"Contaminated starter tissue, the doctors said. No time to grow them over."

"The doctors?"

"*The* doctors. John Shroud, Valentin Parini, and Eamon DeVries." They had worked out of the Service hospital in Rauta Shèràa. They had rebuilt her after the crash, gave her strange eyes and numb limbs, and remained together after the war to form Neoclona. Now, they controlled all the hospitals in the Commonwealth that were worth a damn. Jani tilted her head back and counted out the drops of film. *One . . . four, five.* She held her lids open for ten seconds, then looked in the mirror. Her purple-black eye gazed back with teenage clarity.

Evan cleared his throat. "Don't you think you should do the other one?"

"I just did it three days ago. Barring incident, the stuff lasts seven to ten."

"I think you should make sure."

Jani watched Evan in the mirror until he turned away. After some hesitation, she peeled, poured, mixed, and counted. "Are you sure you want to go through with this?"

"That sounds hopeful." He turned back to her. "Does that mean you've decided to come at least as far as Padishah?"

"Amsun's too close to Whalen. I'd feel better a little farther out."

"How will I know when you feel you've gone far enough?"

"You won't." Jani dabbed away a drop of film former that had spilled down her cheek. "I'll just be gone."

"That sounds familiar." Evan hoisted himself on the counter next to her sink. "Sorry. Completely inappropriate."

"Yes, it was."

"What's past is past. I apologize." He fingered the soap dispenser. "So, how've you been?" He shrugged off Jani's incredulous look. "I've been weighed down with work the past two days. This is the first chance we've had to talk since I rescued you from that hellhole."

"I'm fine, Evan."

"Really?"

"Really." Jani's back twinged, and she leaned against a urinal for support. "You?"

"Fine."

"I'm sorry. About your wife." The words came haltingly. She'd never had a talent for saying the right thing; anything she thought of now seemed inappropriate. Death didn't just alter. It razed. Annihilated. "Your children, too. That was tragic."

"Yes. Thank you. Not a day goes by that I don't think of them." Evan looked at her and sighed. "You've wanted to ask me something delicate for days. I can tell. Go ahead."

There were no right words for this, either. "We heard gossip out here in the beyond. That you and Lyssa had problems.''

''Yes, we did. For the most part, however, our marriage functioned.''

''Sounds mechanical.''

''Most Family marriages are.'' Evan's eyes glinted. Sapphires in snow. ''I don't recall you as the type to be drawn in by rumor.''

''Rumors blossom and seed all the time. They don't all result in the convention of a Court of Inquiry.''

''I told you, Cao and Ulanova want me out.''

''You must have really ticked them off.''

''I don't quite have your talent for alienating the opposition, but I'm working on it.''

''There's something you didn't tell me. Something you left out.''

''And what could that be?''

Jani leaned more heavily against the urinal. She could feel the cold porcelain through her thin coverall. As cold as her right hand. As cold as the chill that gripped her.

''Is something wrong, Jan?''

''This concerns Knevçet Shèràa, doesn't it?''

''I don't know. But I bet you could find out.''

''You bastard. You set me up.''

''No, I gave you A and B and let you reach the logical C. The setup was all yours.'' Evan glanced at his timepiece. ''We better get going.'' He pushed himself off the counter, then turned to wash his hands. ''I'm sorry, Jan, but if I'd mentioned Knevçet Shèràa back on Whalen, you'd have bolted. I couldn't let you do that.''

''What am I walking into?''

''Nothing that endangers you. I'm the one in trouble. You're assumed dead, remember?'' Evan gripped the rim of the sink. ''Jani, your own family wouldn't know you. That's how different you look. Hell, I didn't know you.'' He reached blindly for a dispo towel. ''And I knew you better than anyone.''

''Better not call me 'Jani' anymore. Stick to Risa.'' Jani tossed her bottles into her bag and gave her eyes one last check in the mirror. ''I don't speak Josephani, you know.''

"It's like High Dutch."

"Oh, that narrows it down. Thanks."

Evan unlatched the door. "We're going to walk past a lot of red between here and the shuttle. Will you make it?"

"Yes. I'll just get a bit wound-up. I'll be fine." Jani waited for him to raise the all clear, then followed him into the hall. "Well, that brought back memories."

Evan paused in mid-step, eyes widening as he remembered. "That play. At the Consulate Hall. *Becket*. Intermission. The ladies' was crowded, and you barged in and—"

"Told you to shut up and guard the door. That's how we met." She patted his arm. "You still guard doors pretty well."

They both laughed, a little too loudly and a little too long. Evan offered her his arm as they walked to the elevator bank, then bowed like a gallant as the door opened, gesturing for her to enter first. The other occupants smiled at them, as though the little show had brightened their day.

You set me up, Evan. Jani stepped to the rear of the half-filled elevator and tried not to flinch as he crowded beside her.

Knevçet Shèràa. *Not a day goes by that I don't think—*She leaned against the rear of the car, closed her filmed eyes, and clenched her numb left hand.

"I guess you could consider this a working vacation," Evan said. He nodded curtly to the steward who bustled past him, towing Jani's luggage in a hand-skimmer.

Correction—Risa's luggage. Jani shook her head in disbelief as the steward disappeared into her bedroom to stash the seven brown trueleather bags in her closet.

"I'll unpack while you're at dinner, ma'am," he said as he took his leave, all silver-blond hair and flashing smile. Jani returned the smile to the best of her ability, then turned back to Evan to find him glaring at her.

"But don't get carried away with the vacation part." He walked across the large sitting room and flopped into a lounge chair. "Of course, I don't think I have enough work to keep you occupied for five weeks, and what you do in your off time is your own . . . affair." He smoothed the front of his black uniform tunic and fixed his sights on the wall opposite.

"I'll try to keep the orgies to a minimum, sir," Jani replied quietly.

"That's not what I meant."

"I know exactly what Your Excellency meant. I think I should take this opportunity to remind Your Excellency that, considering certain situations in which I have found myself in the past, if I had been the type to think with my pussy, I'd have been dead years ago."

"Ja—" Evan stopped himself. He rose slowly. "Risa. How vividly put. My apologies. I should know better."

"I think with my head," Jani continued. "If *it* sees the way clear, that is of course a different story."

Evan gaped. He seemed to have trouble deciding what to do with his hands, finally shoving them into his pants pockets. The move caused his tunic to bunch unministerially over his hips. "Dinner," he finally said. "My private dining room. One hour after breakaway. We will have company." He eyed Jani's coverall, an overlarge, chalk brown item she'd liberated from the Whalen transport's lost lambs bin. "We should dress."

"Yes, sir." Jani returned Evan's cool smile and followed him to the door. "Label the forks, so I know which one to use when," she added as he stepped into the hall. The door closed before he could reply, but not before he had shown he hadn't lost his capacity to redden alarmingly.

Jani knocked against the door with her forehead. *Too late to bolt now.* The *Arapaho* was in prebreakaway lockdown—she'd have to trip a hazard alarm. *I've done that before.* But not on a Cabinet-class ship. They had Service crews aboard to put out their fires. She'd be up to her ass in steel blue before the klaxons stopped screaming.

I'm jumping ship at Padishah. She made a circuit of her cabin sitting room, a posh retreat in pale yellow and cream, scanning the shelves and cabinets for anything she could hock. She was examining the contents of an étagère with a pawnbroker's eye when she heard the door open.

"Ma'am." Her steward stood in the entry holding a bottle-filled tray. "Do you require any assistance before dinner?"

Jani straightened. "No. Thank you."

"I thought you might like something to drink."

"Fine." She nodded, larcenous hands locked behind her back.

"A jeune marie?"

"Fine." *What the hell's a "young mary"?*

The young man filled a small glass to the brim with a garnet-colored liquid and handed it to Jani. She raised the drink to her lips, hoping to get rid of him by downing it quickly, when the odor of berries filled her nose.

"Do you like it, ma'am?" His voice held stewardly anxiety. "It's new. From Serra."

"A 'jeune marie' is a kind of berry, isn't it?"

"Yes, ma'am. Is everything—"

"Everything's fine. Please go now. I need to get ready." She fought down a yell as he took his time gathering up his tray and waited for the door to close before sinking into the nearest chair. Her stomach burned. Her hand trembled, causing a stream of red beadlets to slosh over the glass's rim onto the carpet. She hurried to the bathroom, poured the reeking liqueur into the sink, and flushed it down until she could smell only water.

Evan's on his own—I'm jumping ship at Padishah. He didn't need her to get him through his crisis—he was far from vanquished politically. Or personally, for that matter. He had certainly dealt with his own deaths better than she had with hers.

Coping? You're kidding.

Closure? No, her wounds had gaped for eighteen years.

You'd have to execute one hell of an inside-out to set Knevçet Shèràa straight, Kilian. She wasn't that limber anymore.

Jani sat on the edge of the bathtub and unclasped her boots. *But Evan thinks I deserve a second chance.* Of course, since he felt his career was in jeopardy, he'd say anything to get her to help. Just as he'd withhold anything he thought might scare her away. *He thinks in terms of distance to goal and whether goal had been achieved or lost.* Always the pragmatist. Even as a young Consulate deputy, his first time away from home, with every opportunity to go off track, he always kept his eye on the ball.

So? Maybe Evan didn't mean what he'd said about second chances. It didn't follow that it wasn't true. All her records were in secured storage on Earth. Maybe there was something she could learn, something she could discover that would make it not hurt as much. Something she could use to help Evan, and, just possibly, herself.

I don't think like that anymore. Every time I try to help, I fuck up. I'm jumping ship at Padishah. She started undoing the fasteners of her coverall. Her hands stilled. *No, I'm not.* Evan had been right. After almost twenty years, her Family boy still knew her very well. She pondered that disquieting thought as she headed for the bedroom to mine something presentable from the depths of Risa's luggage.

In contrast to the interior of Jani's cabin, the *Arapaho* hallways were simple: undecorated walls of light grey composite, floors of dark grey, footstep-muffling lyno.

Jani hurried after her guide, a frazzled mainline Spacer First Class who had apparently been instructed to *bring Ms. Tyi to dinner without delay.* Her hip twinged with every step. The outfit she wore, a tight, one-shoulder, floor-length column dress in dark blue, had not been her first choice. Or her second. Or her eighth.

Seven damned bags of clothes, and none of them fit! Jani tugged at the dress again as she struggled to keep up with the sensibly booted SFC. Her own sensible boots were hiding beneath her bed—cowards that they were. Her current footwear—strappy, metallic-colored, and high-heeled—had been spared a one-way trip down the disposal chute solely because they were the only shoes in her possession that kept the dress from dragging on the floor.

She and Evan were going to have to discuss hazard pay.

The rough polycotton strap of Jani's duffel bit into the skin of her bare shoulder. Her choice of handbag might cause raised eyebrows among her dinner companions, but she didn't care. Some things, a woman kept with her at all times. *Like her shooter, for example.* She straightened as best she could in her impossible shoes. It had been a very long time since she'd had to look this polished.

"Here we are, ma'am." The SFC slid to a halt before a

double-wide set of sliders embossed with the Interior seal and knocked sharply. The doors opened immediately. She mumbled, ''Good evening, sir,'' and bolted around the nearest corner just as Evan, resplendent in formal black, stepped out into the hall.

''Well, this *is* a change for the better!'' His face lit up as he held out his arm. ''I picked that dress,'' he added as he led her inside. ''I must say, I have excellent taste.''

Jani tugged at the gown's rear. ''It's too tight.'' The back of her neck tingled as Evan lagged behind to take in the view.

''No, not a bit,'' he said. ''Just confirms you still have a waist. Judging from your previous attire, I'd given it up for lost.'' As they walked through the sitting room, Jani heard Evan clear his throat. ''Can't say I agree with that purse, though.''

''Bugger,'' she said as she strode on ahead. The dark green and silver suite was furnished with a tasteful, expensive blend of ornate modern and stark antique. She swallowed a comment that it was larger than some homes in which she'd lived as the odors coming from the dining room made her mouth water. Her step quickened. *God, I'm starved!* Over the past few months, it seemed she could never get enough to eat.

She pulled up short as she entered the dining room. Evan's steadying hand gripped her numb left arm as two pairs of eyes stared in surprise. Jani managed a composed smile. She recognized her dinner companions from the postings in various Guv Halls. *Maybe this dress wasn't such a bad idea after all.*

Evan pushed past her. ''Risa, I'd like to introduce two of the more important members of my staff.'' He nodded toward a tall, dark blond man dressed in a dandyish, pale lilac dinner suit. ''This is Durian Ridgeway, my Documents chief.''

Jani forced herself to extend her hand as Ridgeway pursed his lips and looked her slowly up and down. ''Ms. Tyi.'' The soft cast of his boyish features was offset by the glitter of his blue eyes. ''I've looked forward to meeting you.'' His accent was clipped and difficult to place.

Earth British, Jani decided. She'd thought New Manx, at first, but no self-respecting Manxman would have allowed himself to be seen wearing the curious wad of bright purple braiding Ridgeway had fashioned into a neckpiece. *Clotted octopus,* she thought. Maybe it indicated a sense of humor?

Ridgeway beckoned to a slight young woman who appeared lost amid the furniture. "This is my deputy, Angevin Wyle."

Angevin stepped forward. Her outfit, a fitted copper gauze gown with matching nosebleed heels, seemed to be giving her trouble as well. Jani studied her face. Wide-spaced mossy green eyes, carrot red curls shot through with gold, stubborn chin, all combined to uncover long-buried memories.

I attended school with your father. Hansen Wyle and I were going to change worlds, once. She accepted Angevin's subdued greeting. *Then it all fell apart.*

Evan herded them toward the dinner table, where a first course of glistening vegetable jellies coddled in crushed ice awaited. "I'm glad we could meet now," he said as he helped Jani with her chair. "I don't think we could afford to delay until we returned to Earth."

"Perhaps not, Ev," Ridgeway agreed grudgingly as he assisted Angevin with her chair. "I'm just hesitant to leave documents of this nature aboard an unsecured vessel." He nodded toward the sideboard, where an anodized metal documents case rested.

Jani noted the large case's double touchlocks and felt a pleasant shiver of anticipation. She hadn't had the opportunity to handle close-controlled paper since her Service days.

"If you consider the *Arapaho* unsecured, Durian, we *are* in trouble." Evan speared a tan star-shape with a narrow, two-pronged fork and ferried the wobbly morsel to his mouth. "But I prefer to believe that in this, as in so many things, you are erring on the side of caution."

"Perhaps." Ridgeway tried repeatedly to snag a quivering orange sphere, but the tidbit kept sliding off his fork. "These *méduse,*" he said with a nervous chuckle. "I always have trouble eating these things."

"It's probably afraid of your neckpiece," Angevin Wyle said as she executed an expert forking. She chewed thoughtfully, expression placid, the look in her eyes as flinty as the documents case's finish.

Evan coughed and reached for his wineglass. "It is a bit much, Durian."

Ridgeway fingered his garish neckwear and smiled. Lips only. The sidelong glare he gave Angevin promised a stern lecture behind closed, soundproofed doors.

Thy father's daughter. Jani looked down at her plate to hide her grin. The *Arapaho* suddenly felt very homey.

CHAPTER 4

The balance of the meal passed uneventfully. Make that the imbalance. Embers of conversation sparked fitfully, only to die. Except for her single instance of fashion commentary, Angevin remained silent. Ridgeway was sociable, though guarded, while Evan alternated between expansiveness and distraction as the synergistic effects of lack of sleep and generous servings of five varieties of wine took hold. He had always enjoyed his liquor, but you'd think he'd have known better.

Now is not the time, Evan. After-dinner iced water in hand, Jani left the three behind to talk, or in Angevin's case, listen, shop. She examined the artwork in Evan's sitting room, then paused before an official portrait of the Interior Minister and his late wife. Evan looked thin and worn. His dress tunic hung on his slim frame like woven lead. Lyssa, also in black, appeared drawn and pale. Neither had made any attempt to smile.

"That was taken almost three years ago, a short time after the children died." Durian Ridgeway drew alongside. The tiny glass he held contained a bright pink, presumably lethal, liqueur. "Too soon, in my opinion. They both look ill. It's not the kind of image you want to see scattered throughout the Commonwealth."

Jani glanced into the dining room. Evan was holding forth and gesturing broadly as a seated Angevin Wyle stared and nodded like someone in a trance. *Bewitching, isn't he?* Even after all these years. *You'd think I'd have acquired immunity by now.* "Pity Evan and Lyssa couldn't time their tragedies better."

Ridgeway's eyebrows arched. "I'm sure I sound harsh, but that is part of my job. To observe, monitor, see things which perhaps His Excellency would miss." He drew closer. Jani forced herself to stand still as he brushed against her bare shoulder. "Well, Ms. Tyi, this must all be a big change for you. From a little post on Hortensia to a Cabinet-class ship, all in a matter of weeks. But, you know what they say." He mumbled a few sentences, of which she recognized little and understood nothing.

Servir? Servirat? I'll bet that's Josephani. Her supposed native language, of which she knew zip. "I beg your pardon, Mr. Ridgeway?"

"Would you like me to repeat it, Ms. Tyi?"

"Judging from your accent, I don't think it would help."

He pressed closer. Jani felt his breath in her ear as his chest pushed against her left arm. The numb one. All she felt was the pressure. "If you couldn't understand that, understand this. The contents of the files I will be turning over to you, if revealed, could shake the Commonwealth to its foundations. If anything happens to that paper while it's registered to your control, I will not rest until I personally grind you to fine powder with my bare hands."

"No need to be melodramatic, Mr. Ridgeway."

"I have been with Evan for fifteen years. Since I left school, my primary duty has been to him. I will not stand by and watch everything he's built get blown to bloody fuck-all for the sake of one of his whims."

The fruity odor of Ridgeway's breath filled Jani's nose. Her full stomach gurgled in protest as she forced herself to look him in the face. His eyes watered—the liqueur was apparently as potent as she thought. "If you have anything to say to me, mister, you really should wait until you sober up."

Ridgeway's bleary glower sharpened. "You don't like me, Ms. Tyi. That's fine—I'm not mad for you, either. I don't believe your participation in what I consider should remain an in-House investigation is necessary." He took a step back.

"But we both follow orders, don't we? Live to serve? That's what I tried to tell you before, and so badly, too. I do apologize." He strolled from the portrait to a display case of ornaments, gesturing for Jani to follow. "But now, I think we understand one another. The idomeni have a term for our particular brand of impasse. Esteemed enemy. For now, let us consider ourselves esteemed enemies."

"We'd have to have a ceremony," Jani said, "to declare it properly. There are offertories to the gods, followed by the shedding of blood through ritual combat."

Ridgeway offered a sly smile. "Is that a challenge, Risa? Perhaps later. It sounds very . . . cross-cultural." He reached into the display case and fingered a polished shell. "What do you think of Ms. Wyle?"

She's like her father. "She's like most dexxies. Rough around the edges. Needs some social buffing."

Ridgeway scowled at Jani's use of the slang term for documents examiner. "Buffing," he said pointedly. "Not a day goes by when I don't stifle the urge to throttle her. But considering her background, I make allowances." He returned the shell to its niche. "You've heard of her father, of course?"

"Hansen?"

"Yes. One of only six humans to degree at the Academy in Rauta Shèràa. One of only six to study the paper system with the race that perfected it. What an honor." Jani could hear the envy in Ridgeway's voice. "Then that damned war started, and he had to stick his nose in. What a waste."

Jani struggled to keep her tone level. "From what I've heard, he knew the Laumrau leaders. He knew the Vynshà. I believe he did what he thought best, in order to help."

"And the shatterbox found the building he was in anyway, and the building collapsed on him anyway, and he died anyway, even though he was only trying to help." Ridgeway pushed the display case toward the center of the table. Jani winced as the metal supports screeched against the polished wood.

"Now the idomeni are back," she said, "and you have to work with them. How do you reconcile that?"

"I don't," Ridgeway replied too quickly. "But I do have the opportunity to help the daughter of the man I grew up wanting to emulate." The look in his eyes grew reverential.

"Hansen was more than one of the six. He was One of Six. They were treated like idomeni, constantly being tested—the pressure was unending. But he always came out on top. He was the best." He sighed. "I'm afraid Angevin will have to emerge from under a fairly formidable shadow."

Jani worked her tensing shoulders. "I think," she said slowly, "part of the girl's problem, if she indeed has one, will be in having to deal with other people's expectations."

"True. True." Ridgeway nodded sagely, his sarcasm detector apparently flooded with ethanol. "All we can do is all we can. In the end it's up to her. No one can work magic with someone fundamentally unsuited to the task at hand." He gave Jani a superior smile, his sarcasm synthesizer apparently functioning just fine. "Speaking of which, why don't we get this transfer over with? You realize what I'm handing over to you?"

"Yes." Jani did a mental ten count. "You're giving me sensitive files pertinent to the investigation of Lyssa van Reuter's death, which contain details of His Excellency's life."

"Oh, they contain details, all right. Their contents may shock even a jaded soul like you, Ms. Tyi. We never realize what Mother Commonwealth knows about us until it's too late." Ridgeway offered her his arm. "Shall we?"

Angevin bounded to her feet as Jani and Ridgeway reentered the dining room. "His Excellency's been telling me the most ripping things! All about the idomeni!" Her enthusiasm withered as soon as her eyes met Ridgeway's. She walked over to the sideboard and rummaged through a large leather bag. From it, she removed a sheaf of papers and three pouches, two the size of a man's hand, one much larger.

In the meantime, Ridgeway collected the documents case and carried it to the dining room table. Evan, fresh from making young women's eyes shine, perched on the arm of a nearby chair and graced Jani with a tired grin.

The grin died when he saw what Ridgeway was doing.

We knew this was coming, Evan. Jani pulled her duffel from beneath her chair, cracked the fasteners, and removed her own small, scuffed pouch. *Besides, what can go wrong?* She knew the answer to that. She would just try not to think about it.

The world of close-controlled paper did get complicated at times, but an ownership transfer was one of the simpler procedures. As Angevin Wyle laid out the logs that they each would sign and date, Ridgeway prepared to reprogram the case's touchlocks to accept Jani's prints.

Of course, he'd have to scan her hands and retinas first, and run a comparison check against the various databases each Cabinet-class ship contained within its systems. Criminal. Service. Medical. A matter of procedure. Everyone understood that. Just another form to file away for future audits.

Ridgeway smirked as he removed his scanner from the largest of the three pouches and activated it.

Jani heard Evan fidget behind her. She smiled, which seemed to disappoint Ridgeway. He pouted when she stepped without hesitation into range of the boxlike scanner and held out her hands.

But my handprints aren't the same, are they? Or her retinas. The doctors who had reassembled her had been, after all, very forward-thinking. She watched as a bright yellow light throbbed beneath the scanner's surface. The device hummed, then the indicator display glowed bright, clear green.

"Happy, Durian?" Evan asked, injecting the distilled essence of generations of Familial ennui into his voice.

"Just following prescribed procedure, Ev," Ridgeway said as he stuffed the scanner back into its pouch. "Better safe than sorry." Using a UV stylus, he opened the switches in the document case's control panel, waited for Jani to place her palm against the sensor pad, then closed the switches, locking in her print as the key.

Just like the good old days. Jani glanced at Evan, who winked back. She removed her scanpack from its cracked plastic pouch. The oval device contained a mass of her farmed brain tissue, through which a network of nervelinks and data chips had been implanted. Working together to serve as guideposts on a roadway, the unit and its attachments stored the data necessary to enable its owner to navigate through the documents maze. Her brain-in-a-box, literally. How long had it been since she'd used it as it was meant to be used? In front of her peers, during a high-level documents transaction?

Jani brushed a few flecks of dirt from the scanpack's surface. Over twenty years of use meant that the hand-sized, five-centimeter-thick oval didn't look much better than its container. Scratches dulled its black polycoat finish. Some of the touchpad labeling had been worn away. She examined the nutrient insert slot along the side, then sniffed quickly. No fishy odor, which would have signaled a leak in the spent nutrient broth line, a sure sign of a poorly maintained 'pack. That had never been a problem for her, but accidents did happen. If Ridgeway even suspected she didn't maintain her equipment, she knew she'd never hear the end of it.

Ridgeway looked from his own immaculate tortoiseshell unit to Jani's. "Oh, Ms. Tyi, that *is* a confidence-builder."

Jani shrugged. "The problem with having nice things, Mr. Ridgeway, is that in some of the places I've lived, there are those who would wish to separate them from me. I try to avoid trouble." She turned on her device, waited for the display to activate, then gently slid it over the first of the three forms.

The sensors on the 'pack's underside evaluated the paper surface, analyzed the inks and metal foils decorating the ornate document, decoded the encryptions contained in the chips and prionics embedded in the parchment. *Everything but Luna's phase on the day it was made*—that's what the document would tell her scanpack, which then would compare that information to the data stored in its own chips and cells.

Bright green identification strings scrolled across the display. "It's a current-issue Interior Ministry ownership transfer log, all right," Jani said to Ridgeway. She ignored his glower, affixed her signature to the document, then moved on to the next as Angevin and Ridgeway completed their portion of the first. After all three forms were completed, they each took one copy. Jani stashed hers in her duffel, while Angevin returned hers and Ridgeway's to the leather bag.

"Are we finally finished?" Evan groaned. "I don't know how any business gets completed in a timely fashion these days." He sounded bored, but his face showed the drained relief of a man whose fever had finally broken.

"Yes, Ev, you can go to bed now," Ridgeway said as he jammed his 'pack back into its sheath. He followed up the snappish remark with a smile, but that did little to counter his bundled-underwear edginess. "We will be disembarking late day after tomorrow, at Padishah," he said to Jani. "If you need any assistance afterward, zip us a message through message central transmit. We'll do what we can." He eyed her scanpack again. "I'm sure the equipment you work with leaves something to be desired."

Angevin walked over to Jani, looking at her for the first time with something akin to a smile. "Looks used," she said, pointing to the scanpack's battered case.

Jani nodded. "It has been."

Angevin was about to say something else, but Ridgeway linked her arm through his and led her away.

"Till tomorrow, Ev," he said as they left. "And a good evening to you as well, Ms. Tyi. You will remember what we talked about?"

"What was that all about?" Evan asked after the sliders closed. "Don't tell me—Durian was being Durian." He eased into a lounge chair and ran a hand over his face. Even in the cabin's soft illumination, his skin looked dull. "Forgive him, Jan—he takes damned good care of me in the bargain. And he's worried about those docs."

"You're not?"

"I'm not sure what you'll think of me after reading some of them, but I have to take that chance. Besides, I trust you." He studied Jani for a few moments, his expression neutral. Then he motioned for her to take the seat across from him.

"Like Durian said, in two days we'll reach Padishah. He and Ange will be catching a Service courier that will get them home a week ahead of the *Arapaho*." He took a deep breath. "I need to go with them. Elyas is petitioning to reopen colonial secession talks. Along with the other Outer Circle worlds, they somehow dragged the Jewellers' Loop into the brawl, and that means lots of might and money flying around. The centrists want me home."

Jani said nothing. Instead, she watched Evan's hands, as she had learned to do during their time together. They rested easily on his knees. No nail-picking. No sleeve-tugging. Either he told the truth or he'd learned to hide his lies better.

"I'd been debating telling you for days. Thought if I mentioned it, I'd give you just another excuse to bolt. But I've no choice. Duty calls.''

''You roust me out of my home, close off my escape routes, then tell me you're leaving me alone among strangers for five weeks?''

Evan wrinkled his nose. ''Whalen was no home. And you don't need any escape routes.'' His eyes sparked. ''Besides, I'm more concerned for the strangers than I am for you.'' His stare deepened and his features slackened until he wore the bewildered, slightly stunned expression Jani remembered from their first meeting. ''I wish I could stay.''

If you're going to look at me like that, maybe it's better you don't. Jani tugged as unobtrusively as she could at the bodice of her dress. A waste of time—the silky material snapped back into snug place like a second skin. ''Well, I may be able to work better without you around.'' She snuck a peek at Evan beneath her lashes. He wore evening clothes as easily as other men wore ship coveralls; now, as he unfastened the stiff formal tunic, he looked very agreeably rumpled. *You're still the best-looking man I've ever known.* Yes, and he had very good reasons to go out of his way to make her feel cosseted and comfortable. If it so happened that keeping her cozy could get him laid, he wouldn't turn it down. Remember the pragmatist.

Not fair. Except for that single grumble in the Amsun station bathroom concerning their breakup, he had been silent on the matter of their past. *Sheep's eyes don't count.* Those could be chalked up to a heavy meal and too much alcohol. *Neither do wicked thoughts.* Lucky for her.

''The centrists,'' she said, ''think the colonies will require a lengthy period of adjustment before full independence can be granted. I've heard numbers ranging from ten to one hundred years. Speaking as a colonial, I don't think we need babying.''

If Evan noticed the abrupt cool-off, he hid it beneath a veneer of serious reflection. ''The coalition pushing for these talks is led by a group being advised by Ulanova. They may know how to run businesses, but they don't know how to run governments. They'd need her help, and she'd give them just enough to keep their heads above water until they needed her again. That's not true independence.''

"Maybe it's enough to get them started.''

"You don't know Anais, Jan. Once she'd sunk her claws into that power base, she'd never let go. She wouldn't rest until she was PM of her own little Commonwealth.''

"Funny she doesn't believe she can get what she wants with an Earthbound government,'' Jani said. ''But then, you're fairly isolated with respect to GateWays. You've turned into a planet-sized office building over the years— you've got no substantial manufacturing or shipping anymore. The colonies are where the money is. By comparison, you're stagnant.''

Evan scowled. ''I wish you'd stop saying 'you.' '' He sagged against the cushions and clasped his hands behind his head. ''Are you angry with me? For holding out on you?''

Jani twitched a shoulder. It twitched back. ''A little.''

"I'll be waiting for you in Chicago. You will show up, won't you?''

"Yes.''

He looked up at the ceiling and exhaled slowly. ''Thank you. I'll sleep more easily tonight.'' He stifled a yawn. ''It won't be horrible.''

"It could be.''

"I'll be there. I'll help you.'' He fell silent for a time. Then his eyes came to life again, and he laughed. ''Before you arrived, Durian was filling my ear about Tsecha. Your old teacher's causing quite a stir, apparently. He took one of the embassy triple-lengths out for a spin a few weeks ago. Problem was, nobody knew he could drive. He got as far as Minneapolis before a Service-idomeni pursuit team caught up to him and herded him back to Chicago. They had a hell of a time hushing it up. That's all the anti-idomeni faction needs to hear is that the ambassador flits unguarded through the provinces.''

Jani chuckled as well. ''You're in for it now! Sounds like he hasn't changed. He used to like making himself up as a human in Rauta Shèràa. He even pulled down a job as a Consulate tour guide for a few days. Nobody could tell—his customers kept asking him what colony he was from.''

"Oh shit, I'd forgotten about that. One more thing to worry about—what joy." Evan's expression grew wistful. "Seems odd, calling him *Tsecha*. We knew him as *Nema*. I still think of him by that name." He looked at Jani, his eyes narrowing. "He liked you."

"Yep."

"He thought you were special."

"Uh-huh."

"He had plans for you."

"Evan, if you have a point to make, please do so."

"No. No. Just rambling. Exhausted."

"Too much to drink."

"Hmm." Worry clouded his features for a moment. "How do you feel?"

"Fine."

"Are you sure? You look ill."

"Thanks." Jani rubbed her stomach. It had started to ache. "I just ate too much."

"We've had a few nasty new bugs crop up in the Outer Circle over the past few years. Maybe you should see a doctor."

"*No.*"

Evan held up his hands in surrender. "Ok, ok. Sorry I mentioned it." He struggled to his feet, then helped her gather her bag and case. "Cabin's to your liking, I hope? Your clothes?"

"Nothing fits, Evan."

"Really?" He circled her, studying her in a way not entirely objective. "I did my best. Took your measurements from your old ID and turned it over to my tailor. She seldom errs."

"She made up for lost time."

"I disagree. This dress is perfect." He chucked her under the chin. "Goes with the face." His hand lingered near her cheek. "I'm getting used to it. It fits you. Very 'Queen of the Nile.' " He hesitated, then leaned close and hugged her lightly, as though he feared she'd pull away. "We'll be fine. You'll see." His breath smelled of wine; his neck, of the haygrass-scented cologne he'd always favored. Jani broke the embrace before she wanted to and rushed out the door before

he could say good night. She walked back to her cabin in the
grip of the sensation that she'd just skimmed over a land
mine.

I have to play this at arm's length. She hated to admit how
good it felt to talk to Evan, to someone who knew the long-
submerged Jani Kilian and, if outward signs could be believed, still cared about her as well. It wouldn't take long to
become used to nice dinners and pleasant conversation again.
And anything else that might reasonably follow. Soon, the
roots would go so deep that when the time came to cut and
run, she'd be fixed in place by indecision and fear of what
she would lose. *I can't afford to relax.* Especially now, with
Ridgeway watching her every move.

She turned the corner in time to see her steward emerge
from her cabin.

"Ma'am?" He brushed a hank of hair from his sweaty
brow. "There's a problem with the climate control on this
deck. I've notified Environmental, but they may not be able
to return it to full function until we stop at Padi."

"Oh please!" Jani sagged against the wall. She looked at
the name tag on his left breast pocket. "Mister Ostern. Can't
this wait until morning?"

Ostern thrust a small touchbox toward her. "Oh, everything's under control for now, ma'am. I've jury-rigged a by-
pass." His face glowed with pride. *Look what I made,
Mommy!*

Jani accepted the small device with the hesitation of someone who'd learned long ago there was no such thing as
"free." She looked again at Ostern, shifting from his blinding
smile to his eyes. Dark brown, like chocolate. A warm color,
normally. When brown eyes chilled, the cold came from
within.

Her steward had cold brown eyes.

"I can show you how it works, if you like?" Ostern's
voice, a pleasant tenor, still sounded boyish, but the examining look he gave the documents case aged him several stony
decades.

"No, Mister Ostern, it's all right." Jani hoisted the case
and, smiling sweetly, pushed past him and palmed her way
into her cabin.

"Are you sure, ma'am? I—"

"It's all *right*," she said as the door slid closed. "I think I can figure things out." She paused in the entryway and sniffed the air. It did smell vaguely metallic and dusty, as though various things had gone *plonk* in the depths of the ventilation system.

She removed her shoes. Blessedly barefoot, she knelt in the middle of the sitting room and positioned Ostern's little box on the carpet in front of her. Using one of the spindly heels like a hammer, she smashed the device to bits.

After she tossed the fragments down the trash chute, Jani rooted through her duffel. She pushed aside her magnispecs, assorted scanpack parts twined through a holder of braided red cloth, broken UV styluses, and cracked touchpads, until she reached the scanproof false bottom, beneath which lay her shooter and her devices.

Her sensor looked like a UV stylus, except that the light at its pointed end blinked yellow instead of blue, and it had cost more than such things did when purchased through the usual channels. *One does what one has to.* As long as she'd never hurt anyone but herself, what difference did it make?

She flicked the device on. Holding it before her like a glow stick, she took a turn about the sitting room. *If I were an insect, where would I hide?*

It took the better part of an hour to locate the bug, lodged in the bedroom temperature control panel. Bold of Ostern to set it up so she would activate it herself with his cunning control box. She wrapped the tiny plastic cylinder in a strip of antistatic cloth and buried it in the depths of her duffel. A simple listening device, rather than a full sight-and-sound recorder. In that respect, Ostern had disappointed her. She would have expected more from someone with such cold eyes.

Jani ferreted through her cabin a second time. Reasonably certain she had done all she could to ensure her privacy for the ship-night, she undressed. Her stomach ached in earnest now. Her skin felt clammy. She opted for a hot shower in an effort to warm up, and to wash the food odors from her hair. She stood under the water stream until the utilities monitor squealed an imminent cutoff. Then she toweled slowly, all the while thinking about the garage guy. He'd had stomach problems, too. Nausea. Sweats.

Last thing I need is personal experience with the latest colonial epidemic. They'd become more and more common in the last few years—planet-specific infections which, in all the cases Jani heard about, led to long hospital stays and vague medical mumblings about mutating viruses. Well, she'd had enough doctoring to last a lifetime. Anything she had, she'd fight off herself.

She trudged into her bedroom and dug one of her Service tee shirts out of the warren of drawers. The white polycotton still looked new, even after twenty years. *I remember when I got you.* She pulled the use-softened shirt over her head. *I'd just graduated OCS, surprising one and all.* She smiled. Some memories, at least, were pleasant.

One of Six for tongue of gold, Two for eyes and ears.

"It had nothing to do with brains or rank, Ridgeway—we were all on the ball back then," Jani explained to her furniture. "And we needed our little games, to keep us sane."

Three and Four for hands of light, Five and Six for Earthly might. They each had their own special method for keeping the Laumrau Academy administrators off-balance. Senna and Tsai possessed their "hands of light," their talents as musicians, which ranked them quite highly as far as the born-sect idomeni were concerned. Aryton's and Nawar's "Earthly might" derived from their Family connections.

"But Hansen was the *Ambassador*," Jani said, stressing the point for the benefit of her bedclothes. True red hair was extremely rare among the idomeni's major sects. Red in all its variations being a holy color to them, they were inclined to believe any human gifted with such to be possessed of talents in many areas. When trouble brewed in Rauta Shèràa's human enclave, Hansen was always called in to help lift the pot off the boil.

"And I always went with him." Kilian, with her knack for understanding idomeni languages and mannerisms, and her ability to fade into the background. *I'll talk*, Hansen had always told her, *you just watch*.

"You get used to watching." She crawled into bed, duffel and documents case in hand. She unlocked the case and pulled out black-jacketed, confidential Interior files, arranging them in a semicircle on the blanket.

Then she activated her scanpack, her original, unadorned, idomeni-made unit, awarded to her personally upon her graduation by the being who now called himself Tsecha. Then, as now, he served as chief propitiator, the religious leader of his sect. Thus empowered, he had compelled his order-loving, xenophobic people to accept his dictum that humanish be allowed to school with them. Work with them. Even live with them, if isolation in an enclave two kilometers from the farthest outskirts of Rauta Shèràa could be called "living with."

Scores of humans had studied various subjects at the rigorous Academy. But the Six had been favored, and Jani Kilian and Hansen Wyle had been the most favored of all.

Not that she recalled any envy. If anything, her fellow documents trainees had been happy to allow her and Hansen the bulk of Nema's attention. And of his plotting. *Grim Death with a Deal for You*, Jani had dubbed him, much to Hansen's delight. But he had been theirs to laugh at. After all he'd put them through, they'd felt entitled.

And now he's back. And still causing trouble, according to Evan. *If all you think he's interested in is the occasional joyride, have I got news for you.*

She cracked a file seal and glanced down the table of contents of an Interior budget report, then scanned the file. Her 'pack worked without a hitch, as it had since the day she'd received it. "Anytime you want to compare equipment, Mr. Ridgeway, you just say the word." With that, Two of Six, the Eyes and Ears, set to work.

*By the time the patient arrived on Earth, she had
already entered the acute phase of the condition. This
phase, which is characterized by physical malaise and
extreme neurochemical imbalances, played itself out
over the seventy-two-hour period predicted during lab
trials.*

> *—Internal Communication, Neoclona/Seattle,
> Shroud J., Parini, V., concerning Patient S-1*

THE FIRST DAY

CHAPTER 5

"Do you have anything to declare, madam?"

Jani edged away from the half-opened door, which led to the Customs check-in booths reserved for "personal interviews," and left the young Commerce staffer and her husband, both sweaty and shaken, to their fates. *They know you're smuggling something, dears—may as well give it up.* Once a Customs inspector began addressing you formally, all bets were off.

My guess is collectibles or jewelry. Jani had followed the couple since they'd docked at Luna. Well dressed and parcel-laden, they had shunned the bullet cars that would have taken them to the shuttle docks' VIP section in minutes, preferring instead the hike through two kilometers of walkways.

Jani had followed them, curiosity egging her on even as fatigue set in, aggravating her limp. She watched them shift packages and whisper frantically, and waited out their frequent restroom stops, stifling the urge to sneak up behind them and shout, *"Boo!"* Instead, she'd trailed them into the deceptively comforting confines of the lounge, and waited.

Within minutes, a Treasury Customs official, dark gold uniform making him look like a tarnished elf, interrupted the pair's exploration of the buffet and led them away.

The restroom stops tipped Customs off. Scancams lined the public walkways of shuttle stations, but they were unobtrusive and easily ignored by fatigued travelers now a mere five-hour hop from home. Amateurs. Like any game, smuggling had its rules. You followed them, or you paid the penalty.

She cut down the short hallway and entered the spacious lounge. Collecting a cup of tea and a sandwich from the extravagant buffet, she searched for a seat near the wall-spanning window. In the distance, the Lunar shipyards gleamed in the unfiltered sunlight with molten force, drawing the attention of most of the waiting passengers as construction sites always did.

Jani settled into a recently vacated chair, the documents case between her feet, duffel in her lap. Residual stranger-warmth soaked into her lower back. She took a bite of her sandwich, some sort of smoked fish with herbed mayonnaise. *Good, but Lucien could have done better.*

Lucien. Pascal. Her excellent steward's real name. After several more failed attempts to bug Jani's cabin, followed by futile efforts to gain access to her duffel and documents case, he had proposed a truce, which she had accepted. Life aboard the *Arapaho* became more conventional after that, though no less interesting. Watching Lucien operate within the strict hierarchy of the Cabinet ship's Service crew had proven educational. He never broke rules. He never bucked authority. But things got done his way, usually by people who should have known better.

He had even finagled her some Interiorwear that actually fit, like the grey-and-white wrapshirt and trousers she wore. A courtesy, he had told her, from one professional to another.

I almost preferred it when he was trying to gig me—it took my mind off my work. Evan's files. She understood why he had been so reluctant to let her see them. There had been some dealings with a junior member of the Justice Ministry that wouldn't have borne the weight of a public inquiry, as well as personal financial hopscotch of the sort that implied tax evasion. It had taken her almost two weeks just to sort out the intricacies of the accounting involved. The NorthPort Haárin could have learned something from Evan's financial advisor.

But even so, she'd seen worse. Certainly nothing to merit a death. There had already been too many. First, Evan's and Lyssa's children, drowned during their efforts to sail an antique boat during a summer holiday. Two boys and a girl—ages fourteen, twelve, and ten. Martin, Jerrold, and Serena.

Then came Lyssa. Official record confirmed the gossip. The woman's behavior had become increasingly erratic over the past two years. Unexplained disappearances. Rumors of drug abuse. Hushed-up accidents.

But all the documents scanned within normal variation. Nothing to suggest tampering. Nothing to merit a murder. Have I proved your fears unfounded already, Evan? As things now stood, Lyssa died a broken woman's death, driven by past tragedy.

Jani watched construction workers flit along a future commercial transport's spindly framework, one beat ahead of the immense robot ganglion that did the actual hoisting, joining, and fastening. No matter how well-programmed the 'bot, however fuzzified the thinking, human supervision was still required. No robot was capable of seeing the overall picture. Ultimately, it only knew what it was told.

Jani watched a moon-suited human dodge and weave about one of the arms like an armored gnat . . .

I sense an effort to lead me by the nose.

. . . ensuring that the arm moved in the correct direction and hit the chosen target.

His initials are Durian Ridgeway.

Jani finished her sandwich. She hoped she hadn't wasted almost five weeks working with half the data, but she knew that hope was misplaced. She had slipped an urgent meeting request, coded to Evan's attention, into the queue of scrambled messages transmitted to Chicago every half hour. But she doubted she would receive a reply before her shuttle left in—she checked her timepiece—forty-five minutes.

"Do you have anything to declare?"

Jani turned toward the voice. On the far side of the lounge, Customs clerks moved among the waiting passengers, logging colonial purchases, calculating tariffs, handing out receipts. She exhaled with a shudder. Augie notwithstanding, she hadn't been breathing very easily the past few minutes. But she could relax now. The sending-out-of-the-clerks meant all those who merited more personal attention from Customs had already been winnowed.

I wonder how my young couple is doing? Had the body cavity scans begun? Attorneys been contacted?

"Do you have anything to declare?" Chipper voices grew closer. Paper rustled. Recording boards chirped. "Anything at all?"

If you only knew.

"Nothing?"

Not an issue, now. You had your shot and missed. Go away.

"Are you quite sure?"

Yes. My secrets remain mine. I am Jani Moragh Kilian. Captain. United Services. C-number S-one-two-dash-four-seven-dash-one-seven-nine-D. Sideline Service, assigned to Rauta Shèràa Base, First Documents and Documentation Division. Not a real soldier.

"Anything else?"

Eighteen years ago, in a place called Knevçet Shèràa, during the height of the idomeni civil war, I killed my commanding officer in self-defense. His name was Rikart Neumann—Colonel—Gisela Detmers-Neumann's uncle. She and others would perhaps take exception to the self-defense argument, but since they're aware of the events that precipitated the shoot-out, they may not dare voice such.

"Do you have anything to declare?"

The Laumrau panicked when they learned of Neumann's death. First they lobbed "pink"; the microbe infested and disabled all the weapons, environmental, and communication arrays. Then came the shatterboxes. The Laumrau had secrets to bury, which are none of your concern. All you need know is that, in the process, they buried my corporal. She died when a wall collapsed on her. Corporal Yolan Cray, Mainline Service, Twelfth Rover Corps, C-number M-four-seven-dash-five-six-dash-two-eight-six-R.

"I'm ready, miss—please continue."

One idomeni day later, I killed twenty-six Laumrau in an effort to save my remaining troops. The deaths were not "clean" as far as the Laumrau were concerned. No human had ever become involved in one of their skirmishes before— the resulting disorder upset them. Since I had violated the Bilateral Accord, the Service would have turned me over to the idomeni for trial followed by inevitable execution, but—

"I'm sorry, miss, could you speak up, please?"

—but the transport carrying me and my troops from Knev-çet Shèràa to Rauta Shèràa exploded on takeoff. Lift-array failure. Everyone gone. All her real soldiers. *I know their C-numbers, too.* All fourteen of them. *Do you want to hear them, too?*

"That's not necessary, ma'am. Please continue."

I, however, did not die. Not medically, anyway. *Three doctors salvaged me from the wreckage, for reasons that would shock you to your core. They pieced me together and hid me in a hospital basement in Rauta Shèràa's human enclave. As I healed, the tide of civil war turned, and the Laumrau lost to the Vynshà.* Laumrau descended to Laum, and Vynshà ascended to Vynshàrau. No one fights to avenge the deaths of the losers, not even the well-ordered idomeni.

But they remembered. They called her *kièrshia,* she'd learned later. Toxin. *You don't want to allow me within your perimeter—everything I touch dies.*

"Do you have anything to declare?"

The pennies on my eyes.

"Do you have anything to declare?" The smiling Customs clerk stationed himself beside Jani's chair, recording board in hand, beaming in a way that reminded her of Lucien.

"Just these." Jani removed some pieces of truesilver jewelry, purchased in a hurried swoop through a pricey Felix Station shop, from the side pocket of her duffel. With cheerful efficiency, the clerk scanned the information from the still-attached price tags into his board's data bank and totaled the tariff. Jani just as cheerfully rattled off the Interior account to which the tariff could be billed.

Rule One: Always have something hefty to declare to throw them off. Transaction completed, receipt tucked away, Jani settled back and watched the construction workers hover and dart like metallic bees around a skeletal hive. *Take it from an old smuggler.* She sipped the tea, winced at its bitterness, and waited for her boarding call.

"Admit it, Jani. You'd never seen anything like it in your life. All those old skyscrapers! All that history!" Evan bustled her out onto the glass-walled balcony that adjoined his office and pointed out his view, which included both the Chicago skyline and the nearby lake. "I hope you got a chance to see the memorial to the Greatest War on the way in."

Jani took in the curious array of oddly shaped buildings, all obscured by wind-whipped snow. "You mean 'The War of Family Aggression,' don't you?"

"There were no Families back then, Jani," Evan said patiently.

"No. They came later."

"I seem to recall us having this discussion before." Evan sighed. "Politics aside, it's worth a visit. It's a liquiprism obelisk that changes color on the hour. Really quite striking."

"Evan, I don't know if you've noticed, but it's not sight-seeing weather." Jani looked out at the lake, which had taken on a churning, milky grey life of its own. "If this balcony wasn't enclosed and well heated, we'd be icicles within seconds."

"Yes, but it's home."

"Not for me." She turned her back on his fallen face. "Sorry—didn't mean to rain on your birthday." She hesitated at the office entry. *Why do I feel like I just kicked a puppy?* "I'm sure it must be very nice. In the spring."

"Oh, it is." Evan hurried to her side. "The parks. The arboretums. You'd love it here in the spring." He escorted her back into his retreat's soothing blue-and-green depths. "I gathered your ride here from O'Hare was more exciting than you may have liked."

"That's an understatement." Jani sank into a chair across from Evan's desk. "Nothing like a collision with split batteries to disrupt the flow of traffic on a twelve-lane skimway. Then the HazMat unit came. Then this storm. At least it held off until after I landed." She shuddered. "I think my driver has a death wish. I'd yank her license."

Evan perched on the edge of his desk. "Quite an indictment, coming from you. I blamed my first grey hairs on our sojourns through Rauta Shèràa." That little *bon mot* launched, he eased behind his desk and kicked back. "Chicago is the Commonwealth capital, Jani. Over seventeen million people live within the metroplex limits. I can't tell you the exact square kilometers offhand, but the number borders on the ridiculous.'' His look turned concerned. ''I hadn't considered culture shock. Are you?''

''Shocked by the wonder of it all? I'll live.'' Jani massaged the hard knot in the back of her neck where augie had planted his foot. She had coped with the throbbing red lights on the emergency vehicles well enough, but the sirens had gotten to her. She held out her hands. The right one had finally stopped shaking. The left one had never started. *Half-sane, at least, but which half?* ''Does this place have a gym? Exercise helps.''

''Five. I'll get you a pass for the one I use—it has the best equipment.'' He picked absently at his fingernails. ''We have a decent medical staff, as well,'' he added carefully. ''All Neoclona-trained.''

''*No*, thank you.''

''Oh, for crying out loud, stop acting like an idomeni!'' Evan's voice rasped with irritation. ''What, I'm not your physician-priest, so you can't talk to me? When was the last time you had your augmentation evaluated? Any augmented vet who works for Interior has to be checked out every six months and have at least one precautionary take-down per year.''

''Forget it. Look, I received enough doctoring after the crash to last a lifetime. Half my limbs and most of my insides were grown in a tank. I'm sick of the smell of antiseptic, poking and prodding, and white sheets, not necessarily in that order. And forget any damned take-down. No one's going to stick a blinking box in my face and short out my brain for my own good. I've had it. And speaking of 'had it.' '' She gave Evan a brief rundown of her thoughts with regard to his files. His headshaking grew more and more pronounced each time Jani alluded to the possibility that Durian Ridgeway had purposely withheld information.

''I can't accept that!'' Evan's feet hit the carpeted floor with a muffled *thud*. ''Durian knows how important this is. Hell, he has as much to lose as I do if things fall to pieces. He's been cleaning up after me for so long, his nickname around here is *the janitor*. Everyone knows if I show up, he's never far behind. We're joined at the hip—if I go, he goes.''

Oh goodie—I've come between a dog and his man. And between both of them and what? Jani stared at Evan until he broke eye contact and began pushing his pen stand back and forth. "You're still holding out on me." She worked her hands over the brocaded upholstery that covered the arms of her chair. Only her right could detect the changes in texture.

"Jani—"

"Have you forgotten what *I* have to lose if things fall to pieces?"

"*No one could possibly—*"

"I'm wanted by the Service for mutinous murder and desertion. No dust has ever settled on that warrant. It's reposted every six Common months without fail in every colonial Government Hall. Wherever I happened to be, I'd stop by, keep myself company."

"I know it must—"

"Funny how oddly comforting I found it at times. Like a touchstone—"

"Will you shut up!" Evan's face had taken on a hunted look. "I didn't want to tell you this. Knowing how you may react, I'm still not sure I should." The pen stand jerked and shook. "Exterior's looking for you, Jan. I arrived on Whalen only twelve hours ahead of a cruiser carrying members of Ulanova's executive staff. I heard rumors of a Service ship trolling the area as well, but I couldn't confirm them."

Jani crossed her legs to ease the pressure on her lower back. *You'd think a Cabinet House would have better chairs.* "Why now, I wonder?"

Evan's brow furrowed. "You don't seem surprised."

Jani shook her head. "My record states, 'missing, assumed dead.' The gulf between that and 'declared dead' is very wide." She poked her numb left arm. "No remains were ever found. No indestructible Service ID chip was recovered from the wreckage and canceled out. The Admiral-General doesn't know for sure I'm dead; therefore, I am alive. That's why the outstanding warrant. That's why a rep gets sent out to follow up every rumor of my existence. I killed my CO. Then I violated the Bilateral Accord by interfering in idomeni affairs. Those are two biggies, Ev. You may think they've given up on me, but you're wrong. They're not going to rest until they nail me to the wall.''

Evan's expression grew confused. "What I don't understand is how Shroud and his buddies managed to keep you hidden? What did they think they played at?''

I remember them standing outside my door, when they thought I couldn't hear. Laughing, calling one another Dr. Frankenstein. No, she took that back. John never laughed. "I don't know how they did it. I think it was all a game to them; an escape from the boredom. Most of the humans had been evac'd by that time. They had nothing to do. So they built themselves a friend.'' She walked over to the bar and poured herself a glass of water. She gulped the cold liquid, felt it cool her from within. It took her some time to realize Evan had remained silent. She turned to find him staring at her.

"What do you mean by 'friend'? Tell me what I'm thinking didn't happen. Please tell me they didn't—''

"They didn't, Evan. Parini's homosexual and DeVries only likes blondes with big tits.''

"What about Shroud? I knew him back then, you know. From his visits to the Consulate. He was strange then, and he hasn't improved with time.''

"I knew him, too. A little.'' If encounters in the entryway of Nema's house counted as "knowing.'' *He'd mumble, "Hello," and stare at the floor.* Poor John. Funny the things she remembered. How hands that performed the most delicate medical procedures could turn so clumsy when working under a different sort of pressure. "It's over. Why worry about it? What am I going to do, sue for malpractice?'' She returned to the bar and poured herself more water, this time adding ice.

"I guess I understand your medical phobia now,'' Evan said. "I'm surprised they let you escape.''

"They didn't. I slipped away during the final blitz.'' Jani leaned against a bookcase. The odor of the leather binding seemed especially sharp, almost meaty. "Remember?''

Evan nodded slowly. "The Night of the Blade. The Vynshà sent the Haárin into Rauta Shèràa first. Debriding the wound, they called it.''

Jani picked up the thread. "They had set up observation

points in the hills. I could see the halolamps flashing signals to the Haárin in the city center."

Evan gaped. "They let you walk the streets!"

"I wasn't walking. More like limping double time." She tried to smile. "They didn't want humanish at that point, anyway. They had other concerns." She looked at Evan, sitting hunched over his desk. "Where were you?"

"The sub-basement of the Consulate. We'd been down there for eleven idomeni days. Almost two weeks. The Service got us out at dawn, as the Vynshà entered the city proper. They'd just declared themselves 'rau,' and set fire to the ring the Haárin had erected around Rauta Shèràa's perimeter. We could see the flames from the transport windows." He swallowed. "There were bodies in that ring."

"Not all of them were dead, either." Jani walked away from the bookcase. The odor of the books was making her sick to her stomach. "The ring of souls released by cleansing fire. Supposed to guarantee peace and protection until the next imbalance of power." She looked out the balcony window. The wind still whipped, blowing so much snow that the view looked like a malfunctioning holoVee screen. A roaring gust rattled the panes.

It was Evan's turn to visit the bar. He ignored the water pitcher and reached for the bourbon. "That convergence on Whalen may not mean anything. The way things have been going lately, a display of any type of proficiency with things idomeni would have been enough to attract attention. Ulanova may just be looking for translators." He poured himself a single shot, downed it, then paused to catch his breath. "I slipped a decoy into NorthPort—one of my own people—to distract them." He frowned. "She was one of my best Vynshà-watchers. I'm going to miss her. Probably take us months to get her back."

"Sorry for the inconvenience."

Evan smiled. He hefted the bourbon decanter as though testing its weight, then set it back in its place in the bottle rack. "I think I know what Durian removed from the files. And I know where to find it. You'll have it by tonight."

"Are you going to confront him?"

"No. Not yet. He's not here now, anyway. He and Ange

are flying in later today from London. A visit to his family, I believe." He flinched as another gust shook the balcony panes.

That was Hansen Wyle exploding out of his grave. "A visit to *chez* Ridgeway? *Really?*"

"Durian's relationship with Angevin is completely professional," Evan huffed defensively. "You just don't like him."

"He doesn't like me either. He tried to trip me up on the *Arapaho*. He threw some Josephani at me. I pretended I couldn't understand his accent."

"Did you have a chance to study those language discs I slipped into your documents portfolio?"

"That's not the point!"

"No. No, you're right. I'll have a talk with him." He leaned against the bar. "Jani, nobody here knows you except me. In any case, no one who knew you eighteen years ago could place you now. Your face is completely different, your hair. You've lost weight—hell, you even look *taller.*" His aimless stare came to rest on her and sharpened. "You're safe. I'll keep you safe."

Jani raised her glass in a mock toast, took a last sip, and headed for the door. "I need to walk off my Chicago driving adventure. I'll see you later."

"Jani?"

She turned to find Evan had opted for the second bourbon after all.

"You really killed Riky Neumann?"

"Yes."

"But he drew first? It was self-defense?"

"His hand went to his holster. I wasn't going to wait to discover whether he was serious or just bluffing. Considering I'd just threatened to declare anarchy rules, relieve him of command, and place him under arrest, I don't think he was simply trying to gauge my reaction."

"Anarchy rules? *You* were going to take over command?"

"The integrity of the documents in my care was threatened. I saw no other alternative. I was within my rights."

Evan downed his second shot. His face flushed. "You killed him over a paper issue?"

"You're upset because he was a Family member?"

"He was my father's best friend. I grew up calling him Uncle Rik."

"And I served under him. Apparently he made a better uncle than commanding officer." Jani rifled through her pockets for her key card. Her duffel and documents case waited outside in a locked desk. "I'll see you tonight. In the meantime, I think I'll explore." She left without looking back. She knew what she'd see if she did. Evan, with his puzzled expression, liquor-fueled curiosity, and unspoken question. *Why, Jani?*

Because when the first patient died, Neumann lied when I asked how it happened, and when the second patient mutilated himself, he told me the truth and expected me to go along. Jani recovered her bags from the desk, took comfort in their weight and shape. But it didn't last. Her mind had set off down another trail, one she tried to avoid but never could for long.

Human patients. At the idomeni hospital. At Knevçet Shèràa. She leaned against the anteroom doorway until the arrival of a flock of staffers forced her to brace up. Then she struck out in search of someone who could tell her where her room was.

CHAPTER 6

Jani sat in the living room of her suite, which occupied a substantial portion of the second floor rear, Interior House Private, and listened to the blizzard's relentless assault against her windows.

After requesting assistance from the occupants of an office down the hall from Evan's, she had soon found herself being passed like a human baton from one black-clad staffer to another. Interior House Main, the Ministry headquarters, was a twelve-story-high, two-kilometer-long city-in-miniature, and Jani felt sure she had been ferried through every centimeter of hallway, lift shaft, and underground skimway before being deposited within the confines of her latest home.

I could stop here for a while. Lots of green, icy on the walls, dark and patterned for rugs and curtains. Flooring and furniture in blond truewood; lamps and accent pieces in black, burnished copper, and emerald. The artwork, realistic seascapes and white curves of Channel School sculpture, were either originals or damned good reproductions.

Makes a difference when you enter through the front door, doesn't it? Figuratively speaking. Judging from the sounds filtering through the sealed windows, Jani didn't expect to see a Chicago front door for at least four months.

If I'm here that long. She sagged farther into her chair. The prospect of getting up seemed as daunting as that of leaving Chicago, post-augie jitters having given way to travel lag. She closed her eyes and tried to nap, but nosiness began sending "let's explore" jolts through her system. She answered the call and started opening doors and checking drawers.

Her bags had already been unpacked, the contents distributed among chests, armoires, and a walk-in closet the size of the NorthPort tracking station. A door she thought led to the bathroom actually opened to a fully applianced kitchenette. Jani checked the cooler and found it stocked with the fruit drinks and snack foods she vaguely recalled mentioning to one of the staffers as her favorites. She cracked the seal on a dispo of helgeth and took a tentative sip. The frothy purple juice tasted crisp and slightly astringent. She polished off that container and half of another before resuming her search. She hadn't realized how thirsty she was.

Another door, palm lock in place but not yet activated, led into a small office. The room contained a desk, also lockable, on which sat a workstation with a secured Cabinet link, the newest model parchment imprinter, and a vase of fresh flowers. Jani stashed the documents case in the desk, tested the chair, then drew aside the curtain and looked out at the storm-whipped lake. *An office with windows—you've skipped up a few grades, Captain.*

She wandered into the bathroom to wash her hands, took one look at the multijet shower, and soon stood beneath pounding streams of hot water. Thus refreshed, she rooted through drawers for clean clothes, and pounced on a set of charcoal grey ship coveralls Lucien had scrounged for her. She dug out a matching tee shirt emblazoned across the front with the legend CSS *ARAPAHO* and freed her scuffed, black, steel-toed boots from the civilized confines of one of the armoires. Working a towel through her damp hair, she collected her duffel and returned to her office.

She activated all her locks using a UV stylus she had liberated from the *Arapaho* inventory. That task completed, she tried to return the stylus to its scanproof pocket in her duffel, but something stiff and sharp-edged slipped into the space and dug into her hand, blocking her.

Jani eased out the holocard, taking special care to avoid bending it. As she tilted the card back and forth, the two holographed sailracers swooped and soared like fighting birds. The brilliant purple-and-blue sails reflected the light like colored mirrors, while the racers' multihued wetsuits shimmered with pearly iridescence.

So, Risa, what's your real name? I've told you mine—it's only fair you tell me yours.

Lucien, I'll tell you mine when you tell me who you're working for.

Jani turned the card over and studied the blank writing surface. Lucien hadn't signed his farewell to her, but then, one could hardly have expected him to leave a traceable signature. For her part, Jani had bug-scanned the card immediately. Twice. A show of respect. From one professional to another.

She propped the card against the vase, tilting it until the two racers were displayed to their best advantage. Then she shouldered her bag, locked her office, and set out to explore.

Jani paused in a sunroomlike walkway which, according to the large display in the center of the tiled floor, joined the Colonial Affairs Offices with Employee Services Section Two, the area she had just left. She stared at the network of connected mazes glowing in yellow and green on the display screen, groaning when she realized she was looking at the ground-floor map only. She touched a pad on the side of the display frame. The mazes shimmered and altered to form the second floor.

She touched the pad ten more times.

I'm not lost—I'm buried. Outside, snow sheeted against glass walls and tornadoed into curves and crevices, reinforcing the illusion. Jani again flipped through floor plans, this time with a better idea of what she wanted.

Five hours later, she emerged from the Library the proud possessor of the passcard and linkcodes necessary to access confidential Cabinet references from her office workstation. She had also arranged for the delivery of several Earth-based and colonial newssheets, and impressed the head documents librarian sufficiently to ensure preferential treatment whenever she submitted a special request.

She'd also stolen a magazine.

I'll give it back. Jani's duffel banged against her hip accusingly, its sides bulging with the addition of an expensive, paper-bound gossip holozine, the slick cover of which bore the brutally unretouched image of a glassy-eyed, disheveled Lyssa van Reuter. *I'm surprised Evan allowed this on-site.* But librarians were a notoriously independent-minded lot, and the public's morbid curiosity regarding the hard life and violent death of one of the more hologenic Family members apparently extended to those who should have known better.

The holozine's title had struck her as particularly ludicrous. "Lyssa—A Life Tragically Cut Short." As if a life could be cheerfully cut short. Maybe they'd explain that novel concept in next month's issue. Jani hugged her duffel close as she boarded the first elevator she came to. She felt a common thief, but she didn't want Evan to know what she read. She'd bet her 'pack he'd asked the Library to inform him of what she checked out. Even independent minds had to follow direct orders from Cabinet Ministers.

The elevator started down. Jani checked her timepiece and wondered at the possibility of hitching a ride into the city. Just to look around, get her bearings. It could prove interesting, now the blizzard had finally stopped.

But first, she needed food. She pressed the second-floor pad again. There was a cafeteria on that floor, as well as an Interior-subsidized grocery store. Her stomach rumbled in anticipation of a very late lunch.

Her absent gaze fell on the car's indicator. It had flickered when she touched it, but the display above the door showed she had bypassed the second floor and was continuing down. Jani punched floor pads, then tried to activate the override, but her efforts to halt the car's descent failed. She tried to push through the ceiling access panel. No go.

The indicator continued to flash. ONE. GROUND. BASE-ONE.

She was heading for the sub-basements. According to the touchpad display, Interior Main stretched five floors below ground level.

BASE-TWO.

Sub-basements were extremely well-secured. They were designed, after all, to serve as disaster shelters.

BASE-THREE.

"You should have taken the stairs, idiot." She dug for her shooter, then tried to crack the seals on the car's ceiling lights

with the grip. The thick safety plastic resisted—only two of
the four lights succumbed. The car didn't plunge into darkness—more a cloudy dusk. It would serve.

BASE-FOUR.

Jani disengaged her weapon's safety, then braced against
the car's rear wall. Feet shoulder width apart. Both hands on
the grip. Maybe they wouldn't expect her to stand out in the
open. Maybe they wouldn't expect her to shoot.

Direct line of fire—aim for the chest.

BASE-FIVE.

The door swept open. Durian Ridgeway, windblown and
agitated, squinted into the car. "Who the—*oh*. Good afternoon, Ms. Tyi. This *is* a restricted-use lift, in case no one
informed you."

"Sorry," Jani replied as she secreted her shooter in her
coverall pocket

He glared at the car ceiling. "What in bloody hell happened to the lights?"

Angevin Wyle bustled in behind him, weighed down with
shopping bags. "Hello, Risa." She joined Jani in the rear of
the car. "Why's it so frickin' dark in here?"

"Angevin." Ridgeway thumped the touchpad in the vicinity of the fourth floor. "Language." He didn't bother to ask
Jani which floor she wanted. The door closed like a judgment,
and they ascended in silence.

The door opened to reveal a mob. Jani found herself surrounded by aggressively helpful staffers who first sought to
separate her from her duffel and, when that failed, tried to
usher her down the hall toward a large conference room. At
the sight of the reporters, holocam operators, and Security
guards milling at the room's entrance, she executed a sloppy
but successful *excuse me* ricochet spin-off. The move propelled her away from the conference room and past Angevin,
who was engaged in heated conversation with a sulky young
man who appeared determined to confiscate her shopping
bags.

Jani skirted around a corner and down an empty hall as
images from the display map paged past her mind's eye. She
wandered up and down halls, avoiding guards, searching for
a stairwell or secondary elevator that wasn't alarmed.

Close-controlled floors have one and only one nonemergency entry—slash—exit which means if I want to get out of here without lighting up the whole damn complex, I have to walk by the cams and have my face transmitted to every damn colony—shit!

"Ms. Tyi!"

Jani turned to find Durian Ridgeway rushing toward her.

"Have you seen Angevin? She's disappeared!" His ruddy face flushed as he palmed into several of the offices, searching for his wayward aide. "The meeting begins in five minutes, and she has all my notes. The Deputy Prime Minister is here. Angevin needs this exposure, damn it, but every time she gets a chance to put herself forward, she's nowhere to be found!"

What Angevin needs more than anything are six months' pay and an hour's head start. Jani leaned against the wall and watched Ridgeway pace. "Sounds important."

He nodded. "Emergency session. Called by Langley." His mouth twisted around the Deputy's name. " 'We'll meet as soon as you get back,' he said. 'Nothing important,' he said. Then we pull into the main parking garage to find vans from every major news service parked there. We had to flee down to the subs to avoid being blitzed. *Bastard*." His voice took on a desperate edge. "If you could help me find Angevin, Ms. Tyi, I would be very grateful."

Jani gave him a halfhearted salute, hurrying away before he felt compelled to say, "please." She picked a hall where most of the doors lacked palm locks. She tapped lightly on a couple, then pushed open one labeled, FURNITURE. The room lights had already been activated, brought to life, no doubt, by the furious motion taking place atop one of the desks. Angevin, her long skirt bunched up over her hips, had her bare legs wrapped around the arching back of the young man with whom Jani had seen her arguing a few minutes before. He wasn't sulking now.

Jani kicked at a nearby trashzap, sending the metal bucket clattering across the floor. "Durian!" she hissed before forcing the door closed. She took off down the hall, rounded the corner, and barreled into an agitated Ridgeway.

"What was that noise, Risa?" he asked as he tried to dart around her.

"Just me being clumsy," Jani said as she gripped his arm and spun him around. "Angevin's down on the third floor. The parts bins." That seemed reasonable. Documents examiners always fretted over their scanpack functions, especially before important meetings and transactions. "She'll be on her way back up within a few minutes. I ran into someone who saw her go down. There."

"I hope she doesn't show up stinking of broth. Who told you she was there?"

"One of the Security guards." *Please don't ask which one.* "Angevin gave him a message to give to you. I intercepted." Jani heaved an inward sigh as she felt Ridgeway's arm relax.

"Well, nice to know she hasn't lost all sense of responsibility." He eased out of Jani's grasp and smoothed the sleeve of his jacket. "Back to work, then. Thank you, Ms. Tyi." With a curt nod, he walked off in the direction of the conference room bustle.

Jani waited until she felt sure he wouldn't return. Then she hurried back around the corner and tapped on the storage-room door. "He's gone."

The door cracked open. The young man slipped out first. He glowered at Jani, looked past her down the hall, then whispered over his shoulder, "'S ok."

Angevin crept out, jacket in hand. "Please don't tell Durian," she rasped as she struggled into the snug-fitting topper. "He'll kill us if he finds—"

"Don't *fookin'* beg!" The young man's Channel World accent could have blunted complexed steel. "We airn't done nothin' wrong!"

"You both shut up." Jani leaned close to Angevin. Her frazzled appearance could be written off as travel lag, but no one could mistake the smashed berry stains surrounding her swollen lips. "Collect your gear, splash some cold water on your face, and get your ass to that meeting."

Angevin rushed back into the storage room, reemerging with her documents bag in hand. "Please don't tell—"

Jani waved her quiet. "You told a *male* Security guard to tell Ridgeway you had gone to the parts bins. I ran into the guard and told him I'd deliver the message. Got that?" Angevin nodded wide-eyed as Jani pushed her down the hall.

She watched her disappear around the corner, then sagged against the wall. Her neck seized up as she tried to flex it.

"We airn't done nothin' wrong."

Jani turned slowly to find the young man still scowling. He'd pulled a flat copper case from the inside pocket of his tunic and removed a nicstick. "Airn't seen each other for over three bloody months." He stuck the gold-and-white candy-striped cylinder in his mouth without cracking the ignition tip, shoved his hands in his trouser pockets, and started pacing.

Upon close examination, he proved good-looking, in a pouty, dissolute choirboy sort of way. Thick, straight auburn hair covered his ears and collar and flopped over his forehead. His skin had an office pallor, his uniform black boots needed polishing, and he slouched. *Boy, I bet Ridgeway hated you on sight.* "You Channel Worlder?" Jani asked.

He wheeled. "Yeah!" He stepped close, until his nose was only centimeters from hers and she could smell the spiced odor of his unignited nicstick. "So the fook what?"

Jani looked into his eyes, the same mossy green as Angevin's. More bloodshot, though. "What's your name?" she countered softly.

The question, or the manner in which it was asked, seemed to throw the young man. His jaw worked. "Steve. Forell."

"Jersey? Guernsey? Man?"

"Guernsey." He took a deep breath. "Helier."

Jani smiled. "I've been to Helier. A beautiful city." *If you were born with antifreeze in your veins.* "And what do you do here at Interior, Mr. Forell?"

The smile began in the depths of the narrowed eyes and quickly worked down. Steve Forell shook his shaggy head to help it along. Relaxed and grinning, he looked all of twelve years old. A gamy, street-wise twelve, but twelve all the same.

"Screw that—you're trying to redirect me attentions." He worked his nicstick like a toothpick. "I'm a dexxie, like Ange. Xenopolitical branch. Work with the idomeni. Schooled at Oxbridge Combined." He tugged at his hair. "The xenos came looking for redheads and scooped me up."

"Colony boy at an Earthbound school. You must be good."

"I am." The grin flickered as Steve glanced down the hall in the direction Angevin had gone. "Not good enough, though, according to some." Then his smile vanished and instead of looking street-wise and twelve, he looked lonely, scared, and five and a half.

See what happens when you learn names. You get involved. Jani leaned harder into the wall. *I do not have the time.* Her back ached now, and the elevator episode coming so soon after the traffic adventure hadn't done her post-augie nerves any favors.

"What's the matter with you?" Steve asked. "You look fit to pass out."

Jani massaged her tightened scalp. "Can you get me out of here?" She forced a smile, and felt her travel-dry skin crinkle under the stress. "I'm not cleared for the close-controlled floors. The elevator won't listen to me."

"Surprised Durian didn't have you tossed out a window." Steve pushed his way back into the storage room, emerging with Angevin's shopping bags. "Here." He shoved two of the slick plastic sacks into Jani's arms and gripped the remaining bags with looped thumbs and forefingers only. "He even picks out her clothes," he grumbled as he glanced at the bags' contents. "We'll leave them with the door guard. Meeting'll go on for hours, anyway."

They walked back to the elevators. The area had been cleared of cams and reporters; a pair of guards stood sentry by the closed conference-room doors. They eyed Jani warily, but relaxed when Steve walked over and handed them the bags.

"What now?" he asked as he rejoined her. He flipped open a panel beside the elevator and punched in a code sequence.

"I haven't eaten since the Luna shuttle. That was over ten hours ago. Just point me toward the food."

"You need dinner?" Steve brightened. "I could do with some dinner. The cafeteria on Two is the best one. That's where all the nobbies eat." The doors closed, and he blinked in surprise. "What the hell happened to the lights?"

CHAPTER 7

"Your government takes issue with the bidding, nìRau?"

Tsecha remained very still in his low bench seat, conscious of the sidelong glances of the others at the table and the more direct, fear-filled stare of the man who had spoken. Humanish eyes. He should have grown used to them by now. *But so much white—like death-glaze.*

He crossed his left arm over his chest and lowered his chin. "The bidding, we are most content with, and truly, Mister Ridgeway." His voice rumbled, even in both tone and pitch and, he felt, unaccented. He was most proud of his English. "My Oligarch wonders only of the lapse in security. He fears it happening again."

Ridgeway shook his head in a show of impatience, obvious for even a humanish. "NìRau," he said, "Morden nìRau Ceèl has our word it won't happen again."

Tsecha remained calm as the other humanish at the table shifted in their chairs. Some exhaled loudly. He stared openly down the large wooden oval at Durian Ridgeway, but felt no pleasure as he watched the man's tired face flood with color. It had always been too easy with that one. "Yes, Mister Ridgeway," he replied, "but you also gave your word last year. And your office gave its word last month in your name. You pledged your word to research this company's documents, and you failed. What value is your word, Mister Ridgeway? I ask you that."

The room itself seemed to sigh in response. Then the man at the table's head, Deputy Prime Minister Langley, spoke.

"In Durian's defense, Staffel Mitteilungen took us all by surprise, nìRau. They purposely delayed obtaining their start-up registration until the end of the fiscal year. Many of our new businesses do this for the tax advantage. StafMit did it in hope that, in the flood of applications, the screening committee Durian chaired would miss the fact that via a blind trust, Gisela Detmers-Neumann held a significant financial stake in the company."

Tsecha looked directly into the Deputy PM's eyes. *Dark Langley, as the night is dark.* If they were as idomeni, Langley's eyes would look as two black pits. He sat rigidly, his seat, like the seats of all the humanish, elevated above Tsecha's. The positioning of the chairs, the humans' stiff, formal posture, were meant to display respect. But he had never detected either the gentleness of friend or the wary regard of esteemed enemy in any of those in the room. What could he sense? Fear? Definitely. Dislike? Perhaps. *They do not want me here.* That was indeed unfortunate for them. Here, he was. Here, he would stay.

"Tax advantage, Mister Langley?" Tsecha placed his hands palms down on the tabletop. Red bands trimmed the broad cuffs of his sand white overrobe, making it appear as though blood flowed from his wrists. His ring of station glimmered on his finger, the jasperite also reminding him of blood.

"Yes, nìRau." Langley's thick, black eyebrows arched with some vague emotion, but he offered no accompanying gesture or change in posture to indicate which it was. Puzzlement? Surprise? Or perhaps the man felt embarrassment concerning the question? Who could tell with these government humanish? Their faces were as blocks of wood, their gestures, when they bothered to gesture, meaningless flailing. "Taxes," Langley repeated. "The saving of money."

"Ah." Tsecha spread his fingers. Wrinkled. Age-spotted. He touched a thread-fine scar near the base of his left thumb, the remains of a blade fight with an esteemed enemy, now long dead.

à lèrine—the ritual combat that declared to all idomeni the hatred between two. So many such bouts had he fought in defense of his beliefs—the scars etched his arms, his chest and shoulders. They had thinned and faded over time, as he had. He had grown so old, waiting. "Yes," he said, with a nod he hoped Langley comprehended. "I know humanish have great interest in money, and truly. That interest has been displayed to idomeni in times past."

The room sighed again, for those reasons all humanish knew, yet would not speak. In an effort to placate, Tsecha bared his teeth to the Deputy PM. Smiling, to humanish an expression of most benign regard. Why then did the man squirm so?

"We've been through all this, nìRau," Langley said. Indeed, he seemed most displeased. His jaw worked. He gripped the arms of his chair.

"Yes, Mister Langley, we have."

"Our purpose today is to discuss the Vynshàrau's reluctance to allow StafMit the opportunity to bid for contracts to install communications equipment in the Haárin settlement outside Tsing Tao."

"Yes, Mister Langley, it is."

"Since Mister Ridgeway's committee approved StafMit's preliminary registration, thus bringing them to the Haárin trade council's attention, I asked him here to—"

"To *trap* him, Mister Langley." Tsecha dropped his words slowly, carefully, like stones into still water. "And to embarrass Mister van Reuter."

Plink! Ridgeway stared at him openly, unsure whether to be grateful or to fear what could follow.

Plink! Langley exhaled with a shudder, his anger a solid thing that one could hold in the hand.

Plink! The other humanish at the table stared at their hands, in the air over each other's heads, anywhere but at one another.

Tsecha pressed his lips together to avoid baring his teeth. He most enjoyed telling humanish the obvious truths they so feared. It shocked them so.

"NìRau, I would have thought this neither the time nor the place, but perhaps—"

Tsecha shut out Langley's drone. He had heard the arguments before at too many meetings, could recite them as he did his prayers. It would have surprised the humanish to know if the choice had been his alone, Tsecha would have allowed

Detmers-Neumann and her fellow outcasts to welcome him to this damned cold city, to sit and watch him speak to the shivering crowds. *But when her first openness failed, she tried to worm, to sneak, to . . . to . . .* Tsecha's command of English failed him. He only knew that blood had asserted itself as it always did. Gisela proved she shared skein with Rikart, and truly. So, just as truly, would he never acknowledge her.

His gaze flitted from one tense face to another, finally coming to rest on the female sitting next to Ridgeway. Blood asserted itself, or did it? He tried to will the red-haired young ish to look at him, but she kept her eyes fixed on her lap. Angevin. What did such a name mean? *Not-of-Hansen?* How much Tsecha missed her father, as well as the one who worked with him. His green-eyed Captain.

If they were here, what meetings we would have! But Hansen, Tsecha's brilliant Wyle of the godly hair, was dead, and the man's daughter could not compare.

And Kilian . . .

Tsecha looked down at his mottled hands. He thought so much of age lately. Death. All these meetings brought such thoughts. All this talk with as-dead humanish was enough to drain the hope from any living thing. And he had had such hopes once, had seen the future in two faces. But one was dead and the other, according to the increasingly impatient word of all his experts, had to be as well.

But they never found the body. Though his Temple rejoiced in their belief that Jani Kilian had died in fire, Tsecha had nursed the slight doubt he had sensed in the humanish soldiers who had told him of the crash, grasped it like a handhold in a wall of sand. Had fire destroyed his toxin? He hoped not, with each progress report he received with shaking hands. He prayed not, over each of his six daily sacraments. With each bite of sacred food, he begged the gods to answer him. *Send me my kièrshia, please*, he wove his entreaty around Langley's continuing thrum, *before they bury me.*

And when his Captain had returned to him . . . ah, then, would there be meetings!

CHAPTER 8

Jani followed Steve into the dining hall and waited as he tried to figure out where to sit. In past lives, this hadn't posed a problem for her. *When alone, one-seat table, dark corner, facing the door.* The dictum had been drilled into her head by frustrated mainline Service instructors unprepared to deal with a documents examiner who felt it her primary duty to plant herself within view of the cashbox and watch the way the staff handled the money.

But then, for eighteen years, the scorned procedure had become second nature, an acknowledgment of a threat that, if not always acute, had staked a permanent claim in Jani's mind.

Well, now was the time for something new. Unlike the long, bench-seated tables she had always encountered in cheap public eating areas, the tables here were small and round or small and square, each covered with silver cloth, decorated with a vase of real flowers and surrounded by no more than eight flexframe chairs. The room itself, an expansive arrangement of tiered, skylit ceilings and windowed exterior walls, would easily hold a thousand. It appeared about half-full now, the mealtime din dampened by soundshielding.

"How's this, then?" Steve asked as he claimed a window table. The outside view of the House gardens was stunning, but he showed where his priorities lay as he turned his back on it and pointed out a nearby table filled with upper-management types. "Sit here long enough, whole world goes by."

Her growling stomach urging her to *please eat now*, Jani settled next to Steve and shoveled in a few steaming forkfuls. Then the tastes of the salmon steak and steamed fresh vegetables hit her, and she slowed down. A meal like this deserved some respect—this wasn't a pickup from the *tamè* stand across the street from NorthPort's Guv Hall.

"Good stuff, eh?" Steve asked after a few minutes.

"Hmm." Jani swallowed, then pointed toward the sea of diners with her fork. "So, which are the nobbies?"

In quick succession, she received capsule descriptions of several department and division heads, the general tone of which led Jani to conclude the gossip rag in her duffel had lost a giant when Steven Forell opted for the documents corps.

"Shut up!" She coughed into her napkin as he regaled her with a tale of the novel use to which the head of the Farms Bureau had once put his diplomatic courier service.

"'S true." Steve's broad grin reflected a raconteur's joy in an appreciative audience. "You could hear 'em all up and down the hall. Some limp-dick from the Ag Ministry came here and threatened to have him classified as an animal-research facility if he didn't knock it off." He pushed away his empty plate and maneuvered the chair across from him so he could use it as a footstool. Then he picked up his nicstick from its perch on the edge of his tray and crunched the ignition tip between his teeth. "Thanks for covering for me and Ange," he said, his face obscured by spicy smoke. "'Preciate it."

Jani pushed away her own cleaned plate and sat back to observe the passing parade. "Wasn't the smartest move, considering all the people milling around."

"Weren't my idea, either." Steve's shoulders hunched defensively, his good humor dissipating with the smoke. "Always supposed to be the randy young buck's idea, innit? Havin' it off on desks." He sneered. "I had dinner reservations at Gaetan's tonight. Treasury Minister eats there." He took a pull on his nicstick. Jani watched the thin dose line move halfway up the unit's shaft. "I know how to behave. Be nice if some people gave me a chance to prove it."

Jani watched a cluster of well-dressed manager-types scud

past. "Is it that important to you? To pretend you're one of them, act like they do?" Unpleasant scenes from her Service past flashed in her memory. "Do you think you need to do it to keep your job?"

Steve bristled. "I don't act! Why should I pretend, anyway? I'm just as good as any of them."

"Not to them." Jani began tearing her dispo napkin into tiny bits. Talking about Earthbound–colony relations always made her shred things. "You don't sound like them, and you don't act like them. You're branded on the tongue and in every other way you can think of. Our great-great-etceteras lost the Greatest War, remember? That's why we got kicked out in the first place. We're the problem children. Forever and for always." She picked up a sprig of herb from her plate and stuck it in her mouth.

Steve edged straighter in his seat. "You sound like a secessionist," he mumbled, eyes locked on a pair of high-level staffers walking by the table.

"More a realist than anything. The day we get them to take notice won't come until we can bleed them semiconscious for using our GateWays and importing our goods. And for reeling in our best brains, convincing them they have to come here if they want to be somebody."

"They've started jailing secessionists, you know." Steve had, Jani noted with bemusement, toned down his accent considerably.

"There are a hell of a lot more of us than there are of them," she said. "How many jails they got?"

Steve exhaled with a shaky rumble. "Witch. Mam warned me about girls like you." He tossed his spent nicstick onto his plate. "I'm changing the subject. Not real comfortable talking politics. Always get that swimming-in-shit feeling after a while. Ange told me your name. Can't place your accent. Where you from, Risa?"

Jani hesitated. "Tyi's a Josephani name." *J'suise Acadienne, en actual.* The name of her home world sounded strange to her. Over the past eighteen years, she'd called herself everything *but* Acadian.

"Never been to Josephan," Steve said. "Heard it's nice.

Bit off, rebel like you doing for the Minister. Everyone knows you're one of his spooks."

Oh, they did, did they? Jani surveyed the dining hall. About three-quarters full now, and no one, she noticed to her chagrin, wearing anything remotely resembling ship coveralls. Like it or not, she'd have to start dressing properly to avoid attracting attention. "Spook's a general term. The work I do is more specialized."

"Oh yeah? Do tell."

"Investigations of particular interest."

"As opposed to general butting-in?" Steve pushed his tray back and forth. "And what interesting bit of biz are you investigating at the moment?"

"You're the gossip expert. What have you heard?"

"That you're looking into Lyssa van Reuter's death." Steve ignited another 'stick. "Thought that were an accident."

"Might still be."

"But you don't know yet?"

"Not until I have a chance to see all the data."

"Data? You make it sound like an experiment."

"It could have been, to someone." Jani watched the side of Steve's face as she spoke. He appeared relaxed enough, if solemn. But then, he had a lot on his mind.

"She had problems," he said. "Or rather, you knew she had problems, but she never let on."

Jani thought of the bleary-eyed face on the holozine cover. "Except when the holographers were around?"

"Timing." Steve waved weakly to someone at another table. "I'm afraid if the Lady had problems, they were with timing."

"You sound as though you liked her."

He hesitated. "I never worked with her."

"But you must have friends who did. How did they feel?"

"She were Family. No brothers or sisters. Used to being the center of it all, if you know what I mean."

"Difficult to work with?" Jani knew it would be best for the investigation to remain neutral regarding Lyssa, but being Anais Ulanova's niece could have had the expected nasty influence. "Spoiled? Demanding?"

Steve ignored the question. "So, madam," he said, pushing his chair away from the table, "shall we go?"

They left the cafeteria to find a small crowd had gathered in the glass-sided walkway. Steve elbowed a path to the paned wall, frowning as he checked his timepiece. "He's leaving early. Wonder what happened?"

Jani looked over his shoulder toward the white-robed figure crossing the secured skimway oval two stories below. Whispers of "It's him! It's him!" buzzed about her. Her heart thumped.

"He doesn't look real happy." Steve shook his head. "You can tell by the set of his shoulders, how slouchy he is."

Jani's own spine straightened in self-defense. Nothing activated her urge to confess to everything and brace for the worst like the slumping amble of a pissed-off Vynshàrau. *No, this is Nema.* Jani watched the ambassador slip into the rear seat of an off-white, triple-length skimmer. *Chief propitiators do not get pissed; they become enraged.*

"I hope Ange is all right." Steve pulled on his tunic hem. "When things don't go well, Durian takes it out on her."

"What was the ambassador doing here?" Jani wedged beside him and watched the idomeni vehicle drift away like a land-hugging cloud. "You'd think there'd have been notices or something." She thought how close she had come to being shoved into that damned conference room. *Evan, why the hell didn't you warn me!*

"Langley were responsible for that. He says Interior has the best layout for meeting with Tsecha—the secured conference rooms are furthest away from any and all eating areas and food-storage facilities." Steve recited the policy with bland formality. " 'Course, doesn't mean our man should be allowed to attend these meetings, seeing as the flies are settling on the bloated corpse of his career and all."

"*Steve.*" Jani pressed a hand to her aching stomach. She'd definitely overeaten.

"Langley's one ham-handed wanker, 's all I can say. Likes twisting his little knife." Steve gestured toward the spot where the idomeni skimmer had been parked. "I wonder what he thinks of all this. Thought about asking him a couple times, figured I'd be gigged for bleedin' cheek."

"You've met him?"

"Nothing one-on-one. Sat in on some document-transfer protocols. Harmonizing paper systems. That'll be the bloody day—they run rings around us." He tugged at his bangs. "He stared at my hair, like they expected. Gave me a nod. I feel sorry for the old codge."

"Why?"

Steve gave an uncertain shrug. "Because he's so out of place here. I mean, he's the only member of his delegation who even tries to communicate directly with us. The rest of his crew just passes everything directly to the translator corps. But . . ."

"But?"

"He talks about the time before the war a lot. What went on at the Academy. What he tried to teach his students."

Oh hell. "Such as?"

Steve forced a laugh. "He thinks we're all going to be the same someday. Us and the idomeni. That living together will cause us to blend."

"Blend into what?" As if she didn't know.

"A hybrid race. Rauta Haárin, Tsecha called it." Steve tried his best, but he garbled the Haárin *r*, coughing it up from the back of his throat rather than trilling it. "A brand-new sect."

"You can't blend beings together like ingredients in a bowl," Jani said as she did her best to avoid looking at the reflection of her filmed eyes. "It doesn't work that way."

"You might be right," Steve said. "I ran it by a friend of mine. Genetics therapeutician. She thinks it's a joke." He frowned and toyed with a fastener on his tunic. He tried to appear sure of himself, but Jani could sense his confusion. How would the word of a human rate against that of an alien ambassador, one who possessed a most unique brand of charm?

Like a tsunami with legs. Oh, yes, she remembered it well.

"He makes a strange kind of sense, though," Steve said. "He says that idomeni and humanish both think they control their environments, while in reality, the environments control us. Our environments want order, and order means everything the same. He thinks our worlds will force change upon us, set it up so we'll have no choice but to hybridize." His stare grew dreamy, as though he focused on something far away.

Jani tried to laugh, but it caught in her throat. "You have let him get into your head, haven't you?" She had to wave a hand in front of Steve's face to get his attention. "Look, he's a religious leader. Charismatic and persuasive and sure he speaks the truth. Sincerity doesn't make him right."

"He's good though, Ris. 'We shall change or we shall die, and truly.' That's what he said. He really believes it. You can tell the way his eyes light up." Steve shook his head. "Maybe it is all about politics. Maybe he's just looking for humans who could lobby for his policies."

"He does know his way around a Council chamber." Jani looked at the place where Nema's skimmer had been parked. She could sense his presence, like a ghost forever seeking the thing that would allow it to rest. Humans had names for behavior like that. Fervid, when they felt kind. Fanatic, when they tired of mopping up the blood. But if you denied that part of Nema, you denied the charm as well. And felt the loss, as though you'd disappointed your champion. "Humans don't have the maturity to deal with Tsecha. We took an incredible risk allowing him here."

"What do you know about him?" Steve turned to her, eyes shining. "Have you ever met him?"

Shit. "No. I've just heard things. I know he changed his name after the last war."

Steve shrugged off that piece of old news. "Avrèl nìRau Nema, it used to be. They told us about that in the prep courses. Didn't tell us why, though, exactly." They were the only two left in the walkway now. He took the opportunity to ignite a nicstick. "Said it had something to do with the war. New government, new name."

Something to do with the Temple authorities pressuring him to sever every link to a past they found disordered. How had they felt when their chief priest informed them of his new name? Tsecha. Sìah Haárin for fool. *Depending on the accompanying gestures, of course.* Jani could imagine him announcing his new skein and sect names, arms at his sides, hands obscured by the folds of his overrobe. Palms open, thumbs extended. The Vynshàrau equivalent of crossing his fingers behind his back.

"He's probably the most knowledgeable Vynshàrau where we're concerned," she said. Experience in dealing with humanish—that had to be the reason the idomeni risked sending him. Even now, the Council must be training his replacement.

"Yeah, he tries to be as human as he can. Always just misses, though." Steve bared his teeth in an apelike grimace. "I mean, he comes at you with that smile, holding his hand out for you to shake, and it's like—"

"Grim Death with a Deal for You," Jani said. And what deals he offered.

Someday, nìa, you will be Rauta Haárin. Then you will replace me. As chief propitiator, you will ensure the blending continues. You will guide souls along the Way to the Star. Tsecha had sounded so sure of himself, as always. He knew the gods were on his side. Fervor. Fanaticism.

They had stood on the Academy veranda after the graduation ceremony had been completed. Nema had awarded Jani a ring, as he had each of his Six. A lovely thing, crimson jasperite set in cagework gold, an exact duplicate of his ring of station. Everyone else's had fit, but hers had been too small. So he had explained what needed to happen in order for hers to fit.

He had been genuinely surprised when Jani handed the ring back to him. Confused. But he thought he could compel her. She told him she didn't liked being forced to play pawn in someone else's game.

This is not a game, nìa. This is life as it must be.

The sound of Steve's chuckling brought her back to the present. "Grim Death. That's great!" He flipped his spent 'stick into a trashzap and paced up and down the walkway.

Outside, the dusk-darkened sky was laced with orange and purple. In the distance, charge lot lights had activated. Jani looked at the wall clock in surprise. "It's still afternoon. It's getting dark already?"

Steve stopped in his tracks. "Yeah. Bloody winter. Nothin' to look forward to but nothin'." He looked at her expectantly. "You got plans?"

"Work, for a while. I'm lagged as hell. Probably be asleep

before long.'' She made a show of stretching. ''You never answered my question about Lyssa.''

''Hmm.'' Steve strolled down the walkway. ''Where you going now?''

''Executive offices.'' She fell into step beside him. ''I need to pick up some docs.''

''Anything planned for tomorrow?''

''Not sure. Why?''

Steve looked at her with the sort of grin that drove Earthbound girls to desktops. ''You know that saying about one good turn,'' he said, disappearing into an unmarked stairwell.

CHAPTER 9

Jani found Evan waiting for her in the Interior executive wing.

"Get settled all right?" He ushered her down the painting-trimmed hallway and into his office. "How's your room?" He had changed into civvies. His blue pullover matched his eyes. Unfortunately, the color also accented the hollows beneath. "Hope you've found everything to your liking."

Jani watched him close in on the bar. She refused his offer of a drink, noticing glumly that he still opted for straight bourbon. "Why didn't you tell me about Nema?" she asked, following with a quick rundown of her near miss. "I was an eyelash away from being pushed into that room. The physical changes wouldn't have thrown him at all—he would have known me instantly."

Evan dragged another chair over to the visitor's side of his desk. He sighed and motioned for Jani to sit.

"It caught me by surprise, too." He lowered his lean frame into his chair as though he feared the cushions had teeth. "Langley doesn't bother to inform me of his visits anymore. I must allow him access to that portion of the Main House whenever he requires it. He seems to require it whenever it causes the most inconvenience." He scowled and sipped his drink. "What a coincidence."

"You could have told me."

"I tried! I called your suite. You didn't answer. Knowing the kind of day you'd had, I assumed you were taking a nap. You always slept like a rock." He offered a faint, knowing smile. "I'd been in meetings all afternoon—I had no idea you'd come back here. How did you get into the secured section anyway? I hadn't arranged for your clearance yet."

"The elevator let me ride, but it wouldn't let me steer." Jani pressed her fingers to her temples. Her scalp felt two sizes too small.

"Somebody must have overridden the security controls in order to get people up from the subs more quickly. At least we'll know to be on our guard for next time. Langley usually times these little invasions every six to ten days. My staff didn't expect him until early next week. I guess it was just Cao's way of saying, 'Welcome home.' " Evan rocked his glass back and forth, clinking nonexistent ice. "Do you need me for anything tonight—"

"No—"

"—because I'm busy. Social commitment. A dinner I don't want to eat hosted by people I despise. Welcome to the glamorous world of top-level government." He set down his drink. "I have what you came here for." He rose and walked back to his desk. "Don't want to waste your time."

"You're not." Jani watched Evan's shoulders work beneath his sweater. He had never been exactly strapping, but he looked bonier than she remembered. "Have you eaten anything today?"

"I had lunch," he replied vaguely as he opened a drawer and withdrew a thick, scuffed binder. "I found these in the parts bins, locked away in a drawer." He silenced Jani's protest with a look. "I know as a nondoc, I shouldn't be allowed in there. Don't ask me how I gained access—you don't want to know." He set the files on the table between them.

Jani hefted the binder into her lap and examined the black cover. She flipped the cover open. Her palms felt damp. *Call me Pandora.*

"Please don't read it now." Evan advanced on the bar again. "Take it out of here."

"Evan—"

"You don't understand how much it sickens me to know you're going to read that. But you have to, don't you? It's your job. It's what I asked you here to do." His voice had taken on a formal tone. Very van Reuter. "So you had better go do it."

Jani tucked the binder under her arm and headed for the door. "Enjoy your dinner." She paused in the doorway and looked back at him. "Bicarb lozenges are great for masking liquor breath, by the way."

Evan reached into his pants pocket and pulled out a half-empty foil-wrapped cylinder. "I've been buying them by the case for years," he said, raising his glass to her. Jani closed the door before she had to watch him drain it.

Against all logic, her stomach started growling as she mounted the Private House's sweeping main stairway and wended through the second-floor hallways toward her room. Her appetite had increased markedly over the past few months. *Must be the cold weather.* She was considering the possibilities her cooler offered when the faint smell of fresh coffee brought her to full alert.

On the table outside her door, she found a tray laden with what apparently constituted the House's version of an evening snack. Next to the swan-necked silver ewer containing the coffee rested a plate of sliced fresh fruit, a keep-warm basket filled with sweetened bread, and a three-tiered dish containing colorful miniature cakelets and cookies.

Jani wrestled through the door with her duffel, the file binder, and the tray, determined to shovel everything into the room at once even though she knew it would go much more smoothly if she'd just put something down. She staggered back-bowed and lopsided to the bed, depositing her burden just before straps slid and binders freed themselves and whomped onto trays.

She popped an anise cookie into her mouth as reward for a job well done, then activated the suite's music system, pressing the pad beside her bed until she found something appropriately calming. Mussorgska, she guessed, as strings swelled and faded. Not the current fashion, but comforting. Judging from Evan's behavior when he turned over the binder to her, she would need some comfort soon.

She pulled off her boots, carried the tray into the kitchenette, and poured and arranged. Soon, she was ensconced in her office, steaming mug in hand, feet on desk, binder in lap, scanpack within easy reach. She'd closed the curtains to block out the night, but left her office door wide open. She wanted to feel cozy, not trapped.

She opened the binder, glanced over the stripped-down table of contents, then paused to read more carefully as familiar terms caught her eye. *Initial Hopgood Analysis—Page Four. Insertion and Activation—Page Nine.* She set down her coffee and read further. *Dobriej Parameters. Physical Markers. Final Scans—Page Twenty-One.*

Jani thumbed through the hefty binder. "There are a hell of a lot more than twenty-one pages here!" She browsed psych evals, handwritten notes, Neoclona emergency calls, and wound up staring at the Commonwealth Police report of an accident that occurred at the van Reuter summer compound north of Chicago. A boating accident in which three children died.

A blast of woodwinds jerked Jani upright. She hurried into the bedroom and killed the music, then fixed herself a drink. Water. With lots of ice. To quell the burning in her stomach.

She returned to her office. From the recesses of well-stocked drawers, she removed a pad of paper and several colored pens. On the first sheet of the pad, Jani roughed out a three-column grid, then wrote, "Initial Hopgood" and "Insert and Act." in the first, "Dob," "PM," and "Finals" in the second.

The third column, she left blank.

Four hours later, the third column remained blank. Jani stared at the empty space, debated going through the binder one more time, then shook her head. She hadn't found what she sought because it wasn't there to find.

She walked to the window and drew aside the curtain. The night sky was clear, the glitter of city illumination reflecting sharp silver-gold off the lake surface. She cracked the weather seal and let frigid air wash over her. When her face felt the way her left arm always did, she closed the window and massaged the blood back into her cheeks.

After a few minutes, she returned to her desk and wrote, "Augmentation of Martin van Reuter" across the top of the grid. Every report needed a title, even the ones you couldn't finish.

During her postcrash recovery, she had learned more about her augmentation than she ever wanted to know. The physical reactions it induced had sped her recovery in some ways and hampered it in others, and John Shroud had been adamant she learn its idiosyncrasies along with him. *I can't believe you waited this long,* he had said. *Willful ignorance will only harm you in the long run.* So she forced herself to read the files he purloined for her, memorized the terms, the sequences, the whys and wherefores.

The evaluations had begun during her first month in OCS. She'd been a borderline case. Hopgood analysis confirmed her tendency toward vivid dreams. One Service physician had expressed grave concern over the activity seen in certain regions of her thalamus during Dobriej sensory-input testing.

But when the war came, the Service augmented Jani for the same reason they did all their eligible personnel—as a precaution. The enclave should have bugged out as soon as the fighting began. *But we had a GateWay station to protect, commercial interests to oversee.* Besides, the opportunity to observe the orderly idomeni at war proved too great a temptation. *To walk ignored past battles like figurines in bell jars. To be protected by the simple fact it wasn't our war.*

Of course, it couldn't last. *We watched with our faces pressed against the glass. Before we could stop ourselves, we'd broken through.* Learned names. Become involved.

Jani escaped to her sitting room. Desperate for voices, she activated her holoVee, flipping through the channels until she found a broadcast of a soccer match. The Gold Round of the last Commonwealth Cup. She watched bright blue Serran and red-and-gold-striped Phillipan jerseys dash up and down the field as the crowd roiled and roared.

I shouldn't have been augmented, but at least I was old enough to adapt. She sat on the couch, watched the colors flicker, listened to the ebb and flow of noise. She ate a balanced diet. Kept hydrated. Avoided conflict whenever possible. *I haven't had a precautionary take-down in almost twenty years.* And she'd never need one. *I know the difference be-*

tween right and wrong—no altered neurochemical cascade is going to push me over the edge.

Someone like her was supposed to be the worst-case scenario, the absolute limit to which a dodgy technology could be pushed.

So, whose decision was it to test a prototype personality augment on a three-year-old boy?

What did they think they were doing? When they enhanced what they believed to be Martin's authoritative tendencies, were they surprised when he fought with playmates and flew into tantrums when his wishes were thwarted? Were they astonished when he attacked his father with a lazor at the age of six, or when he pushed his little brother down stairs at eight. Repeatedly tried to force himself on his mother, then his sister, beginning at age eleven?

When they did everything they could to enhance Martin's feeling that he, and only he, was the van Reuter heir, were they shocked that he planned the murders of his brother and sister?

But the storm got you before your parents could. Given the justifications for Martin's behavior she found in the psych evals, it would have been interesting to see how *la famille* van Reuter would have worked out from under that one. And they would have. The pattern had been set.

Jani pondered Martin's blank third column. She had constructed the same sort of chart during her hospital stay, filling her own third column with the terms for post-augie analysis and counseling. In her case, they led to the conclusion that a mistake had been made, but that Captain Kilian, an Academy-trained documents examiner in whom the Service had invested so much, would just have to be taught how to adjust.

Poor Marty—they just turned you loose on an unsuspecting world. Then buried the evidence and prevented the unsuspecting world from figuring out what the hell had happened. *Evan didn't even allow an autopsy.* The miniscule masses, buried next to Martin's amygdala, would have shown up during the examination of his brain. They had formed from the components injected into his ventricular system, produced all those neurotransmitter analogues whose names Jani had managed to forget. Tried to forget. Would forget, eventually.

She worked a finger beneath her hair at the place where skull met spine, and felt the tiny, raised, round scar. The secondary depositions near her thyroid and adrenal glands had been minor discomforts compared to the insertion of the primary augmentation. Having her head immobilized in the stereotaxic restraint had shaken her up, and she'd been a grown woman. How would that damned skull-cage have affected a toddler?

And the headache afterward . . .

She fixed her attention upon the soccer match. Phillipi's star right wing had just scored what would prove to be the winning goal. The screen filled with the raucous tumble of a red-and-gold pile-on.

Jani switched channels, flicking past serials, documentaries, and travelogues before coming to rest on a real-time news transmit. *Live—from the palazzo of Treasury Main*! She watched the florid-faced Treasury Minister, the stark Exterior Minister, and several tightly wrapped colonial governors approach the eager throng of reporters like hikers nearing the edge of a cliff. The governors kept their replies short, while Treasury Minister Abascal entoned the antisecession line in which Prime Minister Cao believed so firmly.

But Exterior Minister Ulanova held sway as always. As soon as she approached the Veephones, the governors fell silent and Abascal's mouth contorted in a dyspeptic smile. No, the PM's views on colonial autonomy did not alarm Exterior, Ulanova said in her warm alto, nor did Cao's unwillingness to entertain opposing views mean all talks on the subject would cease.

Then Ulanova relinquished the spotlight, and Evan sauntered to the fore, his clear eyes and healthy color a testament to the liberal ingestion of both black coffee and dehydro boosters. He ignored a question concerning Lyssa's death and launched into a point-by-point disassembly of Ulanova's views.

"Oh, Evan." Jani listened as he reaffirmed every point he'd made on the *Arapaho*. He left out his beliefs concerning Ulanova's ambitions, of course, but the intimation was there if you knew what to listen for. "I don't think that's what Anais had in mind." She watched the Exterior Minister's visage grow stonier as each verbal missile Evan launched made target. "You spiked her, Evan. This was your chance to play nice, and you bit your playmates and kicked sand."

A flash of silver-blond captured Jani's attention. She watched Lucien Pascal lean over Exterior Minister Ulanova's shoulder and whisper in her ear. The woman nodded sharply; Lucien responded with the smile Jani knew so well after five weeks on the *Arapaho*.

"*Roc cui'jaune*," she whispered to the smug face on the screen. "That means 'stones of brass,' you son of a bitch." Lucien bent forward again, allowing her a clear view of the red lieutenant's bars adorning his Service tunic collar. "A mainline spine." She squinted to see if she could pick up the tiny gold letter in the center of the bar.

"I spy with my little eye a letter *I*. Intelligence. Wonderful." Jani switched off the holoVee and stared into the blank screen. "What the hell have I walked into?" She slumped against the soft cushions and studied the ceiling. Then she went into the kitchenette and applied herself to the still-warm bread, washing it down with another healthy dose of coffee. Afterward, she cleaned her dishes, zapped her trash, stored the uneaten food, and scrubbed until everything shone and even her old drill instructor could not have found fault.

Then she returned to her office and studied her columns. After a while, she flipped to a clean page, and wrote, "Lyssa's death—Martin's augie" along the top. When Lucien's sailracers distracted her, she slammed them facedown on the desktop. When she grew too exhausted to hold her head up, she stretched out on her office floor, duffel by her side, and slept.

CHAPTER 10

"His troops would follow him anywhere, but only for the entertainment value."

Tsecha stared at the sentence until his eyes felt desert-dry. Finally, he admitted surrender with a rumbling sigh and reactivated his handheld. The small unit had long since gone dormant; he had to rock and jostle it before the blue activator pad glowed and the display lightened.

You are as me, grown most old. Tsecha entered codes and file keys both by voice and input pad, pausing frequently to allow the readout time to catch up. He practiced his English counting as the time passed.

Then, one after another, the words scrolled across the display, the looping curves and complex crosshatches of High Vynshàrau. Tsecha savored each nuance, every shading. Even after so long, he found his self-made dictionary most educating.

Entertainment. He read the line again. *This officer's troops intend to watch from a distance, as though he walks a stage.* That implied they did not trust him. A poor thing, such mistrust. A threat to order. Why then did the Service maintain the officer?

Why did humanish do so many foolish things?

"*Aháret.*" Tsecha spoke aloud the Pathen Haárin word. *Why?* An unseemly question in the Pathen tongue. It implied the gods did not know what they did. He stared for a time at the bare, sand-colored walls of his room. Sand—such a comforting hue.

How I miss heat, and truly. Heat, bright sun, and the bloom-laden trees of home. Relasetha and ìrel, fierce yellow and blessed red. The images he held in his memory seemed so much richer than the paper and paint ones that rested within niches in his walls.

I came to this damned cold place for a reason. Why now did that reason seem as hard to grasp as Service English?

Tsecha toyed with his handheld. So much easier to grasp. And so much did it contain. Notes, translations, and definitions of his three most favored humanish tongues, English, French, and Mandarin. He ran a finger along the unit's scuffed, gouged black case. *So much we have been through—peace and war, the death of that which I was and the birth of that which I became.* He looked at the handheld's screen. It flickered. The display fragmented. Half the words lost all meaning, while some took on meanings quite strange. He bared his teeth. *I say you tell me jokes to ease my mind. But my suborns call you broken.*

Once he had, with great reluctance, allowed one of his communications suborns to attempt to transfer the knowledge in his aged device to one of the new bracketed-neuron models much valued by Vynshàrau intelligence. Tsecha had almost screamed himself when his unit whistled and screeched as the young female attached the interphases and initiated connections. He had torn it out of the transfer array just in time, she admitted later. Any longer, and his old friend would have . . . would have . . .

The connections had aged, the suborn said. The neural sheaths contained too much plaque, there had been too much cell death. A transfer was not possible. *At this time, nìRau.*

At any time.

We have aged together. He stroked the plastic case, which felt warm and smooth as flesh beneath his fingers. *Perhaps together, we were meant to die.*

"Ah, you think of death again!" Tsecha rebuked himself aloud, in English. The language worked quite well for such. Its sharp, throaty sounds, aided by so much tongue and tooth, forced one to pay attention.

"So pay attention to this." He paged through the copy of the Service Officer Fitness Assessment, combing for more sentences that would challenge his knowledge and his repository. "The humanish think these words funny, and truly. Why?" It crossed Tsecha's mind that his hosts would be surprised to find an idomeni studying the personnel files of active officers in their military, but he felt it a point to be ignored. He wished to perfect his English, and Hansen Wyle had told him much of the language's meaning could be found in such humanish government files as this, in places "between the lines."

So shall I search. Between lines.

Tsecha put down the file he held and opened another, paging through sheet after sheet until he came to the entry with the latest date.

"This officer should go far. I'll drive."

Tsecha stared and studied. This statement, he felt he understood. *Another incompetent—with so many, how do the humanish survive?* He closed the assessment and set it on the table beside his chair. He would have to remember to ask of his intelligence suborns where exactly they had obtained these files. They had insisted most strongly that their infiltration of humanish systems was not suspected. *But the humanish enjoy laughter so much.* A game, perhaps? Tsecha bared his teeth. Such, he understood most well.

He rose slowly from his rigid metal-and-wood seat, wincing at the popping sounds his aged joints made. He twisted and stretched his spine, worked blood and feeling back into his limbs. Humanish complained of uncomfortable idomeni furniture, but pain kept one sharp. Such did all believe. All idomeni, that is. Humanish were different. They could not accept the mind-focusing ability of pain.

He padded across the bare tiled floor, the same soft color as his walls. He opened a large wooden cupboard and stored his files in one of the touchlocked compartments of which his suborns knew. Then he pushed aside carved panels and etched veneers and opened a touchbox that contained things of which they knew not. Inside rested a ring, twin to his own ring of station, and a much thinner sheaf of documents.

Tsecha picked up the ring, held it under the light, savored its glisten. Then he returned it to its resting place and removed the documents. *Moragh*, he thought as he opened the file. *I must find a humanish to tell me what means,* Moragh. He had already sought the meanings of his Captain's other two names and had come away from each quest still wanting. Perhaps the key was in *Moragh.* There had to be some hint, some foretelling, somewhere. Surely his Captain could not have faded away without leaving some type of trail. Some type of sign for him, who believed.

I fought the Laumrau for you. You are all that is order to me. Tsecha returned to his chair and paged through the pale blue Service parchment. Long ago, some of the sheets had been stained by smoke, then by flame-retardant foam. Their surfaces shone greasy grey and mottled in his room's sunlike illumination.

I paid much to the Haárin to recover these from your Service base. His debriders, dispatched to search the cleansing flames of Rauta Shèràa for any paper they could find. *But all they found was this small amount*—Tsecha riffled the few stiff pages—*because even your own wished you erased.*

Even though he knew the words as he knew his born-sect and skein, Tsecha read Jani Kilian's Officer Assessment.

Insubordinate. Typical dexxie know-it-all. Stiff-necked colonial. Doesn't belong in a uniform. As ever, he could find no humor in Kilian's file.

A muffled, metallic sound stole his attention. Softly, at first, then more loudly, the cloth-wrapped bell that signaled the cook-priest's visitation rang its dull, late-evening song. Tsecha continued to comb the papers. Soon would come last sacrament, then sleep. He had not much time.

Where are you, my future? He read the passages which dealt with the Service's search for their officer, their condemnation of her disorder, their fear she would be found first by the Vynshàrau. *Mutiny . . . murder . . . conspiracy . . . forgery . . . assumed dead . . . body disappeared . . . door-to-door search . . . no sign.* Acadian, she was, but later, they searched for her there and found nothing. Rebellious, she was, but they continued their searches to this day on their colony planets and found nothing.

Words as written, ink on paper, Tsecha read and ignored, continuing his own search for the sign from his gods, his own quest for his Captain. In his own nothing. Between the lines.

THE SECOND DAY

CHAPTER 11

The "thank-you" Jani's back gave her for spending the night on her office floor was countered by the opinion expressed by her right hip and thigh. She limped into the bathroom, shedding clothes along the way.

Another hot shower—two in less than a day. A giddy surfeit of hydrodynamic riches. All wasted, unfortunately. Afterward, she only felt battered and slightly feverish. Never had so much hot water done so little for so few.

Travel lag. Had to be. *Over a month of artificial gee—it's never the same, no matter what they say.* She dug through drawers and shelves, searching for an outfit that didn't make her look like graveyard shift in the engine room, finally settling on a dark blue trouser suit. The color made her appear ill, but the cloth and cut of the outfit whispered "expensive" with an Earthbound accent. She could wander Interior halls at will in a getup like that. Besides, the trouser legs were cut wide enough to fit over her boots.

Jani buttoned the roomy jacket, flexing her shoulders as she checked herself in the full-length mirror. Keeping her hands in her pockets hid the fact that the sleeves were uneven in length, with the right one too short. She glumly examined the crooked breaks in her trouser cuffs. She looked all right. Businesslike. Unconcerned with fashion, as though—

"As though I'd been hurled from a speeding skimmer." She tamped down her damp curls, vowed to check out the cosmetics selection in the Interior stores, and gave the contents of her duffel a last check.

Just before she left, Jani glanced toward the comport light on the end table by the bed. No blink, which meant no message from Evan. She thought of Martin's files, locked in her desk. *Yeah, I probably wouldn't be eager to talk to me, either.* Her stomach rumbled, and she tried to recall the quickest route to Interior House Main. She'd take her meals there today. However averse Evan was to seeing her, the feeling was mutual.

Jani had found the second-floor dining hall extremely attractive the previous afternoon, which was why she avoided it now. Nobbies were to be avoided at all costs. Ridgeway. Angevin. Even Steve.

She rode elevators and scaled stairs until the signs meant nothing. DISPOSITION AND WAREHOUSING—FIELD ASSESSMENTS—CODES AND STATUTES. She ducked into the first breakroom she came to, and was treated to a view of skimmer charge lots and maintenance sheds through the single grimy window. She grabbed a tray, loaded it with single-serve dispos from the glass-fronted cooler and headed for the darkest corner of the deserted eating area.

Don't forget to face the door. Jani sat down, looking up just in time to see Durian Ridgeway enter.

"Good morning, Ms. Tyi." He strode toward her, not seeming at all surprised to find her in such a remote region of Interior Main. "Getting to know the layout of the place, I see." He was dressed in a black day suit and white shirt that had the same effect on his complexion that Jani's outfit had on hers. He sat down across from her and started toying with the spice dispenser.

"You've been following me," Jani said.

"Strictly speaking, no. I just had people keeping an eye out for you." He frowned as she continued eating. "You certainly don't seem the worse for wear, considering."

"Considering what?"

"You read Martin's file, didn't you? Evan gave it to you, didn't he?"

"Yes, and yes, again."

Ridgeway's ears reddened. "It's too early in the morning for flippancy, Ms. Tyi."

"On the contrary, Mr. Ridgeway, I am most serious."

"Then you agree with my estimation of the negative impact the release of that information could have on his career?"

"Oh, yes."

Ridgeway sat back with the edgy posture of one who knew there had to be another shoe teetering on the brink somewhere. "Evan would like to see you. After you finish your breakfast, of course."

Jani reached across the table and took the spice dispenser from his hand. "He can kiss my ass." She slid the spout around to the white-pepper compartment and sprinkled some on her melon. "I'm not interested in his explanations."

"He's your Minister, Ms. Tyi. When he says, 'jump,' it's your job to ask, 'how high.' "

"And yours to hold the measuring tape, Mr. Ridgeway. What a valuable man you are."

Ridgeway stared at her. Then his gaze flicked to her tray. "Would you mind telling me why you just put pepper on your fruit?"

"Because that's the way I choose to eat it."

"You know, Ms. Tyi, I don't think you're quite well."

Jani shook the spice dispenser over her bowl until the melon looked sand-dipped. "You can kiss my ass, too."

"Spit and show me where, Risa dear," Ridgeway replied coolly. He turned toward the breakroom entrance. "Colonel Doyle. Could you come in here please?"

Three guards dressed in mainline winter polywools filled the doorway like a steel blue eclipse in triplicate. A tall, rangy, dark-skinned woman with a shaved head stepped forward, her eyes on Jani, one hand on her shooter holster. "Sir?"

Ridgeway stood up. "It's always been up to me to clean up Evan's little errors in judgment, Ms. Tyi. Perhaps you should keep that in the back of what passes for your mind." He tugged on his jacket cuffs. "Shall we go?"

Jani looked from Ridgeway, to the guards, then back again. She knew she could get past them all and out of the room before any of them knew what had hit them. Augie was telling her how. She would sustain damage, of course, but she'd been damaged before. She wouldn't die. She'd never die. She'd tried it once. It didn't take. *I could let them have it for you, Marty. Show them what an augie can really do.* In the body of an adult who knew the drill.

A sour burning rose in her throat as she stood. "You've left me no choice, Mr. Ridgeway," she said, ignoring his smug smile. As he turned his back to her, her eyes locked on the place where his thin neck met his undeveloped shoulder. *Perhaps later, Marty.* Who knew what could happen later?

Outside, Jani excused herself and hurried to the nearby lavatory, Ridgeway's order to "hurry the hell up" ringing in her ears. She reached the toilet just in time, losing her breakfast in a few rapid heaves.

When she finished, she pressed her sweat-damp face against cold ceramic, closed her eyes, and tried not to think how a thwarted augie would take out his displeasure on a three-year-old boy. Or how the three-year-old boy would re-act. It never paid to think along those lines. A person could go crazy if she dwelled on things like that.

She cleaned up quickly, then rejoined her escort. Two of the guards bookended her, while Doyle brought up the rear. Ridgeway, of course, led the procession. Jani kept her eyes on the spot between his shoulder blades. The point bobbed up and down—he had an annoyingly bouncy gait.

She slowly relaxed. She'd encountered her share of Ridgeways in Rauta Shèràa, walked in more than one promenade to the principal's office. She shoved her hands in her pockets and swallowed down the last hint of bile. She needed freedom and access to do the job asked of her. Despite what Ridgeway wanted, Evan could only afford to bust her so far.

Evan waited for them in his office anteroom. Jani had to allow him some credit—the look he gave Ridgeway and the guards would have stopped a howling mob in its tracks. *It's a gift—comes with the nose.*

Ridgeway held up a hand. "Evan, let me explain." Pedantic tone. Mistake.

"An armed escort," Evan replied, very quietly. "Of my guest. In my house." Small "h." Easily discerned. He'd chosen to take it personally. He looked at Jani. "And what crime was committed?"

Ridgeway floundered. "She was insubordinate!" he finally sputtered.

Evan shrugged. "Of course she was, Durian. It's part of her charm." He stepped past Ridgeway, who watched him with mouth agape and walked over to Colonel Doyle, who seemed preoccupied with the pattern of the carpet. "Virginia."

"Sir." Doyle cast a sidelong glance at Jani and winced.

"Ms. Tyi is to be allowed free access to all parts of the House." Capital "H," this time. "I was remiss in handling that. I'm taking care of it now. You'll help me see to it, won't you?"

"Yes, sir."

"She is a professional, as are we all. Despite what you may have been told, you have nothing to fear where she is concerned."

"Yes, sir." Doyle looked at Jani again. In contrast to her dark skin, her eyes were surprisingly light, a pale gold-brown. "If Ms. Tyi will come by and see me afterward," she said flatly, "I'll see she's taken care of."

"Of course." Evan smiled. The temperature of the room rose above subarctic. "Now, Risa and Durian and I need to talk." He nodded toward Colonel Doyle, who shot Jani a last, reappraising look as she herded her two subordinates out of the anteroom.

Ridgeway erupted as soon as the door closed. "How bloody dare you! You made me look a fool!"

"You never needed any help from me in that regard!" Evan's voice shook. "We're all three of us on one level from this point on. In it up to our necks!" He spun on his heel. "We'll talk in my office, where it's secure."

Jani tried for a seat on the opposite side of the room from Evan's desk, but he blocked that move with a glare and gestured to a chair near his own. Next to Ridgeway's. Jani settled in and looked around. At least the bar was closed up.

"Well?" Evan planted his elbows on his desk. He wore the same sort of severely cut suit as did Ridgeway, but black was his color. It enlivened his complexion, gave his slim frame a solidity it didn't possess on its own, and invested his anger with the authority of worlds.

Not a great way to start the day.

"You already know my feelings." Ridgeway jerked his head toward Jani. "You'll be sorry you brought her into this. Mark my words."

"So you still decline to consider my side of things." Evan waved off Ridgeway's protest and turned to Jani. "And are you, Ms. Tyi, sorry you were brought into this?" A soft light filled his eyes. "You don't look pleased."

Jani teased at her right cuff. Try as she might, she couldn't pull it past her wrist. "Whose idea was it?"

Evan didn't need to ask which idea. "Does it matter? I was his father. It was my responsibility."

Ridgeway chuffed in disgust. "Go ahead—play the martyr. If you still think you can afford it." He looked at Jani. It took an effort—she could almost hear his spine crack from the tension. "It was Acton. He'd been kicked out as king, so he tried for kingmaker. He'd heard about some personality-enhancement work being done by researchers who'd broken off from Neoclona. Similar to combat augmentation, though with a different focus."

Evan cut in. "The secessionists were making noise even then. Nawar had just scrabbled his way back into power, won the interim election by a landslide. The feeling at the time was that he'd be Prime Minister for life. I'd taken the wrong side in a domestic appropriations dustup, so I was in the political doghouse. Dad ran scared. He didn't think he'd ever see a van Reuter in the Cabinet again."

Jani gave up on her jacket cuff and began tugging on her pants. "Any Neoclona hack and slash will tell you augmentation is exactly that, an enhancement of what's already been formed. Whoever told your father they could shape the personality of a three-year-old was a lying butcher, and he was a fool to believe them." A cold-blooded, megalomaniacal fool. But she herself had been gouged more than once by the Old Hawk's beak. "Did Lyssa know the details?"

"We believe so." Ridgeway and Evan answered simultaneously, then Ridgeway picked up the ball. "She was a physician, after all. Not a Neoclona affiliate but still well regarded. I'm sure she only suspected some type of standard behavioral dysfunction at first, but when the true nature of

Martin's problem became known, she plunged into denial as readily as the rest of us. It began slowly. We thought it a phase, a bid for attention, especially after Jerrold and Serena were born. We thought he'd grow out of it.''

Jani yanked on her right trouser leg—a high-pitched rip sounded as lining gave way. "You—" She tried to count to ten, but lost track after *three*. "You took an infant who had no true grasp of right or wrong, no firm moral foundation, and engineered him to automatically, at all times, put his own survival first above all things—"

Ridgeway's face flared. "I had nothing to do with it—"

"—and you thought he'd grow out of it!"

"*You're out of line, Tyi!*"

Jani stormed out of her chair, her stomach on fire. "*Kiss my ass, you son of a bitch!*"

Evan rushed around his desk and thrust an arm between them. "*Quiet!*" He leaned hard against Jani, pushing her back into her chair. "I don't give a damn how you two feel about each other. When you are under this roof, you will treat one another in a civil manner. You will not use any of my departments like little toy armies in your vendettas," he continued, catching Ridgeway's eye, "and, like it or not, you will work together. I need you both. If I have to grind you both into one meaty lump and drag in Neoclona to make a sensible person out of the mess, I will.''

Jani fixed her eyes on the floor. She could hear Ridgeway's hard breathing slow.

Evan took his time returning to his seat. When he finally spoke, Jani heard the smile in his voice. "I won't ask you to shake hands. I'm no physicist, but I understand the concept of fission." His chair creaked. The silence stretched.

After what seemed hours, Jani looked up to find Ridgeway staring at Evan, naked pleading paling his ruddy face.

"Tell her, Durian."

"Oh, Christ, Ev—none of that can matter."

Evan looked at Jani, the shine in his eyes almost feverish. Dying for a drink, probably, but he wouldn't take one while she and Ridgeway were there. "The fact is, Risa, my late wife was suborned by her unfortunately not-late aunt to serve as an in-House verifier. How Ulanova managed to work around Lyssa's swan dives off the sobriety shuttle is anyone's guess, but Colonel Doyle and Durian uncovered evidence that, for the past several years, my loving spouse kept Exterior well informed of the goings-on here.''

Jani pondered that kernel of information. *He kept that from me because he knew if he told me, I wouldn't have come.* ''How much of worth could Lyssa have revealed? You didn't use her as counsel, did you?''

''Not per se. But I underestimated her influence, her access, her—''

''Her hatred.'' Ridgeway's voice tremored. ''She hated us all. Blamed us all. Lyssa became expert at pointing fingers and slathering on guilt with a trowel.''

Evan pressed his thumb and forefinger to the bridge of his nose. ''Durian.''

''It's true, Evan. No use denying it. She turned this House into a civil-war-in-a-jar. God, the lies she told, the people she sucked in. We had to purge entire divisions—we had Exterior-trained operatives running our departments! To tell you the truth, Ms. Tyi, we still don't know if we got everyone.'' His metal stare raked her. ''We don't know who could still be out there, lurking.''

Jani's stomach rumbled. She pressed a hand to it to quiet it. ''I don't recall any of this in the files you gave me, Mr. Ridgeway.''

''I gave you what I was told to give you. Information about Evan.''

''Which was incomplete, as well.''

''Yes.'' He didn't bother to explain or apologize. Those points worked in his favor, since Jani would have believed neither. ''But now, it appears, the House is to be your oyster. Pry with care, Ms. Tyi. That's all I ask.'' He rose. ''I'll earmark the files we've deemed most noteworthy, although you'll want to see them all, I'm sure. Have you ever investigated a death?''

''No.'' *Not officially.* ''I've stuck with paper crimes.'' The memories of her Service work nestled under Jani's ribs, a bundle of warmth. Or maybe it was heartburn? ''Just show me the paper—I'll take it from there. And if I need your help, Mr. Ridgeway—''

"You will have it, of course. Make an appointment to meet with me this afternoon," he said as he swept out.

Evan's groan rattled as the door closed. "It's going to take me days to settle him down. But it will have been worth it. He doesn't like you, but he will work with you."

Jani stared at the closed door. "He thinks I'm an Exterior plant. Any slip I make, he's going to magnify tenfold."

"Who's he going to bitch to? I'll take it all with a transport-load of salt. Virginia and the other execs will take their lead from me." Evan grinned. The years fell away. "He's just jealous, anyway. Do you know what he told me? He suspects you're my mistress, on top of everything else. Thinks I've been keeping you under wraps for years."

"Why would he think that?"

"Because I look so 'contented,' as he put it. That makes him nervous. He likes hungry leaders. In case of a feeding frenzy, he's guaranteed a pile of scraps." His smile wavered. "He saved my life, Jani. When all this hit the fan, I knew I could count on him. I know what he is, what he wants. But there were times when he could've hopped the fence with the others who followed Lyssa, and he didn't. Durian's thrown in with me for better or worse. That's more than anyone else has ever done." He looked at her. "Of course, you would have stuck, if I'd given you the chance. But I listened to *him*." Acton van Reuter's name, unspoken, hung heavy between them. "He chose Lyssa for me. Shows what he knew."

Jani looked toward the balcony. The sun battered through the glass—even from where she sat, she could feel the heat. She'd wanted to throttle Evan only minutes before. Now a part of her just wanted to sit with him, look out at the sunshine, and listen to his assurances.

And fight back the other part of her that didn't believe a word of it. *Steve didn't like Lyssa.* He hadn't admitted it at dinner, but the assumption made sense considering his evasion of Jani's repeated questions. Had Lyssa asked him to assist her in her illegal fact gathering? Had he turned her down?

Had he?

Evan sat up with a start. "I'm actually at loose ends tonight. How about dinner, back at Private? I'll have cook do something colonial.'' He looked at her hopefully. ''About seven?''

''Won't that upset Durian?'' Jani stood and tried to readjust her ill-fitting jacket

''Screw him—I'm entitled.'' He rose and walked around his desk.

''I think I can make it.'' Jani tensed as Evan closed in and slipped his arm around her waist. *Like it never left.* ''Saw your speech last night. I'm surprised Ulanova let you make it home alive.''

''She tried to buy me off. If I threw in with her publicly on the secession-rights issue, she'd disband the Court. Problem is, I didn't trust her to keep her word. I also believe she's wrong.'' Evan opened the door for her, looking out to see whether his staff had arrived. ''Seven o'clock, then.'' He pulled his arm away as voices drifted toward them. ''Considering what else you've learned, I'm happy you're still talking to me.''

''I didn't think I would be,'' Jani admitted. ''The fact your father was involved explained a lot, though.''

''Explained my rolling over and playing dead, you mean.'' He eyed her guiltily. ''What Lyssa did doesn't seem to bother you as much.''

''Vengeful behavior, I'm more familiar with. I understand her feelings. With her training, she could guess what Martin went through.''

''Anything like what you've gone through?'' Evan asked softly.

''Not the same thing, Ev. I could adjust.'' She gave her duffel an absent pat, as though it were an overlarge worry bead. ''When did you know?''

''Looking back, I'd say the signs were there from the start. I just didn't want to face it. I think I even know the day it happened. Dad dropped by out of the blue and took Martin out for ice cream. I've never been able to track where the actual implantation was done, though.'' Evan slipped back into his office and waved to a pair of uniformed clerks who entered the anteroom. ''Dad said Martin needed help. Right away, too, before things got out of hand. My son had shown signs of taking after me, you see. Dad always felt I lacked a sense of purpose, just because it wasn't the same as his.'' He gave Jani a last, sad smile. ''Seven o'clock,'' he mouthed as he closed the door.

CHAPTER 12

Doyle handed over the House access codes with the eggshell grace of someone who didn't like being on the wrong end of the favor stick. Jani accepted them with a quick nod and a minimum of small talk, excusing herself when Doyle's questions drifted toward matters such as "which colony, exactly" had she come from?

She'd also deflected an invitation to brunch.

Not on my bones, you don't. Jani rushed through the Security section, knowing her every move was being monitored. She stifled the impulse to stick out her tongue at a wall-mounted scancam as the front-desk guard coded her departure.

I bet Evan would love for me to find proof Ulanova had something to do with Lyssa's death. That would give him the tool he needed to pry her and the PM off his back for good. Not to mention win Jani some breathing room. In the resulting scandal, who would care about her?

But that doesn't explain what Lyssa's death had to do with Knevçet Shèràa. Unless Evan only steered her to that conclusion to get her to come to Chicago. *Remember the pragmatist—even if he does look great in black.* She used some of her new codes to slip into the controlled Finance section. The division cafeteria was small and, at this between-meals hour, sparsely populated. She loaded a tray and wedged into an odd-shaped corner table with a view of the hallway as well as the door. She was in no mood to be caught twice. She ate quickly, then sat quietly for a few minutes. Only when she felt certain her stomach wouldn't reject her latest offering did she set out on her next project.

Arrange my appointment with Ridgeway. She dreaded the prospect, but the outcry would be tremendous if she didn't show. She coded into the controlled-access lift, noting with relief that the floor indicator stayed lit.

Fixed the lights, I see. Jani grinned at the bright illumination flooding her from above. She stepped into the same fourth-floor lobby she had visited the previous day. This time, the space was empty of both reporters and idomeni ambassadors. She headed down the widest hallway, looking for the largest offices with the best views.

Durian Ridgeway's, of course, proved to be the biggest of all, a commanding corner with views of both the Main House grounds and the lake. Jani made her appointment with a jumpy assistant, restraining an urge to pat the young man's hand when he made an incorrect schedule entry and wouldn't stop apologizing for what apparently constituted a Class X Commonwealth felony in domain Durian.

That task completed, Jani wandered. She checked names on doorplates, sneaked around empty offices, and brushed off curious guards and documents staffers by waving her access cards and sounding indignant—the time-honored way to get into places where one had no business being.

She was debating a visit to the third-floor parts bins when an unmarked door flew open and she found herself staring into Angevin Wyle's tear-stained face. She wore a rumpled Interior trouser suit. No makeup. Even her copper curls appeared tarnished and lifeless. *Bet I know your problem,* Jani thought as she reached into her duffel for more tissues. *A human chimney named Steve.*

Angevin snuffled and straightened her shoulders. "Hullo."

At first, Jani felt tempted to make sympathetic noises and offer womanly advice. But her own love life had never been anything to brag about. Besides, if the well-bred Miss Wyle had displayed the Earthbound behavior Steve hinted at, she deserved to shed a few tears. "If Durian sees you like this, he'll have a fit."

Angevin's chin jutted. "Durian can go drown himself."

She hasn't gone completely over to the enemy, Hansen—

there's still hope. Jani looked up and down the hall. "Where's a breakroom—you could use one. I want to talk to you."

"Don't wanna talk."

"Yes, you do. Besides, you need to pull yourself together. You look like hell."

"Fuck you."

"See." Jani thumped Angevin on the back just hard enough to set her in motion. "You're feeling better already."

They bypassed the crowded department cafeteria. Instead, Angevin led Jani down a dead-end hall and into a converted office furnished with mismatched castoffs. In one corner, a bandy-legged table held an ancient brewer, supplies of cream and sugar in cracked plastic containers, and a tiny cooler decorated with a scrawled snack schedule.

"Does Ridgeway ever come here?" Jani asked as she looked around.

Angevin shook her head. "Nah, he hates this place. Thinks it's a pit. He's been trying to have it closed down for months, tells us the regular cafeteria is good enough for everybody. But we block him. Durian can lord it over civilians as much as he wants, but try telling the head of Interior Tax Form Compliance that she can't have her coffee and doughnut wherever she pleases and you're going to have a fight on your hands."

A few scattered souls already occupied the room, talking, perusing newssheets, rustling through paperwork. Angevin exchanged greetings as she led Jani to an unpopulated corner.

Jani sank into a semicollapsed lounge chair. "How far back does this room date? Since the Lyssa purge?"

"Yeah." Angevin gave her a startled look. "It got to the point that the cafeteria . . . sometimes there just isn't a room big enough, you know?" She sighed. "They don't teach you how to deal with things like that in school."

"Are the ones who come here still under a cloud?"

Angevin snorted softly. "If there was even a hint of an intimation of a possibility, Security met you at your desk and you were gone." She sat back in her squeaky chair. "The ones who come here—it's just our way of giving notice that we disagree with how things were done. It didn't have to be the way it was. Whatever happened to due process?''

"That only applies to official criminal charges.''

"Then whatever happened to letting people explain? Most of them thought they were doing official Interior work—that's how she set things up to look!'' Heads turned in Angevin's direction. She blushed and fell silent.

"You're Ridgeway's right hand,'' Jani said, "but you're accepted here.''

"I'm Hansen Wyle's daughter. That means something, from what I understand.'' Angevin looked around the room. "Maybe if I hang here long enough, someone will tell me what that something is.''

"Considering how closely Ridgeway controls you, I'm surprised he lets you come here.''

Before Angevin could answer, the door opened and Steve Forell entered with a young woman in tow. As soon as she saw them, Angevin's eyes filled. "Excuse me,'' she mumbled. Hands jammed in pockets, she exited just as Steve and his friend worked their way over to Jani's corner.

"Good morning, Ms. Tyi,'' Steve said as he claimed Angevin's chair. "I hope we didn't interrupt anything important.'' His look of wide-eyed innocence disappeared when he noticed his companion still standing shifty-footed beside him. "Crike, sit down,'' he said, pushing the girl into the empty seat next to Jani. She was as tall as Steve, with straight ash blond hair hacked at chin length. She had overwhelmed her pointed features with heavy makeup. A sweeping dark blue skirt and matching jacket hung on her thin frame.

"I'm glad we caught you up,'' Steve said. "I left you a message on your House line, but this works much better.'' He tossed an exasperated look at the young woman, who sat rigid, eyes locked on his face. "This is Betha Concannon— she's Guernsey, too. She were also Lyssa van Reuter's personal documents examiner. I thought you might be interested.''

"It weren't official! She just used to have me check things for her. Travel docs—stuff like that.''

In the friendly confines of Jani's Private House suite, Betha recovered both her voice and her ability to move. She paced, activated lights, pawed bric-a-brac. However long the nervous energy had been building, it was all dissipating now. Jani hid the sculptures and other breakables and stayed out of her way.

Steve, meanwhile, prodded cushions, examined furniture, and stared at the Channel World artwork as Jani stashed it. When the poshness became too much to bear, he pulled out a nicstick. She could hear the crack of the ignition tip across the room.

Betha slowed until she fell onto one of the sofas. "It's not like she had me forge IDs or anything. She just used to have me check things, fill out forms."

"What types of things, exactly?" Jani asked. "You mentioned travel docs. Were they hers?"

"For the most part. But a few of the things were old. Ten, fifteen, twenty years." Betha cradled a pillow in her lap. Every so often, she gave it a squeeze.

"Colonial travel?" Jani asked. "Earth vicinity? Where?"

"All over the place. She went everywhere. Elyas. Amaryllis. Kim Chun. Most of the trips were to Nueva Madrid, though. Can't think why the hell anyone would want to go there. All that's there is a Service hospital."

"Well, she was a physician," Jani said. "One could have all sorts of reasons for visiting a prestigious medical facility. How often did Lyssa visit Nueva Madrid? Were the trips quarterly? Six months? Twelve?"

"Every five to six," Betha replied.

"Over what time span?"

"Almost two years."

"How was she before these trips? Excited? Depressed? Apprehensive? Did they involve business? Research?"

"Well, the papers stated she were acting as some type of envoy. Trying to help smooth relations between Neoclona doctors and the nonaffiliated med groups." The rate of pillow-squeezing increased.

"Did that make sense to you?"

Betha shot Jani a surprised look. "Never really thought about it. I were just a drone in the Doc pool—thrilled to get the work."

"Was His Excellency ever present when you put the packets together? To give his wife advice, go over the itinerary?"

"N-no. *No*. But they weren't getting on, you know—"

"Did you sit in on the planning meetings? Trips like these must have involved a great deal of strategizing."

Betha glanced sideways at Steve. "Yes. A couple."

Out of the corner of her eye, Jani could see Steve shift in his seat. "Well, that's a good place to start." She put an enthusiastic kick in her voice. "We'll have agendas, lists of people Lyssa would be talking to, ship crew lists." She waited, her level gaze never leaving Betha's face. "I'm getting together with Durian Ridgeway this afternoon. If you can give me the dates of the meetings to which you went, I can have him get me copies of the minutes."

Steve emitted a strangled groan. Betha kept kneading the pillow.

"No one knew about you and Lyssa," Jani finally said. The sound of tearing interrupted her. "Months and months go by, coworkers all around you getting the hook," she continued, as Betha surveyed the ripped pillow in mute dismay. "Yet you manage to scoot through the barrage unscathed. Pretty good maneuvering for a drone, considering anybody with any sense would have swept you out at first pass."

"So Betha weren't the Lady's *official* dexxie." Steve, who no longer appeared quite so smug, sat up straight. "He were shipped out to a colonial post during the height of the troubles. No one's heard from him since." He pointed to Betha. "What did you expect her to do—turn herself in?"

"None of the paper you did for Lyssa went through Durian's office, did it?" Jani asked the sick-looking Betha. "At first, it was just a few small favors. She was, after all, the Lady. Maybe your ticket out of the Doc pool. Then, finally, after the favors began piling up, getting more and more complicated, more and more risky, you asked her what the hell was going on?"

"*Hey*," Steve shouted, "I brought her here as a favor—!"

"Be quiet." Jani turned back to Betha, who still clutched the ripped pillow. "That's when she threatened you. Told you what she'd do to you if you didn't keep your mouth shut?"

After a long silence, Betha spoke. "If you already know

so much, why ask me? If you already know what happened, what chance do I have?''

More of one than I did, when Riky Neumann cornered me. "You filled out the travel docs for Nueva Madrid?"

"Yes."

"You didn't register them or obtain Durian's approval?"

"No. She asked me not to. She said she'd handle it."

Steve buried his head in his hands.

"In the meantime," Jani said, "Lyssa went through her regular dexxie for another set of travels docs, the ones her husband and her staff knew about. *Those* were the envoy papers. Same times, same location, different purpose."

"Yes," Betha said. "She said if I told anyone, she'd make sure I got deregistered. At the very least."

Steve cleared his throat. "You think the Lady were sick? Getting some type of medical treatment she didn't want the Minister to know about?"

Jani jerked her head in Betha's direction. "She vetted the return-trip papers, I assume. I think you should ask her."

"I don't think it could have been anything serious." Betha started picking out the pillow stuffing and worked the feathery foam between her fingers. "I don't have much experience in medical records—just my school courses—but I never saw any patient copies of referral documents, or codes for consultation summaries." She shrugged weakly. "Besides, she never seemed nervous or anything. Once, she even said she were taking a vacation. 'Going surfing, Betha' she told me. 'Going to learn how to surf.' "

Jani felt the clammy grip of nausea that had nothing to do with food. She might not yet know who killed Lyssa or why. But she knew how. "How many times did she mention surfing?"

"Two, three times."

Steve ignited another nicstick. "Does that mean something?"

"Maybe." Jani paused. "How much room do we have to maneuver? Any audits coming up in the foreseeable future?"

Steve moaned as Betha worked to her feet. "The general audit starts next week," she said.

"Next week!" Jani smothered a groan herself. "Seven

days until your paper house gets blown down by the big bad wolf.'' She worked her neck, listened to the bones crackle. When general auditors fired, they seldom missed. She'd have to move pretty quickly if she wanted to help those two morons remain in the Registry. And out of prison. ''That leaves us with lots of ground to cover in a very short time.'' She rose as quickly as her aching back would allow. ''Leave me alone to think. I'll track you down when I need you.''

''No reason why we should help you,'' Steve huffed, hands in pockets, slouch in full, sagging bloom.

''Felony documents fraud,'' Jani said, pointing to Betha, ''and accessory after the fact,'' she added as she gripped his sleeve and pulled him toward the door. ''Besides, you'd rather have to do for me than anyone else you've ever known.'' She met Betha's *not again* look head-on. ''Well, if you had said no in the first place, you wouldn't be in this mess.''

Betha fingered the worn edge of her jacket cuff. ''How? She were the Lady. I'm just . . .'' She pulled a thread from the frayed edge. Her shoulders slumped. ''How could I say no?''

Same way I did. No, Colonel Neumann, sir, I will not sign off on your faked medical files. No, Colonel Neumann, sir, I will not fill out the transfer justification for your faked files.

No. No. It did get through, eventually. One way or another. Jani escorted the somber duo to the lift and smiled at them as they boarded the car. Steve looked away, while Betha stared at her like a trapped animal.

The stare jarred Jani. She remained in the hall as the lift doors closed, trying to punch holes in memories that insisted on forcing their way to the surface. Gawky, sloppy Betha. *Take away the bad makeup and trim the hair into a Service burr, you've got Yolan.* Corporal Yolan Cray, who would have been—Jani did a quick mental calculation—thirty-seven Common years old now.

She returned to her suite. After clearing away pillow remnants, she closed herself in her office, righted Lucien's card, and stared at it. *Were you trying to tell me something, Lieutenant?* Sailracing. Before the self-propelled sailboards had been perfected, the racers had to rely on Mother Nature.

Windsurfing, they had called it then. *So Lady Lyssa learned to surf.* Learned to ride what Jani and her fellow augies had called, in grandiosity born of fear, the solar wind. Learned to smell berries the year 'round, hear colors, see sound, feel the blood flow in your veins. Learned that no matter what, dying was for others, but never for you.

She freed the gossip holozine from its hiding place in her duffel. Along with the childhood pictures, wedding portraits, and images of the great lady in decline, some ambitious soul had constructed a timetable of the last few years of Lyssa van Reuter's life. Jani studied the timeline. Public battles with Evan and other minor embarrassments filled in the gaps between the major blowups. Skimmer accidents, disappearances, extended visits to sanitariums run by unaffiliated meds. But never a Neoclona or Service facility. Never someplace where they could tell.

Every few months, another crash. Another disconnect with reality. It happened sometimes, with those who had been augmented when they shouldn't have been. *So she started taking herself to Nueva twice a year to have her brain reset.* Had the flashing lights shoved in her face and went bye-bye. Jani had hated take-down—a minute of fast-forward hallucinations followed by a week of "what's my name" loginess. *No more for me.* Not ever.

Any augmented vet who worked for Interior had to be checked out every six months, with at least one precautionary take-down per year. Evan had said so himself. He was aware of the pattern—you'd think the timing of Lyssa's trips would have sounded a chord with him. Then again, maybe not. Lyssa wasn't Service—any rumor that she had been augmented would have been laughed off the newssheets.

Oh my Lady. Why? To understand what Martin went through, why he did the things he did? Or was it to torture herself, punish herself for allowing it to happen? Jani poked absently at her numb left hand, ran a live finger over dead flesh and bone. *I wish I could have met you first, Lyssa.* She could have told her it wouldn't help. Nothing did.

CHAPTER 13

"NìRau?"

Tsecha suppressed a fatigued sigh as he lowered into his chair. Since before sunrise he had stood, still and straight, praying before the embassy's dominant altar. Now he could see the sun through one of the room's narrow windows, risen three-quarters to prime, its reflection off the lake a painful jolt to his long-closed eyes.

"NìRau? It is the Exterior Minister. Ulanova." Head held high in respect, Sànalàn, Tsecha's religious suborn, stepped into his sight line, a needle of light against the black stone of the altar wall. "She has been scheduled, nìRau, but we may send her away, as before—"

"No, nìa." Tsecha used the gentlest refusal his tongue and posture would allow, but the young female's reaction showed that even so she resented the interruption. Her shoulders rounded, her head tilted forward. Even then, she stood taller than he, fine-boned as a marsh bird, her skin the sand gold of her body mother, a central plains-dwelling Sìah. "This day, I must see her, I think." Tsecha continued to watch as his suborn's shoulders slumped farther. "You do not like her, nìa?"

"She is as a wall." Sànalàn now straightened, raising her cupped right hand chest high in question. "How can one promote order who withholds so much?"

"Such withholding is much admired by humanish."

"Ah." The narrow shoulders relaxed, the arm dropped to the side. "Humanish admire odd things." Sànalàn turned to lead Tsecha out of the altar room. "Which explains much, and truly."

Tsecha held back argument and followed his suborn. She wore a floor-grazing overrobe of bronze metalcloth; the material shone as a mirror. The altar room's bloodstone columns, black altar, sand-hued walls, the humanish sun and lake themselves, curved across Sànalàn's back as she walked, as though the world itself clothed her.

Tsecha bared his teeth in satisfaction. *Humanish grow most still when they see my nìa.* Sànalàn's hair, which matched her skin in hue and her robe in shine, had been drawn back into the tight, braided knot of an unbred Vynshàrau. Her eyes, Tsecha recalled from her embassy identity badge, were large and green.

They call her a walking Chinese porcelain, he remembered, thinking back to the humanish holo of the embassy staff's arrival ceremonies which he had watched. It pleased him greatly that humanish compared his nìa to something of Mandarin, for such promoted connection between alien and idomeni, a sense of order most greatly to be wished.

A sense of order which, Tsecha prayed, remained after his meeting with Ulanova.

Sànalàn led him to the entry of one of his less favored meeting rooms, but declined to open the door. "She will speak to you of Amsun GateWay tariff issues."

"To be expected, nìa."

"Then there are the humanish sicknesses. She will ask if we are, too, affected."

Ah, but that even I do not know, nìa. The Council I represent will not tell me, even when I demand. They believe if they do not speak of such sicknesses, those sicknesses will disappear. They have become most humanish in that regard.

The suborn placed her left hand over her stomach, as protection for her soul. "She has no right to ask of such things. As always, she will give nothing, and expect everything."

Tsecha gestured in affirmation. "The humanish are afraid, nìa. They do not yet understand the truth of what happens. So very few are ill now, but—"

"If humanish took their honor in preserving order, they would not so fear the death of the body." The suborn straightened and began to stroke patterns in the air, invocations against demons. So shaken was she that she did not offer apology for her interruption. "Their fear of death will destroy us all this time, and truly. They will strike at anything to save their lives. It is a most ungodly thing."

Tsecha reached out and gripped Sànalàn's hands, stilling them. "You speak of things you do not understand, nìa. You were not born when we first learned of the fear." He longed to look his suborn in her green eyes, but that would jar her to the roots of her soul, and such he could not afford to do.

"It is you who do not understand, nìRau." Sànalàn spoke slowly, boldly, as she tried to work free of his restraint. "So say the Temple. So say the Council. You took in humanish, not knowing their fear. Trained them in our ways, not understanding their fear. Paid almost with your life, for not destroying that fear when the gods allowed you the chance. You understand nothing! So say the Temple! So say the Council!"

"And what do you say, nìa?"

"Their words are mine." The uncertain tremor in Sànalàn's voice betrayed her, but she was of Sìah, and Sìah were most stubborn. "You understand nothing."

Slowly, Tsecha relaxed his hold on his suborn's wrists. "But that is why I speak to Ulanova, nìa. Because I who understand nothing understand her best." He spoke as humanish, with no gesture or change in stance, his tone flat, allowing his meaning to hide itself between the lines. Then he left his suborn to uncover that meaning as best she could and entered the meeting room.

Inside the sparsely furnished space, Exterior Minister Anais Ulanova met him as any suborn Vynshàrau would have: in the center of the room, posture most straight, chin high, eyes closed. Tsecha had himself just spent many humanish hours in that most uncomfortable position. He wondered how long Ulanova had been standing such, or whether she had been sitting until she heard his discussion with Sànalàn end.

Most humanish of me, to think in this way. Cynical, Hansen had called it. But the door to the meeting room was not soundproofed. To the best of Tsecha's knowledge, supplemented by the work of his Intelligence skein, the Exterior Minister possessed no strong devotion to any deity and little regard for the other ministers. *So what means this respect of hers?*

Tsecha bared his teeth, extended his hand as Hansen had taught him long ago, and summoned forth his best English. "Glories of the day to you, Minister Ulanova!"

The Exterior Minister's eyes snapped open, widening even more as Tsecha drew nearer. She tottered, took a step backwards to regain her balance, then held out her hand as well. Her lips curved, but she did not bare her teeth. "Glories of the day to you as well, nìRau," she said, her low voice pleasing to Tsecha's ear, though not precisely respectful. "I am so glad we could meet together at last." The skin of her hand felt cool and dry, her grip loose.

Cucumbers. The harsh humanish sound pleased Tsecha's internal ear as Ulanova's voice did the external, but why the peculiar word should enter his mind now . . . ? *My handheld.* It remained behind in his rooms—it could not help him now. *I am alone with the wall.*

Ulanova began the discussion, as was fitting. "Please extend my thanks to your suborn for her assistance in arranging this meeting, nìRau. I realize the notice was most short, and truly." She led Tsecha toward two metalframe seats placed in one corner of the room. "But we have received news of an alarming nature from our Outer Circle agents. I felt you should be informed." The Exterior Minister worked onto her tall seat with difficulty, appearing almost as a scuttling insect in the dark brown uniform she wore for her embassy visits. She was only of average height for a humanish female, which made her shorter than an adult Vynshàrau by half an arm's length. "This news may affect us both greatly, nìRau," she finally said as she edged upright.

Tsecha found himself focusing on Ulanova's feet, as always. *So far above the ground . . .* "Yes, Minister. Sànalàn mentioned your concerns of the Amsun GateWay."

"I lied to your suborn, nìRau."

Lied. Tsecha tore his attention from Ulanova's dangling feet and looked into her face. "Lied," he repeated aloud, as darkest brown eyes looked at him in turn.

"She's alive, nìRau."

"She?" He felt a tightening in his soul and took deep

breaths to calm himself. "Of whom do you speak?"

"Of Jani Kilian, of course, nìRau. She was seen on an Outer Circle colony by the name of Whalen's Planet. It has one major population center in its northern hemisphere, a town called NorthPort."

"NorthPort, that is—"

"Yes, nìRau, the site of one of the major Haárin settlements." Ulanova's tone implied no apology for the interruption, as was usual. "She was, in fact, on quite good terms with several of the Pathen Haárin high dominants, especially a shuttle broker named Genta Res. It was he who told my agent of the Captain's existence."

Tsecha tugged at the sleeves of his overrobe. The loyalty of Haárin—*tidal*, Hansen had called it. And yet . . . "I suspect, Anais, that ní Genta was threatened perhaps with cancellation of business permits before he felt the need to inform your agent of the existence of the Captain. Allow me to save both our staffs much time by lodging my protest of such with you now."

"She is a criminal in your government's eyes as well as mine, nìRau. I thought this news would please you." Ulanova's tone grew harsh. "I have known for some time that your search for her has spanned years."

"*My* search, Anais. Not my government's."

"Is there a difference, nìRau?"

Tsecha smoothed the folds of his white overrobe, the red trim of his cuffs providing the only true color in the drab surround. "I was chosen to succeed Xinfa nìRau Ceèl as chief propitiator of my sect eighty-five of your years ago, as a most young one. The Laum had just claimed power from Sìahrau, and none believed Vynshà would ever rule over idomeni. Thus was I chief propitiator when we were only of Vynshà. If we become only of Vynshà again, chief propitiator I will still be."

"NìRau, I didn't mean—"

"To be in government serves only a purpose. For you as well as for me, I believe, Anais, and truly." Tsecha maintained an even, humanish tone throughout his speech, ending by baring his teeth and sighing. An advantage, perhaps, to being as a wall. If he had ever given this type of speech in

Temple or before Council, embellished with the full range of Vynshàrau gesture and posture, so that every emotion and feeling of his was revealed . . . *I would again be fleeing from mixed-sect mobs demanding my life. Of that I am most sure.* He breathed in deeply in an effort to slow his pounding heart. *My Captain lives.*

Anais sat in silence. She had decorated her small hands, narrow as Vynshàrau but lifeless white, with several large-stoned rings, which she toyed with in turn. "We tracked Captain Kilian to a small Transport Ministry hostel located in what one might generously refer to as NorthPort's business district, but one of Interior's people beat us to the goal. My best man was able to catch up with her and work on her for over a month. He is positive we were put on the wrong scent, but I have been at this game longer than he." Stones flickered in the light. "Very soon, I expect to be proven correct. We will have her, nìRau."

Tsecha suppressed the urge to bare his teeth. Anais thought herself so subtle. When she grew angry, she spoke in ways she felt idomeni would not understand. *But I had my Hansen, and I knew my Kilian.* His living Kilian. Quick, yes, and suspicious, as she was always. *Are you quite sure you will have her, Anais? You have not the skill to read between her lines.*

The Exterior Minister continued. "Later, my agents hooked a red herring in NorthPort. She turned out to be an Interior staffer on holiday. On holiday—in bloody NorthPort! Studying the Haárin, she claimed. Sent there by Evan to cross me up, no doubt. Although I suppose it may have been true— she is one of his Vynshà-watchers." Ulanova's mouth curved. "Vynshàrau, nìRau, of course. Stupid of me. No offense meant."

But your very life is an offense, Anais, Tsecha thought as he nodded his acceptance of her apology. "So you suspect van Reuter protects Captain Kilian now?" he asked. "Is that a surprise?" *It is not, to me.*

"Considering their linked pasts, yes and no." She pounded her thigh with a jeweled fist. "If I only knew where he'd stashed her! That man has allies all over the city, though with all those unanswered questions concerning his wife's death, perhaps not as many as he used to."

"Yes." Tsecha nodded. He had read accounts of the death of the Interior Minister's dominant, in fact only, wife. *Such a disordered life.* But there was blessed order in death, at least. "I rejoice in the Lady's death, for it has brought her peace, and truly. May Minister van Reuter find such order as well." He felt Anais's eyes on him again, their glitter hard as the stones on her fingers. Did she believe he wished van Reuter's death as a convenience for her? The thought angered him. "Thank you for the word of the Captain, Anais. What else must we speak of? My time for first prime sacrament draws most close, I believe." He wished to be at peace when he took sacrament, as well as later, when he planned. *So much planning—so many meetings!*

The Exterior Minister again worked her rings, studying him through narrowed eyes. "There has been the first death, nìRau. On Elyas, in the town of Zell, near the Haárin settlement. An older man, a shopkeeper. His family was able to get him to the Neoclona facility on Amsun before he died. The doctors there believe some type of environmental toxin is to blame, but no one can determine what this man ate or drank or touched which could account for his illness."

"This is the first and only death?"

"But not the first *sickness*, nìRau. There were two more in Zell, a husband and wife, and a young man in NorthPort. The symptoms were the same. Digestive problems and body aches, followed by mood disturbances, psychotic episodes, rapid wasting. In the case of the young man, his liver needed to be replaced."

Ulanova's shining gaze moved about the bare room, focusing on nothing. "We will, in deference to your sensibilities, refrain from asking you to question your physician-priest skeins as to whether any idomeni have likewise taken ill these past months. But we do need to know what types of soil and water treatment the Haárin have in place in Zell and NorthPort, nìRau. We need to know what sort of untaxed trade is taking place between your people and mine. Specifically, are your Haárin selling food to my colonists? Food that is proving to be more than an exotic delicacy, but that is poisoning them? I realize your religions and cultures all dictate care and secrecy with regard to the production of your foods, as they do with your treatment of illness, but we need that information. You must comply with our requests. An order is required. Through your Council, and coming from you.''

"You know what the answer will be, Anais.''

"Then we will expel the Haárin from the Outer Circle.''

"And we will expel humanish from Samvasta and Nèae, and all will go as before.''

"We need that information, nìRau.''

"You know it already, Exterior Minister. Do not come to me for confirmation you have obtained from your own. Your doctors keep you well informed, this I know, and truly.''

"No, nìRau—''

Tsecha bared his teeth quite broadly. "Ever since their first work in Rauta Shèràa, your Neoclona doctors have worked as they pleased, Anais. DeVries, and Parini, and your most excellent Shroud. You keep their secrets from idomeni. Why should idomeni behave as different?''

Ulanova looked Tsecha in the eye, her stare most steady. "Because idomeni, I think, want what we in the Commonwealth want. A well-ordered future.'' She stepped down from her high seat. When she stood most straight, she seemed not as short as Tsecha knew her to be. "This is what I assume, nìRau. To the best of my knowledge, your government does not share your vision of the future.'' Her gaze probed like a physician's instruments. "They know what you believe, and still they sent you here.''

Tsecha bared his teeth. He welcomed the opportunity for open discussion, the chance to speak as idomeni. "Yes, Minister. All on Shèrá know my beliefs.''

"That if we share worlds long enough, eat the same foods, drink the same water, we will begin to change? The idomeni will become more human and the human will become more idomeni.''

"Until, in the end, we will be as one people, Minister. Such is order, greatly to be wished. All the same, in the end.''

"Hybridization.'' Ulanova's eyes dulled. "John Shroud

testified before the Cabinet last month on just that subject, nìRau. He believes the idea laughable.''

''Does he, Minister? That is most interesting. When he labored in his basement in Rauta Shèràa's humanish enclave, he believed quite differently. So often would he visit me at the Academy, to argue the beliefs he does not believe in anymore.'' Tsecha remembered warm breezes, the sweet odor of lamptree, the raised voices. ''Even then, his research told him the benefits of combining. Of hybridization. 'Humans could live two hundred years, nìRau,' he would tell me. How pink his face grew as he spoke. Even now, I remember the pinkness.''

Ulanova stood very straight and crossed her arms. ''But his research led nowhere, nìRau.''

''Indeed, Minister?'' Tsecha gestured in disregard. ''This is why he and DeVries and Parini govern their hospitals as Oligarchs, watch over the Commonwealth as propitiators? Because John's research has led nowhere?'' His hands trembled. Such joy to be had, in open disputation. ''But he still thinks his new humans could be changed as he wills, and remain most as human. He thinks he can take the advantages of combining and give nothing in return. So little he understands of order. So little he has always understood.'' An even more joyous thought occurred to him. ''Did you ever ask John Shroud, Minister, whether *he* knew where Jani Kilian is?''

Ulanova closed her eyes and began to massage her forehead. ''Doctor Shroud assured me—''

''Did he, Minister!'' Such joy Tsecha felt, he interrupted without apology. ''So well John assures. He assured my Hansen, just before my Hansen died. And he assured me, just before the Haárin entered Rauta Shèràa and the sect dominants demanded my death. 'I do not have her, nìRau,' he said. 'She died in that transport crash. Nothing left but ashes.' Thus did John Shroud assure, while in his basement, his new human healed.''

Ulanova's eyes snapped open. ''If my hunch proves true, nìRau, and your Captain turns up, I will first use her to destroy Evan van Reuter. Then, she will face court-martial, and if I have any say in the matter, she will be executed for the murder of Rikart Neumann.'' Her lip curled. A humanish smile. The smile of a wall. "Ironic, if that augmentation which helped her survive the crash only served to keep her alive for me."

Tsecha bared his teeth. "My Captain was augmented for one reason only, Minister. So she would be alive when I needed her. So she would live until her time had come. Her time to succeed me. Her time to take my place as chief propitiator of the Vynshàrau."

Something shimmered in Ulanova's eyes. Was it fear? "In your own way, nìRau, you are as fanatical as our most radical religious leaders." Her tone hardened. "What you believe can never come to pass."

"Such is as it will be, Minister. Whether *you* believe or not is of no importance. You will come to accept or be left behind. As the Laum were left behind, and as all will be left behind who do not accept order. Order must proceed, Minister. Order is all."

"It is good I understand you, nìRau," Ulanova said softly as she looked down at him. "Now, with regard to your refusal to supply information concerning illegal Haárin trade, please allow me to save both our staffs much time by lodging my protest of your behavior with you now."

"Your protest is noted, Anais." Tsecha remained seated, his hands twisted through his overrobe to stop their shaking. *But my Captain lives, as I prayed, so lodge your protests where you will.* Double meaning, he knew, in those words. Between the lines. Hansen would have been proud.

CHAPTER 14

Jani sat at her desk, office door closed, curtains drawn against the distractions of sun, calm lake, and cloudless sky. Her workstation screen flashed in silence, its conversation input option shut down, alarms muted. Feet propped on her desk, touchboard cradled in her lap, she leaned forward to advance the shifting screen images with a stylus.

Then she hit the wrong section of the touchboard and dumped herself out of a sensitive region of Commonwealth systems. Exasperated, she leaned toward the screen too quickly and almost dumped herself out of her chair.

Voice would go faster. Jani berated herself as a series of Lyssa's files disappeared in a rainbow flash. Then she rehacked her way through the document tangle, once more by touch.

She had known dexxies for whom workstations provided the bulk of daily verbal exchange. For some, it had been a conscious choice; for others, it had just worked out that way.

Could have worked out that way for me. It's easy, and safe, and I could win all the arguments. There were plenty of jobs out there for a paper-savvy fugitive with an antisocial streak. She could have lain lower over the years.

But she needed to hear real voices. Or, more to the point, voices she knew to be real. Perhaps the difference was subtle, one for philosophers. But she'd seen more than one augmented colleague done in by that difference during her time on Shèrá.

Hearing things is a bad sign. Seeing things was worse.

That meant all those neurochems whose names she kept try-ing to forget were building up in her head in vain search of release, a condition more properly known as augie psychosis. Sometimes reversible, if you excised the implants in time, but most times, not. Shroud had begged her to keep watch for the signs of impending problems, to come to him when she felt she needed medical help.

Of course, her dear doctor had begged for a lot of things. *What a couple we made—at the time, we added up to one normal person.* Anyone's guess who contributed the bulk of the normalcy. Jani watched documents flick across the screen. She tried to avoid thinking of her medical history, which seemed equal parts tragedy and farce. There had been some good science in there as well, of course—it just got over-shadowed. *I'm a walking tribute to some amazing minds, I suppose.* Galatea to three Pygmalions. *No, one Pygmalion, and two Frankensteins.*

A nested display sharded into prismatic chaos. With a groan, Jani flicked the workstation into standby mode. She walked to the window, swept the curtain aside, then gasped as the molten glare of sun on snow blasted through the glass and shocked her roomlight-adapted eyes. She buried her face in the curtain, patted away the tears, then eased her lids apart and tested the filming for the looseness that signaled stress fissures.

She blinked, waited, then looked out the window again. As well as the lake and city skyline, her view included the Private House grounds; snow-coated terrain banked and rolled around season-stripped native trees and shrubbery, forming a land-scape of white sugar and dark chocolate. *You need to get out more,* Jani persuaded herself as she headed for the door.

"Cabin fever, huh?" The Interior staffer who helped Jani into the *one-size-adjusts-for-all-yeah-right* snowsuit nodded in commiseration. "Bites us all after a few days." He led her to the house's rear entry, cocked an eyebrow at her refusal of a skimmer for a trip into the city, and shrugged at her determination to "just take a walk."

"January in Chicago—it ain't for sissies," he said as he closed the door behind her.

Neither's taking a walk in some of the places I've lived, mister. Jani lowered the light transmittance of her goggles until her eyes stopped watering. Each stride cracked like stuttershot as her boots broke through the snow's crusty white surface. Within minutes, she'd cut across a flat, well-trampled expanse that would be a billiard table–like lawn come spring, and entered a less-traveled area of sparse woodland and ravine.

Even when inhaled through her humidifier mask, the air possessed a peppermint clarity. With every breath she drew, Jani felt her head grow clearer. After weeks of recycled ship and station air, she grappled with the urge to strip off her constrictive headgear and feel real wind in her face again. Then she checked the weather sensor on her right sleeve. *Windchill—forty-nine below. Cancel the blow for freedom.* Even after years of adjusting to their quirks, she didn't trust her revamped nerve endings' ability to warn her of impending frostbite.

The landscape glittered with fairy-tale desolation. She bounded over fallen trees and ambled down the ghosts of trails. When a squirrel darted into her path, then stopped short, tail twitching, she rummaged through the pockets of her community snowsuit in case someone had left something edible behind.

"Hang on," she said to the creature, which responded by launching itself across the path toward the remains of a storm-shattered tree. Jani watched it disappear just as her gloved hand closed over something crunchy. "Succcss—you should have waited," she called after the departed creature as she examined the smashed packet of crackers. With the grace of a beneficent monarch, she tore the packet open and sprinkled the crumbs near the base of the tree.

Her good deed for the day accomplished, Jani continued down the path. Every ten meters or so, she'd glance up at the treetops and wonder where Evan's Security force had stashed the buggery. If her sense of Colonel Doyle was as spot-on as she believed, someone was monitoring her heart rate and blood pressure at this very moment.

The distant shooter-crack of snapping branches didn't alarm her at first. She assumed a large animal, some type of ruminant. Or perhaps a member of the Interior grounds crew, who could fall into that category as well. *Not nice—everyone here has been very good to you.* With the exception of Ridgeway, of course. No one could mistake him for a cud-chewer. *Although the cloven-hoofed part—*

In the middle distance, hidden by trees, a high-powered skimmer shut down with an insect whine. Jani executed an about-face and started back toward Interior Private. She could just glimpse the house's roof between the trees.

My shooter is in my duffel, and my duffel is in my office. Good place for it. She ground her teeth and focused on the red brick chimneys, poking up through the slate roof like feathered badges. A beautiful house, really. Too bad she hadn't stayed behind to take a better look at it. Designed to appear hundreds of years old when it was really no more than twenty or thirty—

Branches fractured again. Jani dived off the path and behind a fallen tree.

If that skimmer turns out to belong to grounds crew clearing trails after the storm, I am going to feel mighty stupid. Not to mention look stupid. *Getting an eyeful, Ginny? Think Evan's guest is a loon yet?* She glanced around at the bare trees. No cover. No place to run. Not that she could make any time through the knee-deep snow, anyway. *Anytime, Colonel. Come collect the idiot.*

She gloved through the snow for anything that could serve as a weapon, but could uncover only brittle kindling. She waited for augie to kick in with the familiar calming cascade, but felt only the dry mouth and roiling stomach of growing panic. The air she gulped through her mask tasted only of bracing sharpness. And through it all, the broken thought worked through her racing mind, like subtle static, barely detectable . . . *I'm not right—this isn't right—it's not working right.*

Her berries didn't seem to be in season now. Who'd have thought in the end even augie would have let her down.

A short distance away, snow crunched. Jani nestled closer to the log, grateful for the shadowy color of her snowsuit.

The footsteps stopped. "Risa?"

Jani, hands working under the log, paused in mid-grope.

She'd managed to half-bury herself in snow, uncovering a couple of small rocks as a bonus.

"Risa? I know you're here. I saw you take a header." Twigs snapped. "You're wasting time."

Jani looked up just as Lucien Pascal, dressed in full Service winter camouflage, leaned over the log. "You have a lot of nerve, coming here," she said as she sat up, rocks clasped in still-buried hands. She jerked her head toward the house. "You know you've been seen."

"Depends who's watching." Lucien's breath fogged the clear humidifier mask. He smiled, which she'd learned on the *Arapaho* wasn't necessarily a good sign, and held out a mottled white arm. "Could you come with me, please?"

"I'd rather not."

Lucien's arm hung in midair. What did his eyes, obscured by darkened goggles, look like now? Jani knew she'd see more warmth in the rocks she held. "I wish I could say you had a choice," he said, his voice muffled by the mask. "But I'm afraid you don't."

He was probably right. Without augie stoking her, Jani knew she didn't stand a chance in a hand-to-hand with him. She curled her legs beneath her in a semicrouch and considered her options. *He's got a full head, fifteen years, and at least twenty kilos on me, he's armed, and he has a vehicle hidden nearby that he could use to chase me down.* Add to that the fact that Exterior infiltration apparently extended to Private House as well as Main. *They must have contacted him as soon as I stepped outside.* Which meant he must have been waiting for an opportunity to get to her since she'd arrived. *And he's probably not alone—must be a backup out there somewhere—*

"So?" A hint of self-satisfaction flavored Lucien's voice. "Are you going to come quietly?"

In reply, Jani hunched her shoulders and shot forward at a forty-five-degree angle, cannoning into his midriff and pounding her rock-loaded fists into his solar plexus.

Lucien emitted a gratifying "oomph" as he stumbled backwards, but his jacket, well-padded and lined with impact absorbers, took the brunt of Jani's blows and cushioned his fall. He grabbed her by the shoulders before she could straddle him, rolled her, and rammed her to the ground.

Something hard, large, and pointed impacted Jani's upper back. Her "oomph" came much louder than Lucien's since her civilian snowsuit didn't come equipped with bumpers. Gold lights novaed and died before her eyes. Seeing stars— amazing how damned literal that term was.

"What the hell—" Lucien struggled to his feet and backed away "—were you trying to pull?"

The sound of his labored breathing wended through Jani's pained daze. *Took 'im by surprise on my own—augie, who needs you?* She tried to raise up on her elbows, but slumped back as some invisible giant planted his foot squarely in the middle of her chest. Then jumped up and down. *Me, that's who.* She attempted to draw breath through the suffocating mask, then to tear the clear shield away, but an upper-back cramp stopped her short. Vanquished, she closed her eyes, pulled in the occasional pained gasp, and waited for the fire in her lungs to go out.

Lucien made no move to assist her. He brushed snow and dead-leaf confetti from his suit, freeing his shooter from an inside holster in the process. "You aren't going to try to jump me again, are you?" He approached her gingerly, free hand extended. "Rolling around in the snow with you might have its attractions, but it's too damned cold right now."

"Sweet-talker." Jani waved him back and rose as best she could on her own. "Bet you say that to all the prisoners." She turned and kicked weakly at some dark ridging poking up through the snow, revealing the embedded rock that had knocked the wind out of her. "Lead on, Lieutenant."

Lucien stilled at the mention of his rank. Then he motioned with his shooter for Jani to walk on ahead.

Progress proved slow. The trail sloped and rose; Jani's back cramped with every jolting step, every strained breath. For a time, the only words spoken were Lucien's terse directions as he told her which way to turn. Then, as they approached the clearing in which he had stashed his skimmer, he drew alongside. Jani noted he had holstered his weapon. "You were going to brain me with a rock," he said, sounding genuinely upset. "I stole underwear for you."

"I wouldn't have hit you hard. Just enough to slow you

down." She swallowed a moan as her back seized. "Honest."

Lucien cut in front of her and popped the skimmer passenger door. The vehicle was a newer sport model: satin-finish silver exterior, black-leather interior, and *very* low-slung. This time, when he offered Jani his arm, she took it. "Anything broken?" he asked, as she inserted herself into the cockpit.

Jani shook her head, slowly at first, then more vigorously as the pain in her upper back receded to a duller, more manageable ache. Augie to the rescue. *Now you show up.* "I'm too old for this crap."

"That's what you get for jumping poor unsuspecting lieutenants." Lucien slammed the gullwing shut and hurried around to the driver's side.

Take your time. Jani stared at the vehicle's dash, which resembled a GateWay-certified transport control array. *Not like I could skimjack this thing anytime soon.* She lifted her arms as high as she could, pulled off her goggles and mask, pushed back her hood, and worked a hand through her matted hair.

Lucien fell into his seat and yanked his door closed. Security seals whunked and hissed; the changing cockpit pressure made Jani's ears pop. "Fancy skim for a looie," she said, as he freed himself from his own headgear and gloves. His mussed hair gleamed in contrast to the cabin's dark decor. "Surprised someone from the A-G's office hasn't rapped your knuckles."

Lucien jabbed at the vehicle charge through three times before he hit it. "I have permission."

"I know. Saw you and your permission on the 'Vee last night. You make quite a couple." She mouthed an "ow" as the skimmer rose with a jerk and banked sharply, causing her to ram against her unapologetic driver. "I finally got the meaning of your little card," she said as they flutter-glided down a slope. "Your sailracers. Off to surf the solar wind. You're trying to tell me a certain someone was augmented." Lucien jerked the wheel again, and she banged into her door. *And if you think I'm going to tell you who it is, you can go wrap yourself around a tree.* Hopefully, *after* she had disembarked. "I've never been kidnapped before. Are you taking me to Exterior Main? A stronghold outside Chicago? The next province?''

Lucien cocked his head. That was the only reply Jani received as they hopped over a low fence that marked Interior's boundary. Not once during the transit did she see any Interior vehicles or staffers. Anywhere. *Evan, we must talk when I get back.* When she got back—keep the happy thought.

Lucien's wariness lessened as soon as they ramped onto the Boul, the twelve-lane thoroughfare that had welcomed Jani so roughly the day before. He drove fairly well. The skimmer's proximity alarms didn't yelp that often, and he only passed on the right twice. After a few minutes, they ramped down, leaving the pressing traffic behind. The snow had fallen on this quiet world as well, but Jani could see from the bare sidewalks and roofs that staff had already seen to the cleaning up.

Lucien, too, eyed the facades of cream and light brown brick and stone, tiny patches of manicured hybrid greenery filling the narrow spaces between house and sidewalk. ''This is the Parkway,'' he said softly. ''I suppose you could call it a stronghold.''

Jani recalled Minister Ulanova's stern portrait in the Amsun Station gangway. *I can't say how much I'm looking forward to this.*

They stopped in front of one of the buttercream manors. In the center panel of the double-wide front door, Jani spotted the gold-enameled oval centered with the black double-headed eagle of the Ulanovs. As a uniformed Exterior staffer hurried out to take the skimmer, she and Lucien disembarked and made their way up the narrow walk.

The doors flew open. A dark-haired young woman rushed out onto the landing.

''*Lucien!*'' She wedged between him and Jani, imprisoning his arm in hers. ''Where have you been? Milady has been calling for you every five minutes—the hell of it!'' She pushed Lucien ahead of her through the entry, then tried to close it on Jani. ''You go around the back,'' she snapped.

''*No*, Claire, she comes in the front.'' Lucien shook himself free of his petulant escort and ushered Jani into the mirror-lined entry hall. ''Now go tell Her Excellency we're here.''

His not-so-gentle shove propelled Claire halfway down the hall. "*Bâtard*," she spit as she disappeared through an open doorway, her kittenish face aged to cat by a nasty glare.

"My thoughts exactly," Jani said as she turned to Lucien, who had developed an interest in the gilt frame of a mirror. "Stoking fires upstairs and down. You're asking for trouble." The dig elicited only a bored shrug. "What does Ulanova want from me?"

"You'll know soon enough." Lucien's eyes held the dull cast of ice left too long in the cooler. The *Arapaho* seemed a long time ago. A very long time.

CHAPTER 15

A still-pouting Claire poked her head into the hallway and motioned for Jani to follow. They passed through a series of sitting rooms, each larger and more ornately furnished than the last, ending up in a *salon grande* with crimson fabric-covered walls and museum-quality furnishings. Jani looked at the muraled ceiling and berugged floor. *Everything's freaking red—I dub thee the Bloodshot Room.*

"You wait here," Claire said as she departed, whipping her waist-length hair like an animal repelling flies.

Jani shrugged off her snowsuit jacket, gave up on the pants, then flexed her neck and worked her stiff shoulders. An odd languor had settled over her, an unsettling contrast to her usual post-augie jitters. *At least I won't go bouncing off these goddamn walls.* She listened for approaching footsteps, then stared blearily at the fragile glass and porcelain contents of the cabinets.

When that palled, she switched her attention to the wall decor. She contemplated several holos, their colors calibrated to resemble the mutedness of old oils, before stopping in front of the portrait of a young man. He wore a plain tunic in Exterior burgundy; his clipped hair shone white-blond. Full-lipped, his professional smile held a hint of dry humor. Jani couldn't see the color of his slanted eyes, but a long-forgotten fragment of Commonwealth gossip told her they'd be brown.

"That was my late brother-in-law, David Scriabin, at the age of twenty-five."

Jani twisted around. Her upper back cramped. She hadn't even heard the door open.

"He had just been elected First Deputy to Exterior Minister al-Muhammed." Anais Ulanova stood in the doorway, eyeing Jani with cool cordiality. Unlike many public figures, she was just as imposing in private. Medium height, very thin, she wore a long-sleeved, floor-length black gown of stark design. Weighty gold hoops hung from her ears. Her short, dark brown hair glistened in the room's soft light, its swept-back style accentuating her aquiline nose and wide-set eyes. Lyssa van Reuter, thirty annealing years on.

"Your Excellency," Jani said, with a shallow bow that was as much as her balky back and colonial sensibility would allow.

Ulanova's dark gaze shifted to the portrait, and softened. "He became Minister himself only five years later, the youngest Cabinet member in Commonwealth history. That was the year my sister and he married." She waved languidly toward two nearby chairs set at opposite ends of a long, low table, on which rested a silver beverage service. "You'd like a refreshment? Coffee, perhaps?"

Jani sat down, her stomach grumbling as the rich aroma of truebean reached her. "With all due respect, ma'am, if our positions were reversed, I doubt you'd drink anything I offered."

"Be rude if you wish, Ms. Tyi," Ulanova said as she poured. "But it is a cold winter's afternoon, and I need my coffee." She sat back, cup and saucer in hand, her posture impeccable. "Lieutenant Pascal will be joining us shortly." A smile flirted with the corners of her thin-lipped mouth. "Off seeing to things he could just as well leave to his staff. He really is the most . . . thorough young man."

Jani waited until Ulanova raised her cup to drink. "He's fucking Claire, too, you know. He's snaking you with her just like David Scriabin did with your sister."

Coffee sloshed, spattering Ulanova's dress. Fifty years in the public arena served her well—the pain that flashed across her face disappeared instantly. "I never would have suspected you a wallower in common gossip," she said slowly as she dabbed at her skirt with a linen napkin.

"Oh, I understand the situation was rather uncommon, even by Family standards. You and Scriabin had set the date and picked out the silver, next thing you know, you're a sister-in-law." Jani tilted her head in the direction of the Scriabin portrait. "The resemblance to Lieutenant Pascal is startling. Are they related, or do you breed David look-alikes on a farm somewhere?"

"If this is the way you intend to play, Ms. Tyi, please be advised I earned my letter in the sport before you were born."

"I intend to disclose fully to Minister van Reuter this conversation as soon as I return to Interior House, ma'am."

"My *ex*-nephew-in-law is an incompetent drunkard who has, in the grand tradition of his family, surrounded himself with a staff comprised of children and counter-jumpers. If you think your informing him of our meeting will help you in any way, you are doomed to disappointment."

"Your concern is duly noted, ma'am. Thank you."

"Why did he bring you to Earth?"

"A long-overdue vacation, ma'am."

"Lieutenant Pascal believes otherwise. He was quite taken with you, Ms. Tyi. I can't recall when anyone impressed him more."

"My thanks to the lieutenant for the vote of confidence." Jani rubbed her cheek and smothered a yawn. *She ordered Lucien to jump me. She knows I'm augmented, or made a damned good guess. She wanted me post-augie. She wanted me off my game.*

"Are you sure you won't have coffee, Captain? Or perhaps you'd prefer something stronger? You appear drawn."

Jani caught the tip of her tongue between her teeth, then shook her head. "Captain? I don't have a rank. I'm not Service." She forced a conciliatory smile. "I've only just come off a long-haul, ma'am. I don't recover from those as quickly as I used to."

Some emotion flared in Ulanova's eyes, the last flickers of a dying fire. Then, with a complete lack of fuss, she filled a cup from the coffee ewer and thrust it at Jani.

After a pointed pause, Jani accepted the coffee. The cup's holopattern caught the light as she drew it near; minuscule iridescent snowflakes seemed to tumble down the smooth white sides. She took a healthy swallow of the black, foamy brew. Strong. Sugared. Bracing. Lovely.

Ulanova's measured voice slithered past her strange torpor. "I can be a powerful ally, Ms. Tyi. The reverse also holds true."

"With all due respect, ma'am, why tell me?"

"Evan brought you here to perform an investigation. All I ask is that you inform me of your findings as you do him."

"You're asking me to betray my Minister's confidence, ma'am. What am I worth if I do that?"

"I've never been one to begrudge practicality." Ulanova raised the lid of one of a trio of small dishes and removed a tiny, multicolored cakelet. "And coming over to the winning side before the last decisive battle seems to me the height of practicality." The stiff icing crunched like frozen snow as she bit down.

"I wasn't aware we were at war, ma'am." Jani finished her coffee down to the bitter, grainy dregs.

"Trust me, Ms. Tyi, when I tell you we have a situation developing of even greater concern than the secessionist threat." Ulanova refilled her cup and pushed the cake server toward her side of the table. "Have you ever heard the name *Jani Kilian*?"

Only a few thousand times. "No, ma'am, it doesn't sound familiar."

"Knevçet Shèràa?"

Poor pronunciation—too much buzz in the "ç." "Is that an idomeni phrase?"

"Rikart Neumann?"

"Everyone's heard of the Neumanns, ma'am."

"Acton van Reuter," Ulanova said, a shade too loudly.

"My minister's late father." Jani popped a cakelet into her mouth. "The Old Hawk. Died about four years ago. Age of sixty-seven. David Scriabin was only sixty-four. NUVA-SCAN patriarchs don't seem to live very long these days, do they, ma'am?"

Ulanova arched a stenciled eyebrow. "Perhaps the word *treason* may serve to fix your attention, Ms. Tyi. Treason, and premeditated murder."

Jani's jaw stalled in mid-chew. *I had my reasons.* "Ma'am?"

Before Ulanova could explain further, Lucien entered. He covered the distance to their table in a few rapid strides. "Your Excellency," he said, handing her a sheet of parchment.

As Ulanova studied the document, her expression grew more and more somber.

"Do you recall our recent discussion of Commonwealth kidnapping laws, ma'am?" Lucien asked as he dragged a chair tableside.

Parchment crackled as Ulanova's grip tightened. "Thank you, Lieutenant."

"We've wasted this lady's time," Lucien said, gesturing toward Jani, "and entered tricky legal territory in the process." He served himself coffee, then dug into the cakes, popping them into his mouth one after the other. "Kilian's dead. No one could have lived through that explosion." He had combed his hair and shed the snowgear. He now wore a snug turtleneck the color of rubies and Service winterweight trousers striped down the side in the same rich hue.

Mainline stripe. Jani swirled her cup. *Mine was sideline white.* She checked his footwear. Sensible boots, like hers, though in better shape. Black. Mirror-polished and steel-toed.

Ulanova handed the paper back to Lucien. "The woman's ID chip was never found," she said. "Her death is assumption only."

Lucien staged another assault on the cakes. "Analysis of the wreckage showed that a pulse bomb had been placed directly over the transport's main battery, beneath the front of the passenger compartment." He glanced at Jani. "Anyone sitting in the front of the craft was vaporized. The ID chips the recovery crew did find were as badly damaged as any they'd ever seen. It was their opinion Kilian's was obliterated."

Ulanova snorted. "That has never happened!"

"There's a first time for everything," Lucien replied.

Maybe, if I'd been sitting in the front. The memory of the transport cabin air's ozone tang burned Jani's throat. *But I was way in the back.* Jammed between the rearmost seat and the bulkhead, wrists bound to ankles, head between her knees. She could almost feel the rumble of the directionals shuddering through her dainty salon chair—

Pulse bomb?

"Ms. Tyi is just what she says she is, an Interior field agent," Lucien said. "Kilian's dead. Murdered along with the rest of the Twelfth Rovers."

Jani leaned forward slowly and set her cup on the table.

Ulanova grew thoughtful. "Some would maintain Kilian's death was an execution. My friend Gisela Detmers-Neumann, for one. You've heard of *her*, I assume, Ms. Tyi?" Her gaze sharpened as she shouldered on. "But innocent people died in that explosion, as well. Rescuers and rescued—loyal Spacers all. A great scandal, one to shake the foundations of the Commonwealth, the trust between those who administer and those who defend."

The explosion wasn't an accident. It had been planned, by someone who couldn't allow the events that transpired at Knevçet Shèràa to become known.

"I've been trying to connect Acton van Reuter to that transport explosion for nine years," Ulanova said. "He died before justice could be served directly. But I will accept his son in his stead, Ms. Tyi. Someone who could bring me proof Evan knew of his father's guilt and covered it up would earn the Commonwealth's gratitude as well as mine."

Jani grooved her right thumbnail into the lifeline of her numb left palm. *She called you a loyal Spacer, Borgie.* Rose pink carrier bled through the abraded synthon, forming a string of tiny, liquid pearls. *Isn't that nice of her?* "I'm sorry, ma'am," she said as she massaged away the sticky liquid. "I don't mean to appear thick, but I don't understand what you and Lieutenant Pascal are talking about."

Lucien stared straight ahead. Ulanova regarded Jani for a long moment, then pushed back the lids of the other two servers. "We also have fruit tarts and biscotti, Ms. Tyi," she said. "Unfortunately, the lieutenant has been greedy enough to eat all the cake." Her sidelong look at Lucien held murder. "No surprise there, it seems." She rose. "We have apparently detained you unnecessarily. Allow me to extend my most heartfelt apologies. The lieutenant will see to any compensation you feel is merited.'' She swept out of the room in a swirl of black.

Jani stared after the departed minister, her stomach gurgling its own farewell. Then the sound of muffled laughter claimed her attention. She turned to the chuckling Lucien.

He gave her a thumbs-up. ''Good job,'' he offered around a mouthful of fruit tart. ''The quieter she gets, the madder she is.'' His shoulders shook. ''She's really pissed!''

''You can both—'' Jani stopped as her stomach gurgled again, this time more urgently. Cramps rippled through her abdomen. Cold sweat bloomed and beaded. ''Where's—'' She clamped a hand over her mouth as the saliva flooded.

''Oh shit!'' Lucien grabbed her by the shoulders and herded her toward the door. ''Not on the rugs—not on the rugs!'' He pushed her out into the hall. ''Second door on the right!''

Jani stumbled into the bathroom, reaching the sink just in time. She kept her eyes closed as she vomited. She groped for the faucet and cranked it open, washing away the rancid stench, replacing it with the clean smell of flowing water.

Heavy footsteps closed in from behind. ''Are you all right?'' Jani jerked as an icy lump touched the back of her neck. ''Steady on—it's just a coldpack.'' As the chill soaked through her shirt, her knees gave way. She sagged to the tiled floor, Lucien providing just enough support to keep her from cracking her head against the plumbing. Her emptied stomach gave a last trembling lurch. She moaned and rested her cheek on the cold floor.

''Do you need a doctor?''

Jani opened one eye. *What is it about me and men and bathrooms?* Lucien sat atop the marble vanity, legs swinging from the knee. Back—forth—back—forth. The motion nauseated her anew. ''No.'' She closed her eye and tried to feel whether her filming had fissured. ''What the hell was it, and where?''

Silence. A sigh. ''Ascertane. Glazed inside your coffee cup.'' The sound of a fastener being worked, a bottle seal being cracked. ''I don't understand your reaction. Ascertane's a mild anti-inhibitory—you're not supposed to know you've been drugged. You're just supposed to feel happy. Trusting.''

The slide of cloth against counter. Footsteps. "Here. Drink this."

Jani opened both eyes. Lucien and his identical twin slowly merged into a single, blurry-edged figure holding a small dispo filled with yellow liquid. "Stick it in your ear."

"It's for nausea."

"I already have that. Thank you."

"Look." Lucien gulped the tiny draft. "Same bottle. Same damned cup!" He refilled the dispo, swallowed that as well, refilled it again, then placed it on the floor in front of Jani. "Suit yourself," he said as he returned to his perch. "I'm just trying to help." He shoved the bottle into a Service-issue toiletry kit and yanked the fastener closed.

"Yeah, you're a real humanitarian." Jani worked into a sitting position, pausing every so often to give her stomach time to catch up. Then she picked up the tiny cup and sniffed the bright yellow syrup. The harsh lemon odor made her cough.

Lucien glared at her. "It's the same stuff we drank by the barrel during flight training."

"I didn't have flight training, did I?" Jani drained the dispo, gagging as the thick liquid burned her throat.

"I don't understand." Lucien linked his hands around his knee. "I've administered Ascertane a hundred times—all it does is make you blab." He rocked back. "That nausea stuff works fast. Feel better?"

Jani swallowed. Her stomach remained steady. "I think so." She rested her head against the wall and watched Lucien watch her. "I told her about Claire. Just to see her reaction."

His rocking continued without a hitch. "Which was?"

"Surprise. I think I actually caught her unawares."

"So she'll send Claire away. Won't be the first time she's sent someone away." His eyes slitted as he smirked, slanting upward at the corners. "Or the last."

Jani compared Lucien's face to David Scriabin's. His was longer, his cheekbones not as high. Close enough in the dark, though. "You know, David Scriabin and Anais Ulanova were quite the item until he lost his nerve and eloped with her younger, prettier, less ambitious sister. He and Anais never quite called it quits, however. A typical Family mess." She sat up straighter. The antinausea brew had functioned as promised. "So, you aren't her first twenty-five-year-old towhead." She tossed the coldpack back to Lucien. "Or her last."

Lucien caught the pack with one hand. Without a word, he slid off the vanity, placed the toiletry kit on the rim of the sink, and left.

Jani took a few "get-ready" breaths and eased to her feet, using the wall as a support. She rummaged through the kit, liberating a single-use toothbrush and a pouch of oral rinse. "The man's a born looker-after of old ladies." Jani removed the wrapper from the toothbrush. "Of course, if you took him home to meet mother, she'd fight you for him."

Lucien was waiting for Jani in the hall, her jacket in hand. Instead of his Service winter camou, he had opted for the standard-issue snowsuit in an alarming shade of bright blue. The glaring color made him look like an overgrown little boy.

Except around the eyes. Jani looked into the familiar chilly brown stare. She allowed him to help her with her jacket, then followed him silently. Just before leaving the house, she turned. The kittenish Claire watched them from the end of the hall, arms folded, face in the shadows.

Neither Jani nor Lucien donned their facegear before going outside. Instead, in psychic agreement, they made a bareheaded dash for the waiting skimmer, piling into seats and pulling shut gullwings, causing the vehicle to rock as though wind-buffeted. Jani's backache had lessened to stiffness; the short exposure to the frigid air slapped away the last of her sick haze. By the time Lucien ramped onto the Boul, she felt human again.

Near death makes you appreciate the simple things. She studied the Chicago skyline with heightened interest. *Near murder gives them that extra glow.* She savored the buildings of new stone and old glass, their angled, diamond-shaped summits and swirling scrollery. This time around, she even took note of the Greatest War Memorial, its molecular clock coating glowing crimson in the stark winter sun. "Did it take you two long to rehearse?" she asked as the capital zipped by. "My questioning."

"It wasn't my idea." Lucien eased behind a ponderous

people-mover and backed off the accelerator. Their zip slowed to an easy glide. "She flipped as soon as she discovered van Reuter had gone to Whalen himself to collect you. That nailed it. As far as she was concerned, you were Jani Kilian."

"But you didn't think so?"

"On the *Arapaho*?" Lucien shrugged. "You acted like someone with something to hide. But then, don't we all?" He bypassed the ramp that would have returned them to the Interior access skimway. "Besides, I scanned you in this skimmer—it's off now—and compared the reading to the ID we'd lifted from Kilian's Service record. She had it all planned. Confrontation, forced confession, deal. But the scans didn't match, and she couldn't proceed without paper proof." He slowed the skimmer further, until other vehicles actually began passing them. "Aren't you even a little curious why this Kilian is so important?"

Jani watched a distant shuttle descend like a pulse-powered beetle. *Means to an end. Ulanova wants Evan's head on any platter she can find.* "I don't even know when all this was supposed to have happened."

"Eighteen years ago—the last idomeni civil war." Lucien snatched glances at her as he maneuvered off the Boul and into a crowded commercial district. "Laumrau versus Vynshà, winner take all. The Laumrau were winning until this thing with Kilian happened. All sorts of mess bubbled to the surface after she died. Some Family members, led by Rikart Neumann and Acton van Reuter, had apparently agreed to throw their support behind the Laum in exchange for augmentation technology."

It's for the home world, Kilian. Who cares about a few xenogeologists from a colonial consortium no one's ever fucking heard of! Neumann had stood nose to nose with her. His breath, scented from ever-present throat lozenges, had wafted around her in cinnamon-tinged puffs. *Work with me now, you come to Earth with me when it's over. Cross me, and I'll snap your spine.*

"Problem was, the idomeni had never had another race involved in their wars before. Everything had always been very ordered, in as much as a war can be ordered. Organized.

Very . . . well, idomeni.'' Lucien steered into an underground lot and edged the skimmer into a narrow charge station. ''The fact that the Laum had actually courted disorder by dealing with humans staggered all the idomeni. The Vynshà had been getting ripped up to that point, but they were able to publicize what happened and turn it to their advantage. They took the dominant capital of Rauta Shèràa less than four months later.''

Jani followed Lucien out of the garage and onto a moving sidewalk. Pushed along by a swelling crowd, they entered a glass-enclosed mall with a large skating rink in its center.

Lucien tugged on her sleeve. ''Do you feel up to anything?'' He flashed a dark red plastic card that proved, at second glance, to be an Exterior Ministry expense voucher. ''It's on her.'' They wandered over to a snack kiosk that, if the posted prices were any indication, did most of its business with Cabinet expense accounts.

In deference to her iffy stomach, Jani opted for an iced fruit drink. Lucien protested he had an image to maintain with Exterior Contractor Accounts and ordered enough overpriced food to feed them both for the day. They carried laden trays to a rinkside table, doffed their coats, and settled in. Jani's drink turned out to be grapefruit-flavored. Very tart; it stripped the last of the minty oral rinse from her tongue.

Then the assorted aromas from Lucien's side of the table reached her. Fried onion. Grilled beef. Melted butter. ''What kind of technology did Neumann and van Reuter get from the Laum?'' Jani asked as she tipped back her chair and started breathing through her mouth.

''Hints on how to upgrade augmentation technology, in a way that could be better adapted to personality alteration.'' Lucien dug into his food like a starved teenager. ''I don't think it ever worked out, though. Idomeni brain chemistry is different from ours, and they've got that culture of theirs as an external force to keep their antisocial personalities in line. The humans they tried the augie upgrade on flipped. Twelve sheets to the wind. The research petered out years ago.''

But not before Acton sacrificed his firstborn grandson on the R and D altar. Jani crunched ice. ''Who did they test the new augie on?''

"Volunteers, I assume. Research subject stipends can be pretty substantial."

So you don't know everything. Some secrets still lay buried beneath the sands of Knevçet Shèràa. "And what does Kilian have to do with all this?"

Lucien dredged a forkful of fried potatoes through a dollop of mayonnaise. Jani looked away while he chewed. "She was a sideline captain," he said. "Documents examiner. Academy grad, of all things. Reported to Neumann." His tone grew thoughtful. "Anais thinks some kind of double cross occurred. Either they argued over division of the spoils, or Neumann tried to push Kilian out of the deal altogether. All she's certain of is that Kilian murdered Neumann, along with a few Laum who got in the way. What no one realized was, Acton was keeping tabs. He knew he faced prison if any details of his collusion with the Laum got out, so he arranged for the elimination of the one person who could put him there."

But I didn't know. Neither had any of her real soldiers. Jani took tiny sips of her drink, applying it like salve to her tender stomach. *By the way, Ev, you know my little investigation— your daddy is involved. Do you want me to stop now?* Dull pain radiated across her abdomen. She set her glass down with a clatter.

Lucien flinched. "What's the matter?" He tried to smile. "Aren't you having fun? I am."

"You have an odd idea of fun, Lieutenant." Jani turned her attention toward the rink skaters. Most were average at best, but one pair struck her as particularly good. "So, you and Anais are pretty close?" she asked, as the man flipped his partner into the air.

Lucien donned the look of innocence he'd employed to perfection on the *Arapaho.* "Look, I'm sorry if that bothers you, but it's none of your—"

"She ever bring work home?" Jani joined other shoppers in applause as the partner landed cleanly on one edge and spun immediately into a quad-triple combination. The attention she paid to the skating display seemed to bother Lucien. He tapped his fork against the rim of his plate, remaining silent until she looked at him.

"Sometimes," he said.

"She chairs the Cabinet Court Board of Inquiry?"

"Uh-huh."

"Think you could get me a copy of the Court Summary of Investigation of Evan van Reuter?"

"Why?"

Because Acton van Reuter tried to kill me to prevent his dealings in illegal idomeni technology from being known. He used that technology on his grandson. His grandson died. Then Lyssa had herself augmented. How much more deeply had she explored what happened to Martin, and why? Who had she spooked? *This didn't die with Acton van Reuter.* Which meant someone else was involved in what had happened at Knevçet Shèràa.

And that someone had murdered Lyssa.

"Because," Jani replied, "the Court Summary contains the documents references for all the evidence examined. Once you have a doc reference, you can track it down in systems."

"You can't do that without Court-level passwor—"

"That's why you're going to supply me with those, too."

Lucien segued from innocence to indignation. "I'm an Intelligence officer in the mainline Service. I signed the Commonwealth Secrets Act."

"Despite those obvious shortcomings, I still think you capable of carrying out simple theft."

"It's illeg—"

"So is kidnapping, as you were so kind to point out. But you don't see me belaboring the point. Not yet, anyway." *Acton van Reuter tried to murder me.* And slaughtered her real soldiers in the process. *Who else knew the story?* Who had Lyssa flushed from the undergrowth before she went on that final bender?

"The Summary hasn't been issued yet. It's still in draft, no final Court seal. Not as grave a sin." Suddenly, Lucien grinned. If you ignored his eyes, you'd think it was your lucky day. "If I get it for you, what do I get in exchange?"

"The Commonwealth's gratitude."

"Not yours?" He cupped his chin in his hand and leered politely.

Jani reached across the table and brushed a finger along his arm. "Considering your penchant for gadgets, do you by any chance have something that could secure a workstation?''

''I'm sure someone at your level in Interior would have secured—''

''I want to make sure.''

Lucien's smile tightened. ''Will you please stop interrupting me.''

''It needs to be a portable jig, something I can move from machine to machine.''

''I don't take orders from you.''

''No, but you'll do it, if for no other reason than that some day you'll be able to tell Anais all about it.''

Dead eyes widened. To call the look ''surprised'' would have been overstating the case. But awareness would do, appreciation that she knew Lucien better than he thought, that he didn't fool all the people all the time.

''I'll see what I can do,'' he said after a while. ''Will there be anything else, General?''

''No, I think that should do it for now.'' Jani finished her drink. ''Thanks for the snack. I'll be in touch.''

''Where are you going?'' Lucien scrambled for his coat. ''I thought we'd spend the afternoon together.'' Judging from his flustered behavior, rejection was an unfamiliar experience. ''Like we did on the *Arapaho*, remember?''

''I have things to do.''

''How will I contact you?''

''Not directly. I'll send a runner for the paper and the jig. I don't think we should be seen together anymore.''

''Just squeeze me dry and cast me aside, huh?''

''You got it.'' Jani patted his cheek in farewell. Then she darted into the midst of the milling shoppers. She heard Lucien call, ''Damn it, Risa!'' but she didn't look back, and she didn't slow down. She knew how to lose herself in a crowd.

CHAPTER 16

In response to the repeated inquiries of your staff, I regret to inform you, nìRau . . .

The note had been written on Ulanova's personal stationery, Tsecha noted. Thick, stone-colored parchment nearly idomeni in quality, edged in black and topped with a bird possessing two heads. The minister's family symbol. *Two heads. Two faces.* He bared his teeth. He was becoming quite good with double meanings, and truly. Perhaps the day would come when his old handheld would no longer be needed.

. . . that the matter we discussed earlier today has, unfortunately, not been resolved. After further inquiry, it has been determined that my initial conclusions were in error.

"She fooled you, Anais." Tsecha walked slowly to his favored chair and sat carefully to prevent the angled frame from poking him. "But she fooled all you humanish. Until that last evening at Knevçet Shèràa, your kind thought you knew Captain Kilian most well."

This avenue of exploration, regrettably, appears closed at this time. Rest assured, nìRau, and truly, that I will keep you apprised of any new developments. a lète ona vèste, *Nemarau. Anais Ulanova.*

Glories of the day to you, Nema. Tsecha reread the letter once, then again, his gaze drawn repeatedly to the final line, the curves and slashes of his born language. Quite adequate High Vynshàrau—the proper accents, the appropriate phrasing for his skein and standing. He could find no fault with it. Some Exterior suborn must have labored most diligently to produce the deceivingly simple phrase. And yet . . .

You did not know me in the time before, Anais. You have no right to call me by my born name. He would answer to few idomeni who referred to him as Nema. Not even from his less-favored chosen humans, Tsai and Senna, Aryton and Nawar, would he tolerate such.

My born name is for the very few. Esteemed enemies, some. Most favored, others. Hansen Wylc, if he had lived, would know him only as Nema. *And my toxin.* His excellent Captain, whom Ulanova had apparently misplaced.

Tsecha settled back against his unforgiving cushions and set the Exterior Minister's letter on the chairside table. Such careful wording, on unofficial paper. *She would not seem so tall now, I think.* Ulanova had stumbled, and badly.

Yet that morning, she had been so sure.

Humanish like my Anais do not state themselves strongly without reason. So between the morning and the afternoon, she had been thwarted, but how? *To whom may I speak of this?*

Tsecha looked across his room. His newly acquired comport, a bulky hybrid hastily adapted by his dominant Communications suborn to function within Commonwealth systems, rested on his inscribing table.

His newly acquired, *unmonitored*, comport.

He had had a most difficult time convincing his Security of his need for such. But he had, in the end, persuaded. He had, after all, once convinced a mixed-sect mob that, whatever they may truly have wished, dismembering him with long blades and adding him to the soul circle burning around Rauta Shèràa was not part of it. Thus had he sidestepped death. And if so death, why not Embassy Security?

Tsecha approached his comport as though it were a piece of engine wreckage which could explode. He had not yet used it, and the instruction provided by the Communications suborn had lacked detail. He touched the activation pad, feeling a tingle of accomplishment as the display shimmered.

He released the touchlock of one of the drawers and withdrew a folded sheet of parchment. True idomeni paper, smooth as metalcloth, its color the soft pink of the inside of a cavashell. Tsecha unfolded it, laid it on the desktop, and watched the creases lessen, straighten, then disappear completely until only the handwritten series of humanish numbers and letters marred its surface.

The code had been carefully acquired, requested with many others so that Tsecha's agents would not suspect its worth. He tapped it into the comport touchpad, then pulled his favored chair tableside as a series of low, ringing tones told him the connection had been made.

Moments later, rainbow light splayed across the display, assembling to form a most familiar face. "Glories of the day to you, Physician DeVries," Tsecha said.

Watery dark eyes, downturned at the corners, squinted, then widened. "*Nema!*" The sagged face, too much pale skin on too little bone, quivered. "How in hell did you get this number?"

"I bought it, DeVries."

"From whom?"

"As you said to me once, long ago, ah, sir, that would be telling."

"Son of a—" Eamon DeVries's jaw clamped, cutting off the balance of the insult. *Something of my lineage,* Tsecha thought, *of that I am most sure.* Although the most unseemly of the three doctors who had founded Neoclona, the man had always been, in a fashion almost as idomeni, comfortably predictable.

He bared his teeth, but not very much. "I could only obtain your satellite office code, unfortunately, Physician DeVries. Physician Parini's, I could not—"

"He's out of town."

"—nor could I Physician Shroud's. Most unfortunate, in that case, because he is the one to whom I must speak."

DeVries sat back and folded his arms across his chest. "I would rather," he said slowly, "be strung up by my nuts over a bonfire than tell John *you* want to talk to him."

"Find him, Eamon. Tell him."

"I can't disturb him." Flaps of skin shook back and forth. "He's in the lab."

"In the lab!" Tsecha folded his arms as DeVries had. "Still? After so much time? Is it true what is said, that he sleeps within, eats within, never leaves?"

"He works, Nema. You remember how he works."

"And I remember as well what he works on. Who does he hide in his basement now?" Tsecha revealed his teeth more as DeVries's face ceased its movement. "Physician DeVries, if you possess any sense, you will tell John Shroud I wish to speak to him."

DeVries muttered of "ruined days" and "hell to pay," and disappeared.

Tsecha stared at the blank display. *Perhaps I pushed too greatly?* And now Eamon DeVries would alter his code. He resigned himself to planning yet another subterfuge. Fortunately, his Security could probably find DeVries's new code as they had this one. From a humanish female who sold. Hansen had been the first to discover that with Physician DeVries, there could always be found a female who sold.

The display flickered again. Tsecha stiffened as the face formed. Just as familiar, this face, but some humanish compelled more attention than others. He nodded toward the display. "John."

Eyes, pale blue as ice, glinted. "My God, it really is you. I thought Eamon had been dipping into the drug bins again." Long-fingered hands combed through lazored hair which shone as a young one's. White hands. White hair. Rimed eyes the only color in a white face. A body wrapped in death-glaze.

John Shroud is an . . . albino. Yes, that was the word, and truly. Tsecha forced himself to look the man in the face. Still so sharp the bones, like Vynshàrau, skin taut as paint over muscle and bone. "Yes, John, it really is me."

John bared his teeth. They glistened even more than his hair. "It figures you'd get hold of *Eamon's* code. The idiot scribbles it on everything short of restroom walls." And the voice. *A back-of-the-cave voice*, Hansen had called it, *the word from the bottom of the well.* When an idomeni possessed such a voice, it was said to come from the center of the soul, but whether one could say such in John's case, Tsecha did not know. Allowing the man possession of a soul seemed, as again Hansen would have said, a stretch.

"Well, points to you, Nema." John tilted his head well to his left, until he looked at Tsecha sideways. Unseemly familiarity in that, but such was his way. "Imagine seeing you again after all these years. Such a pleasure, I can't begin to say. I have to get back to work now. See you in the newssheets." He drew up straight. A hand flicked toward a touchpad, to end the connection.

"*John!*" Tsecha gripped the sides of his display as though doing such could trap the man within. "If I wanted to find her, how could I?"

John's hand stilled. Pale eyes stared. Such a color. So cold. And artificial, the result of filming. His born eyes were pink. *Lab rat, they called him, in youth.* That knowledge always seemed to give Hansen such pleasure.

The bone white hand lowered. "Who are you talking about, Nema?"

"Her, John. *Her.* I believe she is alive."

John's face deadened even more. "You believe? You don't know?"

"That is why I ask you. Her paper is yours. Her history. How would you search for her? How would *you* confirm she lives?"

John sat back, hands to his mouth, fingertips pressed together. The movement allowed Tsecha a glimpse of the shortsleeved, collarless white shirt he wore. The trousers, Tsecha knew, would be white as well. *Medwhites*, humanish called them. John's favored clothing. During his time in Rauta Shèràa, he seldom wore anything else.

"Assuming I care," John said, "why should I tell you?"

Oh, you care, John. "Ulanova wants her . . . arrested, I believe is the word." Tsecha released his display, sat back, paused. Periods of silence seemed as important in humanish speech as in some idomeni. *We like to let things sink in,* Hansen had taught him. "She believes it is the wish of the idomeni for that arrest, as well. But I possess no such wish."

"Are you sure your people feel the same, Nema? I seem to recall a few riots concerning that very wish. Demands for your own arrest. Oh, for the good old days." John struggled to bare his teeth but failed. "Why does Anais want to arrest her?"

"The Exterior Minister requires her as a tool only, I believe. To destroy Evan van Reuter."

John's barely visible eyebrows arched. "Evan? Is that secession issue heating up again? I remember Anais thinking her van Reuter problems would end when Acton died. Guess not." Bony fingers tapped against cheekbone. Tsecha almost expected to hear the click. "Unless the rumors about old Ev being responsible for Lyssa's death are true. But even then, would Anais care? She and Lyssa despised one another because of that scandal over Lyssa's father." He frowned. "Unfortunately, Val's my muck and sludge specialist, and he's unavailable."

Tsecha bared his teeth with enthusiasm. "Please allow my glories of the day to the most excellent Physician Parini when he returns from his vacation."

John's frown grew. "You always liked him, didn't you?"

"I found him always most seemly, yes."

"But you hate him as well?"

"Yes to that also, John. As a most esteemed enemy, how else could he be regarded by me?"

"Hmm." John worked his hands together as though he held something he wished to mold. "Sh-she . . . always tried to explain that to me. I didn't understand then, and it still makes no sense."

Tsecha eased against his lumpy cushions. "But you never possessed the wish to learn of idomeni. You only possessed the wish to take from idomeni. Most disordered, John. Balance must always be maintained."

"So says the priest." John's face turned most as a wall. His hands ceased movement. "You're no stranger to taking, Nema. If you'd been allowed your way, if that bloody war and your bloody Temple hadn't stopped you, how much would you have taken from them? From Wyle? From—especially from—" His jaw continued to work, but no sound emerged.

Tsecha looked into John Shroud's ungodly eyes. "I do not take, John. I possess no wish to possess. I only allow what must become to become. As a propitiator, I can do nothing else.''

''The future as you see it? A race of human-idomeni hybrids with you as its spiritual leader?'' John laughed quietly. ''Hundreds of years ago, a human who said things like that would have been burned at the stake. Your people had the right idea, Nema. Maybe we are more alike than we realize.''

Tsecha sat heavy in his chair. ''Why must I always explain as to young ones? We must merge together. In the end, all will be as one. All the same. So it must be, John, for the journey to the Star to be complete.''

''Your journey! To your Star! We don't believe in your Star!''

''But yet you began the journey yourself, John. The first span in the bridge was built by you. You are as responsible as I for what she will become. What we will all become.'' Tsecha's heart pounded hard and slow in his chest. Not since he had worked to persuade the Council to name him ambassador had he felt so alive. ''I always felt you reasoned as a physician, of course, in your experimentation. You wished to heal her, to improve her. Hansen believed, though, something most different. 'He just wants another freak to keep him company,' is what he said.''

Shroud's hands drew apart slowly as he sat forward in his chair. ''Hansen Wyle,'' he said through his teeth, ''was as crazy as you are.''

''My Hansen was most sane, as I am. We tried so to find her, but you hid her well. And now, you who hid her should know how to find her. How would I know her? For her good, for yours, for us all, do you not think I should find her first?'' Tsecha inscribed shapes in the air to ward off demons. He could not be as humanish, now. ''My Captain. My suborn. She who will follow me. Your Jani. How will I know her?''

John stared at him. Even his hate could not warm his eyes. ''She's dead.'' His hand flashed white motion, and his face fragmented.

Before the man's image faded completely, Tsecha reentered the code. Several times. But after each attempt, the display only flickered as the comport audio emitted a series of low beeps. *So quickly you work to thwart me, John.*

He berated himself for revealing his soul so to the humanish, but it could not be helped. They merely spoke of what was already well-known—why did saying truth aloud matter so to humanish?

If they do not speak of it, it does not exist. If they do not think of it, it goes away. Illuminating thoughts, perhaps. Explanations of humanish behavior. But not logical. Tsecha relaxed into his chair, allowing the framing to stab him where it would and thus focus his mind. *They are not as idomeni.* But in some future time, they would be. *And idomeni will be as they.* Rather sooner, that inevitability, if his Council's behavior with regard to the idomeni sicknesses was indication. The thought made him hesitate. *John and I as one.*

From far away, the tones announcing his late-afternoon sacrament sounded. Tsecha rose as quickly as his bent, inflexible seat allowed, but not before resetting the comport for internal communication and notifying Security of his wish for a conference.

John and I as one.

Tsecha pressed his open left palm against his stomach, a gesture of supplication. Perhaps, for one of his standing, to understand fully was not to be, but the gift of some intimation struck him as most seemly—

John and I as one?

—and greatly to be wished.

CHAPTER 17

A jovial "Come in, Risa" sounded through the door just as Jani raised her hand to knock. The panel swung open in a whispery combination of mechanics and the brush of door edge over expensive carpet. She stepped onto the dark grey pile and experienced the fleeting sensation of the ground giving way beneath her as her boots sank in to just below the ankle.

Original artwork she recognized from holozines decorated the light grey walls. As she crossed the room toward Ridgeway, ensconced behind his desk, she was treated to a wall-spanning backdrop of the lake, tastefully muted through glare-filtering scanglass. *Large body of water as office accessory—very nice.*

Ridgeway made no effort to rise until Jani reached his desk. Only then did he execute a quick half-up-and-be-seated. His smile held the same consideration. "Nice of you to be so prompt," he muttered breathlessly as he gestured for her to sit. "It's been a hell of a day." An errant lock of hair provided emphasis by flopping over his forehead.

Hope I helped. Jani smiled wanly and held her tongue.

"I do try to promote an environment which is conducive to cooperation, Risa—"

I doubt that.

"—and Lord knows I'm no micromanager—"

I'd have guessed pico-.

"—but is it too much to expect a reasoned approach to tasks at hand? Circumspection? Forethought? Is it too much to ask of people that they think things through?''

As though on cue, the door opened, and Ridgeway's aide entered. He still looked like the enemy artillery barrage had stretched into the third day with no end in sight. Jani shot a "take heart" grin at him, but he avoided her eye as he placed a black-edged file folder on the desk in front of Ridgeway.

"Thank you, Greer." Ridgeway's smile curdled as he opened the folder, positioning it so Jani couldn't see what it contained, and paged through it while Greer exited silently. Then, eyes bright and predatory, he leaned across the desk and splayed the folder's contents over the bare, polished bloodwood in front of her. "A rendezvous in the snow," he said, triumph causing his voice to quaver. "How romantic."

Jani surveyed what lay before her. Sceneshots—one short sequence per panel. Snippets of action, intercutting middle distance and zoom, replayed themselves every few seconds in a rolling series. The holographer had been selective. The first display showed her diving behind the log, but not her scrabble for rocks. The angle and replay speed of the second sequence made her attempted flattening of Lucien look like a playful shove. The third scene stopped just as Lucien flipped her on her back. The overall impression given was, to say the least, incriminating.

Just some playful precoital wrestling. Never mind the wind-chill—lust conquers all. Jani pulled in a slow, painful breath. She'd checked the condition of her stiff upper back in a rest-room mirror upon her return to Interior Main. The dinner-plate-sized bruise had bloomed nicely, thank you, Lucien.

The fourth scene showed her and the lieutenant making their way down the forest path, the angle of the shot hiding the shooter trained on her back.

"Circumspection." Ridgeway clucked softly. "Fore-thought. You aren't the first slimy little traitor to lack either of those vital qualities." His gloating smile threatened to split his face in two. "Your ass is mine now, Tyi. Evan won't let you get away with this."

Jani looked from Ridgeway to the sceneshots with a lack of concern that bothered her in an abstract way. It was as though she watched the missteps of a character in a play. Augie picked the damnedest times to overstay his welcome.

Ridgeway apparently wondered at her reaction as well. His smile wavered.

"Interesting," she managed, eliciting sounds of choking from across the desk. On another level, her mind raced. A frame, but by whom? *Ulanova?* She seemed petty enough, jealous of what she perceived to be Lucien's attachment. *But you'd think she'd try to wring something out of me before hanging me out to dry.*

"Ms. Tyi, you are in a great deal of trouble, you know. I've been informed the man in these sceneshots is mainline Service. An Exterior Ministry Security officer."

Could be the PM. Keeping tabs on her prodigal van Reuter, trolling for tidbits. *Or any of the other ministers, for that matter—they wouldn't even have to be anti-Evan, necessarily.* Hell, anyone who could adapt a holoremote to get past sensescan could have taken those shots. Newssheets. Gossip rags. Lucien, the gadget expert, for the hell of it.

Bâtard, indeed.

Ridgeway cocked his head. "Are you listening to me, Ms. Tyi?"

Jani sat back. Her chair was designed to make the occupant feel off-balance—spindly, hard of seat, and tilted forward slightly. It didn't work. For visitor intimidation, Ridgeway should have tried idomeni furniture. Jani had, on countless occasions, sat through hours-long Academy exams in chairs that had treated her back in much the same way Lucien had.

"I doubt you did this," she said to Ridgeway, indicating the panels. "If you had, I don't believe you'd have bothered to show them to me first. You would have gone directly to His Excellency." She gripped her armrests as a helium bubble expanded in the depths of her skull. "And here you probably felt like Christmas made a second pass." She took a deep breath in an effort to dispel her lightheadedness. "Sorry to disappoint."

Ridgeway leaned so far forward he was in danger of pitching out of his chair. "You are a traitor—"

"Speaking of traitors," Jani interrupted, "I've come upon something interesting." The calmness of her voice fascinated her. She'd never been adept at extemporaneous self-defense— the results reflected in her Service record. Augie never bothered to kick in at those lower stress levels. So why was he being so helpful now? "His Excellency's father apparently made hash of the Bilateral Accord some years ago. He colluded with the Laumrau during the idomeni civil war and managed to have some of their augmentation technology smuggled back to Earth. Martin, it seems, paid the bulk of the fine for that particular violation."

"Careful how you speculate," Ridgeway said. His eyes still shone, but his voice had weakened.

"The technology came from a research hospital, a place called Knevçet Shèràa." Jani bit out the *c* as Ulanova had, gave "Shèràa" the two-syllable treatment instead of entoning the double-*a* upturn at the end, and sat on her hands to avoid gesturing. God, she hated sounding like an Earthbound hick. "Rumor has it that in order to eliminate possible witnesses, he ordered the deaths of the Service troops stationed there. Just imagine, multiple counts of premeditated murder. Oh, and let's not forget the treason." She smiled. "Nice to have something in common with a man of Acton van Reuter's standing, I suppose."

Ridgeway licked his lips. "Acton's dead," he said. From his tone, he didn't seem altogether sure.

"Yes, but the sins of the father, Durian. They matter to idomeni, and they make humans sit up as well. The shrapnel from this bombshell just might take out our boss." She looked into Ridgeway's eyes. *Don't tell me you didn't know.* Oh, he knew—knowing went a long way toward explaining his lack of cooperation in providing her Evan's documents.

Ridgeway fingered his chin. "Risa—"

Oh, it's "Risa" again, is it?

"—I don't know what to say." He appeared genuinely thoughtful. "Lieutenant Pascal told you this?"

So, no one traced me to the Parkway—sloppy. That implied a stationary cam, perhaps in the Private House. Well, it saved a lot of explaining, although it did make Jani wonder how secure her office really was. "The information was there for the taking." No reason to disclose who offered it.

Ridgeway's manner became very clipped. Perhaps he associated that with professionalism. "Did Pascal attempt to interfere with you in any way while he served as your steward on the *Arapaho*?''

Now it was Jani's turn to sound surprised. ''So you knew about that?'' Ridgeway's stare offered no reply. ''Nothing I couldn't handle.'' She thought back to her lunches with Lucien. They had spent most of the time laughing over whatever human weakness he had exploited that particular ship-day. ''I think he'd grown used to manipulating through his looks and charm. I saw no reason to disabuse him of his notion.''

Ridgeway nodded sagely. ''Brave of you.''

Jani shrugged. ''Solo older woman coming in from a long-term colony assignment. He probably figured me for an easy target.'' She looked away from Ridgeway's developing smirk. *I'll be sorry I said that.* Big mouth returns. Looked like augie had finally folded his tent.

Ridgeway swung his feet onto his desk. He'd changed clothes since their morning altercation. His pale green socks peeked through the gap between his black half boots and coal grey trousers. They matched his loosened neckpiece, which in turn contrasted nicely with his medium grey shirt. *Occupant as office accessory—very nice.* The look he bestowed on Jani wouldn't have qualified as friendly. More like superior, but without the gloat. ''Will you continue to see this man?'' He wasn't quite able to control the lively curiosity in his voice. The idea of operating as a pimp for the House seemed to appeal to him.

''I'll play it for as long as it runs,'' Jani replied blandly.

''It bothers me that Ulanova has zeroed in on Acton again.'' Ridgeway pursed his lips. ''She'd gone after him once before, of course, but that was before his death. Oh, dear Anais had her claws out for him—make no mistake. Back in the Dark Ages, he alternated between undercutting Scriabin business concerns and aiming Anais's younger sister at David Scriabin. Unfortunately, David was engaged to Anais at the time. The scandal when David and Milla eloped was horrendous. Poor Anais never really recovered from the humiliation.'' He glanced at Jani and smiled coolly. ''I appreciate your help, Risa, really I do. I understand what it must have taken out of you. Do you suppose any of this may tie in with Lyssa's death?''

Jani stifled a yawn. Her head felt heavy—a nap sounded tempting. But she wanted to visit the Library. Then she needed to get ready for dinner with Evan. "It was implied to me that several Families were involved in the importation of the augmentation technology. If you believe Lyssa had discovered what had been done to her son and was trying to figure out who was responsible at the time of her death . . ." She let the sentence peter out, punctuating the silence with a raised eyebrow.

"Good God!" Ridgeway became positively buoyant, no doubt envisioning how many of Evan's rivals he could scuttle by linking them to a murder plot. "I'm going to have to meet with Colonel Doyle as soon as possible." He sat up straight and tightened his neckpiece. "Well, you've blown my evening all to hell, Risa, but I think the results may well prove worth the inconvenience." He hesitated noticeably. "You're welcome to sit in, of course."

"You—" Jani stopped her personal commentary in time. "You are too kind, Durian, but I'll be dining with His Excellency this evening." She ignored his arch look. "By the way, those files we discussed this morning. Could I have them, please?"

"Of course." Ridgeway grinned. Grin, hell, he bubbled. In a week, he'd be telling people hiring Risa Tyi was his idea. "In fact," he said, "let's get some drudgery out of the way now."

A few intercommed orders to the frazzled Greer later, Jani found herself in possession of a Class A Interior expense voucher (no manager approval necessary unless she tried to buy something substantial, like Chicago), parts bin and repair chits, and other pieces of paper and plastic designed to make the favored Interior employee's life easier. The promised files, however, were held up in document limbo. Jani would have to wait for those until tomorrow. Ridgeway apologized profusely as he walked her all the way to the outer-office door, adding they would have to have dinner "very soon."

Can't wait. Jani trudged down the hall, wondering what exactly she had opened herself up to. True, she'd gotten Ridgeway off her back, but it crossed her mind he might attempt to reap some of the benefits he thought her to be bestowing on Lucien and Evan. She wandered down the wrong hallway, backtracked, then found herself standing before the doorway leading to the alternate breakroom. *What would I do?* Probably whatever he wanted. Ridgeway, Jani sensed, was the sort of man who thought staking a claim in a woman's vagina locked up the rest of her as well. A risky assumption, but fortunately, not a rare one. On more than one occasion, her continued good health had depended upon her working that assumption to its limits.

Sometimes, it's whatever gets you from here to there. She was glad to find the breakroom empty. She spent a few minutes straightening the snack table, then cleaned and reloaded the brewer. Soon the aroma of fresh coffee filled the room and her stomach, having recovered from its bout with Ascertane, responded by growling each time she inhaled. She rummaged around for a cup, then settled into a battered corner seat.

Ridgeway let me off easy. He could have bounced me off three walls and the ceiling besides, and he caved as soon as I brought up Acton.

Nimble little counter-jumper, Anais Ulanova would have said. *Knows how to keep his feet under him.* One option, if Ridgeway felt Jani had uncovered knowledge he wished to keep buried, would be to shower her with bounty. She reached into her shirt pocket for the expense voucher. Silver, in contrast to Lucien's red, with a discreet scripted *a* in the lower left hand corner that she hadn't recalled seeing on the lieutenant's card. *Anything within reason, and maybe a thing or two without,* Ridgeway had said when he handed it to her. *Just be discreet.*

"But diddle an account once, and I'm all his." Jani repocketed the thin plastic card. "He thinks." If she put her mind to it, she could divert half of Interior's liquid assets into a float-rebound maze before the Comptroller's office had a chance to reconcile her first transaction. Working with the Haárin had been an education in more ways than one. She wouldn't think of doing it, of course. But it was nice to know she could.

When I'm good, I'm very, very good. When she was bad, she could make Lucien look like a stiff. Still, the ease with which she had gotten around Ridgeway nagged her. But then, her idea of what constituted "difficult" differed from most peoples'.

My Academy final exams were oral. In High Laumrau. Not one idomeni on the examining board, not even Nema, looked her in the face. Instead, they watched her posture, her hands, the way she moved. Listened to her tones, lilts, phrasings.

Pauses after her replies stretched for ten minutes or more, then suddenly questions would pile on questions, with no chance of a request for clarification being honored, or even acknowledged. The exam lasted for nine humanish hours, with Jani knowing every step of the way that only one other being in the room wanted her to succeed. And also knowing for that very reason, he dare not make a move to help her in any way.

I learned as idomeni. Which had made it damned difficult to slip back into the humanish way of doing things. Back to the world of subtext. Hidden meanings. Things left unsaid, glossed over. *The world between the lines,* Hansen had called it. He'd been able to move between idomeni and humanish without breaking a sweat, but there had been a very good reason for keeping Jani off to one side. *A typical socially backward paper pusher—I gabbled, and I blurted, and I explained too much.* To go from a culture where everything you say is understood instantly to one where you could talk for hours and not say a goddamned thing had rattled her. She had fit with the idomeni so well, she thought.

"Until I proved myself most human." She sipped her coffee, grown cold in the cup. *Too easy.* The coffee tasted greasy and harsh. Jani flushed it down the sink and set out for the Library.

It proved a happy accident that she ran into Angevin Wyle in the journal reading room. She had been trying to figure out how to contact her without using the Houseline or risking another encounter with Ridgeway.

"Hullo." Angevin leafed without interest through a documents journal. "What's up?"

"I have some info for you." Jani beckoned her toward a pair of chairs in an isolated corner of the room. "About those sailracing lessons we talked about. It'll give you a chance to get out of here for an hour or so.''

''Sailracing? I never—'' Angevin lowered herself to the edge of her seat. A flicker of life animated her pinched features. ''What's going on?''

''I need you to contact someone outside Interior. You have to do it from a public comport in the city. He'll meet you to arrange the transfer of some things he's obtaining for me.''

''Why don't you use the courier service?''

Because I don't trust the courier service. Jani debated the best handle by which to grip Angevin for this detail. ''The Doc Control administers the courier service, and I don't want Durian to find out I had contact with this guy. He works for Exterior.''

''Durian. Phfft!'' Angevin cradled her chin in her hand. ''Is this guy good-looking?''

''Oh yes.''

''Even better.'' The young woman fluffed her mashed curls. ''Any particular place I should contact him from?''

''The only spot I know in the city is the mall with the skating rink.''

Angevin wrinkled her nose. ''That tacky place.'' She rummaged through her small shoulder bag, liberating a colorstick and a mirror. ''I'll call him from the Galleria,'' she said as she applied bright copper to her lips with a few deft strokes. ''What's his name?''

''Lucien Pascal. He's in Exterior Security.''

''*Lucien.*'' Angevin waggled her eyebrows. ''Oo la la.''

''Blond. Brown eyes. Your age. As tall as Minister van Reuter. Make sure to mention the sailracing—then he'll know you came from me.'' Jani hid a smile behind her hand as Angevin applied the colorstick to her cheeks as well. ''I appreciate this.''

''Yeah, well, I need a break. Supper meeting coming up. Then I get to confer with Durian again.'' Angevin crossed her eyes. ''Speaking of Durian,'' she said nonchalantly as she continued to apply her makeup, ''what are you getting from this Lucien that might upset him?''

Jani leaned back in her seat. Her battered shoulders

cramped. "Job-related things," she replied through clenched teeth. "Just stuff."

Angevin dabbed at the corners of her mouth. "Things. Just stuff. For the sake of my Registry standing, I don't want to know the details, do I?" She studied Jani over the top of her mirror. "Durian doesn't like you. He thinks you're trouble. He told me, and I quote, 'His Excellency has taken in a stray who will turn on him,' unquote. Durian tends to be melodramatic, but he didn't get where he is by being wrong a lot." She tossed the mirror and colorstick back in her bag. "Does this involve Lyssa van Reuter's death?"

"I thought that had been ruled an accident," Jani said.

"Oh, we're going to be that way, are we? Maybe I should beg off and let you arrange your own damned transfer."

Please don't. If Angevin didn't agree to help, Jani knew she'd have a difficult time finding another runner. Steve and Betha certainly wouldn't oblige, which meant she'd have to pick a suitable stranger and bribe him or her with nontraceable cash chits. And you could not get a dummy chit from a Cabinet House bank booth, no matter how many *a*'s you had on your expense voucher.

Assuming Lucien comes through with something worth paying for. Assuming he had anything to come through with. Courts of Inquiry weren't exactly known as fountains of useful information. Anything good had a tendency to be kept in the Family. "Why do people wonder about Lyssa's death?"

Angevin wandered to the window behind Jani's seat and stared into the winter darkness beyond the glass. "There were rumors."

"That her death wasn't an accident?"

Angevin nodded. "That it was murder. The big one for about a month was that His Excellency finally got so fed up with her that he arranged a mishap. When that led nowhere, everyone whispered about how much Anais Ulanova and Lyssa's mother hated one another over the mess with Lyssa's father, and that Anais waited until he died to murder Lyssa in revenge."

"That hypothesis sounds bizarre enough to be popular," Jani said with a dry laugh. "Doesn't jibe with the fact Lyssa worked for Auntie, though."

"How about the rumor Lyssa was really Anais's daughter by Scriabin." Angevin's lip curled. "Durian laughed till he cried when that one started circulating."

"Sounds like one he'd start himself."

"Doesn't it, though?" The young woman's tense face relaxed in a grin. "Nice to know we have the same opinion of my boss."

"So why work for him?"

Angevin shrugged. "Means to an end. Building the old Cabinet pedigree." She grew serious. "Last thing my dad would have done, according to all who knew him. When that's the case, sign me up."

Oh Hansen—maybe she doesn't mean it. Jani looked up at Angevin's somber face. *Oops.* Maybe she did, at that.

"What type of man," Angevin continued, "would leave his wife and child behind in order to school in a place that didn't want him and meddle in things that didn't concern him? That's my mom's slightly biased viewpoint."

"What's yours?"

"Every time someone who knew him sees me, they tell me how much I look like him. Then they stand back with this shit-eating grin on their face and wait for me to do my Hansen Wyle imitation." Angevin tugged at a flattened curl. "I don't know what they want me to say. I don't know what they want me to do. I never knew him. I don't remember him. To me, he's a few holos and a name in the first page of the Registry." She looked down at Jani. "You're about the age he'd be now. You've lived out for years. Did you ever meet him?"

Jani swallowed hard. "No."

"I wonder if he'd have ever met anyone in secret to arrange an iffy transfer?" Angevin shouldered her bag and moved away from the window. "I have to go to my office and get my coat. Then I'll be off."

Jani made an effort to elevate her dampened mood. "If I see Steve," she said, "do you want me to mention you're going off to see another man?"

"Steve can go to hell and take Betha Concannon with him," Angevin replied flatly as she strode out of the reading room.

Is that a yes *or a* no? Jani lacked recent experience in the

Rules of War as they applied to battling lovers. *Maybe I'd better mind my own business.* She wandered around the reading room, paged through several journals, and arranged to have copies of technical updates sent to her suite workstation.

"Well, that used up a half hour." She debated conducting a search through Interior stacks, but doubted she'd uncover anything worthwhile in any legally accessible areas. She needed to get her hands on locked-down paper, documents that had been removed from public access. She didn't dare try that without Lucien's jig. If she tried and failed to bull into a controlled Cabinet system, the alarm would be raised. And if Ulanova discovered the burrowing attempt originated from Interior . . .

"We'll wait for Angevin." Jani limped along the convolve of short halls and aisles leading from the reading room to the main body of the Library. The technical dissertation section always proved the least visited area of every bibliodrome she'd ever visited; Interior proved no exception. She wandered down aisle after aisle of leather-bound dexxie theses, encountering no one, checking the quality of the couches and chairs along the way. "Do what you can when you can," she said with a yawn as she stretched out in a particularly comfortable lounge chair, "including nothing." She worked her duffel beneath her head to serve as a pillow and closed her eyes.

CHAPTER 18

It seemed only seconds had passed when Jani felt a sharp poke in her rib cage. Her hand shot out and closed around a wrist—a startled yelp filled her ears. She opened her eyes to find a gape-mouthed Angevin standing over her.

"Sorry," Jani said as she released her. "You surprised me." She sat up slowly. Her stiff back complained anyway. "How did you find me?"

"I work here, remember?" Angevin eyed Jani warily. "You want to ditch a meeting, you hide in the dissertation section." She massaged her wrist. "Damn it, that hurt!"

"I said I was sorry." Jani felt her cheeks burn. *You're in civilization now, remember? No one's going to arrest you in your sleep.* That was Evan's promise, anyway. "Want some friendly advice?"

"What?"

"Don't surprise people who do sneaky work in the Commonwealth's name. We tend to overreact."

"Now you tell me." Angevin dragged over a chair and sat down. She had already draped her coat over a nearby planter and set an assortment of bags on the floor near Jani's lounge. "Oh well, I'm sorry I sneaked up on you," she said hurriedly. "Never happen again, that's for sure." She remained quiet for a time, her hands folded in her lap. "I've brought that *stuff* from Lucien," she finally said.

"He had it ready!" Jani struggled to her feet, trying to decide which sack to root through first. "He gave you all these?" she asked as she reached for the nearest bag.

"No! That's mine." Angevin slid to the floor and wrested the bag from Jani's grasp. "These are mine, too," she added, indicating the others. Then she removed a battered yellow sack from the hidden depths of the melange and handed it to Jani. "This one is yours."

Jani stared from her single parcel to the impressive array spread out before her. "You went shopping?"

"Well, after I called Lucien I had to wait for him, didn't I? Then when he showed up, he said there was something he needed to buy, too. We worked fast." Angevin held up a pullover and eyed it skeptically. "I thought you said he was good-looking."

"You don't think so?"

"No. Good-looking for men equals average. Lucien is not average. Lucien is gorgeous." Angevin tugged at her rumpled shirt. "You could have warned me—I'd have changed. Not that it would have mattered. All he did was ask about you."

"Really?" Jani peeked into her bag and opened the plastic pouch containing the jig. The device's beige case shone back. "What did he want to know?"

"The usual. 'What's Risa doing tonight? How's she feeling? What did she tell you about me?' " Angevin had draped the pullover across her chair, and was now examining the seams on a pair of trousers. "I thought I was in prep school again. Introduction to the Lovelorn."

"Sorry." Jani stuck her finger in a shallow depression in the jig's side. It squealed in response, and she shut the bag hastily. "I thought it would be fun for you."

"Oh, he hit on me. Asked me out to dinner. But I could tell his heart wasn't in it." Angevin cast dubious glances at the bag in Jani's lap as she continued to fuss over her purchases. "All your *stuff* in good shape? Nothing missing?"

"Everything's fine," Jani said as she gathered her duffel and bag and rose to her feet. "Where are the workstation carrels?"

"I'll show you." Angevin assembled her booty. "Follow me," she said as she jostled down the aisle.

"You can tell me the way—I'll find them."

"I don't mind." Angevin led the way through the Library,

fielding greetings from other patrons and offering comments on the state of her day.

Jani, for her part, avoided making eye contact with anyone. A disturbingly large number of people seemed interested in the reason for her presence in the Library. One young man, thwarted in his attempts to engage her in conversation, cursed her under his breath, calling her van Reuter's hatchet.

"You've become the topic of the day," Angevin said. "Some folks think you've been brought in to do the final post-troubles cleanup."

"That's ridiculous," Jani muttered. The workstation carrels, she was relieved to see, were located in a quiet area of the Library. She followed Angevin into one of the small rooms and immediately closed the door.

"Sorry about the gauntlet," Angevin said. "Like I told you, the place has become a rumor mill."

Jani sat down in front of the workstation display. "I just didn't think I'd be caught in the grinders." She set her bags on the desk, then looked over at Angevin. "Thanks for your help," she said. "I don't want to keep you from your meeting."

Angevin made no move to leave. She set her parcels on the floor, then massaged her palms where the handles had bitten. "Can I ask you a question?" She waited for Jani's nod. "You carry a 'pack."

"Yes."

"You're in Registry. I looked you up this afternoon."

Good job, Evan. "Your point?"

"You don't act like a documents examiner. You keep popping up all over the complex. Asking questions. You act like a verifier. You worry people."

"I don't mean to," Jani said. "Look, I'm working under His Excellency's mandate. Anything I ask someone to do is completely legal. You have nothing to be concerned about."

"I'm sorry, but friends of mine who swallowed that line before found themselves suspended. Or deregistered. Or worse." Angevin folded her arms and ground her heels into the thick carpet. "What are you doing here?"

"You took part in the documents transfer on the *Arapaho*, Angevin. I think you have a pretty good idea."

"You're supposed to be looking into Lyssa van Reuter's death," Angevin said. "Outside eyes, according to Durian, on the lookout for things that could hurt His Excellency. Is that really the whole story?"

"Like you said, Durian didn't get where he is by making mistakes."

"You know, I helped you. The least you could do is level with me."

"What makes you think I'm not?"

Angevin gathered her bags, her cheeks flaming. "Next time you need *stuff* picked up, you can get it yourself," she said as she hustled out of the carrel.

Jani sat still for a time, staring at nothing. *What the hell is going on here?* She should have been able to disappear within the hugeness of Interior, but the people she encountered were stretched tight emotionally, sensitive to every intrusion. *And the only buffer I have is Evan.* Evan, who didn't communicate with his staff. Evan the drunkard. Evan the target. Evan, who people thought capable of murdering his wife.

But that's a discounted rumor.

Why had it been a rumor at all?

Jani pulled the yellow bag into her lap. First, she removed the jig, then a thick documents pouch adorned with the crimson Exterior seal. The seal had been tampered with—the color had blotched and the Ministry emboss had puckered.

Lucien must have worked in a hurry. Jani cracked the ruined seal and removed the weighty sheaf of Cabinet parchment. TOP SECRET had been stamped in the margin of the first page. COURT OF INQUIRY adorned each header. The word *draft* was nowhere to be seen.

Lucien had stolen Ulanova's copy of the Court's final report.

"You don't mess about, do you, Lieutenant?" It crossed Jani's mind the sort of distraction Lucien must be providing to keep Anais Ulanova from discovering his crime; stomach churning, she hurriedly activated her scanpack and began a confirmation check of the report. Knowing the lieutenant, she realized that he relished the danger he'd put himself in. But the line between worthwhile risk and recklessness was hairthin. If she had to walk the report through the snow herself, she'd make sure Lucien had it back in his hands in the morning. Even if he distracted Anais to the point of mutual exhaustion, the minister would have to look for the document eventually.

"All green," she breathed as she scanned the final page. Not a dummy report assembled to throw off an office mole, but the real thing. She quickly leafed through to the appendix and studied the ID strings of the evidence used in the compilation. *SRS-1* jumped out at her again and again. Service papers, issued by First D-Doc, Rauta Shèràa Base.

"I probably imprimateured some of those." Jani removed the jig from its bag, then gave it a once-over with her debugging stylus. *It's not that I don't trust you, Lucien—I just have a healthy respect for your sense of whimsy.* She stared at the doughnut-sized device's featureless case, trying to figure out how to attach it to the workstation. Finally, she touched it to the rear of the display, staring in wonder as it remained in place. After a few seconds, it emitted a barely audible squeak. Then a soft green light glimmered from its depths.

Jani took a deep breath and activated the workstation.

"Passwords, Lucien," she said as she worked her way from Interior House systems into general access Exterior. "I need passwords." She scrabbled once more through the bag, but found it contained only a small box wrapped in silver paper.

"Damn it!" One of Angevin's purchases, no doubt, accidentally dumped in the wrong sack. Jani was ready to stuff it back in the bag when she stopped and took a better look.

This is posh Galleria gift wrapping, huh? Wrinkled paper. Crooked seams. Curled corners where the sealant had been sloppily applied.

Jani ran a thumbnail beneath the paper seaming, unwrapped the box, and smoothed the gift wrap. Scrawled passwords filled the white underside of the paper. Random strings of letters and numbers. Proper names. Places. The occasional foul word.

"You don't believe in keeping it simple either, do you?" She set the sheet of passwords beside the display. Then, with some trepidation, she opened the box.

. . . he said there was something he needed to buy, too.

The toy soldier was small, six or seven centimeters tall. Exquisitely crafted. Every button had been brushed with silver, each microscopic medal glazed with colored enamels. He wore modern dress blue-greys: steel blue crossover tunic and grey knife-creased trousers cut along the sides with the requisite mainline red stripe. The hair visible beneath his brimmed lid glimmered pale blond; his right arm was bent in a permanent salute.

"Are you trying to tell me something?" Jani examined the figure for any sign Lucien had inserted something untoward in the tiny body. She scrabbled again for her sensor and scanned the figure as she had the jig.

"Disease-free," she said, placing her new mascot beside the touchboard. Then she flexed her fingers like a musician warming up, keyed in the first of the purloined passwords, and began mining history. As she cut through the protective barriers of bomb shelters and mazes, she could almost imagine herself in the small office in the hospital, digging through the patient records Neumann hadn't managed to hide. For an instant, the burnt-leather tang of shooter gloves stung her nose. She sensed Borgie standing behind her, reading the screens over her shoulder as he had then. She twisted around in her seat, heart pounding, but of course no one was there.

Of course. Jani checked the carrel door to make sure Angevin had closed it. Only then did she return to work.

If the curious had found Jani unresponsive before her disappearance into the workstation carrel, they found her damned near aphasic when she emerged, an hour and a half later.

I'm sorry. Very sorry. She offered silent apology to the librarian she brushed past, the young man who smiled and offered, "Hello." Yes, they had their own reasons for wanting to talk to her, but she had the experience to work around their concern. She could have calmed their groundless fears with a few well-considered words, convinced them it was safe to let her fade into the background where she belonged. The problem was that she didn't trust herself to speak. No telling what she'd say. That always happened when she was very, very angry.

You're a lying bastard, Evan van Reuter. You don't give a damn how Lyssa died—you dragged me here to help save your father's reputation.

She rode the lift down to the third floor, keyed through the triple sets of doors, then let her nose guide her to the scanpack parts bins. The residents of the floor had no doubt grown used to the characteristic odor of spent nutrient broth, but the undercurrent of rotted fish managed to have its nasty way with Jani's temper-churned gut. She leaned against the doorway leading to the bins, one hand over her mouth, as nauseated as any first-year intern. It would only get worse once she went inside; she knew from experience the only odor-killing ionizers on the floor would be positioned at the exit. A dexxie was allowed to clean up for the civilians, but when in the land of your ancestors, you sucked it in and proved yourself worthy.

Cursing softly, Jani pushed through the door. The idomeni, with their food issues and general delicacy, handled it so much more intelligently. Ionizers everywhere—the air in the Academy parts bins had smelled boiled.

Place looked better, too. The term *bin* proved an apt description for this area, which resembled an overfilled tool kit. No windows. Low ceilings. Narrow aisles lined with open work shelving. Repair carrels ran along one side of the enormous room; on the other side, the check-in desk and order-entry booths competed for space.

Jani tried to duck into one of the booths. She accidentally caught the eye of one of the clerks, however, and soon found herself the focus of several pairs of helping hands. Good news traveled fast.

"Are you sure this is the part you want, ma'am?" one of the clerks asked as he read her scribbled order.

"Yes." Jani tightened her grip on her duffel, shaking off yet another eager soul's offer to stash it behind the check-in desk. "Is there a problem?"

"Mr. Ridgeway's orders, ma'am. We need to inform him when someone checks out an old-time chip."

"Oh, really?" Jani circled to the clerk's side of the desk and waited for him to key Ridgeway's code into his comport. Chimes sounded—the man's face filled the display. "Durian," she said, "I'm checking out a revised GB-Delta twenty-year chip. I understand that's a problem."

Ridgeway stared at her pointedly, the seconds ticking away. "Good evening, Ms. Tyi," he said at last, smiling stiffly. Then he took a look at his timepiece. "Shouldn't you be getting ready for dinner? His Excellency hates to be kept waiting."

The words *His Excellency* elicited shocked whispers from the clerks. Jani gritted her teeth. "If we can settle this quickly, I'll be spot on time."

"Yes." Ridgeway glanced off to one side and shrugged quickly at someone. "I'm in the middle of something myself." His smile disappeared. "Must you do this now?"

Ginny Doyle chose that moment to move in beside Ridgeway and stick her head in the display range. "Hello, Ms. Tyi."

"Colonel."

"Digging into the archives, are we?"

"Trying to, if Grandma here will give me the sign-off." Jani looked into Ridgeway's narrowed eyes. "You aren't going to force me to resort to shoplifting, are you?"

One of the clerks gasped. Another snickered.

On the display, Doyle's grin twitched. "You know," she said, resting a hand on Ridgeway's shoulder, "I wouldn't put it past her."

"We'd nab her at the exit."

"Perhaps, but we are due for a systems drill this week. Let's give her a shot."

"We don't have time for that crap now, Virginia." Ridgeway looked down at his desk, his fingers drumming on the shiny wood. "Simon."

The clerk who'd been waiting on Jani stepped into display range. "Sir?"

"Give her the goddamned thing." Durian's image shrank to a pinpoint of light.

Foot-shuffling silence reigned for a time. Then Jani brought her fist down on the desk. "Well, you heard Grandma," she said to the startled faces surrounding her. "Give me the goddamned thing!"

The transaction was sorted out in record time. Smiles

turned from polite to genuine. *Durian, Durian, how thee are loved,* Jani thought as one of the clerks appointed herself her guide to the repair carrels. *I should have tried this in the Library.*

The young woman led her down the hall. "Is the smell getting to you?" she asked. "You looked a little green back there."

"It's been a while since I've visited a bin this size," Jani conceded.

"These help," the clerk said, handing her a small plastic-wrapped package. "We keep them for the civvies, but the smell gets to everyone once in a while."

Jani examined the small packet. Nose plugs, menthol-infused. "Thanks," she said as she inserted them.

The clerk stopped in front of one of the carrels and handed Jani the key card. "It's the only one open. Nobody else wants it." She jerked a thumb toward the door next to Jani's. "Your neighbor smokes up a storm. It seeps into the shared vent. People swear it screws up their 'packs, but there's no proof—"

"Smokes?" Jani stopped in front of her neighbor's door. "Is this Steve Forell's carrel?"

"Oh God, you know him?" The clerk shook her head. "Just yell if you need help. Make sure you open the door, first—these rooms are soundproofed." She flashed a smile. "If Grandma calls, we'll let you know," she said as she left.

Jani waited until the clerk was out of sight before she knocked on Steve's door. "Open up. It's Risa." She waited. Knocked louder. "Steve. Come on."

The door slid open. Steve blocked the entry. "What the hell do you want?" Behind him, Betha sat at a small table, a nicstick dangling from her lips. They both looked exhausted.

"You two been busy?" Jani stepped past Steve into the carrel. Her nostrils tingled as the clove stink of the nicsticks worked past the menthol. "Smells like you've been busy. I'm not surprised. They'll yank both your 'packs as soon as those fake documents surface unless you can hand them something bigger."

"Yeah, well." Steve flipped his spent nicstick into the

trashzap. "We've only got your word for that, don't we?"

"That's why you're both huddled in here smoking your brains out, because you only have my word."

"She's right, Steve," Betha said. "I looked it up." Her voice lowered. "The shortest sentence I could find were ten years in Lowell Correctional. That were for only one violation. I jazzed the Lady's docs—" Shaking fingers ticked off the total. She sagged into her chair when she ran out of digits.

Steve slumped against the carrel wall and slid to the floor. "Yeah, well if it goes to hell, we can just blow off, can't we? Hide out in the colonies, with our own. Doing for our own." He nodded firmly. "Pushing paper on the home world—how bad could that be?"

"How bad do you want it to be?" Jani pulled the other chair up to the table and set her bags down on the floor. "From that point on, all your work would be non-Registry. You could never use your 'pack again. You could never sign your real name to anything. And you wouldn't be doing for your own. You won't even be able to *see* your own, because any contact with them would be traced." She sat down carefully. Her stomach ached. Her back hurt. Her anger had ebbed. She felt old.

It had been fourteen years since she'd last tried to contact her parents. No one had been home, so she'd been transferred to a staffer from CitéMessage. That had struck Jani as odd, since her parents had always subscribed to the standard account with autoservice. She disconnected in the middle of the staffer's insistent request for her name.

The Service cruiser bearing the Admiral-General's seal had docked at Chenonceaux Station eight days later. Jani, who had decided to wait it out at the station before trying another call, had huddled behind a vending machine and watched the uniforms stream into the shuttle bound for her hometown of Ville Acadie. "You will," she paused to allow the tightening in her chest to ease, "never be able to go home."

A year passed before Jani worked up the nerve to touch down at Chenonceaux and try again. She had tapped out the code with a sweaty hand, disconnecting as soon as she heard her father's voice sing out, "*C'est Declan!*"

"If you're smart," she continued, "you'll stay away from

paper altogether. But that's hard to do when it's all you know. If you're lucky, you'll find work in some high-turnover post, like shipping tech. You'll fill out manifests, track transports. Monitor warehouse inventory." The words caught in Jani's throat. She *hated* warehouse inventory. "If you're not lucky, which is most of the time, you'll be at the mercy of every cheap crook who susses out the fact you're in trouble. So you'll do what they want, when they want, for whatever they choose to pay you, if anything. Because you'll both know one anonymous call to any Cabinet annex is all that stands between you and a prison cell. Have I made myself clear?"

Betha stared at her, round-eyed and blanched. Steve freed another nicstick from his pocket, wrinkled his nose, and shoved it into his mouth without igniting it.

"So." Jani paused to pat her eyelids. Her films had absorbed the clove smoke and her eyes felt grainy. She pressed lightly, until the tears came. "I'd like to ask you some questions, if you're agreeable." She waited. "Betha?"

The young woman sighed. "What?"

"Can you still access the paper Lyssa had you work on? Not the Nueva trips—the other stuff. You mentioned older documents." She knew all she needed concerning the details of Lyssa's visits to Nueva. They were indeed scheduled takedowns. *Surmise confirmed—aren't we the genius?* Ulanova had had her niece followed on her excursions. According to the Court report, Lucien had been quite the busy bee for eighteen months prior to Lyssa's death. So now she had the means and the opportunity nailed. *But I still need the damned motive.* And motive meant paper. Jani looked at Steve. "How about you?"

"I don't have them anymore, and they're probably beyond his security clearance," Betha said softly. "I don't think he can help you."

"You don't know what my clearance is!" Steve shot back.

Betha fingered a skirt pleat. "It would have to be at least Orange, possibly even Blue. Only Ridgeway's immediate staff rates Blue." She never looked at Steve. "Sepulveda. Zalestek. Wyle. They all rate Blue."

"I take meetings with the idomeni ambassador!" Steve

shouted. "Anything I need to find, I'll find. If I care to," he added hastily.

Jani looked at Betha, who regarded her in turn, her expression blank except for a faint quivering around the eyes. It could have been a guarded attempt at a wink. Or just a tic.

"I'm also looking for Consulate papers from our Rauta Shèràa days," Jani continued, "dating from just before the war to expulsion." The section of the report dealing with Acton had covered a respectable span of time, but Jani had still found significant gaps. "Duty logs would be good. Communication logs. Anything indicating who talked to whom and when." She pulled her scanpack from her duffel and set it on the table along with the recently purchased chip. "Think we can meet tomorrow?"

"We're not demanding, are we?" Steve worked to his feet. "We can meet here at fourteen-thirty. I'll be upgrading." He stretched. "So why can't you just pull this paper yourself?" he asked. "Why step up the flame under our arses?"

"Fewer questions this way," Jani replied as she rose and walked to the carrel's environmental control panel. "You both have reasons to go where you'll be going. I make people nervous, apparently, and I don't have time to muck about laying groundwork." She touched the lightpad; everything in the room took on a bluish glow as the antiseptic lighting kicked in.

"What are you doing?" Steve asked.

Jani increased the ventilation setting—the carrel grew noticeably cooler. "Surgery."

"You can't do that in here till the air flushes out!" Steve stuffed his hands in his pockets and pouted. "People bitch about the smoke."

"Hell of a lot cleaner than some places I've worked." Jani returned to the table, pulled her tool kit out of her duffel, and set out instruments. Then she cracked her container of nerve solder and poured a few drops of the thick brown liquid into a heat cup. "Scanpacks are hardier than you think." *Trust me.*

Betha stationed herself at Jani's shoulder. Steve sat down at the table, fascinated in spite of the circumstances. "What are you loading?"

"Something that can read what you're going to find for me." Jani pressed her hands flat against the sides of her scanpack and squeezed. The cover ID'd her prints and sprang open. "A new chip's been added to those docs over the years. I needed new hardware." Nestled in its case, the fist-sized mass of brain tissue shuddered beneath its protective pink dura mater.

"What kind of chip?" Betha asked.

"Family mark. The kind used in private papers." Jani felt beneath the scanpack for the master touchswitch. She set the switch to CHILL, then shut down the battery that pumped nutrient through the brain like a miniature heart. The healthy pink color of the dura mater remained, but the brain's trembling slowed to an occasional shudder.

"Whose?" Steve asked.

"Won't know until I can read the paper." *But I can make a damned good guess, Evan.* "What's the call on that chip?"

Steve held up the chip's antistatic pouch and squinted. "Five-eighths, nine to two, bleeds to death, flash activate."

Jani clamped the oxy feed lines to the fifth octant region of the brain, then closed the nutrient web. The shuddering ceased. Using microforceps, she peeled back the dura mater and anchored it to one side with a butterfly clamp, revealing a raised freckled line of chips and nerve bundles. She activated her laser knife, cut away the old two-nerve chip, and drew a thread of nerve solder from the ninth nerve lead to the second, forming an eight-nerve circuit that would drive the newer, more powerful chip.

"Family chip, eh? You be diggin' where you shouldn't, Ris?" Steve asked, his stare fixed on the table.

"Wouldn't think of it," Jani replied. The fried-meat smell of nerve solder worked past the nose plugs. Tiny puffs of smoke streamed upward as she picked single pinholes in the tissue. Using her forceps, Jani set the chip in place. The hair-thin anchors fit perfectly into the pattern of holes she had cut. She attached the ends of the solder thread to the chip, baking them into place with touches of the knife.

"Not bad," Betha said.

"Don't know why in hell they make an edition chip a 'bleeds to death.' Every time a new version comes out, you risk killing your 'pack on fire-up." Jani reactivated the battery, then touched the knife to the chip, breaking the seal. The chip activated with an emerald flash, then faded to the pink-tinged grey of the surrounding tissue. Slowly, Jani reopened the oxy lines, then set the master touchswitch back to NORMAL. The octant revived with a rippling shiver.

Betha exhaled slowly and massaged the back of her neck. "You think there's something in this House got to do with the Lady's death?"

"I know there is," Jani replied.

"Not an accident?"

"No."

"You think she were augmented." Betha smiled at Jani's look of surprise. "I remember your reaction when I told you about her 'surfin'.' Asked an ex-Service friend what it meant. He told me. You think all her trips to Nueva Madrid had something to do with the augmentation, that she died because something happened to it." She grew serious. "Because somebody did something to it."

"It's possible," Jani finally said.

Betha walked to the door. "You mean yes. Why don't you say what you mean." She turned to Steve. "See you later."

"Where you going?" he asked.

"Work. I'll be in one of the spare offices if you need to talk." Betha smiled weakly. " 'Bye."

"She's smarter than she looks," Jani said as the door closed.

Steve drew close. "Weirdo 'pack you've got there," he said. "Dull lookin', like a lump of mud. Tsecha's got somethin' looks just like it. His thing's like a dictionary. Got a couple human languages in it."

"Coincidence," Jani said as she swept her gear back into her duffel.

"Don't tell me that! I seen it! I've sat in meetings with him. Watched him tap at the damned thing."

Jani stuffed the yellow sack containing the Court of Inquiry report into her duffel. "Have you talked to Angevin today?"

Steve's eyes widened. He stood up, rocked uncertainly from one foot to the other. "Nah," he finally muttered. "Don't have time for her crap. It's all over. It's done."

Jani rose, then closed in on Steve until she stood toe to toe with him. "You don't want her linked with you in case you get arrested."

Steve tensed. "Won't get arrested. Be gone long before then." He chewed his unactivated 'stick. "That story. That were just a story, weren't it? 'Bout what it's like. I mean, you're just a posh little Cabinet cracker—what do you know about rough?" He offered her a hide'n'seek smile—now you see it, now you don't. "Were just a story, weren't it?"

"Oh yes." Jani focused on the floor. "You found me out. Blatant exaggeration, just to scare you." She walked to the door. "Tomorrow," she said. She glanced at her timepiece as she headed for the lift. She'd be late for dinner with Evan. After he heard what she had to say, he'd wish she'd stood him up.

CHAPTER 19

Jani ignored a staffer's efforts to announce her arrival and brushed past him into the Private House dining room. Evan, who had been sitting with his back to the door, stood up unsteadily as she cut across the room to the portable bar.

"Jesus, you do bang around, don't you?" He smiled tentatively, swirling the contents of his glass. "There was no need for you to rush. First chance I've had to be by myself all day. Gave me a chance to catch my breath."

Jani poured herself a glass of water and watched Evan sample his drink. She had always known him as a steady drinker. The official term was *maintenance alcoholic*, according to the Court of Inquiry report. He was on a regimen of alcohol dehydrogenase boosters and nutritional supplements and had a replacement liver waiting for him in Neoclona-Chicago's organ storage bank. Every year, he had a battery of tests to monitor for signs of incipient alcoholic psychoses. He was on record as saying he had no intention of curbing his drinking. He would do as he pleased; it was up to his cadre of highly paid physicians to keep him functional.

He looked Jani up and down. His grin dimmed. "I thought you'd dress like you did on the *Arapaho*. I was looking forward to it." He had certainly gone the full formal route. Black evening suit. Gleaming white shirt with onyx fasteners. The only thing missing was the red rose in his crossover lapel.

"You don't give a damn what happened to Lyssa. For the last two years of her life, you and she barely spoke." Jani walked over to a serving cart. Too much time had passed since her last meal. Her stomach ached as though she'd been punched. "You found out the Court had initiated an investigation of your father's conduct during the idomeni civil war. The van Reuter reputation was at stake. You needed someone with experience in Rauta Shèràa paper to do a minesweep, help you bury incriminating Service documents Acton recoded as private paper. Enter yours truly." She snagged a warm roll from one of the baskets and bit into it. "You thought I'd help you cover for him to save my ass. Need I remind you that your Uncle Rik made the same mistake?"

"Who have you been talking to?" Evan shrugged off Jani's answering glare. "Anais has tried to engineer my father's ruin many times. She's always come out looking the fool."

"My transport crash was no crash at all. Anais has proof Acton arranged to have a bomb placed on board. He was involved with Neumann in the illegal acquisition of augmentation technology from the Laum at Knevçet Shèràa. They tried to pull me into the mix. I said no. When Rikart pushed, I pushed back harder." Jani closed her eyes. She could smell it again, the singed-leather stink of shooter gloves. "Acton pushed back hardest of all."

"Wishful thinking on Anais's part."

"I was there, Evan, remember?"

"My father was many things. But he believed in Lady Commonwealth. He would never have slaughtered her soldiers."

"Knowing what happened to Martin, how can you stand there and say that to me?"

"Knowing what happened to Martin gives me every right. The van Reuter men were always ripe for sacrifice, Jan. That's our job—it's an honor reserved for us alone. Dad would never have deigned to share the glory." He walked to the bar and refilled his glass. Four fingers of bourbon—no water or ice. "I'm not denying what happened to you. I certainly can't deny Rikart's involvement. But nothing my father did is anyone's concern but mine. He did not become aware of the Laum technology until after the war. Martin paid the first installment on that bargain. Serena and Jerrold paid the second, Lyssa, the third. I'm responsible for the balance, to be repaid in my own currency." He took a large swallow. "Anais has come up empty with this search of hers for years. Now, all of a sudden, she thinks she's gotten lucky."

Jani perched on the edge of a dining-room chair. Took a bite of bread. A gulp of water. She'd eaten this way too many times. Mechanical, tasteless refueling, choked down just prior to getting the hell out of town. "Yes, but this time she had Lyssa acting as Interior mole. Your wife had good reason to hate Acton. She wanted the entire Commonwealth to know what he'd done to Martin."

"It never occurred to her that she could damage her own reputation in the process. People would ask how she could have allowed it to happen. I tried to explain that to her, but she wouldn't listen to reason. I'm a magnet for women who refuse to listen to reason." Evan walked slowly toward Jani, stopping when he came within arm's reach. "Durian told me about your forced excursion this afternoon. Don't you see what Anais is trying to do? She's trying to drive a wedge between us, convince you it's safe to throw in with her."

"She may have a point." Jani brushed crumbs from her fingers. The bread rested like ballast in her stomach. "The Court will be releasing its findings one week from today. The final summation contains a demand for your resignation."

"How do you know that?"

"I read the report."

A host of emotions played across Evan's face as Jani's words sank in. Surprise. Elation. Anger. Fear. "Aren't you the enterprising one," he finally said, his words strung out like beads on a wire. "How did you manage to obtain it?"

"Never mind." Jani picked out another roll. "Besides, I don't have it anymore." Technically, that was true. She had stashed it in the women's locker room next to Interior's main gymnasium. "You don't sound surprised."

"I had my own artfully acquired copy delivered into my hands earlier today. Neatest piece of fiction I've read in years. I noted several gaps in the evidence. They seemed to coincide with every point the Court needs to make its case." Evan sighted Jani with the cobalt stare that had swayed voters for two decades. "Did Anais provide you with your copy of the report, by any chance?"

"Why would she do that?"

"She'll use you, Jan. She'll take what she can, then lock you up and throw away the code."

"And you're offering me so much more, aren't you?"

"I can offer you anything you want." He sat in the chair next to hers, still taking care to keep his distance, not to allow anything he did to seem threatening. "I never stopped caring for you. I never stopped wishing things had worked out differently. My life with you in Rauta Shèràa was the best time of my life. I want that life back."

"Evan, don't lie to me. You brought me here to salvage that old bastard's reputation."

"I brought you here to take care of you!" His fingers tightened around his glass, the knuckles whitening. "To make it up to you, for everything you went through. I had a house in the city picked out for you. A job, if you wanted to work. I had it all planned."

"I don't need anyone to take care of me. I can take care of myself."

"I've seen your idea of taking care of yourself. I've seen what it's done to you. Leave the thinking to someone else."

But thought is all I have. Planning. Outwitting. The art of seeming to give in when actually giving nothing. She'd read her Service file in the library carrel, through shrewder, more discerning eyes. *I'm what I've always been, only more so.* "I don't like to be beholden, Evan. I prefer to pay my own way." Jani stared at him until the arrogant gleam in his eyes degraded to uncertainty. "In my own currency."

Evan sank back in his chair. The skin on his face was greyed, the hollows beneath his eyes, deepened. "Has Anais identified you? Does she know you're Jani Kilian?"

"No. She had me scanned. The current pattern doesn't match my Service ID."

"Well then, what can she do to you? How can she threaten you? Don't let her scare you—she has nothing!" He touched her at last, resting his hand on her knee. "Just keep your mouth shut and wait her out. Follow my lead—I've brazened my way through more than one full frontal assault in my time." Taking her silence for agreement, he pressed a touch-pad alongside his place setting. Uniformed staffers entered by way of a narrow access door and began serving the first course.

"So what did you do today?" he asked when they were again alone. "Besides getting yourself kidnapped and purloining top secret Cabinet documents."

"Just mucked about." Jani fished a mushroom slice out of her soup. Fungi, she had learned over the past few months, were *not* an option. "Visited the Library."

"You seem to have made some interesting friends." Evan filled his wineglass to the brim. "Durian told me you've been seen with Steven Forell. Durian has a great deal to say about Mr. Forell, none of it complimentary."

"Durian wants to wrap his slimy paws around Angevin Wyle. He blames Steve for keeping that from happening. If he knew how Angevin really felt about him, he'd spin in his well-appointed seat for a week." Jani ate what she could of the soup, then tested the green salad. When she looked up, she found Evan studying her, chin cradled in hand. "What?"

"How long have you been here?" he asked.

He's so close. He wants me to reach out and touch—Jani felt the heat rise in her face; she looked down at her plate. "Little over a day." The salad contained chopped apple. She reached for the pepper mill instead.

"So much news acquired in a little over a day. Tell me, are there any other love affairs affecting members of my executive staff that you think I should know about?"

Jani regarded the mill in her hand. It had a decidedly suggestive shape. "Well, the head of your Farms Bureau used to holo himself screwing assorted animal life in his office. He's not doing it anymore, though. AgMin shut him down."

Evan's eyes widened. He sat back and clamped a hand over his mouth.

"I hope we're not having lamb or chicken tonight," she added peevishly.

His shoulders shook. Gently, at first, then more and more violently. He'd always been a remarkably quiet laugher. He'd turn red and choke before he'd make a sound.

Jani continued eating. After a minute or so, she reached over and thumped Evan between his shoulder blades. He inhaled with a wheezing gasp.

"I don't remember—the last time—oh shit, Jan, don't ever do that to me again." He wiped his tearing eyes with his napkin, then sat quietly, his hands over his face. "I remember the night—they threw us out—of the Consulate bar—oh hell." He started up again, though much more weakly. "You'll stay here, won't you?" he asked when he'd finally summoned the strength to talk in complete sentences. "If they can't ID you, why leave?"

Jani examined the spice dispenser. Something called *ground habañero* had a lightning bolt beside the name. She sprinkled it liberally on her salad. "What if you're forced to resign?"

"Then I'll resign. Move back to the house in the Bluffs, play the gentleman of leisure. Answer my question, Jan."

"Gentleman of leisure. You'll go crazy." She coughed. The habañero wasn't bad.

"I won't go crazy if I know you're nearby. I'd sleep easier tonight if I knew I could count on you. Can I?"

"Why would you think you couldn't?"

Evan pressed a hand to his temple. "You're deflecting me. One eye on the exit, just like always. I could afford your evasions in Rauta Shèràa. I can't afford them now. Can I count on your support or not?"

Always the pressure to give and give . . . in exchange for what? She wasn't the only one who hadn't changed with time. "Blind loyalty's a quality I can't afford, Evan. Tell me what to expect."

"These situations tend to follow a pattern. No one will officially acknowledge my existence for about six months, although my real friends will send notes and such, just to make sure I'm keeping body and soul together. Then I'll start getting visits. Old allies asking for advice. Old adversaries checking my pulse. Within a year to eighteen months, I'll be ready to make a run at a deputy Cabinet seat. Next thing you know, it'll be like I never left."

"Sounds formulaic."

"It happened to Dad. It's happened to me before." Evan stirred his soup, which he'd barely touched. "It's just politics." He watched her eat, his brow wrinkling. "You used to tell me how spicy your mother's cooking was." He pointed to her salad plate. "I never thought that was what you meant. Lacks subtlety, at least from where I'm sitting. What's going on?"

Jani looked down at her salad. "I don't know what you mean."

"The chef aboard the *Arapaho* had some interesting things to say concerning your culinary requests."

"You had crew reporting on me?"

"No. Durian did."

"Durian did?"

"I'll admit he may not have had the purest motives, but when I spoke with him a few hours ago, he seemed genuinely concerned." Evan propped his elbows on the table and tented his hands. "He suggested I ask you a few questions. For example, are you drinking a lot of water—"

Jani set down her refilled glass. The third. No, the fourth—

"—and are foods that you'd once been able to eat with no reaction making you sick now?" Evan jerked his chin in the direction of Jani's salad. "Have your tastes changed, become what most of us might consider odd? Have you been experiencing body aches, abdominal distress—"

"You sound like John Shroud." Jani tried to laugh. "Interrogations every third day, same hour of the morning, same crummy therapy room." If she closed her eyes, she could visualize the bare, dark tan walls, the restraint-bedecked myostimulator squatting in one corner like the hulking torture device it was.

Evan disrupted her grim vision. "Jani, one colonist has recently died from a condition which began with the symptoms I described. The symptoms you're evidencing. I wish you'd see a doctor."

Jani examined her hands. Her right one shook a bit, but that was only because she was angry. *The garage guy's stomach always hurt.* Well, hers did, too. *He threw up a lot.* Ok. *He tried to kill his grandmother with a lazor.* Except his grandmother had been dead for twenty years; he exhausted himself annihilating a pillow. Hepatic dementia, the doctors had called it. They had a name for everything.

I have never tried to kill any dead female relatives. Hah— had them there. Besides, everyone in NorthPort knew the garage guy became sick from eating Haárin food. Lots of people on Whalen tried Haárin foodstuffs at least once. Jani had been eating it for years—it wasn't her problem. She attacked her water again. "Well, I wish you'd do something about your drinking," she said as she came up for air. "We can't have everything, can we?"

On cosmic cue, two staffers entered. They cleared and carved silently, but with many covert glances toward the table.

"Here's a deal for you," Evan said after they left. "I'll face my little problem when you face yours." He cut into his roast beef. A smile flickered. "Not lamb or chicken," he said.

"I'm not sick." Jani drove the point home by adding habañero to her meat as well. "I'm sorry if my colonial taste offends your Earthbound sensibilities, but don't compound your prejudice by calling it a disease."

"Have it your own way, Jan," Evan replied. "For now." They finished eating in silence, then adjourned to the adjacent sitting room for dessert and coffee. He carried his cup to the bar and, with a pointed look at Jani, added a generous splash of brandy. "Do you want to talk about Lyssa? I'm sure, since you read the report, you have questions."

Jani swallowed a belch. It felt as though a hot coal had lodged beneath her sternum. "I had already guessed she was augmented. The Court report research confirmed it. I think she had it done in order to feel what Martin had gone through. But she didn't have the right brain chemistry to withstand the stress. It was all pretty easy to figure, if you knew what to look for." She explained about the gossip magazine's crisis timeline. "Someone saw their chance and took advantage. It didn't take much to make her death look like an accident."

Evan leaned against the bar. "You'd think it would have helped her, don't you?" he said, his voice dead. "The Service uses it to build better soldiers—you'd think it would've helped her cope."

"Lyssa should never have been augied. Her mental state was already precarious, and it only got worse. Even frequent take-downs weren't leveling her out—she was headed for augie psychosis. If she'd been Service, she'd never have made it past the initials. She'd have been typed as a likely burnout and kicked out of the program.''

Evan smiled grimly. ''Augie burnout. I used to hear that phrase in meetings.'' He looked at Jani. ''Burnouts hallucinate to a greater degree than regular augies. Borderlines, too. Like you?''

''Depends what you mean by hallucinate. My problems are with smell, mostly. I catch a noseful of berries whenever I get aggravated. Never heard voices, thank God. Never saw spiders crawling out of the walls.''

Evan approached her with the slow step and unfocused eye of a man on the way to his own execution. As he lowered himself into the chair next to her, he exuded the same beaten-down wariness she had felt toward the myostimulator. *This needs to be worked through. This needs to be done. But that doesn't mean we have to like it.*

''A year after the children died, I visited Lyssa's suite without calling first. We had reached the point where we called first. She was sitting alone on her bed. She looked so happy— I thought she'd drugged herself. Being a doctor, she had access to the staff infirmary.'' His spiked coffee rested on his knee, its surface rippling.

''She was talking. To them. She saw me eventually, or at least *sensed* me. Didn't Martin look nice in his school uniform, she asked? He'd just told her he wanted to be a doctor like his mum. I slipped out as quickly as I could.'' He hoisted his cup. ''My drinking, to that point, hadn't been too bad, but it did pick up from then on.''

Jani sipped her coffee. ''You didn't know?''

''About the augment?'' He shook his head. ''Not until I read the report today. Like I said, I thought she'd been drugging.''

''You'd been exposed to it so much in your day-to-day, I'm surprised nothing clicked.''

Evan leaned back in his chair. ''I blocked it out, I guess. Didn't feel I had the right to inquire. I figured by that time, Lyssa and I were each entitled to the pit of our choosing. I didn't even ok an autopsy—that's what set Cao on the warpath. But I felt she deserved that . . . privacy. A last kind gesture from me, to make up for all the others.'' He looked at

Jani, his eyes reflecting the depths of his own abyss. "This may sound horrible, but I think whoever killed her did her a favor. Every once in a while, I wish they'd show me the same consideration." He refilled his cup from the ewer.

Jani shifted in her chair. She was angry. Her back ached. Her stomach had begun to rumble ominously. She didn't think she could deal with a drunken Evan as well.

"Don't worry," he said, reading her mind. "Just coffee, until you leave. I promise." He shook a finger at her. "But I must insist you allow me my pit. I've earned it. These past few months, it's become a second home." He gestured toward the curtained wall opposite them. "Here's something you might like." He pressed a touchpad near the tray. The drapes swept aside. "Isn't it pretty?"

A spun-sugar world filled the window. Lit by rainbow lights, with the night as a backdrop, two banked tiers of snow-frosted hybrid shrubs glittered. Some of the dwarf evergreens had been clipped into spires and coils, while others had been shaped into stylized buildings. In the center, a line of graceful, needled shrubs had been trimmed into a suspension bridge, joining the two tiers. "It's pretty," Jani said, but all it looked was cold. She rubbed her aching gut and shivered. She didn't feel very art-appreciative just then.

Evan picked through the dessert tray. "I had it made for Nema; we were supposed to have a reception in the main ballroom after his welcoming ceremony. A bridge for the chief bridge-builder. Obvious, perhaps, but I felt it appropriate." He chewed reflectively. "Cao and Ulanova blocked me, of course. They felt he'd be insulted. As if they'd fucking know. So I had it moved here. Next time those two come for dinner, if there ever is a next time, it'll be waiting. Hell, if the weather's good, maybe I'll have the tables set up under the damned bridge." He touched her arm to get her attention.

"How did you manage? After the children . . . I almost cashed in. How did you keep going?" His hand lingered. It was Jani's left arm. All she felt was the pressure. "What went through your mind? After Knevçet Shèràa. During your recovery. When, you knew you'd lost it all. How did you live?"

Jani pressed down on her aching stomach. "I told myself——" She stalled. That was the point, wasn't it? She'd told *her-*

self, never anyone else. "I told myself that I was the last one. If I died, there wouldn't be anyone left to remember Knevçet Shèràa." This time she pronounced it properly, adding the right-handed gesture that mimicked the sweep of the sand dunes.

Evan's hand tightened on her arm. "You're remembered, Jan, if it's any consolation. I've seen the files. They fill a two-meter-long shelf in the Judge Advocate's office."

"That's not the remembrance I mean." Jani grew still; even her stomach quieted. "I remember the heat. The blowing sand. The sense of dread when I walked into Eva Yatni's room." She had been the first patient to die. She'd plucked out her eyes and plunged her thumbs into her brain. Neumann called it suicide.

"I remember another patient named Simyan Baru. I watched him peel the skin from his cheek like it was a piece of fruit. I couldn't get in the room to stop him—it was locked. So I went to see Neumann to get the code. He wouldn't give it to me. We had a talk. You know what happened next."

"I remember when Baru and two other patients escaped. We tried to treat them as best we could, but they were too far gone. Hallucinating. They thought we were Laum, come to kill them. They jumped Felicio and Stanleigh and stole our people mover. The only transport we had. We had nothing to knock it down with, no way to repair it if we did. I watched it disappear over the rise. I saw the flash after the Laum chased it down.

"I remember the whine of the shatterboxes. My corporal's death. The last night, ordering Sergeant Burgoyne to take everyone into the basement. I said it was because of the threat of further bombing, but I looked at him and he looked at me and I *needed* that look he gave me." That last flame lick of hope, driving her forward.

"Jani?" Evan's voice rasped. "You don't have to tell me this if you don't want."

What does want have to do with it? "I left them behind, and I went outside. I checked my shooter. I said a prayer. *à Yestha raùn.* Preserve my soul. I cut my left arm from wrist to elbow, sopped up the blood with a rag, staked the rag near the front door of the hospital. *Chäusen tha sè rau.* Shelter my soul—keep it safe." The stiff red braid rested in her duffel now—somehow, it had found its way onto the transport, surviving both the explosion and the crash. John Shroud had recovered it from the wreckage and returned it to her. "It was so still. So quiet. I knew Knevçet Shèràa was important to the Laumrau. They needed to take it back from us, reclaim it from humanish contamination. That meant it was a Night of Conjunction—sacrament and prayer before a decisive battle. Even the guards were sequestered in their tents. I remember the silence as I walked over the rise and into their camp."

"Jani—"

"I remember . . . twenty-six expressions of surprise on twenty-six faces when I entered twenty-six tents and fired my shooter twenty-six times." Shredded the Bilateral Accord and every tenet of idomeni behavior. Slaughtered them one by one in a way no fellow idomeni had ever dared. She remembered how the shooter grip overheated and cooked the palm of her hand. *I became one with my weapon that night.* A real soldier. "But most of all, I remember, I *have* to remember, why. Because it loses something when you write it down." She had to remember the fear she'd seen in her real soldiers' eyes as Borgie herded them down the stairs. Remember that only she possessed the knowledge that would guarantee they'd remain alive to walk back up. "I have to remember, because everyone else seems to want to forget."

She turned to find Evan hunched forward, his face buried in his hands. "Trust me when I tell you, Jan," he said, his voice muffled, "they can't." He rose and straightlined for the bar. "About that promise I made—I take it back." He filled a water glass halfway with bourbon, looked at her, and poured a second. "I never thought I'd say this to anyone," he said as he pressed the glass into her hands, "but you look like you need this more than I do."

Jani swirled the dark caramel liquid. Her films absorbed the ethanol vapors, stinging her eyes. The tears spilled. She tipped back the glass and drank. The bourbon burned down her throat. Desert heat.

"Attagirl." Evan raised his glass in a toast, then followed suit. He drank more than she did, and it seemed to have no effect whatsoever on his eyes. "What do you think would happen," he asked over the top of his glass, "if they found out you were you?"

Jani took another swallow. A sip, really. Her mouth had gone numb. "Court-martial. Execution, probably, unless the idomeni pushed for extradition. They'd probably want to kill me, too. Hell, the line forms in the rear—if they got inventive, they could have a Neoclona team standing by to revive me after every barrage. They could keep it going for years." Poor John—he'd probably offer to fire the first shot. She smiled bleakly. The expression froze as her stomach cramped.

"I won't let that happen." Evan reached out to stroke her arm. Then he pointed to the glazed garden. "Don't you wish you could just press a pad and make everything else disappear. The past. Whatever's outside the door. Just the two of us, and to hell with everyone else."

Jani tried to nod, but the movement started a trail of heat burning up from her stomach. She dropped her glass and bounded out of her chair, leaving Evan behind to stagger to his feet and call after her.

She made it to her bathroom. Barely. Her body let her know bourbon was never, *ever*, to be considered an option again. *Let us sing a song of real soldiers . . . first verse.* She slumped against the toilet as the room spun. *All dead, so you're stuck with me.* Then she lost what balance she had. Her skull impacted tile with a vibrating *crack*.

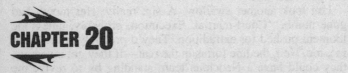

CHAPTER 20

"Here is your seat, sir. Would you like a program?"

Tsecha accepted the small booklet the young female handed him. He fingered a page and frowned. Paper-plastic interweave. Sturdy, perhaps, but no more so than mid-grade parchment. He looked over the polished gold railing and down at the banked rows of seats. *So much red.* Every chair had been covered in material like blood in color, even the less honored ones in the rows above the level of his head, which he had to squint to see in the half-light.

Behind him, doors opened and closed. "The bar is fully stocked," the female continued, "as is the cooler." An expectant silence followed. Tsecha turned to find her standing beside an open food repository which had been set into the back wall of the small space. "There's a seasonal fruit tray," she said, pointing to a multicolored pile, "and cold hors d'oeuvres. There's a touchpad by your seat that will connect you to our service area. In addition, a member of our staff will stop by throughout the course of the evening. If you prefer hot food, or if the bar lacks something, just ask, please."

Tsecha stared at the fruit tray. Such large pieces. All so mixed. Together. After so long, with all he had come to accept, still it shocked him. And just resting there, for anyone to look at, to touch. *And stored with meat and grain.* The words of his esteemed enemies in Temple sang in his mind. *They do not know their food.* A killing insult to any idomeni, even Haárin, but one which meant nothing to humanish.

"Will there be anything else, Mister Hansen?"

Tsecha blinked. His films, the darkest brown he could find, squeezed his eyes, drying them as the winds that blew through Rauta Shèràa. "No," he said, "thank you." He smoothed his humanish neckpiece, black as his evening suit, and curved his mouth without baring his teeth. "I am quite fine."

He did not sit until the female left him. So unseemly, to remain standing in the suborn's presence. The anxiety that plagued him during these excursions coursed through him with his blood. *Not a good idea,* his Hansen of the godly hair had told him the first time Tsecha tried to impersonate humanish. The words *sore thumb* had also been used, although when Tsecha had sought to divine their meaning from his handheld, the definitions made no sense.

Despite Hansen Wyle's misgivings, Tsecha's first sojourn had gone well. One of Eamon DeVries's females had helped with makeup. John Shroud himself had applied the eyefilms. His Jani, who was still a lieutenant then, arrived later to brief him on things a colonial humanish should know. *You'd never pass as Earthbound in a thousand years, niRau,* she had told him, so somber in her stiff uniform. *Don't even try.* She had been more concerned about his excursion than Hansen. Her doubt, more than anything, had driven Tsecha forward.

He had served as a tour guide to a group of the humanish Consulate's high-ranking visitors. He had been commended for his expertise as he escorted officials through the city of his life. In the process, he learned more of humanish behavior than he ever could have from his handheld or his discs.

"I was even given tips." Tsecha bared his teeth as he recalled the pile of chits and the look on Hansen's face as he counted them. *Only you could turn a profit from acting like a jackass,* his godly hair had said. Those words also made no sense. He had not acted as an animal, but most assuredly as humanish. One of the officials had even asked him if he was Phillipan. That had made him feel most proud.

He looked again over the railing. Humanish streamed in through many doors, then wound down aisles and up and down steps to their seats. Some had guides, dressed in dark blue tunics and trousers as his female had been. Others found their own way. A few could not, however, and wandered as though lost. Once or twice, voices rose as small groups waved their arms and pointed to seats. Tsecha bared his teeth. *The number on the ticket is to match the number on the chair.* That, he had learned on his own, only a short time ago, and by himself. Only humanish could turn such a simplicity into confusion.

He stroked the arms of his seat. The cloth that covered them felt as close-clipped fur, pleasing to his touch. *My nìa Sànalàn has told all I am at high prayer.* A series of pleas to each of the Vynshàrau's eight dominant gods, the holiest rite for a chief propitiator. Not even the head of Temple or the secular Oligarch could disturb him at such. *Nor my nìa.* For such did she believe as well. That he lied to his suborn at all did not disturb him as much as that he did so so easily. The change had embraced him already, perhaps, leaving none of its physical signs. *I am one with my kìershia, my Captain. I am toxin.*

Tsecha directed his attention to the front of the huge room. A large drapery, shiny as metalcloth and dark gold in color, separated the audience from the place where the performance would occur. A holodrama, to be performed by images of humanish actors, both living and dead.

He studied his program, which had been printed in the dominant humanish languages, decoding his way between blocky English script and more logical Mandarin. *Tales of Arthur.* An ancient dominant. *A king.* There would be battles on horseback and tragic love. Witches. Dragons. *And a dancing goat.* Tsecha made a gesture that would have shocked his suborns and made Hansen Wyle laugh. He longed for his handheld, if only to inform him what exactly a goat was.

Loud voices and laughter drew his attention. Other compartments like his ran along the curved sides of the immense room. The noise emanated from the third compartment to his right. The curve of the wall was such that he could see quite clearly the owners of the voices. Which meant, of course, they could see him as well.

Anais Ulanova expected to see no idomeni this night. The gown she wore glowed red as molten metal, revealing her body in the way many humanish females preferred. Five others joined her, three males and two females. Tsecha recog-

nized Treasury Minister Abascal and his solitary wife, as well
as Deputy Prime Minister Langley and a very young female
he had once heard some humanish refer to as flavor of the
month. Only this female was most dark, while the one he had
seen at his welcome ceremony had been most light. A seemly
elevation for all involved, he felt sure. Most as idomeni. *Why
then did the humanish laugh so?*

Tsecha looked at the third male, who stood behind Anais's
chair. He wore the uniform of a Service officer. Most young,
he seemed; only the flavor appeared younger. *His hair is almost as John Shroud's.* Tsecha grew conscious of the fact the
male studied him as well. He responded with the slight nod
Hansen Wyle had told him was suitable for such meetings.

The male did not nod back, but continued to stare openly
until Anais claimed his attention by turning in her seat and
gripping his hand. Only then did he smile, baring his teeth
almost as widely as Vynshàrau as he leaned toward his dominant. Quite a seemly pairing, perhaps, if one looked only at
faces.

But Tsecha studied the man as idomeni. The stiffness of
his neck. The angle of his head as he sought to turn away
from the Exterior Minister without seeming to. How his left
hand, hidden behind his back, clenched and worked. Almost
as simple as idomeni, these walls, at times. *Anais's warrior
is not a willing suborn.* Then what held him there, as spikes
to the floor?

With signal flickers, the illumins died. Voices faded. Once
more, Tsecha felt the male's gaze upon him, piercing through
the half-night as a weapons sight. At last, the blessed curtain
rose. The humanish clapped their hands, and the booming,
wheezing disorder that constituted their music began. Even as
the noise buffeted him, Tsecha felt his fear leave. With such
as Anais's unwilling warrior near, he felt more comfortable
in the dark.

*If my Temple knew me to be here, I would be made Haárin,
and truly.*

The hologram actors, clothes aglow with too-vivid color,
voices more measured and clear of tone than any humanish
speech Tsecha had ever heard, displayed the story of the king.

The Vynshàrau worked against the aggravating comfort of his chair. If only there were some humanish he could trust, who could explain this king to him!

Why is he dominant, this Arthur, when he has no more sense than a young one? His dominant wife had agreed to elevate a suborn male, who had chosen her freely. Such was a most seemly occurrence, greatly to be wished; yet the king looked upon it as betrayal, a threat to order. Then there was a skein member, a nephew, who sang of injustice and plotted murder even though he was true suborn and had no right to rule. And suborns who wore clothes of clanking metal and rode off on meaningless quests, for objects, leaving their own skein members behind, confused and grieving.

The tragedy is the disorder! An illumin shone on the pad near Tsecha's chair. He slapped it dark. Let his blue-clad female take her offerings elsewhere. He thought of the food repository behind him as, onstage, the actors sat down to a banquet. How they ate and drank and shouted as the humanish audience laughed and cheered.

He watched food pass from hand to hand, from one plate into many mouths, and felt an ache in his soul. Two actors dressed in scraps of dull cloth scuttled across the stage after a chunk of meat discarded by a dominant, tearing at it as animals. Just then, the hot, spicy odor of broiling drifted into Tsecha's compartment from another. His stomach lurched. He forced himself to stare at the carpet at his feet as his eyes watered and his throat tightened.

He barely staunched a cry as behind him, a soft tapping sounded. "Compliments of the theater, Mister Hansen," a voice muttered through the thin door. "If you pad me in, I can set it up for you."

Tsecha lowered to his hands and knees and crawled across his own floor as the beggars had across theirs. He pressed his face against the door, breathing through his mouth to shut out the stench of food not his own. "Go away," he rasped. "I want nothing."

"Compliments of the theater, Mister Hansen," the voice persisted, like the yammer of demons. "A signature is required, even if you turn it down. Procedure, sir."

A signature. To breathe, the humanish needed signatures.

But if I open the door, I can leave. Escape the small compartment. Flee into the cold, cleansing night. Tsecha stood, scrabbled with the latch, flung the door wide and stilled as he looked into the face of Anais's warrior.

"*NìRau ti nìRau.*" The moonlight head glinted as it tilted very slightly to Tsecha's right. An angle indicating true respect, but with no implied intimacy of friend or enemy. "Is this performance boring you as much as it is me?" He crossed his right arm in front of his chest, palm outward.

Tsecha glanced at the designators on the man's collar. Red bars. Mainline lieutenant. Yes, this officer had greeted him in quite the correct way, and truly. *a lète ona vèste, Nemuruu*—his Anais's source for High Vynshàrau had, with no doubt, come from a place much closer than an office within Exterior Main.

"I could see you, even in the dim light." The lieutenant led Tsecha from an upper-level theater exit and into a glass-covered walkway suspended above the street. "You began fidgeting during that scene in the stables, where Lancelot fed his horse as he sang about Guinevere. After that, I waited fifteen minutes, then came by to pay my respects." He turned, hands linked behind his back. Even in the dark, his hair shimmered. "Actually, nìRau, I'm surprised you lasted as long as you did. Makes me wonder what you were trying to prove."

"Prove?" Tsecha slowed, stepping around the man as though avoiding a hazard in the street. "I am curious only, Lieutenant"—he edged just close enough to read the man's name designator—"Pascal. I wish only to learn of those with whom I have been charged to deal."

"Well, in the dark, you appear humanish enough. And your English is exceptional, nìRau."

"It is not a complicated language, Lieutenant." How easily he lied. But what could Pascal know of his handheld, or of his quest to read between lines?

"You consider Mandarin Chinese much more respectable, for its structure and order." Pascal proceeded down the walkway, beckoning Tsecha to follow. Beneath them, skimmers darted in the night like huge waterflicks, following the phosphor trail of the well-illuminated roadway and bright buildings.

"And French, for its sound." His pace quickened as he stepped off the walkway and down a narrow flight of stairs. Then came a series of winding indoor hallways.

We are in a building now—and I am most lost. Tsecha hurried after Pascal as they passed through door-lined halls and lobbies much as those in Interior Main, though smaller in scale. The other humanish he saw were male. Some stood in the halls and talked; others emerged from rooms in pairs or groups. At times, curious glances came to rest on Tsecha, but most seemed directed at Pascal. He ignored the attention, the occasional reaching hand or calling of his name. Instead, he walked on as though alone until he stopped before one of the identical doors, removed a key card from his tunic pocket, and coded his way inside.

The room contained only a bed, a frame chair, and, in a tiny alcove, a humanish sanitary room. "No food," Tsecha said. "I am most glad."

"People don't come here to eat, nìRau." Pascal unbuttoned his tunic and massaged the grooves the collar had pressed into his neck. His undershirt, to Tsecha's surprise, matched the red stripe running down the sides of his trousers.

"Has your Service altered its uniform code, Jeremy? I thought only white shirts were allowed."

The lieutenant sat down on the bed. "A small freedom. One of the benefits of a Cabinet posting." He looked at Tsecha with narrowed eyes. "Why did you call me *Jeremy*?"

Tsecha sat in the frame chair. The seat proved nicely rigid, but he wondered the purpose for the buckled fasteners on the chair's arms. "One of the men outside called to you in that way. Is that not your name?"

"Sometimes." Pascal's lips curved in the way Eamon's did when he felt he had been clever. "It's handy to have access to a place like this. At times, you need to talk to someone, but neither of you wants the true nature of your discussion known. So, you come here. Much better than a cabinet interrogation room. Rather like hiding in plain sight." He looked over at Tsecha. "My real name is Lucien, by the way, though I'd prefer you didn't use it here."

"But your name is on your tunic, most easy to see. How difficult would it be for someone to learn your true identity?"

It would have taken Hansen no time. Of that, Tsecha felt most sure.

"I know. It's just the principle of the thing, nìRau."

I am between lines. "It is disorderly."

Lucien bared his teeth and laughed. "Actually, *disorderly* is a more appropriate term than you'll ever know, nìRau."

"Indeed." Tsecha looked out the room's tiny window, but there was nothing of interest to see, only the filtered illumins of buildings he did not know. "Anais will notice you are gone?"

"I told her I had a call. She's learned to accept my devotion to duty." Lucien continued to massage his neck. "Speaking of devotion to duty, nìRau, have you had any success with your search?"

Tsecha shifted in his seat. He valued the focusing ability of discomfort, but he would not try wearing close-fitting humanish trousers again soon. "My search?" He touched his eyelids. They had begun to itch.

"For Jani Kilian."

"Kilian? Who is—"

"Anais has been looking for her for months. She thought, for a time, that she had her." Lucien rose and walked to the window. "Maybe she did."

Tsecha rubbed his eyes again. He shivered—it had grown very cold as well. He clapped his hands together to warm them. "Who is this Kilian of whom you speak, Jeremy? Are you sure of your names? You possess so many. They must be easily confused, and truly."

Lucien turned. For the shortest time, his face held no emotion. Then his teeth flashed and he raised his right hand in a Haárin gesture of irreverence. "*Touché*, nìRau." He refastened his tunic, wincing as he clasped the collar. "Well, we never had her, and you didn't want her if we did. Nothing lost."

Tsecha again pressed his fingers to his eyelids. The films had begun to prickle, but at least that made his eyes water. He would have to find a heavier jacket for these humanish evenings, one that protected him from the icy Chicago air. *The inset read, WINTER WOOL.* Would he have to learn to read between the lines of clothing labels as well?

Between the lines.

Ah.

"Well, I'm sorry to have wasted your time, nìRau," Lucien said. "But if we're lucky, that damned play might be over by the time we get back to the theater."

Tsecha remained seated. The chair proved quiet focusing. He had even developed a tolerance for the trousers. "Lucien, if you found this Kilian, what would you do with her?"

"Bring her here," the man answered after some time, "just to see the look on her face." Under Tsecha's steady stare, he hesitated. "I wouldn't hurt her." He stepped into the sanitary area and removed a comb from his pocket. "It's all theory, of course, isn't it, nìRau?" he said as he arranged his hair. "Seeing she's dead."

I understand this Lucien now. Could Hansen even have done so well? "How humanish talk. When they wish something not to exist, they execute it by not speaking of it. And when they want something more than their own life, they invent it from nothing by speaking of it at all times." Tsecha bared his teeth as Lucien turned to him, again expressionless. "But we have more than nothing here, do we not? She hides in plain sight. Where is she?"

"She's dead."

"Where is she!"

Lucien continued to comb his hair. "Safe, for now. In plain sight." The hands stopped. "Could you shelter her, nìRau, if necessary?"

"No." Tsecha again scratched the skin on his hands, then stifled a sneeze as his face started to itch as well. "But I know one who could."

"One who could. Does that mean you still talk to your friend, John Shroud?"

Tsecha shook his head. As an esteemed enemy, yes, but as a friend. . . . He shivered again, this time not from the cold. "I do not speak to Physician Shroud as a friend."

The lieutenant thrust his comb back into his pocket. "Well, the next time you don't talk to him, don't forget not to ask him about that illegal trial he never performed three years ago. The one where he studied the effects of Ascertane on some of the chev Haárin living on Elyas."

Don't forget . . . not . . . never. Tsecha took a deep breath. His head cleared even as the inside of his nose tingled, forcing him to fight back another sneeze. *So the rumors were true, John—yet how you denied.* "Trial? Ascertane?"

"A mild truth drug, nìRau. The Haárin can't tolerate it. Doesn't do a damn thing to get them to talk, and makes them violently ill besides. Tell him—" Lucien stopped, then gasped out another breath. He seemed surprised he could see the puff of air. He groped in his trouser pocket and pulled out a tiny black box, touching it so the red illumins on its surface dimmed.

"Is that a recording device?" Tsecha asked, most carefully.

"No, nìRau, an override. They're a specialty of mine. This one lets me take over a room's climate control. I can cool a room down." Lucien coughed. "Dry it out."

Tsecha gently prodded his eyelids. "Do you so value disorder, Lucien?"

"In myself, no." White teeth shone. "But I enjoy inspiring it in others." He opened the door, leaving the room before Tsecha, as was most proper. "Some advice, Mister Hansen," he said, as they stepped into the hall. "As much as I admire your daring, you shouldn't try a stunt like this again."

"My disguise is not good?"

"You're too distinctive-looking. Your posture. Your attitude. I wouldn't advise a repeat performance." Lucien led Tsecha down the hall, ignoring once more efforts made by other males to claim his attention. "But I can find you quite good makeup. And I can coach you. Escort you around Chicago. Show you the ropes, so to speak." He smiled. "Our first conspiracy. The first of many, I hope."

Tsecha studied Anais's unwilling warrior, now his own most willing guide. Another Hansen had found him, another teacher of humanish ways. *What can you teach me, Lucien?* He nodded to the young man, who smiled in a way Hansen had once warned him of. So bright. So wide. *Butter wouldn't melt in his mouth.* Interesting. *He tells me I do not look humanish. I, who have passed for Phillipan. He lies to me already, and keeps me from my Captain.* Oh yes, he could learn much from watching Lucien, and truly.

They left the building by a different walkway. Tsecha

looked up into the night sky, picking out the brighter stars through the city glare and filtering glass.

"How did you get here, nìRau?" Lucien asked. "Just out of curiosity."

"I drove, Lieutenant."

"*Again!*" Lucien skidded to a halt. "Where did you park?"

"In the theater charge lot." Tsecha rummaged through his pockets, removing a chip of brown plastic. "I have a stub."

"Yes. Well." Lucien took the plastic piece away from him, then removed a small comunit from his pocket and keyed in a code. "I'll see you and your vehicle get back to the embassy. Separately." After a few hurried words, he repocketed the device. "How did you get out of the embassy in the first place?"

"I told all I would be at prayer. Thus would I be left alone. I knew when the guards would be at early-evening sacrament. I knew which exits were not fully scanned." Tsecha felt his inside jacket pocket, where his own black box rested. "I knew what to do when they were."

"And your clothes?"

"Hidden in the Exterior Security outpost which shares our property border. If such were found in my quarters, I would be made Haárin, and truly. But if such are found in a humanish place . . . ?" Tsecha hunched his shoulders in a most humanish shrug.

Lucien smiled. Differently, this time. Often had Hansen smiled at him in that way, when they spoke of changes to come. "You're quite different than I imagined, nìRau."

"Have you ever been in a war, Lucien?" Tsecha guessed the answer, but waited for the man to shake his head. "One learns the most alarming things in a war. You think you forget them, but you do not. They wait in your memory. They never leave." *This I know, as does my hidden Captain.*

Lucien stared at him in question. But before Tsecha could explain further, the skimmer the lieutenant had summoned glided up to the curb. Tsecha eased into the well-cushioned backseat, which, if not as demanding as a Vynshàrau chair, compensated by being as comfortable as a Vynshàrau bed. As the vehicle drifted down the street, Tsecha closed his eyes. The next thing he knew, the humanish was calling him awake, telling him they had reached the embassy.

contaminated by being in contact with it in Wendelin Beer-
helter system differed and at the street lamps a motor chugged.
The following is braced. Transformers have called up her visitor
taken just then had reached the cableway.

THE THIRD DAY

THE THIRD DAY

CHAPTER 21

What do you think, Eamon?

Still the ugliest girl in the bar, John. DeVries's *r*s rolled like pebbles down a hillside. Jani felt his breath abrade her newly grown cheek as he leaned closer. *Not enough booze in the Commonwealth to make me take that home.*

She can hear you, Eamon. John's voice rumbled, the warning growl of a watchdog.

I know. Jani could hear the smile in DeVries's voice. *So what?* Brutal chill washed over the fresh skin of her torso as he yanked down her sheet. *I still think we should have given her bigger tits.*

No words after that. Sounds of a scuffle. DeVries's startled yelp. The whine of a door mechanism being forced open, then closed.

Footsteps.

Don't listen to him. John pulled up the thermal sheet and tucked it under her chin. *You're beautiful. Val made sure.* Then came silence. The hum of a skimgurney. Another trip to another lab. Another immersion tank. More jostling, jostling, jostling. . . .

"God damn you, Risa!" The mild rocking ramped to a Level Ten landquake. "Wake up! *Now!*"

Jani's head pounded. She forced open one eye. Saw red. Hair. Glowing in too-bright light. "Where's John?"

"Who the hell is John?" Fingers worked into Jani's hair, tilted her head up.

White white ceiling ceiling oh shit—! Her stomach shuddered. She closed her eye.

"Oh no. Don't you dare pass out on me." Skittering footsteps like fingernails on glass. Running water. "Stay awake this time, damn you!"

Cold. Wet. On her face, her neck, her hands. She opened both eyes this time as she licked away the droplets that had fallen on her lips.

"Are you thirsty?" Angevin's face lightened. "Good. Thirsty, I can handle." She stared at the soggy washcloth as though it had appeared by magic, then folded it and laid it across Jani's forehead. "Be right back."

Jani blinked, testing her films. The cloth slid down her face and settled in a drippy wad in the middle of her chest. Cold water soaked through her shirt, darkening the blue to black. She shivered.

"Where the hell is—" Angevin's voice bounced into the tiled bathroom from the kitchenette. "Oh, I found it—never mind." Sounds of running. "Is this ok?"

Jani turned her head. Carefully.

Angevin stood in the doorway holding a filled glass. "It's helgeth. Is that ok? I saw all the dispos in the front of the cooler—figured it was your favorite."

Jani nodded. Worked her stiff jaw. "Ye—yes. Thanks." She struggled into a sitting position and wrapped her shaky hands around the glass. The first swallow stripped the film from her mouth and some of the haze from her brain. "What time is it?"

"Two in the morning. At least it was when I—" Angevin glanced at her timepiece. "It's two-twenty now. I found you here on the floor. You came to a couple times, but you kept drifting out again. You've got an awful knock on your forehead. Scared me. I thought you had a concussion. What the hell happened to you?"

Out for almost six hours, eh? Jani forced herself to sip the juice. What went down in a hurry had a nasty habit of coming up the same way. "How did you get in here?"

"Housekeeping let me in." Angevin squatted on the tiled floor. She wasn't dressed for an early-morning call. In her green-velvet evening suit and pearl jewelry, she looked like an upper-class cricket. "I said you had some papers Durian needed, but that you weren't answering your comport. Everybody knows Durian—they let me in out of sympathy."

"You found me unconscious on my bathroom floor and didn't call a doctor?"

"No." Angevin wavered under Jani's hard stare. "I kept thinking about Lucien, about what I picked up for you. If anything happened to you, Durian would have found an excuse to search your suite." Worry dulled her eyes to brown. "I didn't want to get you into trouble."

"Thanks." Jani took a larger swallow of juice. "What's going on?"

"All our staff meetings have been canceled until further notice. Durian's been bumping all his appointments, but no one knows why."

"He saw me this afternoon." Jani hesitated. "Make that yesterday afternoon."

Angevin sat down on the floor and plucked the washcloth from its damp resting spot in Jani's lap. "He's been making lots of calls to other Cabinet Houses. No one's returning them. We were supposed to have a working dinner with the head of Commerce Doc Control tonight, but they canceled with about an hour's notice. Durian ordered me to stay put in my office, but he won't tell me anything." She twisted the cloth, sending more water dripping to the tile.

Jani drained her glass, then flexed her neck and shoulders. She could almost feel the sugar flood her bloodstream. "He met with Colonel Doyle."

Angevin shook her head. "He saw her, but not for long. Ginny teaches an advanced judo class three nights a week. A friend of mine takes it. Ginny was there tonight, same as always." Her eyes lightened to mossy ice. "What's going on?"

"What do you mean?"

"This involves Steve, doesn't it? He's in it up to his ears, isn't he?"

Jani rubbed a smudge on her glass. "I have no way of—"

"Don't give me that crap!" Angevin threw the cloth to the floor and bounded to her feet. Her green demiheels clicked on the glassy floor like finger cymbals. "He's been pulling some scam with that bonehead Guernsey buddy of his. Betha. I tried to warn him about her, but would he listen? Hell, no. I mean, what am I, anyway? Just a 'posh little anti-colonial Earthbounder' who doesn't understand what it means to have to work my way up!"

"That's what it sounded like to me," Jani muttered.

Angevin crouched down and grabbed a handful of Jani's collar. "Well that just shows you don't know everything either. So he's colony—it bothers him a hell of a lot more than it bothers me!" She released her, then started patting the rumpled material back into shape. "So," she said, her eyes on her task, "how bad is it?"

Jani took a steadying breath. "He could go to jail for a very long time. Betha jazzed paper for Lyssa. Steve helped her cover it up."

"Fuck. And the general audit's next week." Angevin sagged to the floor. "Why?"

"Loyalty to another Guernsey kid. The need to show up a system he hates and wants to join at the same time."

"Yeah." Angevin picked up the discarded cloth and twisted it into knots. "So how did you find out so much? Did Steve tell you?" She gave the cloth a particularly strong yank.

Jani gave a quick rundown of Lyssa's possible discovery of Acton van Reuter's dealings with the Laumrau. "If we can prove Lyssa was killed because of what she knew, I think we hand the Cabinet Court a much bigger problem than two low-level dexxies jazzing docs. They won't get off scot-free, but since they were involved in bringing a much greater crime to light, they won't sit in jail until they're eighty, either."

"And you trust Betha to see this through?"

"What else can she do? If she goes to any of her superiors with things as they now stand, she's screwed. I also tried to impress upon her the fact that, if she flees, her life on the run would be hell."

"Might work." Angevin made a sour face. "I have my doubts." She stared at the floor for a moment. When she looked up, her eyes were glistening. "Why did he shut me out? Why didn't he tell me?"

"In case it went to hell, he didn't want you involved."

Angevin's anxious expression did a slow melt into despair. She buried her face in her hands. "He puts his ass on the line for that cow, but he can't trust me enough to see him through!"

"Accessory after the fact."

"Bonehead." Angevin sniffled into her hands. "Is it too late to volunteer for save-the-idiot duty? I can't just sit around and wait for the ax to fall—I have to do something."

Jani maneuvered into a crouch, stopping every so often to let the private star show between her ears wink out. Her right knee popped as she rose. "You know, he may be doing you a favor."

"Yeah." Angevin straightened without any joints cracking. "But I'm going where he's going." She smiled sadly. "Believe it or not, I actually feel better. I thought Steve dumped me because he started sleeping with Betha."

Jani bit her lip before *extreme stress has made people do stranger things* slipped out. She checked herself in the mirror, dabbed cold water on her bruise, then toweled her face in an effort to rub some life into her ashen cheeks.

"Of course," Angevin continued with brittle gaiety, "if they are having it off, they won't have to worry about jail, will they?" She cracked her knuckles, the sound amplified by the tile into a rapid-fire of gravel crunches. "Let's go," she said as she clicked out of the bathroom.

"Coming, Your Excellency." Jani gave her face one last swipe and tossed the towel into the sink.

Jani wanted to work off the last of her muddle, and Angevin was pumping enough adrenaline to stock Neoclona for a month, so they walked the underground route to Interior Main. It was well populated for that hour of the morning. They passed grocery-laden skimtrollies, laundry and supply skiffs, and other vehicles that inhabited the world beneath the buildings.

All calm on the surface, but down here we have the business end of the duck. Jani walked quietly for a few minutes, her duffel bouncing comfortably against her left hip, when an unpleasantly familiar sound claimed her attention. She pulled up short as an overloaded skiff eased past them, the whine of its lift array pitched dangerously high. She took off after the vehicle, waving off Angevin's protest.

"You're too heavy!" She pointed to the skiff's cargo of a huge, chocolate-hued truewood desk, topped with a bookcase for sauce and a serving table as the tottering cherry. "Break that load down!"

"What?" The driver blinked at Jani as though coming out of a daze. "I'm not going to haul this stuff all the way back to Private."

"No, you're not. You're going to unload that bookcase and table right here."

"Yeah, right," the driver said. "In your dreams, lady."

"Don't. Move." Jani stared at the side of the driver's face, could almost hear the scrape of her grinding teeth. "You've had safety training, I assume?"

The woman's glance flicked down at the vehicle's dash, where the load gauge must have been thumping red like an overworked heart. She hesitated. "Yeah, but—"

"You know the damage that can occur when a mag shield fails in an enclosed space? To systems? To nearby human brains? Yours and those of all the poor innocents who just happen to be walking by?"

"Yea—*yes*, but—"

"Not to mention what could happen if the hyperacid fumes from blown battery cells ooze along for the ride?"

"Yes, *ma'am*, but—"

"Break that load down. Now." Jani bit back the *spacer* just in time. Although it would have fit. The woman, close-cropped hair greyed at the temples, coverall sleeves and pants legs knife-creased, had suddenly developed the wild-eyed look of a person who had thought her order-taking days long over. She stepped off the skiff, grapplers in hand, and started unloading the table. The task began in grudging silence, although the words, *thought I left this behind at fuckin' Fort Sheridan* drifted down to Jani as she and Angevin continued on their way to Main.

"What the hell—?" Angevin glanced back at the muttering driver. "You really did whack your head, didn't you?"

"What do you mean?" Jani asked. The last traces of nausea had passed, taking with it the fuzzy-headedness and trembling in her thighs.

"Were you in the Service? Jeez, she almost saluted you."

"No, she didn't."

"I saw her arm tense. She wanted to." Angevin shook her head. "*I* wanted to." She gave Jani a worried look. "Or maybe she just wanted to belt you. But she didn't. What are you? I mean, really?"

I don't think I know, anymore. Fingering through her sense of calm, Jani sensed an unwelcome edginess, the feeling of being *au point*. She sensed the business end of her own duck paddling furiously, quacking for her to wake up. *Something is wrong with me.* Something more than travel lag, a stomach unsettled by stress and years of strange foods, a back wrenched by too many cheap mattresses. "I'm just an Interior staffer on special assignment," she answered hastily, as she recalled again how the garage guy had behaved in the days before his collapse.

"Yeah, ok. Whatever you say." Angevin fell silent for a time, then piped, "Wish you could bottle that voice—I'd buy it and use it on Durian."

Muscles aches. Disorientation.

"He'd shit himself. Twice."

Mood swings? She'd been so tightly wrapped for so long, how could she judge? *Chronic indigestion? Oh, hell.*

"Then I'd use it on Steve. He'd never cut me out again."

Am I really sick? Jani shivered, even though the tunnel air felt comfortably warm. *Dying?* She heard Angevin mutter something about stupid shoes, and followed her to a vacant two-seater parked at a mini-charge. Without thinking, Jani got in on the passenger side. Angevin could drive. She didn't feel up to it.

CHAPTER 22

Angevin's office, at the opposite end of the wing from Durian Ridgeway's, at first looked like a smaller version of her boss's grey aerie.

It was only upon closer inspection that the differences became obvious. Instead of Durian's great art, Angevin had hung holos of family and friends on her walls. From a well-lit place overlooking the sitting area, Hansen Wyle's face, young enough for the uninformed to think him Angevin's twin brother, smiled down.

She's doing ok, Jani thought at the portrait. *She's got your mouth and your temper, and your knack for sussing people out. It's going to take some effort for her to shake off Ridgeway, but she's got a colony boy to help her. You'd like him, I think. Too bad you're not here to wipe the Earth glitter from his eyes.*

"Tell me what you're looking for." Angevin sat down at her desk and activated her workstation. "I've got top-level clearance—I can find you anything you need."

"Can you get into Cabinet Court evidence files?" Jani dragged a chair around to Angevin's side of the desk.

"Oh, you don't ask for much, do you?" Angevin fingered her way through one color-coded screen after another. "This is going to be a one-shot, you know. As soon as systems sense me in there, they'll shut down and trace back."

Jani dug into her duffel for Lucien's jig. "This should help," she said as she attached the device to Angevin's workstation. "I've got passwords, too."

Angevin accepted the piece of wrapping paper with held breath. "That goddamn toy soldier," she said as she read the list of words. "I am not going to ask—I do not want to know." She uttered the first few passwords, then paused. "Where are we going?"

"Rauta Shèràa," Jani said. "Both Base and Consulate. SRS-1 designates."

"This is what you were doing in the Library, wasn't it?"

"Yes. I had to quit before I could finish."

"What do you think you'll find there?" Angevin looked directly at her display, uttered a few passwords in Hortensian German, then turned back to Jani as she waited for the codes to clear. "A signed letter from Acton van Reuter confessing to everything?"

Jani rubbed her face, then looked around for a source of something cold to drink. "A few communication logs with the right dates and names could serve the same function." She couldn't spot any ewers or coolers and made do with a trip to the bathroom sink. "I know when his Excellency was putting in his time at the Consulate, his father checked up on him on a fairly regular basis." *Boy, did I know.* She filled a large dispo from the tap, drained it, and filled it again. "Acton must have had a source or two there. It was a well-known fact he didn't approve of his son working so far from home."

Angevin nodded. "Yeah, I heard he was a real stick. Durian calls him The Old Hawk. Like he was some kind of god."

"If you were an Earth-firster who believed in keeping the colonies on a short leash, he was." Jani returned to her seat, dispo in hand. "Prime Minister Cao was a disciple of his, whether she'll admit it now or not. Her first major seat was on Acton's Back Door Cabinet—that interim election he won after Nawar was forced to resign, right after the idomeni kicked us out. Cao served as Deputy Finance Minister, I think."

Angevin toyed with her touchboard. "Maybe she just played up to him to get her foot in the big door. Wouldn't be the first time an old blowhard got sucked down his own pipe."

Jani pretended not to hear Angevin's tacit admission with

regard to Durian Ridgeway. "Cao tries to sound more moderate now," she continued, "but she's coming down pretty hard on Ulanova's efforts to expand the concept of colonial semiautonomy. Not that I think the Exterior Minister's motives are pure."

Angevin folded her arms, her eyes fixed on her flickering screen. "Durian thinks she wants to be some kind of empress. Of course, he's just repeating His Excellency's opinion. If he had to choose between Empress Ulanova and political oblivion, though, he'd crown her himself."

Jani hid her grin at Angevin's assessment of her superior. *What does Nema think when he looks at you? Does he look for a copy of Hansen and come away disappointed?* He never grasped how different it could be for humanish, especially a pretty humanish female laboring under her legendary father's shadow. But Hansen the iconoclast appreciated the rebel. Would he have understood that his daughter was being as daring in her way as he had been in his?

But you know how she really feels—she's got your face on her wall where she can see it at all times.

"We're in the index." Angevin's fingers drummed against the arms of her chair. "There are executive staff comlogs and junior up-and-comer comlogs. Affiliated Service staff. Security." Her eyes widened. "There was even a kitchen comlog. Had to be, I guess. We must have had a hell of a time shipping food into Rauta Shèràa."

Doe, you just said a mouthful and a half. Jani had been involved in negotiating the supply shipments. That was due in part to her training and education, but also to the fact that the Laumrau had seemed afraid of her even then.

I was Nema's, and the first skirmishes had already taken place in the Vynshà strongholds in the south. The Laumrau felt sure the chief propitiator's Eyes and Ears would deliberately botch a shipment schedule, sending the wrong type of humanish food into Rauta Shèràa at the wrong time. That would have brought severe dishonor upon their blessed dominant city, providing the Vynshà with a compelling reason to force the Laumrau to relinquish their power. *Maybe I should have screwed up. I could have saved us all a great deal of trouble.*

"Try the executive staff logs first," she said to Angevin. "The Old Hawk was status-conscious, even when it came to snitches."

"Strong words, Risa. Almost as though you speak from personal experience." Angevin keyed in Jani's directive, then tossed her an inquisitive look. "Durian said you've spent your entire career 'working out.' Did you ever cross paths with our minister's late daddy?"

Paths, words, swords. Jani weighed her words. "The occasional order trickled down. I was pretty low-level back then. Didn't suffer many direct hits."

"Were you ever on Shèrá? My dad spent eight years there, with school and his work as Laumrau liaison. That's why it surprises me that Durian admires him so much. He and Acton van Reuter were constantly at each other's throats. It wasn't until I was at university that my mom finally told me about some of the battles they'd had. Maybe she thought it would scare me, keep me from studying paper. She told me van Reuter actually threatened my dad with a treason charge if he didn't cease and desist in his efforts to improve idomeni-human relations."

Jani dredged her memories, trying to separate the things she could have heard through the intelligence grapevine from those only a deep insider could know. It wasn't easy—like trying to cleave a single person and keep both halves alive.

"Acton had Laumrau support in that, actually," she finally said. "Everyone at the top of the tree gets scared when the ground beneath starts shaking. Parallels what's going on now. The Vynshàrau are having a hell of a time bringing the Haárin to heel, even though Haárin have been Vynshàrau hounds for the past several generations. And of course, we have the colonial problem."

"On the macro and micro level." Angevin made a wry face as she entered a series of rapid keyings. "This isn't working."

Jani strained for a better view of the display. "What's wrong?"

"Don't look at it!" Angevin gave Jani a one-armed shove that propelled her back into her chair. "My retinal lock's activated. If the display senses you looking at it, it'll shut my workstation down, and I'll need to get Ginny Doyle here in person to get it back up." She exhaled with a shudder. "Ginny gets very 'Colonel-ly' when she's rousted out of bed at three in the morning." She barked a few more commands at her screen, then slumped back in defeat. "It won't let me in. I'm using all the words you gave me, and it won't let me in."

Jani edged forward as much as she dared. "What's the reason code?"

"PM-seven eighty."

"Lock-down by the Prime Minister?"

"More than that. An examiner's lien. They're not even letting the members of the Court look at it now." Angevin's voice dropped to a whisper. "They know we're here."

"Not if that jig's working like it's supposed to." Unless Lucien had set her up. Jani took another gulp of water. What she had consumed so far sloshed in her stomach like an internal sea, whitecaps, undertow, and all. "I've got Ulanova's passwords. She's driving the Court—if she can't get in, nobody can. Back out and try again." She watched Angevin work. As the minutes passed, she grew conscious of a distinctive aroma. "I think we have company," she whispered.

"What?" Angevin scowled as she picked up the scent. "That jerk." She turned toward her door. It was just barely ajar, the crack scarcely visible.

"Don't you arm a proximity alarm when you work late?" Jani asked.

"Why bother? Who the hell can get up here?" Angevin punched her touchboard, activating too many pads at once and eliciting a squeal from the helpless electronic array. Then, faint as the clove scent in the air, a smile of triumph flicked to life. "You may as well come in, Steve," she called out. "We know you're there."

The seconds ticked by. Then the door eased open and Steve stepped inside. He still wore the clothes he'd had on when Jani had last seen him, but the overall effect had now degraded to distinctly-rumpled-and-needs-a-shave-to-boot. Portrait of a young man who had bought dinner from a machine and slept in his office.

"I were just walking by," he began lamely, the telltale

nicstick smoking weakly in his hand. "Saw lights. Wondered what were up." His eyes chilled as he looked at Angevin. "My my, aren't we dressed fancy for the office." He sneered. "Oh. Right. Stupid of me. You had a *dinner* tonight."

"It was canceled."

"Oh. That's too bad." He smiled too brightly at Jani. "Well, Risa, you're looking well!"

Jani eyed Angevin, who looked quite pinched around the mouth. "Thanks, but I don't see how that's possible. Angevin found me on my bathroom floor. Too much to drink at dinner." She fingered the tender bruise on her forehead. "I doubt I look any better than you do." Steve winced at that, while Angevin stiffened. *Good—piss them both off.*

Silence filled every available space. Angevin sat with her arms crossed, eyes fixed on her bare desktop. Steve rocked slowly from one foot to the other.

"She told me." Angevin jerked her chin toward Jani. "I had to hear it from a stranger. You couldn't tell me."

Steve stepped toward the desk, one foot in front of the other, like a man on a balance beam. "Didn't want it to rub off on you." He flicked the nicstick into the trashzap. "Didn't want you to go through what the others did during the purge."

"So you hooked up with *her*? Talked about it all with *her*? And left me to wonder what the hell happened?"

"Betha needs a friend." Steve toed the carpet. "Needs support. You're different. You're a *Wyle*. You don't need anybody."

Angevin closed her eyes and covered her mouth with her hand.

"Well, we both need you now," Jani said. "We're trying to code into Court of Inquiry evidence files and systems won't let us in."

"Oh, *phfft*, you're not getting any of that," Steve said, "it all got seven-eightied about an hour ago. Expectin' an examiner's lien from Cao's head dex any minute now. They're shuttin' us down."

Angevin spun her chair to face him. "How do you know!"

He shrugged. "Everyone's talking about it down the hall. Third shift's in a tizz. Figured it would happen, though. Cao never were happy with all that House paper we shipped her last month. She claimed we were withholding from an Official Inquiry. Her complaint got bumped to your boss for reply." He eyed Angevin suspiciously. "Airn't heard nothing of it since. Till tonight."

"This is the first I've heard of any of this." Angevin glared at Steve. "Just one more thing you couldn't tell me!"

"Don't look at me like that. We were *sworn*!" Steve pulled at his pockets and freed a fresh 'stick. "Doyle stood at the door while we got all the paper together, watched us like a bloody vulture. Ever see her when she's on? All she needs are spurs and a whip." He dragged a chair in the vicinity of the desk, closer to Jani than to Angevin, and sat down with a heavy sigh. "I saw her in my sleep for a week after, bald head shinin'."

"That's exactly the paper I asked you to look for." Jani looked at Steve until he began leaning in Angevin's direction. "I would have appreciated it if you'd have told me you couldn't get it."

Steve cracked the 'stick's ignition tip. "Didn't say that, did I? All I said were you wouldn't be able to access the fiche through Ange's station." He studied Jani through his smoky veil. "I can get the originals."

"You held back Consulate paper from a Court of Inquiry, too!" Jani's temples started to throb.

"I'm sure he had a good—I'm sure he had a reason." Angevin's eyes were now as stormy as Jani's stomach. "Which he will explain to us now."

Steve scooted his chair away from the desk. "The originals we've got here were from His Excellency's private library. Willed to him by his father. Justice is supposed to decide soon whether private papers can be claimed by the PM under a blanket subpoena. Cao wouldn't tell us why exactly she wanted them, so van Reuter told her to blow. Betha and me split 'em up—the Lady had given them to her for safekeeping."

"Lyssa?" Jani nodded. That made sense. A great deal concerning old Acton must reside in those papers. "I want both sets. Where's Betha?" She stood up. "Home?"

Steve shook his head. "Vacant office down the hall. I saw

her a few hours ago. She told me she'd probably be here most of the night, but that she'd have her papers in the morning. I'd bring mine from where I stashed them in my flat. We'd give them to you together.'' He blinked. ''Teamwork, you know.''

Angevin growled. ''Teamwork, my ass! I'll show her teamwork.'' She swatted her workstation into standby, then ran from the room. Steve and Jani looked at one another, then pelted after her.

The vacant office was dark. Its trashzap had been recharged.

''What time do the cleaners come through?'' Jani asked an extremely subdued Steve.

''Eleven,'' he replied. ''She said she'd be here till morning.'' He pulled open a drawer, pushed it closed. ''She wouldn't have run out on me.'' He leaned against the desk. ''She wouldn't have left me behind.'' He pushed a hand through his hair, his eyes wide and lost. Angevin reached out to him, hesitated, then muttered, ''Screw this,'' and threw herself into his arms.

''She probably went home,'' Jani said after a time. ''I'll try to get in touch with her from here. You two try her place, then get some sleep. We'll meet in Angevin's office at oh-eight. Don't forget your half of the docs. Steve?'' She waited in the doorway for some response from the enmeshed pair, finally detecting a hint of a nod from Steve. ''Oh-eight,'' she repeated, closing the door softly.

The grumble in her stomach sounded animal. She stopped at a vend cooler in Doc Control's deserted cafeteria and bought juice and a sandwich. Then she dragged a chair over to the Houseline array in the corner of the room. In between mouthfuls, she made calls. House Security, the desk clerk at the Interior employee hostel, every third-shift manager she could find. The Doc pool. The parts bins. The Library. Every cafeteria in the complex. No one recalled seeing Betha, although the parts-bins clerk remembered her afternoon visit.

Personnel refused to give Jani Betha's homecode. When she dropped Evan's name, they told her she needed Ridgeway's sign-off to get the number.

She left the cafeteria and roamed the Doc Control halls,

checking every vacant office and conference room. The rest rooms, men's and women's. The alternate breakroom. Janitor's closets, storage rooms, stairwells. She stopped short of pushing up ceiling tiles and checking crawl spaces. Harder to cram a body in a space like that. Messier. She didn't want to risk destroying evidence.

You've got death on the brain. Betha's home in bed. Take the hint. Jani trudged to the elevators and rode down to the restricted-access charge lots. On her way to the Main-Private tunnel, a Security guard tried to stop her, but when he looked her in the face he hesitated. Then he stepped aside and let her pass.

CHAPTER 23

The skimmer shuddered as it skirted the border between Exterior and Shèrá property and ran afoul of both sets of tracking arrays. Tsecha countered by applying the barest twitch to the vehicle's controls, redirecting it back within the Exterior domain. The skimmer's agitation, brought on by the confounding signals of two different systems, ceased immediately.

Tsecha's trembling, however, continued for some time. *This godless cold.* Rolling whiteness stretched about him in every direction save the east, where the lake-defining blackness stopped it short.

He searched the approaching darkness for the flicker of Security vehicle illumins. Ulanova's. His own. It made no difference—both would be as enemy to him. He felt for the Haárin-made shooter, a souvenir of his war, nestled in the chest pocket of his coat. *However, I cannot shoot at them.* Such would constitute an incident.

"So long, since I have taken part in an incident." Tsecha bared his teeth fully in the dimness of the skimmer cabin, then almost lost control of his vehicle as the expression degenerated into a jaw-flexing yawn. He had done much since his return from the play, little of which would have received sanction from either his Temple or his Oligarch.

He slowed as he approached the Exterior outpost, activating his black box at the same time. The device, also of Haárin origin, blocked the automated concrete booth's scanning equipment and prevented its outside alarms from activating.

It also took the extra step of misleading the scanners, assuring them they were not being interfered with at all.

The only drawback to the ingenious device lay in the fact the designers believed they understood humanish systems much better than they actually did. The resulting errors in the interference program meant Tsecha had only a very short time to do that which he came to do.

Three humanish minutes, in fact, beginning from the time he first activated the unit.

On average.

So cold! He half jumped, half slid from the skimmer cockpit to the thermacrete slab on which the outpost rested, grunting in relief as his boots struck dry deck. The thermacrete had apparently done its job in preventing any snow from building up around the outpost, but Tsecha still stepped carefully in the pitch-darkness. Heat cells did occasionally fail. Failure here meant ice patches. Padding and shock absorption worked well for youngish, perhaps, but he did not trust them to protect his old bones.

Besides, if he did fall, who would rescue him? *Cats and police*, his Hansen had said, *only come when you* don't *want them*. Tsecha tapped the toe of his boot against the thermacrete, planting his foot only when he felt certain he would not slip. *Tap, step, tap, step*—like the odd, rapid gait of a shorebird, and truly. But he could not fall. He had come too far to risk any mistake.

The door slid partially open. Illumins activated to the dimmest setting. Once inside the windowless concrete booth, Tsecha hurried to the small, plastic-covered bench that served as the supplies bin, cracking the lock with a soundkey that also had been made by Haárin. *What would Vynshàrau have done without our most excellent Haárin?* He pulled the large tool pouch containing his humanish clothes from the recesses of his oversize coat, but before he laid his bundled disguise to rest, he rummaged through the cluttered bin.

Ah! It lay beneath the first layer of half-empty parts kits and battered all-weather gear. Most easy to find if you knew to look for it, knew from repeated visits the position of every object in the bin. A crumpled note. Tattered stone-colored parchment trimmed in dark Exterior red. *My Lieutenant. My new friend.* Tsecha stuffed the note inside his coat, worked his tool pouch to the bottom of the bin, relocked the lid, and hurried outside.

The outpost's proximity alarm illumins fluttered to half-life just as Tsecha threw himself into his skimmer, dying to dark as soon as he jerked the vehicle back within its boundary. He flitted along the border, hopped a pile of construction debris, then banked around a broad stand of winter-bare trees. The embassy appeared, its lakeside face, sheltered from the sight of godless humanish habits, enhanced by large windows, balconies, and enclosed patios.

Tsecha could see no idomeni in any of the windows, but that, of course, did not mean they could not see his skimmer. Not that they would take special notice if they did. The vehicle, after all, belonged to Exterior, and traveled along Ulanova's side of the border.

Tsecha eased back on the accelerator as he approached the Exterior maintenance shed located so conveniently close to his embassy. He coaxed the skimmer into its charge slot with finesse acquired through repetition, then fled across the border at the place his black box told him he could pass unnoticed.

Tsecha returned to his rooms by way of back stairways and little-used passages, Lucien's note resting like something burning against his chest. Not since the war had he felt so. Then, every communication held life and death between its lines. For himself. For his valued friends. And even for a few esteemed enemies, without whose presence everyday life would have become a desolation indeed.

My Lucien thinks I play at a game, I think. Tsecha sneaked into his front room and immediately began peeling away his protective clothing. Then he hurried to his favored chair, the crumpled paper clasped in his hand. On the way, he hesitated, detoured to his worktable, and recovered his handheld from its recess. What if, as Hansen before him, Lucien took it as his godly duty to instruct an idomeni in the nuances of English?

I will need to study this note as I do my files. Tsecha unfolded the Exterior parchment, and stared. What had he expected? An offer of an excursion? A suggestion of how to better pass himself off as humanish? A simple greeting?

He saw nothing like that.

Instead, Tsecha read his language. *His* language, in all its complexity, High Vynshàrau as his Sànalàn might compose if she were male and member of a military skein.

And the words. The phrases. The fear in the lines. Only during the war had he read such, when his sect-sharers had watched Rauta Shèràa from the hills above and Hansen pleaded with him that their time to act had grown most short.

> . . . *get her out . . . am meeting with her "captors" tomorrow evening . . . I can only get her so far . . . am depending on you . . .*

Tsecha's grip on the note weakened and it fluttered to the bare floor. Such familiar words. So did Hansen plan his meeting with John Shroud. *But my Hansen died*, on the morning of his meeting day. Most sorry were the Haárin, to have bombed a building containing humanish. But then, the humanish had left their untouchable enclave of their own free will, choosing to interfere in idomeni affairs. Thus they were no longer blameless in any of this, were they? The chief propitiator's Eyes and Ears had herself set the precedent. That being the case, where lay the disorder, or the blame?

But the Haárin, with their love of disorder, would feel that way, would they not? The members of the Vynshà Temple, positioning themselves for their ascension to *rau*, felt quite differently. They had seen how the godless events of Knevçet Shèràa had demoralized the Laumrau. While they had most willingly taken advantage of their foes' disorientation, such did not mean they wished to chance the same happening to them.

Tsecha felt a tightening in his soul. *They told me Hansen's death rediscovered order, Kilian's death resuscitated order, while my death*—he bent to pick up the fallen note—*my death would confirm order had truly returned.* But he had talked them out of killing him, just as he had earlier talked them into allowing humanish into their cities and schools. The gods had gifted him with the power to persuade. They had allowed him the wit to know when to take action and how.

And they had provided him patience, so he could wait so

long for his Captain to return to him and not go mad.

Tsecha glanced at the timepiece on his worktable. *What do you do now, John?* The city where the man worked—Seattle—was located far west. That meant it was darker there, the middle of night. *Do you sleep, John, or do you work?* He walked across the room to his comport and keyed in a code any humanish with a Chicago city directory could find.

The face of a young, dark-haired male filled the display. "Neoclona Chicago. May I help—" His eyes widened as he realized whose face filled his display. Tsecha bared his teeth to alleviate his alarm, but the action only seemed to heighten his agitation. "May—m-may—oh shit!" The stricken face dissolved from the screen, leaving Tsecha to stare at nothing.

Humanish see bared teeth as reassurance. Hansen said so. Tsecha tried to key in the code of another Neoclona department, but the idiot youngish had activated some sort of lock which made such impossible. Too much time passed as Tsecha tried every code combination of which he could think to break the connection. *I cannot ask the communications skein for help—then all will know to whom I spoke.* He made ready to remove the unit's cover and disconnect its power source in an effort to reset the system. It could damage his unit beyond repair; if his Security had their way, he would not soon receive another. The risk was considerable, but he didn't know what else to do.

Just as he prepared to unclip the display screen from its support, it returned to life with a flash. This male as well, he had never seen. Pleasantly dark, with the facial hair many humanish males grew so easily, clipped to a sharp point at the end of the chin. "NìRau," the man said in a pleasant voice, "John warned me you might call."

"I must speak with him," Tsecha said. "Whoever you are, tell him he is to talk with me!"

"My name is Calvin Montoya, nìRau, and I'm a physician, like John. He has given me some instructions, which he recently gave the heads of all the major Neoclona facilities on Earth." He fingered the hair on his chin. "If you try to contact him through us, we are to tell you to go to hell. If you have any doubts as to what we are saying, John has told us to tell you to, and this is a direct quote, 'Use your goddamn handheld.' That is the message I am supposed to give you, nìRau. I am then supposed to end the call and report the attempted contact to John immediately.''

Tsecha sat back in his chair, nodding as the man spoke. Quite a clear communication. Most as idomeni, and most unlike Physician Shroud. ''Albino John may have given you meaning,'' he said to the face on the screen, ''but Val Parini, I believe and truly, has given you the words. Physician Parini always enjoyed speaking as idomeni. He thought himself most shocking to other humanish as he did so. I am to guess from this he has been called back from vacation? Please greet him for me when next you report to him.'' Then, to ensure all would be taken well, Tsecha ended by baring his teeth.

Unlike the youngish, Physician Montoya maintained his composure, and even bared his teeth in return. ''Alb—John warned me about you, nìRau. Something along the lines of, 'Don't let him get a goddamn foot in the door, or he'll walk out with half the goddamn facility.' I believe I understand his concern.'' He pushed a hand through his hair. ''Now I am supposed to end this call, or John will be angry.''

''John is a stern dominant, Calvin?'' Tsecha always sought to call humanish by their primary names as soon as he learned them. Such a simple act, but it seemed to make them so happy. And cooperative.

''Yes, nìRau, and I do like my job.''

Yes, but you do not wish to end this call, because you are curious. ''And what did Physician DeVries suggest you should do if I contacted you, Calvin?''

The physician's brows arched. He laughed. ''Ooh boy— John warned us about the charm, too.'' He jerked his shoulders, a gesture that could have meant anything, and thus helped Tsecha not at all. ''Actually, nìRau, what Eamon suggested involved tracking your comport signal to its source, then dropping shatterboxes until only a rubble-filled crater remained.'' Calvin's smile disappeared. ''I believe he was joking.''

Left hand clenched, Tsecha gestured in the extreme negative. ''And I know he was not. Your John and your Val, I believe, accepted Eamon into their skein for his technical expertise, not his social.''

Calvin coughed. "I really have to disconnect now, nìRau."

"You must tell John—you *must* tell him I am most concerned!"

Calvin grew very still. At first, Tsecha thought the display had malfunctioned. "Your concerns are noted, nìRau. And they are being explored. Now, I must go." He disconnected before Tsecha could again speak. Most wise, actually. Given more time, bearded Calvin would surely have told him everything he wanted to know.

It is how primary names affect these walls. So desperate are they for order, they interpret such as understanding. Tsecha slumped back in his chair. *But I understand so little.* Throughout his wing of the embassy, the tonal series that signaled time for early-morning sacrament sounded. He rose and listened for the preparatory scrapes and clattering which indicated the presence of his cook-priest and her suborn in his altar room. Tsecha waited until the blessed red illumin flickered above the altar-room door, meaning the room was fit for him to enter.

The meal did not go well. Tsecha ate his grains and fruits in the wrong order, forgot to spice his meats, lost track of his prayers. *Your concerns are being explored.* Hansen had often told him how humanish explored one another's concerns. *The more they claim they do, the less they truly do. It is a well-established fact with our species.*

But he tells me my concerns are being explored, Hansen. Tsecha withdrew from his altar room and headed to his favored enclosed patio. It viewed the lake, as did they all, but if one squinted, one could also catch a glimpse of the Interior compound far down the shore. He had often done so, in days past, when he considered the soul of Acton van Reuter and where it might currently reside.

But now Tsecha stood in his enclosure, watched the illumins far down the beach, and considered Acton's son. *He and my Captain—a most seemly pairing.* Or so it had appeared at the time. *But the father forbade it, and now the father is dead.* His Lucien's words returned to him. *She hides in plain sight, nìRau.* And his Calvin's words. *Your concerns are being explored.*

"Plain sight!" Tsecha hurried from the patio to the comport booths located within the documents repository. No reason to obscure the fact of this call. This call was indeed most seemly.

Tsecha entered the code for Interior House. The young female whose face appeared on the display also maintained her composure—she had spoken with him before.

"Angevin Wyle, please, Sandra."

The female bared her teeth, as Tsecha knew she would, and directed her attention to her House console. Her expression waned. "Ms. Wyle is unavailable, nìRau."

"Do not summon her in her office—she is not there yet."

"No, nìRau, I buzzed her residence. She's not home."

"Where is she?"

"She's left no forwarding code, nìRau." Sandra shrugged. Humanish, in Tsecha's opinion, shrugged too much. "I can leave her a message, if you wish?"

"No. No." He could not wait for messages. Another humanish came to mind. Male, this one. Slumped as the Oligarch. Red hair, though not as godly as Hansen's daughter's. "Steve!" he shouted.

"Mr. Forell in Xeno?" Sandra applied herself to her console. "I know he won't be in at this hour." The female's eyebrows rose. "His private code is blocked, nìRau."

"Blocked?"

"Blocked, nìRau." Yet another strange expression crossed the female's face. Something as a smile, and yet . . . "It means he's home, but doesn't wish to be disturbed."

"Ah."

"I can message them both, nìRau." Sandra's brow now lowered. That meant confusion. Sometimes. "Are you sure you don't want to speak to the head of Xeno? Perhaps His Excellency himself?"

"No, Sandra. Message Angevin Wyle please." He ended the call and returned to his rooms to dress for his appointments. *Today I see the Prime Minister, who will complain of my treatment of Detmers-Neumann, and a delegation from the Xhà Pathen, who will complain of my favoritism toward their brethren the laes.*

Both complaints held truth, of course. *I treat Detmers-Neumann as she deserves and the Xhà as they deserve, and for much the same reason.* Tsecha secured the privacy locks to his sanitary room. *I do not trust them.* He removed the overrobe and trousers he had donned for his excursion to the maintenance shed and prepared to lave. His scars glistened pale in the overhead illumination—he stared at them in his reflection and felt every blade slice him anew. His meal rested as a weight in his stomach, his knees ached from the leap he had made onto the thermacrete, and if John Shroud had, by some godish whimsy, appeared before him at that moment, he would with great joy have snapped the man's neck.

My Lucien knew where she was and did not tell me. His odd Lucien, who enjoyed disorder. Tsecha plunged his arms to his elbows in hot water, felt its steam condense upon and trickle down his face. *I must save her.* His Captain. With his odd Lucien's aid. And he would bury all who tried to stop him, as the Haárin had buried his Hansen.

CHAPTER 24

Jani punched her pillow and turned over. Again. Again. *I will not look at the clock*. She looked. Oh-six-thirty. She'd have to get up soon. The thought wouldn't have seemed so daunting if she had managed to fall asleep in the first place.

She rolled on her back and stared at the ceiling. Her real limbs sagged into the mattress like stalks of lead, while the fake ones felt the way they always did. She kicked off her covers, then rose in stages. One leg over the side. The other. *Sit up. Wait for the room to stop throbbing. Stand. Walk.*

Showering proved a challenge. Her upper back, a skinscape of green and purple centered by a fist-sized swelling, allowed movement, but drew the line at assault by pounding streams of water. Jani faced the main showerhead as she washed her hair and got cleanser in her eyes, thus scuttling her films. By the time she emerged, eyes stinging and back muscles twitching, her stomach had begun to ache. *Can I go back to bed?* She checked the clock again. Oh-seven-thirty. *Nope.* She refilmed, threw on another expensive but ill-fitting trouser suit, and was halfway out the door before she noticed her comport's blinking message light.

Evan had recorded the message well after their aborted dinner. Dressed in pajamas, he sat hunched at the edge of his bed like a condemned prisoner on his bunk. "Jan? I'm asking you, no, I'm *ordering* you to stop. Just stop. Meet me for breakfast, and we'll talk over the reasons. But right now, as your minister, I'm ordering you to cease your investigation." He rubbed his face, pressed his fingers to his forehead.

"Durian showed me some sceneshots, Jan. You and some punk from Exterior. I don't believe the things he told me about the two of you, but judging from the lengths to which he's gone already, I don't think it's a good idea to cross him right now. He'll do what he thinks he has to. That's his job. I'll let him. That's mine." He held a supplicating hand out to her. "I love you. I want to take care of you. Isn't that enough?" The message ended in a twinkling fade, like a dream.

Jani sat on her rumpled bed, duffel cradled in her lap. "No, Evan. It's not." She hit the touchpad and called up the time he had recorded the message. A little after one.

"Having second thoughts about bringing me here, are you?" With equal parts alcohol and Durian Ridgeway fertilizing the seeds of doubt. She hurried to the elevator, then rode down with her finger poised in front of the STOP OVERRIDE pad, ready to block anyone else from coming aboard. She didn't want to share the car with anyone. Especially someone who wanted to take care of her.

Jani entered Angevin's office to find her and Steve sitting at the desk, drinking coffee and talking in low tones. Both wore slacks and pullovers in shades of pale tan which, combined with their hair, made them look like a couple of lit matches.

Jani allowed herself a small feeling of satisfaction. *Nice to see the kids together again.* But an undercurrent of edginess and the thick haze of multiple nicsticks prevented her from thinking all was well.

Angevin confirmed the prevailing mood. "The idomeni ambassador tried to reach me early this morning. The House operator added the notation that he asked for Steve as well."

Steve waved Jani a vague greeting, then busied himself pouring her coffee from a disposable reservoir. "What do you think it means, Ris? Think he's upset we're digging into his old paper?"

Jani accepted the coffee with a grateful nod and eased into a deskside chair. "If he was, he wouldn't call you directly. He'd lodge his complaint using proper channels. First thing you'd hear of it would be when the Xeno liaison called you into the office and tore you a new orifice." She winced as she drank. The coffee tasted as though it had been filtered through a sock. "The ambassador was close to Angevin's father, I believe?" She looked to Angevin for confirmation she didn't need. "Maybe it had something to do with that?"

Angevin scowled. "God, I'd hoped that had stopped." She gave Jani a tired look and shook her head. "He tried to hook up with me as soon as he arrived. I don't know what he expected. I told him, 'I'm not my father, nìRau.' He said, 'I know, nìa—Hansen is most dead.' He's so damned literal."

Steve rocked back in his chair. "That's how their minds work. I told you, if you don't want to talk with him, I will. Knowing how blunt he is, he'll come right out and tell me what's the problem. And we'll proceed from there. I were thinkin' of callin' him after the midmorning sacrament. 'Round ten." He glanced at Jani. "Like to be there with me, Ris?"

"No." Jani choked down another swallow of coffee. "Thank you. I doubt I'd do any good." She ignored Steve's stare, leaving it to blister the side of her face. "We need to get to work. Let's see your paper."

Angevin crumpled a dispo and bounced it lightly off Steve's chest. "Tell her." Her voice tightened. "Or I will."

Steve stood, stretched, and walked to the curtained window. "Mind if I open this? Sun's a bloody bitch this early, but I need to see some light." He swept back the drape, revealing the shimmering lake, clear sky, and the sun hanging in the midst of it all like a self-suspending light set on high. "Not that bad, is it, with the filters in the glass?" He took his time pushing the drape into its niche.

"*Steve*." Angevin reached for another dispo.

Steve thumped the pane with his fist. Once. Again. "Betha's gone, ok! No one's seen her since last night. She never returned to her flat. Her half of the papers are gone, too. I checked her locker. I checked her cubicle. The office she used last night. So that's it. No one's seen her since last night, and the docs are gone. What else do you want me to say!"

Oh shit. "It's not your fault, Steve," Jani said. "We were both sure she would stick." Considering the scenarios running through her mind, Betha's merely running off would be a relief. "Where's your half?"

"My office. Locked in my desk." Steve flinched at Jani's glower. "Didn't want to be seen carrying them. Not with the lien and all."

"Let's go get them."

They had to pass the Doc Control cafeteria on the way to Steve's office. The noise made them pause; the crowd drew them inside. As they pushed their way to the front, sharp voices cut through the swell.

"*Son of a bitch—where the hell is he!*"

"Oh God." Angevin gripped Steve's arm. "That's Durian."

People turned toward them. A few pointed. The sound level dropped as though someone had flicked a switch.

"What the hell's on, Barry?" Steve called out to the stricken young man over whom Ridgeway loomed. "Someone forget to sign a req for toilet roll?"

A red-faced Durian Ridgeway pushed past bystanders. "Where the hell is Betha Concannon, Forell!" Coffee sloshed and work clothes were spattered, but no one made outraged noises. Everyone was too busy staring at Steve. Behind Ridgeway, two fully loaded Security officers shadowed into view, long-barreled shooters gripped in their glove-protected hands.

"Oh fuck." Steve took a step backward, his eyes fixed on the weapons.

"Don't run." Jani made a grab for him, but he dodged with a quick sidestep. "Whatever you do, don't—"

Steve shook off Angevin's scrabbling hands and cut for the door like a sprinter out of the blocks.

"—run." *Right.* Jani spun back around, let her bag slide to the ground, and took a step toward the nearer guard, who had raised her weapon. She gripped the barrel with both hands, tilted it to the ceiling, twisted it ninety degrees, jerked out and in. Gristly crunches cut the air, silencing onlookers' startled cries. The guard uttered a strangled half sob and sagged to her knees, her nose smashed and streaming blood, her fingers twisted.

Back muscles screaming, Jani swung the heavy weapon to her shoulder and aimed it at Ridgeway. Lousy weapon-handling on her part, but his stricken expression was worth a few broken rules.

Angevin waved and pointed toward the doorway. "Behind you. Trouble."

Jani shifted her stance to find Colonel Doyle sauntering toward her. Behind the Security chief, onlookers scattered. "Your friend won't get far, Ms. Tyi. The elevators and stairwells are already locked down." She reached out. "Hand over that weapon—it is not a crowd-control device."

"No," Jani said, "it's not. It's a V-40 Long-Range. Combat weapon. Enough power to punch you into the hallway and me through the wall if I fire. Stupid choice for indoors." She pretended to take aim at a planter. As she hoped, people scurried, ducking under tables and behind chairs.

"If you back around one more table, you're clear to the door," Angevin said. "Do you want me to get the other one?"

"*No!*" Jani shouted. One V-40 was enough. Thing had a kick like a skimmer head-on—it needed a strut support, damn it!

Just stand sideways like you're doin', and bend your back knee a tad. It'll brace you, Captain. You'll be fine.

"Thank you, Sergeant," Jani whispered. She aimed the weapon in Ridgeway's direction again. "Now, we're going to go somewhere and talk about this."

"Like hell we'll talk!" Ridgeway pointed to the door. "That bastard buggered paper with Betha Concannon. Now she's missing. The time for talk is over. I'm ranking documents examiner on-site, and I have cause. I'm declaring anarchy rules now!" He turned to Doyle. "Order a door-to-door! If the little cunt tries to bolt, shoot to kill!"

"Stop. Telling. Me. My. Job." Doyle pointed an accusing finger at Ridgeway. "*You* said the other Cabinet Doc offices were in a panic. *You* said a threat to the Commonwealth existed. Now you've scared off the only person in this building who could confirm either condition, and, mister, until you have confirmation, you do *not* have cause, and you do *not* give me orders!"

Oh good—dissension in the ranks. Does that mean I can hand this disaster-on-a-stick off to someone? Jani lowered the V-40; the other guard's shoulders sagged. She gave him a barely perceptible nod, which he returned. "I will safety the weapon and hand it to Colonel Doyle," she said. "Then we will go to a nice quiet place, and talk."

"You will be under arrest!" Ridgeway sputtered, his face purpling. "You threatened—"

"I just prevented a massacre by your order, Durian." Jani keyed the adjustment diverting the weapon's prep charge. The stock warmed as the heat dissipated. "The pulse packet from this thing could have blitzed half this room. Packets can be unpredictable, you know. I've seen them circle their targets and boomerang back on their source when conditions were right." The conditions involved magnetic interference caused by the lift-array rupture of a troop transport, but no reason to mention minor details when things were going so well.

Jani's words had the desired effect. Around her, outraged mutters rose dangerously high as a roomful of aggravated paper pushers shifted their attention to Ridgeway. She smiled at the nervous man, then handed the V-40, stock first, to Ginny Doyle. "Let's talk." Her eyes met Doyle's, and the colonel's glare turned even stonier. Jani recovered her bag and gave Angevin a smile she hoped appeared reassuring.

Jani, Angevin, and Ridgeway waited in brittle silence outside the cafeteria for Doyle to return from escorting her injured subordinate to the infirmary; they then adjourned to Ridgeway's office. He barked an order that they not be disturbed to Greer, who had witnessed the episode. The young man stood gaping at them until his boss shut the door in his face. "Probably be selling bloody tickets in a minute," Ridgeway muttered as he engaged the lock.

It was obvious he couldn't decide whom to play to. He pointedly ignored Jani as he walked to his desk, instead bestowing a look of professional neutrality upon Doyle. The colonel's narrow-eyed response was far from neutral, and could only be considered professional if you thought of occupations such as assassin. Ridgeway pulled in an unsteady breath as he sat and offered Angevin a wary half smile.

She beamed in return. "I'm thinking of finally taking your advice, Durian," she said in a sprightly tone.

Doyle glanced at Jani and cocked an eyebrow. Jani responded with a *beats me* shrug.

"Oh?" Ridgeway settled back in his chair.

"I'm going to look up those dexxies who went to the Academy with my father." Angevin paced in front of his desk and counted off on her fingers. "Senna and Tsai. Aryton and Nawar. The Big Four. The Hands and Feet and Left Armpit and whatever the hell other assorted body parts they comprise." She planted her hands on the desk's edge. "If anything happens to Steve, I will sic them on you like a pack of dogs. Mom always said I had Dad's mouth. Good a time as any to try it out, don't you think?"

During Angevin's speech, Ridgeway's expression altered from surprised anger to stern disapproval. "You've backed the wrong horse, my dear. That unfortunate young man has a long history of knocking over fences. Your championing him could do your own career irreparable harm. He's a common thug."

Doyle dragged a couple of chairs over to Ridgeway's desk. "Let's reserve judgment until we talk to the boy, Durian. My people should corral him anytime now." She sat, then motioned for Jani to do the same. "I need proof. All I see now is oversolicitous mentoring." She stared at Ridgeway, who scowled and tugged at his neckpiece.

Angevin, oblivious to Doyle's allusion, smacked a fist against her open palm. "He doesn't like Steve because he's colony." She fell into a chair and folded her arms across her chest.

Ridgeway rolled his eyes. "It's gone well beyond that, Angevin. Only an hour ago, I spoke to a friend of Ms. Concannon's. The man is ex-Service. He said she sought him out yesterday afternoon and asked him some rather peculiar questions concerning augmentation. He told me that the nature of the questions, along with Ms. Concannon's obvious distress, alarmed him. He tried all night to get back in touch with her. He even visited her flat. When he couldn't find her, he contacted me."

Doyle tapped a blunt-nailed thumb against her thigh. "It is not uncommon for young people to spend nights in apartments not their own."

Ridgeway shook his head. "It was for Betha, apparently. The poor young woman didn't have much of a social life, according to the man. So easy, to take advantage of someone like that. Lead her on.''

''What are you getting at, Durian?'' Doyle asked.

''Something unfortunate came to my attention a few days ago,'' Ridgeway said. ''It appears our Betha had worked rather closely with our late Lady. The same crap we've been dealing with for the past few months, Virginia. You know the shape we're in. It's taken all my powers of persuasion thus far to keep Justice from shutting down our Doc Control and assigning an overseer. This examiner's lien Cao's doc chief has issued against us means we now have a visit from a Court-appointed auditor to look forward to. Considering the position our Minister is in already—''

Doyle ran a hand over her glistening scalp. ''The unemployment line forms to the right. And Steven Forell, like many of us, is very fond of his job.'' She fixed the sullen Angevin with a level stare that worked on the young woman like a slap. ''I understand Mr. Forell spent a portion of the evening with you, Ms. Wyle. Could you tell us about it, please?''

Angevin shot Jani a pleading look. ''What do you want to know?''

My guess is Doyle knows it all already. Jani pressed a hand to her grumbling stomach. *She just wants to see where you especially feel the need to lie.*

Doyle's smile was deceptively reassuring. ''Just start at the beginning. What time last night did you first encounter Mr. Forell?''

''About three. Maybe a little after.''

''That late?''

''I was with Risa—we were busy.''

Doyle gave Jani a look of mild curiosity, then turned back to Angevin. ''How did Mr. Forell appear to you?''

''Fine. Normal. For him. A little pissed.'' Angevin's eyes goggled when she realized what she had said. ''At *me*. Pissed at *me*. We'd been fighting.''

''But you made up.'' Doyle smiled again. ''This morning at a little after three.''

Angevin exhaled shakily. ''Yes.''

''Then you and he left the compound together, visited Betha Concannon's flat, spent the balance of the night at his apartment, and returned here at seven-ten?''

''You've been monitoring Steve's and Angevin's movements?'' Jani asked.

''Ms. Tyi, we'll discuss your late-afternoon encounter with Forell and Concannon after I finish with Ms. Wyle.''

''Are you questioning me in connection with a crime, Colonel?''

''Not at this time, Ms. Tyi. Merely—''

''Fishing? If the issue is documents fraud, ma'am, you are neither qualified nor authorized to question me. Only a Registry mediator can do that, and since we are, last time I checked, in a peacetime, nonemergency situation—''

''Nonemergency!'' Ridgeway yanked at his neckpiece again. ''We're on the verge of being shut down, Risa—I'd shudder to think what you deem important!''

''No one's life is at stake,'' Jani replied. ''No one has died.'' *We hope.* ''We're only dealing with reputations, which may be ruined at our leisure.'' Gradually she became aware of Doyle, who pounded her chair arm like a uniformed metronome.

''Who in hell,'' she bit out, ''are you to question my authority?''

''Who in hell do I have to be? Steve bolted from the cafeteria only moments before you showed up. You must have seen him, yet you made no move to pursue him.''

''My people are searching for him now, Tyi—the sector-wide lock-down has him bottled.''

''Lock-downs can be evaded surprisingly easily by someone who knows the area. It's amazing how many people seem to know this area. Yesterday, one of the Exterior Minister's goons kidnapped me in full view of Private House. Do you even know of this?''

Doyle's shocked expression answered that question. ''What goon?''

''Stop it! Stop it!'' Angevin pounded her thighs with her fists. ''What has this got to do with Steve! What has this got to do with Nueva Madrid and all that other crap!''

At the mention of Nueva Madrid, Ridgeway took on the

strangled appearance of someone who had just swallowed his tongue.

"Angevin," Jani said, "don't open your mouth again until you've spoken to a Registry mediator."

"But I—"

"Keep your mouth shut."

Angevin rose. "This is bullshit! Steve's in trouble and you're all fighting about rules!" She dashed past Doyle and ran from the office.

"Where the hell is she going!" Ridgeway shouted, as he, Doyle, and Jani hurried into the hall.

Doyle paced halfway down the passage. "She knows where her boyfriend is, I'll bet." She spun on her heel toward Ridgeway. "You said his scanpack needed maintenance, that he'd need to be desperate to bolt without it." She motioned to two guards standing nearby. "Which repair carrel is his?"

The lock-down was tighter than Jani suspected. Or hoped. As they tried to enter the third-floor parts bins, the system balked at accepting even Doyle's palm and key card.

The stink of nutrient broth sent Ridgeway to the front desk for nose plugs. Jani trailed Doyle, Ridgeway, and the green-faced guards past the line of carrels. Only one door stood open. Angevin leaned against the jamb, a hand cupped over her mouth. "He didn't do it," she muttered as Doyle brushed past her into the tiny room. "He didn't do it."

Doyle muttered a heartfelt, "Oh shit," and turned back to Ridgeway. "Notify ComPol. Tell them we need an ambulance. And the medical examiner." As Ridgeway left to find a comport, Doyle whispered some orders to the guards, then gently maneuvered a shaken Angevin into the hall.

"He didn't do it," Angevin repeated like a desperate prayer. "He didn't do it."

Jani remained in the doorway. She could see Betha. On the floor. Far corner. No need to approach. No need to confirm. She had seen more than her share of corpses over the years.

Strange the way a body seemed to crumple in on itself after death.

Jani heard the *clack* of a charge-through being engaged. She turned to see Borgie draw alongside her, his T-40 humming its standby song. He wiped a grimy hand over his mouth. His brown eyes had that hollowed-out look, matched by his pale, sunken cheeks. "She dead, Captain?" he asked, his voice shaky.

"Yeah." Jani nodded, waiting for the next question. She knew what it was, but she waited anyway. *Do you think she felt—*

"Do you think she felt anything, ma'am?"

Jani looked at Betha. Outflung arms. Twisted neck. Her hair dragged around to the far side of her face, making her look close-cropped. Just like Yolan. "No, I don't think so, Sergeant. Looked quick to me." As if she could tell. As if she could find her way out of a goddamn closet.

"We aren't going to leave her like that, are we, ma'am?"

"No, Sergeant, we're not. I'll take care of it."

"Ms. Tyi, who are you talking to?"

Jani turned to see Doyle, surrounded by wary subordinates, regarding her with a puzzled frown. "No one," she replied, "just thinking out loud." When she turned back, Borgie had gone. But he'd left her a gift—the burnt-leather stench of his T-40 scorched gloves. The acrid stink filled Jani's nose. Her eyes watered. "No one at all."

CHAPTER 25

Ridgeway joined Jani inside the parts-bin vending alcove; they took turns draining the water cooler. Jani downed dispo after dispo in an effort to assuage her relentless thirst, but Ridgeway just needed something to wash down the multicolored tablets he tossed into his mouth like candy.

"I recall your saying something about an emergency requiring a body." He popped a tiny yellow ovaloid Jani recognized as a black-market tranquilizer. "Check that point off your list, Risa—requirement met."

"Forell didn't do it."

"You've known him less than three days. I've dealt with him for over a year." Ridgeway made a vain attempt to brush his hair out of his eyes. "Allow the fact I know my people, however little you think of my ability to handle them."

Stick it. Jani looked down the hall. One of the Commonwealth Police officers had set up a dyetape barrier in front of the carrel door. Two others had entered the small room carrying scanscreens and evidence cases. A skimgurney hovered against the wall, its body bag zipped open, waiting to be filled. "Steve's feelings for Betha seemed almost paternal," she said. "I can't accept that he'd turn on her."

Ridgeway gave a tired shrug. "It wouldn't be the first time a mentor turned on his charge, Risa."

"True, but for a relationship like that to turn bad, it needs an edge. The edge just wasn't there. Substitute Angevin for Betha and you for Steve—there's a murder I could accept."

Ridgeway scowled. "Dear, dear Angevin." The black-and-grey shades of his daysuit, combined with his pallor and mood, made him look like an animated pencil sketch. "She chose her bed. Let her lie in it." He reinserted his nose plugs and stepped out of the alcove to take a look at the scene down the hall. "Tell me, my esteemed enemy, would you really have shot me?" The plugs made him sound nasal.

"No. Not with that weapon, not in an enclosed space." Jani considered stopping there, but with an esteemed enemy, one never held back certain truths. "I would have clouted you alongside the head with the butt end, though. But only if you became violent."

"Thank you, Risa," Ridgeway replied. "That makes me feel so much better." They walked down the aisle toward the dyetape barrier. "Are you going to tell me what you were working on with those two? Besides the fact it involved Lyssa."

"Ruining a reputation."

"Oh." Ridgeway stepped close to the barrier, taking care to avoid the trespass sensors and the splattering of marker dye that would follow. "Anyone I know? Or should I say, knew?" He clasped his hands behind his back and lifted his chin. All he needed was a blindfold and a nicstick to complete the effect. "You're going after Acton. The connection with Neumann. What he did to Martin."

"Oh, yes."

"Oh, hell!" One of the ComPol officers stationed outside the carrel entrance turned to stare at them, and Ridgeway lowered his voice. "Forget the scandal. Forget the political hay Ulanova would make of it. How can you think of piling something like that on your Minister, atop all he's been through already?" Anger returned the familiar flush to his face. "Your definition of loyalty appears as novel as your one for emergency. He'd have to resign. In disgrace."

"Have you looked at him lately! He's killing himself, Durian. It may be in a socially acceptable manner, but it's suicide all the same." Jani watched the flickers of multicolored light reflect off the surface of the open carrel door. That meant the forensic techs had set up their screens and were scangraphing the body and the area around it. "Forced retirement could save his life."

"Or end it." The fluttering light had drawn Ridgeway's attention as well. A muscle in his cheek twitched. "I saw him this morning. He told me he asked you to quit your investigation."

"Yes."

"So what are you doing here?"

"I was brought in to do a job."

"And now you've been asked to quit."

"Tell me why I should."

Before Ridgeway could respond, Colonel Doyle emerged from the carrel. Dyetape deactivator wand in hand, she poked and pushed toward them, her expression grim.

"Damn, damn, damn." She massaged the back of her neck, but rejected Ridgeway's offer to share his tablet collection.

"So?" he asked.

"Manual strangulation. ME thinks she died around midnight." Doyle glanced at the cup in Jani's hand. "I could use some water, Ms. Tyi. Could you show me where it is, please?"

As soon as they reached the alcove, Doyle sagged against the wall, sliding down until she crouched on the floor. "Her neck. You could hear it crunch when the ME touched her chin. Then her head just flopped over. There were hemorrhages under her eyelids. Lots of them. Whoever killed her tightened down, then eased up and let her come to."

Jani filled a dispo with cold water. Doyle stared past her when she held out the cup, and she set it on the floor in front of her. "Torture strangulation. Whoever killed her was desperate for something she knew. Or had."

"You don't seem very surprised by this."

"No, not completely."

"Do you think Forell did it?"

"No."

"Then who?"

Jani moved to the other side of the alcove and sat on the floor. "Both she and Steve were working to keep themselves out of jail under my direction. Of the two, Betha seemed the more scared. I think she'd confided in someone else without Steve's knowledge. That person killed her."

Doyle covered her face with her hands. She stared at Jani

through a cage of fingers. "Could you please back up to the 'keep themselves out of jail' part, and explain what you mean by 'direction'?"

Jani wavered. Because the murder occurred on Cabinet property, the ComPol had to work with House Security. If Steve turned up during the search, Doyle would handle his transfer into their eager hands. "Deal?"

"What kind?"

"Stall the ComPol. Don't tell them about Steve. If he turns up, hang on to him."

"How! It's a murder, Ms. Tyi. ComPol is setting up a command center in my office as we speak!"

"He didn't do it."

"According to Durian, Forell had means, motive, and opportunity."

"You'd listen to that jackass?"

"Murder makes me open-minded. Besides, if Forell is innocent, he could be in danger as well. Jail may be the safest place for him."

Jani tried to shake her head, but the rocking motion made her sick to her stomach. "I need him here," she said. "He has special knowledge of past events I'm investigating for His Excellency. Besides, imprisonment for any reason means a mandatory hearing. Unless Steve's able to build a good defense, he faces immediate deletion from the Registry."

"You goddamn dexxies are all alike, you know that! Self-centered morons! Betha Concannon is *dead*. She died horribly. Steven Forell can bundle his botched career with his scanpack and shove them both up his ass!"

"I'm perfectly aware of how Betha died, Colonel. Do you want the real murderer to go unpunished? What happened to your open mind?"

Doyle's jaw worked. She picked up the dispo of water and took a cautious sip. "What do you want?"

"Keep the ComPol away from Steve Forell. Give me two days." Jani waited for Doyle's grudging nod before continuing. "Betha buggered paper for Lyssa."

"Durian mentioned that already. That angered Steve because one bad colony kid ruins it for the others."

"No. Steve was trying to help Betha get out from under.

He knew what she'd done. We were digging into why Lyssa wanted the work done in the first place." Jani straightened slowly and moved to Doyle's side of the alcove so she could talk more softly. "Eighteen years ago, during the last idomeni civil war, several ranking Family members made a deal with the Laumrau. Protection and support in exchange for research involving personality augmentation. Acton van Reuter used what he learned to have his grandson, Martin, augied at the age of three."

Doyle's jaw dropped. "That's what was wrong with that kid? Oh God! You don't augment someone that young—you create a monster." Her expression grew pained. "Five years ago. I had just begun working here. There were several episodes we needed to hush up. One with his sister—" Her look sharpened. "Did His Excellency and the Lady know?"

"I think Lyssa figured it out. I believe she had herself augmented, perhaps so she could better understand what Martin went through." She thought back to Evan's after-dinner confession. "Or perhaps, because of her particular brain chemistry, she knew it would cause her to hallucinate under stress. I think she saw what she wanted to see during those episodes."

Doyle winced. "Her kids?" She sighed when Jani nodded. "But there have been rumors about Acton van Reuter's dealings for years. He prospered in spite of them."

"Rumors are one thing. Betha had paper proof." Jani hesitated. "I'm pretty sure she had paper proof. Private documents from the van Reuter library. The stuff Cao's been trying to get her hands on for months."

Doyle nodded. "I oversaw one transfer. A tense time was had by all."

"Well, the private paper is untouchable until Justice makes a ruling, but if Nawar decides they're actionable—"

"That's the end of the *V* in NUVA-SCAN." Doyle crumpled the cup and tossed it into the trashzap, where it ignited with a soft *pop*. "And Stevie knows what these papers consist of?" She smiled coldly at Jani's affirmative. "Then let's go find Stevie." She stood, then rubbed her knees gingerly. "I remember my old CO telling me what a posh job House Security was. If I ever run into her again, she's in for one heavy-duty bout of reeducation.''

Jani tried to stand, but her sore back balked. She held out a hand to Doyle, who pulled her easily to her feet.

"If what you say about Steve is true, Ms. Tyi, you've just done me out of my prime suspect. Maybe I should add your name to the list, just on general principles.''

"Yours as well, Colonel. Anyone with a vested interest in the status quo.''

"Good," Doyle said as she stepped into the hall. "That narrows down the list to mere thousands.''

Two assistants from the ME's office had just maneuvered the skimgurney bearing Betha's body into the hall. The colonel's eyes locked on the dull green body bag as it floated down the aisle and toward the elevators. Ridgeway stood off to the side, conversing intently with a ComPol detective lieutenant holding a recorder. Angevin, however, was nowhere to be seen. Jani nudged Doyle. "Where's Angevin?''

"Infirmary. Shock combined with the stench in this place. First she was royally sick, then she fainted.'' The gurney disappeared around a corner, and Doyle turned back to Jani. "Were Steve and Betha having an affair? I did hear rumors. Ms. Wyle's temper is a minor legend around here.''

"You've seen Angevin's hands. You saw Betha's neck. Did they match?''

"No." Doyle frowned. "The ME said it had to have been a man, or a very physically fit woman.'' Her grimace altered to a cool smile. "Like you, Risa.''

Jani smiled in return. "Or you, Virginia.''

They regarded one another until Doyle broke the impasse. "I hate to sound petty, but this could not have come at a worse time. My Exterior counterpart, Colonel Tanz, and his executive staff are coming over this evening. Informal monthly meeting. My turn to pour tea and pass cookies.''

Jani's mind raced. Exterior. *The Court of Inquiry report.* Would Lucien be a member of the executive staff? Could she pass off the report to him under Doyle's beady eye?

"I've tried to cancel it this past two days, but Tanz wouldn't let me.'' Doyle started down the hall. " 'Things we need to discuss,' he said, the son of a bitch. Knowing how quickly good news travels in this town, I'm anticipating a lovely evening.'' She offered Jani a tired wave before disappearing around the corner.

Ridgeway, his interview over, brushed past Jani without a word. Then she felt a tap on her shoulder and turned to find herself fixed by the dubious eye of a detective sergeant who just wanted to ''ask a few questions, please, ma'am.''

Jani managed to escape with her pretenses intact. *Lying to police—piece of cake—do it all the time.* The thought of cake made Jani realize how starved she was. She ducked back into the alcove and built a late breakfast from the offerings of the various machines.

If one assumes Ridgeway lit a fire under ComPol's collective ass concerning Steve, Ginny's going to have a hell of a time holding them off. Jani chewed thoughtfully. Two days of stonewalling could prove impossible—one day could be pushing it. *Steve, where the hell are you?*

She watched food wrappers flash to powder in the trashzap and wondered if she'd soon be doing the same. *I saw Borgie clear as day. Heard his voice.* It felt good to see him, in spite of the circumstances and the intimation her health was deteriorating. *Lyssa must have felt that way, as well. Any contact, however fleeting, would serve in the never-ending quest to ease the guilt-ridden ache.*

By the time Jani left the alcove, ComPol had finished searching carrels. One lucky detective captain was donning a cartridge-filter mask in preparation for searching the aquariums, where damaged scanpack innards went to be rehabbed.

Well, the aquariums were technically the most visitor-friendly area of the bins. No static barriers to discharge. No nitrogen-blanketing to recharge. *Just the open-top tanks with their little baby brains.* The aquariums made the rest of the bin area smell like a flower garden. Someone who chose to hide there did so in the hope no one would look for them there. So, of course, ComPol would look there first.

Good luck, Captain—I give that mask twenty minutes, tops. Jani tried her Interior ID in the stairwell card reader. *Bet you burn your uniform, too.* The access light blinked; the door swept aside. Either Doyle had lowered the status of the lockdown, or Risa Tyi's status was loftier than Jani thought. She mounted the stairs, alert for movement of any kind. *Stevie, where the hell are you?* Doyle certainly seemed concerned about finding him, but she would have had him by now if she'd kept her eyes open outside the cafeteria.

If I were Ulanova, I'd want someone like Doyle in charge of my enemy's security. Jani paused to consider the concept, then took the steps two at a time until her cramping right hip told her to knock it off. The fourth-floor door opened for her as had the third. She flashed her ID at a trio of somber Security guards and studied wall maps until she found the corridor that led to the infirmary.

CHAPTER 26

Tsecha shifted against the rigid metal frame of his uncushioned chair and watched the Xhà Pathen representative state her skein's case against the laes. Xhà did not possess the fluidity of Vynshàrau, or even of Laum. The female jerked rather than gestured; her voice sounded as though she spoke in a metal box. Tsecha looked away from her twitching form, focusing instead on a favored sculpture. But even smooth riverstone failed to please him. His back ached. His head throbbed. He had lost patience with the mind-focusing ability of pain.

When the female finished, Tsecha nodded in acknowledgment of her statement of position, then gestured for her to go, neglecting the customary benediction. She hesitated, waiting for the blessing, but he slashed the air again with his right hand. More roughly, this time. An insult.

I will hear of this from the Oligarch, he thought glumly as the Xhà Pathen left him. Pathen-descended Haárin controlled much of the trade with Outer Circle humanish. They also claimed strong loyalty to their former born-sect. Tsecha sensed an upcoming trade slowdown. Perhaps even a strike.

A strike. How humanish of Haárin. *So well do they blend, even now.* Most as hybrid, even without the outward physical signs. The signs he and John Shroud had spoken of such a long time past as they sat on the Academy veranda, warmed by the sun and a blessedly hot breeze, and argued the possibilities of change.

But the reality of change is most different, and truly. The agent of change, his toxin, resided as prisoner within the bounds of Interior and needed to be freed. Did she even know herself to be imprisoned? Tsecha hoped not. Kilian's reactions under such conditions had, after all, proven unpredictable, even by her own kind.

My odd Lucien is to liberate her this night. The thought made him uneasy. He did not fully trust his new guide. His dead Hansen had desired order of a sort, but Lucien seemed most content when all around him were confused. The Tsecha who had fought in a war rose from his cursed chair and massaged his numb thighs. *Confusion* and *rescue mission*, he felt most sure, were not a desirable combination.

His meeting with the Prime Minister had been put off until afternoon, so Tsecha retired to the quiet of his rooms. He studied the space, which appeared much larger than it truly was owing to the sparseness of its furnishings. *My Captain could hide here.* He bared his teeth at the disorder of the thought. *She could sleep under my bed.* During the day, she could labor at his workstation, deal with his tiresome duties, explain to him what he must do to survive humanish meetings.

But what would she eat? The prospect of sharing food bothered him, but if such was what the gods demanded, he would allow his Captain his food. What she could eat of it. *She could grow ill.* He lowered himself into his favored chair and pulled at his red-trimmed sleeves. *She could die.* John had warned of such. The nutritional requirements of a hybrid would change constantly as its body altered. A food that once nourished could act as poison a short time later. A wretched, wasting death, which would bring an end to the future as well as his Captain's life.

No. Tsecha settled back in his chair and contemplated a curve of polished sandwood in a niche across the room. *She cannot stay here.*

A sharp series of tones rang out, jolting him from his reverie. *A call to sacrament?* He glanced at the timeform at his workplace. *No, it is too early.*

The tones sounded once more. Tsecha slowly approached his comport. Across the surface of the device's input pad, illumins flashed and fluttered. "Someone has called me?"

But the unit did not allow incoming messages, and no other possessed his code.

This lacks order. Tsecha activated the device's audio. *Thus do I know who calls.*

"NìRau?"

Ah. "Lieutenant Pascal, this comport does not accept incoming."

A pause. "It does now."

Tsecha bared his teeth and waited.

"NìRau?" His lieutenant sounded youngish now. Plaintive. Then, like the turning of a page, the tone changed, becoming harsh. "I won't be selling it to the newssheets, if that's what you're worried about."

I detect anger. Good to know his disorderly guide could be vexed. He dragged his chair by the comport table and sat.

"NìRau, would you please activate your video?"

"Yes, Lucien." Tsecha fingered the input pad. A side view of his guide's face filled the display. "I am most surprised to hear from you."

"Obviously." Lucien kept his head turned. Below the level of the display, his hands worked.

Tsecha saw a flash of white. Another "Lieutenant?"

"My apologies, nìRau—I'm experiencing a technical difficulty." He at last held up a folded square of cloth and pressed it to the side of his face that Tsecha couldn't see.

"Lucien?"

"Yes, nìRau."

"Lower the cloth."

"No, it's—"

"Lower it!"

Slowly, Lucien did as he was told.

Tsecha touched his own face when he saw the four ragged, seeping gouges that ran from the middle of Lucien's cheek to the edge of his high Service collar. He recalled the humanish custom of sharing their homes with animals. "You were scratched by a pet, Lucien?"

Lucien's lips curved. "You could say that, nìRau." The expression altered to a grimace and he again pressed the cloth to his wounds. "I've had a lousy day so far."

"It will soon become worse."

"Thank you. I wouldn't have known that without you telling me."

"Then it is good we speak now, so I can remind you."

"What would I do without you, nìRau?" Lucien lifted the cloth from his face and stared at the crosshatches of blood. "There's been a murder, nìRau. A young woman. A documents examiner. Kilian knew her."

Tsecha felt a tightening in his soul. "Did my Captain kill her?"

"Why would you think that, nìRau?"

"The past—"

"Is the past." Lucien shook his head. "Kilian wasn't in the Main House at the time of the murder."

"And how do you know this, Lucien?"

"I have a source."

"Ah, a spy."

"Yes."

"Ah." Tsecha looked at his lieutenant, who had now become most as a wall. "This killing worries you."

"Kilian was working with the dead girl, nìRau. They were investigating Lyssa van Reuter's death and its connection to what happened at Knevçet Shèràa." The bright redness of Lucien's wounds made his skin seem most pale. "But we all know the connection. Acton van Reuter and Rikart Neumann were friends. After Kilian killed Neumann, van Reuter arranged the transport explosion. He did it for self-protection and to avenge Neumann's death. But there must be something else."

"Something else?"

"Another connection we're all missing."

"All will be connected in the end, Lucien. Such is the root of order."

"NìRau, I can't use philosophy now—I need facts."

Tsecha slumped against hard cushions. How often had he and Hansen argued of this? *There has to be something else, Nema!* His guide had stalked his rooms at Temple like a hunting animal. *How the hell did the order to blow up the transport get to the depot outside Knevçet Shèràa?*

"Does it matter?" Tsecha spoke as much to his dead friend as to the face on the display. "All we do affects all we know.

A deed performed by one is a deed performed by all.''

"The sins of the fathers, nìRau?''

"Sins are sins, Lucien—they taint the sect as a whole. That is why those who sin most greatly are made Haárin, to excise them from the whole and save the souls of their brethren.''

"Ok then,'' Lucien sighed, "who in Interior House would you make Haárin?''

Tsecha bared his teeth. "My Captain, Lucien.''

Lucien emitted a guttural, Haárin-like sound. "That's not the answer I'm looking for, nìRau, and you know it.''

"But that is the answer you will receive from me. She must be excised from the rest of humanish. She does not belong with you any longer. She must be allowed to become what she must.''

"Which is?''

"She is toxin. The agent of change. She is change's spy.'' He felt a tremor of satisfaction. *I thought of such without my handheld.* He was finally becoming used to this English.

"That's very poetic, nìRau.'' Lucien touched his cheek and moaned softly. "I plan to excuse myself from my meeting tonight and track her down within Main.'' For the first time, he looked Tsecha in the eye. "Eight o'clock, nìRau. One half hour after the finish of midevening sacrament. You must be at your outpost with your Exterior skimmer, charged up and ready.''

So he knows of that as well? Tsecha studied Lucien's face in return. Through the display, it did not seem such an intrusion. *Most as Haárin, my odd one's eyes.* From a sheltered corner of his memory, he heard the tensile song of blades being pulled from sheaths. "Yes, Lucien. For her to live is necessary for us both. You have chosen her as your dominant; thus you owe her your knife.''

"My dominant? Yes, I suppose you're right.'' Lucien cocked his head. The gesture was not as idomeni. He looked as a humanish who contemplated the lines of a sculpture, or an object in a niche. "And you've chosen her for something else. Does she know what you plan for her?''

He knows! How much as Hansen he was, after all. "You know of the blending?'' Tsecha asked. "The hybridization? You know of what is to be?''

"I've read your prewar essays, nìRau." Lucien wadded his bloody bandage and flung it out of range of the display. "I can't say I accept your conclusions."

Ah.

"But you want her to live, and I can't save her by myself."

"I will be there, Lucien." Tsecha watched his lieutenant carefully. "With my stolen skimmer." At that, Lucien's mouth curved upward, as he had hoped. Before he could say more, a more familiar series of chords echoed through the rooms. "I must go now," he said as the last series rang. "Midmorning sacrament. I will offer prayers for our success tonight." He waited for Lucien to nod before disconnecting. The screen blanked. He meditated upon the greyness.

No, not as Hansen. Something quite different, I believe, and truly. He smoothed a hand over the front of his overrobe, then reached for his handheld and picked at the touchpad. But the meanings he plumbed from the device's depths failed to help him. *He chose my Captain.* This young lieutenant whose eyes, whose soul, seemed wrapped in a death-glaze that could not be seen. The clatter of dishes and utensils reached Tsecha through the closed door. He felt a small rush of comfort at the sounds.

He chose me. The summoning illumin shone. He rose. His soul felt heavy. *This strange, dead humanish.* He could not keep his mind focused upon his prayers; he pleaded with his gods for understanding.

CHAPTER 27

Jani entered the infirmary to find Angevin in the midst of an animated discussion with the duty nurse. "How many times do I have to tell you"—she struck the check-in counter—"I'm not sick anymore. I'm fine!" The nurse, tall and heavily built, folded his arms and seemed ready to dig in for the duration.

"How about if she agrees to come back every couple of hours?" Jani leaned against the counter and gave the nurse a commiserating smile. "I know she's supposed to be in shock, but does she look shocky to you? I mean, she has her color back." She leaned close to Angevin, who glared at her. "Her pupils look ok. I can't speak for confused behavior, but two out of three isn't bad."

"I should have kicked you," Angevin grumbled as they departed a few minutes later. Security guards were stationed near the elevators and stairwell doors; every so often, one would pop his head around a corner like a treechuck. "And why do I have to check in? It's so stupid—I feel fine!"

"It's a good idea," Jani countered. "Doyle wouldn't have sent you up here if she didn't think you looked shaky." The thought also crossed her mind that the colonel would want Angevin closeted in a well-guarded place as long as Steve remained at large, but she kept it to herself.

"Doyle just sent me here to get me out of the way. I fainted, ok. It was my first dead body." Angevin snorted in disgust. "Doyle didn't take it so well, either. Saw her swallow hard a few times."

"She's a human being, Angevin. The day she stops swallowing hard is the day she better change professions."

"You didn't even blink! Just stood in the doorway and took it all in." Angevin keyed into her office. The look she shot Jani held envy, but something else as well. As in, *I wish I could do that. I think.* "Did you spot any clues?" She made a show of checking her paper message box. "Anything that could clear Steve?"

Jani thought back to the scene in the carrel. *I spied with my warped little eye . . .* something she'd rather not say. Betha had looked so much like Yolan, and in looking like Yolan, she had brought Borgie back for a little while. Jani flexed her shoulders. Her back felt loose. Her hip worked smoothly. Her stomach had even stopped aching. *You ghoul—a young woman is dead and you react by feeling better than you have in weeks.*

"Where the hell could he be hiding?" Angevin locked the door, then headed for her comport. "He couldn't have had enough time to get off the compound." She activated the unit and checked her voicebox. Message after message bit the trashbin after only a few words. "Where the hell is he!"

"Well, I should hope he wouldn't be dumb enough to leave you a message." Jani dragged a chair deskside. "He'd have to know Doyle would check."

"She wouldn't dare!"

"There's been a murder, Angevin. She can, she would, and more than likely she already has."

"She wouldn't have deleted it, would she?"

"No, she'd let you hear it. Then she'd hope Steve would give himself away to you and you'd lead her to him."

"Fuck." Angevin dropped into her chair. "Risa, he didn't do it." She pulled at the hem of her baggy pullover. "But why did he run away like that?"

"Durian had two V-40s pointed in his direction. The gut reaction of anyone with one working neuron would be to run."

"You didn't." That look, again. "You took it out of the guard's hands."

"I got lucky—she didn't know how to handle it."

"But you did." Angevin's gaze was steady and decidedly

nonshocky. "Don't you have a guess where Steve could be?"

Jani rummaged through her duffel. She pulled out a squat brushed-metal cylinder, twisted the top, and set it on the desk. "This should buy us a few minutes."

Angevin eyed the device skeptically. "What is it?"

"Insecticide."

"She's bugged my office!"

"The court order was probably fiched over here while you were on your way to the infirmary. Just audio, probably. Holofield, they reserve for real crooks." *Like us after today— who knows?* Jani adjusted the cylinder until it rested in a direct line between the two of them. "But don't be surprised if someone from Systems shows up soon waving a repair order you don't remember requesting. The interference pattern this thing emits reads a lot like a transmission from a blown workstation card."

"How do you get hold of something like that?" Angevin's voice held the greedy wonder of someone ready to pull out a recorder and take notes.

"Oh, you can get hold of anything. All depends how much you're willing to give in return." Jani stroked the device with a fingertip. "With regard to Steve, there are a few places I can check."

Angevin shot to her feet. "Let's go."

"Not so fast." She waved the young woman back into her seat. "*You* stay here."

"Bullshit!"

"Doyle has her eye on me sort of. You, she's watching like a hawk. The best thing you can do for Steve is stay here. Work. Make lots of calls. Walk the wing from end to end and talk to everyone you see. Check in at the infirmary every two hours."

Angevin's expression slowly lightened. "You want me to draw attention away from you while you hunt around?"

"It can't hurt." Jani raised a finger to her lips, then swept her device off the desk and back into her bag. "Keep a good thought," she said as she headed for the door. "I'm going to head back to Private for a while." Angevin offered Jani a thumbs-up, then turned back to her comport with a determined glare.

Where are you, Steven, you little jerk? Jani stuck her head in the alternate breakroom and encountered two guards playing cards at one of the battered tables. No one else was in the room; judging from the surprise on the guards' faces, dexxies had been avoiding the place the entire morning.

Every elevator and stairway Jani passed was monitored by at least one guard. She stopped on the second floor and entered the women's locker room next to the main gymnasium. She checked the ceiling directly overhead. *They wouldn't have video in here, would they?*

She dug into her trouser pocket for the tiny key card she had stolen earlier from the gymnasium office and slid the uncomplicated plastic sliver into its lockslot. For the benefit of any viewing device, she rummaged through a stack of washcloths and towels. When she came to the towel in which she'd wrapped the Court of Inquiry report, she rolled it into a loose cylinder and stuffed it into her duffel. She followed with a washcloth and some soap.

She stopped at the sink to wash her hands. *Always have a reason to be where you are.* The soap was black, with the throaty scent of a humid summer night. *I came here to try this soap—I overheard people in the hallway talking about this soap—this soap is legend.* She wrapped the wet bar in the washcloth and stuffed it into her bag.

Only a few employees walked the hall outside the locker room. Jani paused to study the message board outside the gym. Then she stopped at one of the glass panels set at regular intervals along the wide hall and spent a few minutes watching a man and a woman play handball. She felt calm. The rest of the world seemed to be moving just a bit more slowly than she.

She entered a lounge area filled with uniformed and plainclothes employees, sat at one of the small tables, and paged through the newssheet the previous occupant had left behind. When the noise level of the room dipped, she looked up. A pair of guards had wandered in and were perusing the contents of a vend cooler. Around her, she could hear the murmurs. "Murder . . . girl . . . the parts bins." She checked her timepiece. One and a half hours since they had found Betha's body. Well, if Doyle wanted to alarm the entire House and waste manpower in the process, she was certainly doing a good job. Jani watched the guards until they departed. Then she left as well.

Where are you hiding, Steven? Jani shuffled down the hall toward the elevators. She didn't bother to eavesdrop on any of the groups clustered in corners and near doorways. It didn't take a genius to figure out what they talked about.

Fear not, citizens—your friends in Security have it all under control. She rode down to the lowest parking level; once in the tunnel, she hitched a ride to Private on a grocery skim. She rode the elevator to her door and keyed herself inside. The housekeepers had been through, apparently. Her bed had been made and the air possessed the eye-watering scent of cleansing agents. Jani sniffed again and wrinkled her nose. Odd smell for a cleanser. Sharp. Spicy. Familiar.

Oh no!

Out of the corner of her eye, she detected movement.

"Risa?" Steve walked into the sitting room, his cupped hand hiding his smoking 'stick. "Don't yell. I can explain."

CHAPTER 28

"How the hell did you get in here?"

Steve backed away, stumbled, and wound up straddling a footstool. "I said, don't yell—"

"I'm not yelling," Jani said, just a touch louder than necessary. "Start at the beginning. What happened after you ran out of the cafeteria?"

Steve's nicstick puffed feebly. On the nearby coffee table, a small dish contained the remains of several others. "Scarpered down the hall. My office. Grabbed my shit and made for the stairs."

"Did you pass Ginny Doyle on the way?"

"Hell no." He looked horrified at the prospect. "Wouldn't be here if I had, would I?"

Don't be too sure. "The stairway lock let you through?"

"Yeah. Everything worked until I got to the first floor. Heard running. Ducked into a doorway. Saw guards running in all directions. Waited till they'd gone, then tried the stairway door again. Locked. I knew the main exits would be sealed before I could reach them, so I made for the delivery bays in the rear of the House."

"They were still open?"

"Yeah. Food deliveries today. Skimvans inside, filling the bays—skimvans outside lined up ten abreast, waiting to unload. In this weather, they don't shut down for anything. One of the supers saw me and started cussing me out. Told me to get my ass into some coldgear and start unloading. So I did."

"So you got all muffled up and unrecognizable in a snow-suit and nailed yourself a skiff."

Steve grinned. "Lucky, huh? I spent about a half hour un-loading. Worked my way through Oxbridge at the school docks, so I'm pretty good at it. Super watched me for a few minutes, then left to squawk at somebody else. Guards came through every once in a while. One stared right at me, but I looked like I knew what I were doing. No one expects a nance dexxie to know how to handle a loading skiff, do they?" His lip curled. "A few minutes later, I steered the skiff outside, made like the battery were low, and drifted it to a mainte-nance shed. Changed it for a grounds-crew skiff and floated down the access road to here."

Jani found herself listening with respectful interest. Then she thought of Betha, and her mood soured.

"Made for the tradesman's entrance," Steve continued. "Housekeeper leaves coffee and snacks for the Private crews in a little back room. I know because I stop by some days to check for blueberry tart. Outer door's always unlocked. Had to wait until someone came out to refresh the pot—ducked in through the inner door while her back were turned. Up the lift. Snuck in with the cleaners. Here I am." He looked at Jani in surprise. "You know, it really were easy to get in here."

"Doyle will love to hear it."

"Do you have to keep bringing her up?" Steve dug in his trouser pocket and pulled out another 'stick, which he shoved into his mouth without igniting. "How's Ange?"

"About what you'd expect."

"Pissed as hell. Doyle giving her fits?"

"I'm sure she has her under surveillance. I hope you haven't tried to call her." Steve shook his head. "Keep it that way. You both may go crazy in the interim, but if you try to hook up, you're screwed." Jani waited for his affirmative sigh. "So, you went straight from fourth floor to first? Never got off on the third floor? Didn't visit the repair carrels?"

Steve gave her a puzzled look. "Nah. Didn't have no bloody time, Ris."

"When was the last time you were down there?"

"Last night. I stayed a while after you left. Had to turn in my parts req.'' His expression grew guarded. ''Why?''

A thin band of tension stretched from Jani's scalp and down her neck. ''Betha's dead. We found her body in your repair carrel about two hours ago. She'd been strangled. The medical examiner put the time of death at around midnight.''

Steve tried to shake his head, but all he could manage was a palsied tremor. ''Why—why would someone want to hurt her?''

''I think she went behind your back and tried to work a deal with someone.''

''Aw, no—''

''That someone killed her. The way she died suggested the killer wanted something from her.'' Jani sat on the arm of a chair and watched the light play over her boot as she swung her leg to and fro. *Now I feel better. It comes and goes in waves.* She looked up from her mesmerizing footwear and into Steve's frightened eyes.

''What do you mean, 'way she died'? What do you mean, 'wanted something'?''

''I mean it took a while for whoever killed her to kill her. They were trying to extract information from her.''

''Did they get it?''

''I don't know.''

''Well, maybe I can give 'em some of what they need,'' Steve said as he ran from the room.

''Steve!'' Jani rushed after him, reaching him as he disappeared into the bathroom. ''Where do you think you're going?''

Steve had already pulled on one leg of a pair of snowpants. Behind him, the lube-stained jacket lay in a heap on the floor. ''Back to Main,'' he said as he shoved in the other leg, then yanked the thick grey pants up to his waist. ''I'm going to find whoever did this.''

Jani leaned against the doorway, positioning herself to throw a block if things needed to get physical. ''I wouldn't do that if I were you.''

''Yeah? Why not?'' Steve finished fastening his pants and pulled the jacket over his head.

''Because a lot of people back at Main think you did it. Because Ridgeway tried to declare anarchy rules and order you killed if you tried to escape from the compound, and while Doyle countermanded the 'rules' part, I'm not a hundred percent sure about the 'kill' part.''

The furious movement beneath the jacket slowly subsided.

''It's become more than doc-jazzing, Steve. You're wanted for questioning in a murder.''

The jacket sagged to the tiled floor. ''Does *Ange* think—?

''No.'' Jani moved out of her ''brace'' position. Steve didn't appear too eager to leave anymore. ''The first thing she said was, 'He didn't do it.' ''

''But that were the first thing she *thought*.'' He moaned softly. ''She saw Betha?'' He winced at Jani's affirmative. ''Is she ok?''

''She got sick. Doyle sent her to the infirmary. Personally, I think she just wanted Angevin locked up as long as you still ran loose.'' Jani waited for Steve to reply, but he just stared over her shoulder. ''That's why you have to stay here. Someone has committed murder and framed you for it. The case is all circumstantial, but as the old saying goes, 'Enough coincidence will surely hang a man.' '' Steve's eyes finally moved to meet hers. They held the dumb misery of a wounded animal, waiting for the killing blow. ''Let's go into the other room, where we can talk.''

Jani returned to the sitting room while Steve removed his snowsuit. She sat carefully. Her back had begun to ache again. *The wave comes in. The wave goes out.*

''Now, after you bolted you went to the office to get your 'pack and the papers,'' she said, as Steve flopped into the chair across from her.

He nodded. ''Yeah, I had—I usually wear my 'pack on me, but Ange and me, we got in sort of early, and after she parked in the garage, we just stayed put and sat and talked and then—'' A blush crept up his neck. ''You know.''

Jani forced a smile. ''Yeah, I know.''

''And when we got into the building, I realized I left my belt and packpouch in her skimmer. Then we were running late, tryin' to track down Betha, so I locked my 'pack in my desk with the papers. Couldn't carry 'em around in my hand like my orb and bloody scepter, could I? Not with that fookin' lien.''

''Where are the papers?''

Steve's face brightened a bit more. ''They're in the jacket.'' He bounded to his feet and headed back to the bathroom, returning with the battered jacket. ''I zipped it all in here. Thing's got more pockets than a snooker tournament.'' He unzipped and rummaged; soon, the coffee table between them held a scanpack in a scuffed case, an emergency 'pack tool kit, and a file pouch bursting with handwritten notes, general-purpose paper, and—

''Some of this stuff has the Prime Minister's seal.'' Jani fingered a creamy white page. The familiar silky smoothness of government parchment sent a shiver up her arm. ''You've got original docs here. From another damn House! From *the* damn House!''

Steve stilled. ''I know.''

''Eyes-only docs.''

''I know.''

''The Prime Minister's eyes!''

''Yeah, well. She didn't seem to want to use them the way they should've been.'' Steve grimaced in disgust. ''They followed her, you know. The Lady. They knew something were wrong with her, and they just followed her with scans and watched it unfold. She grew up with them, went to school with them. Treated some of their kids. She were one of them, and they just watched while she flamed out.'' He shoved the doc pouch across the table. ''Here.''

Jani flipped open the pouch. ''Who compiled this?''

''Betha. The Lady helped with the personal stuff, but Betha did more than you think.'' Steve's expression darkened further. ''She had ways of getting hold of stuff. She'd visit friends in other Houses and just go wandering on her own. She said the things people left out on their desks would scare you.''

Jani held up one of the PM's documents. ''Are you telling me she just walked into Li Cao's office, and said, 'Excuse me, Your Excellency, do you mind?' ''

''I don't know how she got that.'' Steve fussed with a

jacket zipper. A plastic rasp cut the air. "She wouldn't tell me. Just said she had connections."

She had connections, all right. "Well, maybe she did you a favor by not telling you," Jani said as she flipped through a few more cream white sheets. "We could have found you on the floor next to her." The image stalled Steve in mid-zip. He pushed the jacket to one side, mumbled something about needing a drink, and escaped to the kitchenette.

Jani continued paging through the pile. The PM documents contained information she already knew from the Court report. All of Lyssa's public missteps, and a few private ones, all neatly cataloged and cross-referenced with her trips to Nueva Madrid. *So, Betha didn't reach her own brilliant conclusions—she stole them from an entire team of Prime analysts.* She set the docs aside and rooted through the miscellaneous scraps.

Paper from Interior Grounds and Facilities, listing Lyssa's vehicular mishaps. Liquor bills. A listing of wrecked furniture. *Probably blasphemy coming from a paper pusher, but some things shouldn't be written down.* Physician, wife, mother—all forgotten amid the damning slips of paper. Jani brushed a stack of sheets aside, sending several of them fluttering to the floor.

Hold on! Jani picked up one of the fallen documents. A different sort of shiver moved up her arm. *Consulate paper.* From Rauta Shèràa. She checked the date code in the upper left corner. *I was still at Knevçet Shèràa then.* Yolan was dead, but the rest of them were alive, battered and weaponless, waiting for their Captain to keep her promise and see them safely home.

Jani touched the paper's snow-white body, ran a finger along the bright blue trim. A log excerpt, judging from its margins and formatting, but without a Consulate cipher glossary, it would be impossible to break the code. *They used semi-Rime iterations then.* With her 'pack and a workstation, Jani could crack it eventually. *Could take a day, or a couple thousand years.* She heard Steve clatter out of the kitchenette and folded the document into the inside pocket of her jacket.

"Find anything useful?" Steve asked as he twisted the cap off a bottle of New Indiesian beer.

Jani shrugged. "Nothing we don't already know. I was searching for Consulate paper from eighteen years ago."

Steve shook his head. "That's that blue-and-white stuff? I looked for that. There's none in there. Betha said she had it in her half of the files. Did anyone find it in the carrel?"

"Not that I know of," Jani said. "They could have been wedged beneath her body, or hidden in one of the desk drawers." But the desk had been more a table; none of its drawers could have contained a file pouch the size of the one she held. *And the one I'm holding didn't have any Consulate paper in it when Steve looked through it last night.* "Did you sleep in your office last night?"

Steve colored. "Yeah. Few hours. Didn't want to go home. Don't like sleeping alone."

"What time did you fall asleep?"

"Tennish. I remember because my 'zap's recharge light were blinking, and it weren't when I woke."

"And the cleaning crews come through about eleven?"

"At my end of the floor, more like ten-thirty."

Jani plopped the doc pouch on the couch beside her and sat back. *You had another visitor besides the cleaner.* She could imagine Betha sneaking into Steve's office, finding him asleep, and slipping the most important piece of paper Lyssa had given her into his share of the info tangle. *What were you up to, Betha?* Did she plan to withhold the most vital piece of information from her other coconspirator? *Of course.* But her plan backfired. Her coconspirator knew what to look for, knew what was missing. *I need that cipher glossary.* "I have to go."

Steve stood. "I don't suppose I can go with?"

"Not a chance." She pointed to a stack of paper that had been growing steadily since her arrival. "There's a three-day backlog of newssheets. Please keep your hands off my workstation. I've typed it to me, but I'm sure it's monitored for intrusions. In fact, the whole damn suite could be under monitoring. I try to check it a couple times a day, but it's their playpen. They know tricks I haven't heard of."

"They airn't gonna bug His Excellency's guest!"

"They're not that considerate." Jani walked over to the holoVee and patted the top of the console. "Keep away from this. Don't use the comport, either. We don't want signals coming out of this suite when they know I'm not here to make them. Understand?''

Steve sat down and dug out another 'stick. "Yes, Mother."

"And if you're going to keep smoking, do it in the bathroom." Jani cracked open her office door. "Stash the snowsuit in here. If someone tries to get in here, you may have to dress *tout de suite* and go out the window."

"We're on the second floor, Ris."

"There's over two meters of snow on the ground. It'll break your fall."

"Says you. They're not your bloody ankles, are they?" Steve sighed heavily. "Would they really shoot me?"

At this point, they're so damned spooked they'd take out the entire Cabinet. Jani pulled her shooter out of her duffel. "Do you know how to use one of these," she asked as she handed it to Steve.

"Y-yeah." His mouth gaped as he examined the bulky grip and dated styling. "Crike, my dad has one of these. Thing's a relic!"

"Thanks."

His look sharpened. "He got his in the Service." But his heart wasn't in this particular attempt to badger Jani about her past. He slumped back in his chair. "Would they really, really shoot me?"

Jani left Steve's pained question unanswered and hurried to the bathroom. *A quick splash of cold water on your face can take the place of a nap.* Sure it could. She checked her films in the mirror, then examined her face. *I look tired.* But the garage guy had looked sick. Sallow, clammy skin. Bones jutting. And the delirium. Seeing Borgie as she had didn't qualify as delirium. Hearing him. That was stress. Augie. The sight of combat weapons and dead bodies. She'd be fine as soon as she could manage some sleep. She finished washing up. When she reentered the sitting room, Steve still sat with the shooter cradled in his hands.

"Ris?"

Jani shouldered her duffel. The Consulate paper crackled against her chest as she moved. "Yeah?"

"Are you sure you don't want to keep this?" He held the

weapon out to her, taking care to keep the barrel pointed at the floor. "Betha's murderer may have wanted her and me out of the way for starters, but you're helping us. They might go after you now, too."

"I'll be fine," she said as she locked the door on the worried young man. *Nobody can kill me—I'm never going to die.*

Everybody dies, Captain.

Not me. I tried it once, remember—it didn't take.

She hurried to the elevator. Her touchy stomach shuddered as the car moved down, but the sensation soon passed. She hugged her duffel, imagining the empty slot that usually held her shooter. She felt no regrets over her decision to leave the weapon with Steve. Better he should have it.

The wave goes out . . . the wave comes in.

She wouldn't need it anyway.

CHAPTER 29

Jani keyed into Doc Control's Archive wing. As she studied the nameplates on the doors lining the narrow hall, she rehearsed the reasons she hoped would compel the code-room supervisor to let her see the cipher glossary.

It's an ancient code—no one's used it since the war. Nope, too limp. *I'm cross-checking some old Service disability claims.* Now that sounded asinine enough to be true.

She stopped in front of a plain metal slider guarded only by a simple palm reader. *Bet it lets everyone in.* Getting out, however, could prove tricky if your scan didn't clear. A ready-made cell—no choice but to sit tight and wait for the cavalry to come. She wiped her right palm on her trouser leg and prepared to press it against the reader surface, but before she could, the door slid open of its own accord.

Whoops—la cavalerie c'est ici.

At the far end of the room, Ginny Doyle rose from behind the supervisor's desk. The supervisor, a slender, dark-haired young man wearing sweat-blotched grey civvies, stood nearer the door, in front of a tilt-top worktable. He glowered at Jani, then resumed inserting small data discs into a storage booklet. The iridescent circles glittered in their slots like an overgrown coin collection.

The cipher glossary. But why was Doyle interested in it?

"Ms. Tyi." The colonel's mouth turned up at the ends. Calling the expression a smile would have been charitable. "I was just going to call you." She turned to the supervisor.

"I'll send someone for those discs in fifteen minutes. They'd better be ready."

"Bring me Ridgeway's sign-off, and they will be." The supervisor inserted the last disc in its slot, then closed the booklet with as much emphasis as he could without risking damage to the contents. "No sign-off, no discs."

"We've been over this, mister."

"And I've got a lien hanging over my head, Colonel. Nothing leaves this office without the ranking's ok."

Jani cleared her throat and waited for the supervisor to direct his stiff-necked scowl at her. *No, I don't think the disability-claims approach would have worked with this one.* She pulled her scanpack from her duffel, making sure he saw it. "Rauta Shèràa Consulate, civil war stratum? The cipher glossary for comlogs?"

"You need it, too?" The supervisor looked down at Jani's scanpack. "You're His Excellency's hired shooter, here to clean up after the troubles. Why do you need to see it?"

"My thought exactly," said Doyle, who had perched on the desk's edge. One leather-booted leg swung freely, a glistening play of polished black and silvery reflection. Jani forced herself to look away as the light patterning set off a series of buzzes and cracklings in her head.

"It's for Betha," she said, loudly enough to block out the noise. "It'll help us find out who killed Betha."

The supervisor's dark eyes misted. He jerked a thumb at Doyle. "You're working with her?"

Jani looked at the colonel, who stared back blandly. "If necessary." After a long silence, Doyle responded with a slow nod. Light danced across her dark brown scalp.

The supervisor sighed. "This glossary's directly related to van Reuter family records, so it's covered by the lien. I can only release it on the ranking's signature, and Ridgeway's not available."

"If I supply you with a valid reason and promise not to leave the compound, you can sign it out to me. If Ridgeway told you otherwise, he's wrong."

"Look." The supervisor tugged at his damp shirt. "I can't give you the whole damn glossary."

"How about a single disc?"

"To do that, I need a page code. Do you have a page code?"

Jani removed the sheet of Consulate paper from her inside shirt pocket and handed it to the supervisor.

"You *folded* it," he said, in a tone one might reserve for a slaughterer of baby animals. "Don't you know better than that?" He held the sheet between thumbs and forefingers and unfolded it slowly, as though a quick movement might injure it further. Then he set it down on the worktable and slid restraint bars along the top and bottom to fix it in place.

"Where did you get that, Ms. Tyi?" Doyle stood up and ambled toward the table, her hands locked behind her back. "It matches the description of the paper the PM's been looking for."

"Later, Colonel."

"Ms. Tyi—"

"*Later*, Colonel."

"I hope you didn't catch the code inset chip in the fold," the supervisor interrupted. "That would necessitate surgical repair before I could attempt a full scan. Something this old could take days to heal."

"Codes for that series of sheets were set in the lower left quadrant" Jani said, "just right of quadrant center. I took great care to leave that area smooth."

The supervisor's head shot up. "How do you know that?" He focused his attention on the document, smoothing his scanpack over the surface in the area she had described. "Well, well," was all he said as he took note of the page number on his display and checked it against the index inside the glossary binder. He removed the appropriate disc from its slot and slipped it into an antistatic pouch, then freed the Consulate document from its weighting and rolled it into a loose scroll. "Three hours," he said as he handed them to Jani. "Any longer, and I'll have no choice but to notify Ridgeway."

Jani slipped the items into her duffel. "Shall we go, Colonel?"

When they reached Security, Doyle turned down the executive wing, then stopped. "Wrong way," she muttered under her breath as she spun on her heel and led Jani in the opposite direction. Still grumbling, she palmed them into a small conference room that had been fitted out as a temporary office.

Doyle closed the door just as two ComPol officers bustled past. "They've taken over my office until further notice," she said. "They've seconded members of my staff until further notice. It wouldn't be so bad if they treated my people like fellow professionals, but it seems to be ComPol opinion that this murder is an indication of their incompetence."

Jani lowered herself into the first chair she came to. Her right hand felt weak, her fingers, stiff. Muscles twitched throughout her arm and up to her shoulder. "I bet the first thing they asked was why you didn't have visiscan set up in the parts bins."

Doyle sat down behind an old metal desk. The sides of the desk were dented, the dull brown electrostat paint worn away in patches. "Please! The first thing I asked them was how closely they monitored *their* dexxies. They changed the subject so fast I almost got whiplash." She leaned back, chair creaking in protest. "No offense meant, but everyone knows dexxies are crazy. You try to keep them from getting overexcited and pray they stay away from sharp objects and the personnel files."

"Unfair, Colonel." Jani forced a smile. "Payroll is where you have the most fun."

Doyle's eyes glittered. "When I see Lieutenant Pascal this evening, I'll have to let him know you referred to him as a 'goon.' Lucien's many things to many people, but that, I believe, may take him by surprise. I doubt he'd enjoy being thought of as quite so common." She swung her feet up on her desk. "After we left the parts bins, Durian took great pains to fill me in on what he believes happened between you and Lucien yesterday. Such nice sceneshots." She smiled. "Do you work for Exterior, Ms. Tyi?"

"Funny, Colonel, I've been meaning to ask you the same question."

Doyle's smile froze, but she recovered quickly. "Please, call me Ginny." She stifled a yawn. "You certainly worked dexxie magic with that code-room supervisor. He's never given me the time of day. I love it when a bright boy gets set back on his heels by one of us old girls.'' The glint in her eyes softened, as though she recalled a bright boy of her own. ''Why do you believe Angevin Wyle took the trouble to pay a visit to your Private suite at two o'clock in the morning?'' She was good—the tone of her voice never changed. Neither did her expression of goodwill.

Jani flexed her hands again. The right one began to twitch. ''I thought we'd decided she had nothing to do with Betha's death.''

''But why seek you out at such an odd hour? To discuss her concern for Mr. Forell, perhaps? Her worry over what she'd suspected he'd done? Something she witnessed?'' As the colonel's eyes followed the movements of Jani's hands, she frowned. ''Then an odd thought occurred to me. Just let me say the term 'hired shooter' could prove more appropriate in the end than our supervisor friend could ever have imagined.''

What! Jani hoped the surprise she felt didn't show. She didn't want Doyle to know she'd managed to rattle her. ''You believe I murdered Betha? At my minister's request?''

''Lyssa, too. It explains the special trip to Whalen just to retrieve you. Taxi service from His Excellency himself as reward for a job well-done. I understand you and he had dinner for two at Private House last night.''

Thank you, Durian. ''And why would his Excellency have ordered it done?''

''To make sure the dead remained buried.'' Doyle's expression grew grim. ''You have no idea what it's been like in this House the past few years. Believe me, Risa, as soon as we heard Lyssa had died, a half dozen scenarios passed through this floor like a bout of food poisoning, and every one of them began with the assumption Evan van Reuter *wanted* his wife dead.''

''I never got that impression from him when we spoke of the matter.''

''With all due respect, I only have your word for that and I'm not sure what that's worth.'' Doyle's voice grew eager. The hound on the scent. If she'd howled, Jani wouldn't have been too surprised. ''If I could dig up any evidence whatsoever that you buggered Private security and made your way back here around the time Betha Concannon was killed, I'd walk you down to the ComPol command center myself. You had motive and means, Risa. Anyone who saw you in the cafeteria this morning knows you could make the opportunity."

"And you have a remarkably vivid imagination. Ginny." Jani's stomach grumbled in agreement. "I'm guessing I murdered Betha because she uncovered proof I murdered Lyssa. Very neat. I understand the appeal. I'm a stranger. No one likes me or trusts me. I can see where pinning it all on me would make everyone else feel much better. Pardon me if I decline to cooperate. I've killed no one." *At least, not lately.* "Your problems began here, you'll find your answers here, and I doubt they'll be as neat as you hope."

Doyle chewed on her lower lip. "You've bothered me since you arrived," she said. "Durian told me our dear lieutenant served as your steward during your journey here. Disgracefully bold of my favorite blond, but knowing Lucien as I do, not a surprise. The fact he's taken to you concerns me. He has a long history, Risa. Being his friend is no recommendation."

Jani remained silent. *They think I killed Lyssa. Evan says he brought me here to take care of me, but did he really plan to turn me over for his wife's murder?* Evan's career teetered on the brink—what steps would he take to save it?

Apprehending his wife's murderer, to start?

I'm the outsider here.

"Is everything all right, Risa?"

"Everything's fine."

"Hmm. I don't suppose you'd like to tell me where you got that piece of Consulate paper?"

"No, not at this time."

"You said in the code room that it was some sort of communications log?"

"Yeah. Ingoing and outgoing Consulate calls covering a three-day period. Idomeni days. They're a little longer than ours."

Doyle frowned. "I know that, Risa. Funny that so many calls could fit on a single page."

"Well, every department had its own log. I'm hoping this

page came from the one used by executive staff.'' Jani removed the document from her bag. ''Besides, the assault on Rauta Shèràa had reached its climax during the period this record was made. The Consulate had switched to emergency transmission only, to avoid sniffer bombs.''

''How do you know? Don't tell me you were there?''

Big mouth. ''Common sense.'' In truth, she'd found it out from John. He'd shown great interest in the circumstances surrounding the transport crash and had managed to uncover all sorts of details during her convalescence. ''Why take chances?''

''Indeed?'' Doyle watched Jani activate her scanpack. ''What can I do to help?''

''I'll need a workstation. I assume yours is typed to you?''

Doyle pulled over the wheeled cart on which her sleek unit sat. ''As you said, we're now working together on this, whether we like it or not.''

Jani removed the code disc from its pouch and ran her 'pack over it to break the seal. She then handed the disc to Doyle. ''Here. I'm sure you know what to do.''

Doyle inserted the disc in one of the reader slots; Jani scanned the Consulate document to unlock the internal latches that would have prevented instrument reading. Her new chip functioned smoothly. She handed the unlocked document to Doyle, who set it facedown on a plate reader.

''I hope my station can handle an old code like this without locking down.'' Doyle's fingers moved over her touchboard. ''I can't unlock my own damned machine— I'd have to call in someone from Justice. They'd use Betha's murder and the examiner's lien as excuses to shut me down, too.'' She tapped in a final series, then glanced at Jani. ''Here goes.'' She muttered an initiation code, then held her breath as she watched her display.

Jani moved as close as she dared to the workstation and snatched peeks at the display's edge from the corner of her eye.

After a minute or so, Doyle's display flickered. ''Here it comes,'' she whispered.

Jani watched the edge of the screen. ''What does it say?''

''Just a list of names and dates so far.'' Doyle's eyes widened. "Wow, she *was* there then," she said, partly to herself. "Old school friend. Had a rep as a patho. Always told me she was on staff on Shèrá. Thought she was lying." She looked at Jani, then touched another area of the board. "Let me print you something solid. You look ready to jump out of your chair." Several sheets of paper emerged from a slot in the workstation's side, and Doyle handed them to Jani.

Jani took the papers in her left hand. The one that wasn't shaking. *Two women died because of what's on this paper.* She studied the column of names. Acton van Reuter's name was entered several times, as was Evan's.

Makes sense. Daddy messaging Sonny several times a day, demanding he get the hell out of the line of fire and come home like a good little van Reuter. Jani checked the date-time column. Most of the messages had been sent before the crash, while she had still been trapped at Knevçet Shèràa.

John said the transport had been sent from a Service fuel depot just outside the city. According to Lucien, that's where the bomb had been planted. The site had an odd phone code, an alphanumeric that corresponded to its location on a Service grid map of the area. *N-2-D—*

—1-4-3-7-L. Jani read the rest of the code, next to Evan's name. An outgoing call, made soon after the last in a series of communications with his father.

The buzzing in her head resumed. Intensified.

But he could have been talking to anyone there. The Service personnel stationed at the depot were the primary sources of information regarding Laumrau and Vynshà troop movements. Someone from the Consulate would have had to keep in touch with them regularly.

Don't make excuses for him anymore. Jani reread the entry. The right day. The right time. A short call. Only a few seconds. A call someone expected. A simple order. *Do it.*

"Is something wrong, Risa? You don't look well." Doyle leaned across her desk. "Is it important? What the hell do you see!"

More than two women died because of what's on this paper. Eight patients. Twenty-six Laumrau. Fifteen members of the Twelfth Rover Corps. Rikart Neumann.

And, in ways large and small, though not as important, Jani Kilian.

"Risa! Talk to me!"

You always took orders, didn't you, Evan? Jani heard a rustling to her left. Caught a whiff of burnt leather. She looked up to find Borgie standing beside her chair.

"Got your motive for Lady Lyssa's death now, don't you, Captain? She found out her husband gave the order to bomb your transport. Your old boyfriend. Saving his ass as usual. Keeping his eye on the ball. Not caring who got hurt." His fatigues stank of smoke and sweat. Dirt smeared his face. "I can't tell you anything you don't already know, Captain. Don't give me the wide-eyed look."

"I never would have guessed."

"Ah, bullshit, Captain. You remember what he was. You've been jumpy as a cat since you've been here. Glass in his hand all the time, just like back then. Making excuses, just like back then. Always somebody else's fault, just like back then." He looked at his T-40 and grimaced. "I think it crossed his mind more than once you might be on that transport. But his overbred ass was on the line. First things first—save the tears for later."

"I think you're right, Sergeant," Jani said. From far away, she heard Doyle calling her. No, not her. Someone else.

"Risa, who the hell are you talking to! Answer me, damn it!"

Jani stood up, almost stumbling as her back cramped. She shoved the papers and scanpack into her duffel and headed for the door.

"Tyi! Stop! Drop the bag! Put your hands where I can see them! Turn around slowly!"

Something in Doyle's tone made Jani stop. More than mere loudness. Panic. The kind that had drawn its weapon. The kind with blood in it.

Blood sings to me. I know the words. Jani let her bag slide to the floor, put her hands up, and turned. Doyle had indeed drawn her shooter—the bright red sight fix skittered across Jani's shirtfront like an insect. Better to stand still. Nervous hands made for messy shooting.

"*Roche!*" Doyle shouted. "Get the meds up here now!"

She edged around her desk. "Don't move, Risa—I will shoot."

Blood sings. Strange songs. Jani heard the pound of footsteps in the hallway. Muffled shouts. *Blood talks, too. It asks, "Evan, how could you?"* Amid the voices, Jani heard Doyle call out, "She's in here." Then she felt a cool prickle between her shoulder blades. Then she heard nothing at all.

CHAPTER 30

"Of course you understand, nìRau, that much depends on your people's willingness to let bygones be bygones."

Tsecha looked Prime Minister Cao in the face as he tried to discern her meaning. The female raised her chin in acknowledgment of his attention and curved her lips without baring her teeth. On its own, Tsecha had learned over the past weeks, the expression meant nothing. Cao always smiled.

"I do not understand you, nìa," he said. "Please explain." The female's lips curved even more. *Yes, it is good to have called her nìa.* The only other humanish female he had called by the informal title in this damned cold city had been Hansen Wyle's daughter. *And she had not smiled.* She had shouted, in fact, and stamped her foot. Her voice had grown so loud, embassy Security had wanted to expel her from the grounds. How the young one had cried out. *I'm not my father!*

"Bygones, nìRau." Cao shifted in her high seat. Like Ulanova, her legs were not long enough to provide adequate counterbalance. She tottered and had to grab hold of the sides of her seat cushion to keep from falling. "We will ignore the fact the Elyasian Haárin are trying to monopolize transport refitting in most of the Outer Circle. In return, your colonial Council will cease its attempts to secure full and unrestricted access to Padishah GateWay."

Tsecha nodded, his eyes fixed on the Prime Minister's pale-knuckled grip on her chair. *If I moved quickly, she would tumble to the floor.* He had done such once before, to Ennegret Nawar, during the young male's Academy entrance interview. As Tsecha remembered, Nawar had not thought it very funny. *He bruised his hip, and split his trousers*. Nervous humanish, he had learned, needed to be treated carefully.

"NìRau? Are you listening to me?"

Tsecha studied Cao's round, golden face. Her eyebrows, thin as black pencil lines, had drawn down in puzzlement. "Yes, nìa," he replied. "You will allow my Sìah Haárin to continue to attempt to rebuild your most aged, unspaceworthy ships. In exchange, we the idomeni are to surrender in our efforts to gain more direct access to our Vren colonies, which suffer already from undersupply and dwindling populations. Thank you. Most generous. My Oligarch will be most pleased."

"NìRau—"

"Why do you not say what you mean? Why do humanish never say what they mean? As long as Padishah remains secure, you will have no worry that Haárin will try to settle on Nueva Madrid. Your Service hospital will remain safe from our observation. Your experiments will remain safe from our observation."

"NìRau!"

"We have known of the Ascertane work for some time, Your Excellency." Tsecha's use of Cao's humanish title upset the female, as he knew it would. Every trace of her constant smile disappeared. "We also know of the attempts John Shroud's colonial hospitals have made to recruit Haárin into other medical studies. So much have our outcasts been promised in return for their help. Access to business. Status. I wonder how Albino John is able to offer so much. I wonder who allows Albino John to offer so much."

The pleasing color drained from Cao's face, changing from Sìah-like gold to the bloodless sand of her tunic. Shards of pure color, formed by the lake reflection through idomeni window glass, danced over her face as though small flares burned beneath her skin. The lake itself, Tsecha could see, had calmed, the shore ice that had been shattered by the storm re-formed. A pleasing observation, a well-ordered reflection of the room itself: large, lake-facing, quiet, with chairs even a humanish would consider tolerable. With the exception of his own rooms, Tsecha favored this place most in all the embassy.

Cao breathed in deeply. "Since we're being so open and aboveboard with one another, nìRau—"

Ah, sarcasm.

"—perhaps you would be so good as to explain your actions of the past few days?"

"Actions?" Tsecha folded his arms into the full sleeves of his overrobe and shifted on his low stool. Had they found traces of his presence in the Exterior skimmer? Clothes? Hair? Skinprints? *But I took such care.* Would they be watching his hiding places tonight? *But I have so much to do!*

"The Exterior Minister has complained to me—"

Tsecha held his breath.

"—of your surprising attitude toward our requests for information concerning Haárin soil- and water-treatment systems in our Outer Circle. The reluctance of your Oligarch, of your Council and Temple, didn't surprise us, but we expected more of you, nìRau. Considering your history of kindliness toward us, even during difficult times, we find this sudden lack of cooperation on your part most unsettling—"

Tsecha watched the lake shimmer in the cold sunlight like metal foil. *My two favorites would have liked this room, I think.*

"—if not downright alarming." The Prime Minister paused to dab perspiration from her forehead with a wisp of white cloth she then tucked inside her tunic sleeve. Outside, the air could freeze one's blood, but the temperature inside the viewing room was most pleasant. "This place is set up to remind you of Rauta Shèràa, nìRau?" she asked as she made a small gesture toward the sand-painted walls and sunstone-tiled floor.

"Yes, nìa."

"Even the temperature?"

"Do you not find it comforting?" Tsecha inhaled deeply of the hot, dry air. "I was told you would find it comforting." He had, of course, been told no such thing. The ease with which he lied about such an inconsequence was lessened by the fact that, for the first time since he had arrived in this frozen city, he felt truly warm.

Cao patted her forehead again. "I think you are pulling my leg, nìRau."

"Pulling your leg, nìa?" Tsecha looked at the female's cloth-covered limbs in alarm. He and the Prime Minister sat an arm's length apart—he had not touched her! "I only enjoy the warmth," he admitted, "and wish you to think I provided it for you." A humiliating admission, perhaps, but better that than to suffer such disorder!

Cao drew up straighter in her seat. "The strategy sounds familiar. Which of your Six taught you that particular lesson, nìRau?"

"My Tongue taught me most." Tsecha bared his teeth. "My Hansen."

"I should have guessed," Cao said, frowning. "I watched Hansen Wyle grow up. He schooled with my children. With all due respect, nìRau, learning humanish ways from that man was the equivalent of learning table manners from Vlad the Impaler."

"Vlad, nìa?"

"A long-dead dominant of ours. You would have considered him most disordered." A shadow of a smile revisited Cao. "Do you think much of Hansen these days, nìRau?"

Tsecha felt the female's stare, chilling where the sun had so recently warmed. "I think of Hansen every day, nìa."

"Do you think of any of the the others, as well?"

To lie successfully, Nema, you need to think of it as a game. His Hansen had sat in a room much like this one. Fallow time had come to the north-central regions; rain and wind had beaten against the window like souls screaming for mercy. *The best human liars think of it as a game. Don't think of the importance of what you're saying, or what you're trying to accomplish—if you do that, you'll lose. It's just a game Nema. Just a game.*

"No, nìa," Tsecha answered, "I think of no other." *I am as a young one, playing my game.*

"Exterior Minister Ulanova believes otherwise, nìRau."

A good liar knows how to use truth, Nema. He realizes its value better than anyone. "My Anais, nìa," Tsecha said, "has much of which to worry. Much which gives her trouble." He bit his lip to avoid baring his teeth as his Lucien's stiff posture at the theater sprang up from his memory. "The youngish lieutenant. Pascal."

"Yes." Cao's look held surprise. "Well, if *you* can figure out what's going on, someone had better have a talk with our Anais, and soon." She slid carefully off her seat. The click of her shoes on the bare tile echoed within the room. "I must go, nìRau. Time for my staff to begin the dance with your staff, I suppose. As usual, I have had an interesting time."

Tsecha followed Cao out of the room. In the hall, Sànalàn appeared from the shadowed interior of a side hall and took over the escort duties. Blessedly alone, Tsecha hurried back to his rooms. The time for midevening sacrament was fast approaching, and he had much for which to prepare.

He stripped off his clothing as soon as his doors slid closed and hurried to the sanitary room for a quick laving. Even as water dripped from his soaked head, Tsecha rummaged through his clothing cupboard for that which he needed for his evening's work: the silkweave cold-weather suit which would fit under his clothes like skin and the battered bronze-metal case containing other lessons learned from war.

Tsecha finished dressing. On its cupboard shelf, the metal case awaited his attention. He lifted it, its weight as nothing in his hands, and dumped its contents onto his bed. The two thin Vynshàrau blades he strapped over the sleeves of his coldsuit. The Pathen Haárin shooter he shoved into a pocket in the coldsuit's front. The weapon bulged from his chest as a second heart, but it would be most easy to reach if it proved needed. This he knew from experience.

With an ease he knew would have surprised his Lucien, Tsecha stowed supplemental shooter power packs and assorted scanning and blocking devices within other pockets in the suit. Shielded by the special polymer weave, his weapons would fail to activate embassy scanners. *I am most as Haárin.* He had felt such during the war, when he had allowed Hansen to persuade him to have the suit made. The materials were meant to be used in weapons-systems construction only—the fact a chief propitiator caused them to be used in ways not their own moved beyond disorder and into chaos.

I have always been as Haárin. Tsecha pulled on a fresh overrobe, then sat in his favored chair. *Because of such, I understand my Captain.* After a time, room illumins lulled by stillness darkened to thin half-light. Tsecha felt along his sleeves and touched each blade in turn. Through the altar-room door, he heard the soft sounds of his cook-priest and her suborn as they readied midevening sacrament.

I feel no fear. His hands were dry and steady. His heart did not thud beneath his ribs. *Soon I shall walk into the night, as my Captain did.* The thought should have sickened him, but it did not. He knew, as she had known before him, that a disordered way sometimes proved the only one possible.

CHAPTER 31

She lay on her back. She couldn't move. Efforts to flex her legs caused her right thigh to cramp. A tight strap pressed around her ribs just beneath her breasts, barely allowing her to breathe. A band like bony fingers encircled her right wrist and presumably her left, as well.

Jani opened her right eye and felt the depressingly familiar release of tension as her film split. She blinked. A slimy hydropolymer fragment slid off her eyeball and down her cheek, leaving a cold, damp snail track in its wake.

Well, let's see how much more damage we can do. She opened both eyes wide. Her left film remained intact, but her right continued to fissure. Her vision alternately blurred and sharpened as bits and pieces floated across her eye, then over the side, leaving her right cheek cool and sticky.

After a few determined blinks, Jani's vision cleared enough that she could look around. Up to a point. *Nice ceiling.* Dull white, from what she could tell, since the room's lighting left something to be desired. She lifted her head as high as she could. Darker walls, somewhere in the cheery blue family. In the far corner, near the door, two frame chairs squatted near a low, dispo-littered table. Someone had eaten their meal out of a box. More than one someone, judging from the number of containers.

They ate and watched me sleep? Jani tried to swallow and coughed as her dry throat prickled. Her mouth felt lined with absorbent, her lips, dry and rough. She summoned up what saliva she could and ran her tongue over her teeth. She pulled against her restraints again; her lower back tightened. She sagged back on the bed and tried to gather her scattering thoughts.

Not just any room. I'm in a hospital. Jani could tell from the smells in the air. Chemical. Antiseptic. Freshly cleaned bed linens and an underlying hint of metal. Especially metal. Instruments. Cold, sharp, and always too large.

This is for your own good, Captain.

Jani shivered at the memory of her examinations, embedded in flesh and bone and brought to life by her surroundings. John had gotten to the point where he flinched each time she did, which only made things worse. Val Parini, meanwhile, always examined her with the distracted air of one who had seen the worst, and rest assured, Jani, you aren't even close.

But that bastard DeVries had enjoyed hurting her. At first, she thought herself the unlucky recipient of his warped version of foreplay. But as time went on, she was compelled to conclude the man simply did not like her.

Hell, he hated my guts. He felt I distracted John from their greater purpose. She had heard the arguments. Raised voices in the hall outside her room.

"Open your little rat eyes, John! The A-G wants her, so hand her over. Hang on to her, she'll drag us and everything we've worked for right into the sewer with her. We've learned what we needed from her—give her up!"

Jani stroked the bedsheet. Warm, where her hand had rested. Smooth. Pure white. Like John. He never lost his temper during DeVries's tirades. He'd slip into her room afterward, pull a chair beside her bed, and watch her as she pretended to sleep. Always the same position, legs crossed at the knees, hands folded in his lap. The attitude of a man who owned the store and the street besides.

Hello, creation—my name is John Shroud, he'd said to her the first time she'd opened her eyes to find him there. *Unfortunate name for a physician, don't you think?* His milk white skin had seemed to glow in the harsh light, his voice rumbling from a source nowhere near his heart. Palest blue eyes had glittered like cut crystal. In the stupor following the reversal of her induced coma, Jani had thought him some sort of implacable, medically trained angel.

It was the color of his eyes that did it—turned out they were fake. John's eyes were pink, in reality. He'd been the one who taught her how to film. And how to walk, dress, and feed herself with the aid of numb, twitchy animandroid limbs. *Being a freak has its drawbacks,* he'd told her. *But it has its advantages, as well. Trust me, I know what I'm talking about.*

But he'd never shown her how to burst a restraint. Bad John. Jani pulled against the straps until the pain brought tears to her eyes. Then she raised her head and looked at herself. *I was wearing clothes, wasn't I?* If she had, they'd since been replaced by a plain-fronted white gown. In the crook of her right arm, a raised silver disc glittered in the dim light.

Oh hell—!

Too late. Cued by her increased movement and elevated blood pressure, the sedative pump activated. Jani felt the skin beneath the disc tingle. A heartbeat later, warmth rippled up her arm and across her chest. *I don't want to sleep anymore, damn it!* She yanked again at her restraints, but the straps held fast.

Sweat bloomed on her forehead, under her arms. Chills. Her stomach spasmed. Burning rose in her throat. *I'm going to vomit!* She tried to turn on her side, but the chest strap held her down. *I'll drown in it!* She forced herself still, breathed in slowly and deeply, willed the nausea to pass. Acid harshness percolated to the base of her tongue and stayed there. *For now.* If she continued moving, the pump would administer another dose after a buffer period had passed. Could be thirty minutes, or thirty seconds, depending on the drug.

Jani looked toward the door. Funny no one had checked on her. The sensors in the bed had to be monitoring her vitals. Didn't anyone notice the increased activity?

She worked her hands. The skin on her right wrist burned as she moved. *I'm hurting myself—these shouldn't hurt.* What kind of restraints were these? *Old.* And poorly applied. *I'm not in a place where they're used to strapping people down.* That seemed promising. Maybe they wouldn't know how to handle her if she broke loose.

She pulled against her left wrist restraint. Gently and firmly at first, then not so gently and much more firmly. All she felt was the compression. When her hand became stuck, she tugged harder still. A few muffled cracks sounded. It worked through the narrow opening more easily after that.

Jani held up the hand for inspection. The little finger twitched uselessly, corkscrew-twisted wrong side up. The thumb's movement was barely perceptible. The whole hand had numbed—she couldn't even detect pressure anymore. She loosened the strap beneath her breasts. *Thumbs come in handy when you're trying to work buckles*, she thought as she tried to unlatch the strap she couldn't see using fingers she couldn't feel.

"How's it goin' there, Captain?"

Jani glanced to the side. Borgie sat perched on her end table, cradling his T-40 like a bouquet of long-stemmed roses. "You could help," she replied.

Smoke puffed from the man's flak jacket as he shrugged. "Can't, ma'am. You know that." The fact seemed to desolate him—his hangdog expression appeared even more gloomy than usual. "Yolan's here, too," he said, momentarily brightening. "She's found a new friend."

The chest strap fell away. Jani sat up and freed her right wrist and ankles. "Are they out in the hall, Sergeant? Does that mean you know where we are?" She looked again at Borgie, whose smile faded.

"Can't help you, ma'am," he repeated. "You know that." As Jani struggled out of bed, he stood up and shouldered the T-40. An odd odor wafted about him as he moved. Not scorched gloves, this time, but something familiar that Jani couldn't quite place. Scorched, yes, but not gloves . . .

"Oh, great!" She felt for the back of the knee-length gown and caught a handful of bare ass. "I had clothes, didn't I? Where the hell are they!" She caught Borgie's eye just as he was about to shrug another negative. His shoulders sagged.

"—*bullshit*—!" The sound pierced through the closed door. Jani backpedaled toward the bed, prepared to dive under the sheet if anyone entered, but no one came. Instead, the voices grew louder.

"—see you in hell before I call him in! Once you call in a facility chief, forget it!" A man's voice. Enraged. "—empty bedpans for the rest of my life—!" Jani tasted the panic, as well. Like bile. The taste reminded her of the pump. She worked her index finger beneath the thin disc—it left a raised, bloody welt in the crook of her arm. The itch had taken on a squirmy life of its own, as though worms crawled through her elbow and up her arm.

"You have no choice, *Doctor*!" Another man's voice. No panic, but you could fuel transports with the anger. "Look at the liver enzymes! When did you ever see values like those!"

The doctor countered, voice lower, shaky. "Are you sure you calibrated the blood analyzer properly?"

Silence. Which spoke volumes. "I ran the drug screen," the angry man finally replied. "She'd been dosed with Ascertane sometime in the past seventy-two hours. Her blood contains metabolite NCH-12. The last bulletin we got stated that if any patient turned up positive for that metabolite, we were to notify the nearest facility chief immediately. Now, Doctor, are you going to call Cal Montoya, or am I?"

The doctor spoke, his voice softer, words impossible to discern. Jani left Borgie standing by the door and walked back to her bed. Near the headboard, a wheeled IV rack stood like a skeletal sentry. She hefted it, checked it for balance, swung it back and forth like a baseball bat.

"Heavy, Captain?" Borgie had started poking through the dispos on the low table, wrinkling his nose at what he found.

"Nope. Under control, Sergeant." Holding the rack in her right hand, Jani headed for the door. It swept open for her, revealing a larger room, an examination table, lab furniture, and assorted analyzers. The doctor and his angry colleague leaned over a desk, their backs to her, still arguing. The desktop was cluttered with readout cards, sheets of notes, and stacks of textbooks.

The angry man turned. Jani recognized him. Vaguely. *The duty nurse?* His eyes widened. He reached out to her just as she swung the rack around.

Both men wore medwhites. Jani stripped off the doctor's. Fewer bloodstains. She put them on, then scrounged through the glass-fronted cabinets, uncovering bottles of film former, a white medcoat, scuffed white work shoes. She washed away blood, dressed, refilmed her eyes. Light brown filming. Poor coverage. The greenness shown through—her eyes appeared phosphorescent in the office lighting.

"You look like a crazy wonko, Captain," Borgie said dryly as they left the infirmary. "Get the urge to drop 'em and bend over just looking at ya."

"Control yourself, Sergeant." Jani tried to smile, but one look at Borgie's face stopped her. It had changed in the past few minutes. Blackened in places. Blistered in others. One ear was gone. The peculiar odor that followed the man like a faithful hound had grown stronger. "Am I dying, Borgie?" she asked. "Or am I just cracking up?"

Her sergeant, her dead sergeant, stared at her through cloudy eyes. Cloudier eyes. His dark brown irises grew milkier as he spoke. "Captain, I can't help you. It's all you." His voice rasped with desperation. "*Your* questions! *Your* answers!"

They paused so Jani could get a drink of water from the hall cooler. After the fifth dispoful, Borgie began to fidget, so Jani reluctantly tossed the cup in the 'zap and fell in behind him. The people they passed in the halls looked at Jani's clothing, never at her. No one challenged them, or tried to stop them. *I mean, me. No one's tried to stop me.* Her sergeant had nothing to worry about. He possessed his own unique brand of camou.

Good ol' Borgie, Jani thought as she watched the man's smoking back. "*Sais-tu ou nous allons*, Sergent Burgoyne?" she asked him. *Do you know where we are going?*

"*Mais oui, ma Capitaine.*" Borgie looked back at her as he spoke. His other ear, along with most of his cheek, had burned away. White and yellow blisters glistened in the light.

The acid rose once more in Jani's throat. She recognized the smell now.

Borgie led her through an anteroom and into an office. Expensive paintings. View of a lake. Nighttime. Moon reflecting on rippling water. Jani expected to see a man sitting at the desk, but instead, she saw a woman. A friend. Dead, of course, like Borgie. Funny how that fact seemed to concern her less and less.

"Yolan." Jani approached the desk slowly. Her old corporal still wore her usual startled-deer expression. Her lazored blonde hair was as neatly combed as ever. Her steel blues appeared battered, though. But it was brick dust, not smoke, which puffed from the material as Yolan nodded weakly. The rubble had buried her fairly deep, after all. Oddly enough, her gamine face had remained untouched, but her body . . .

Bones in a bag. All that had been left. Borgie had waited for Jani to turn her back before he fell to his knees and gathered that limp body in his arms. Yes, his relationship with Yolan had crossed every line. Yes, Jani had known, and kept it to herself. The one time she got involved was when Borgie asked her to persuade Neumann not to leave Yolan behind at Rauta Shèràa Base. Neumann hadn't wanted to take her to Knevçet Shèràa. He trusted her even less than he had Jani. "I killed her, Captain," Borgie had cried. His weeping had seemed to sound from the walls themselves, following Jani as she left that section of the bombed wing, dogging her down every hall, echoing around every corner.

I helped, Sergeant.

"We had to come here," Yolan explained to Borgie, who loomed over her in his still-futile effort to appear domineering. "She got scared out in the open. Didn't want to risk seeing him again until she knew she could take it." Her delicate features set in stern lines, Yolan turned to Jani. "Captain or not, you say anything mean to her and I swear, I'll air you out. She's been through enough." The corporal leaned her head back. The chair rocked back as well. It dawned on Jani that Yolan had yet to move from the neck down.

"Fine, fine," Jani nodded. "Bossy-assed mainliner." A flash of movement captured her attention. She turned. "*You!*"

Betha Concannon stood in the middle of the office, her clothing rumpled, her hair tangled. She tried to speak, then winced and held a hand to her throat. Jani saw the steel blue scarf knotted around her neck and looked at Yolan, who regarded her levelly. "She wanted something to cover the bruises. She's sensitive about them."

"Well, bully for her," Jani replied. "She's left her best friend to be accused of her murder. She betrayed everyone she worked with and for. She's a liar and a cheat and an accomplice in Lyssa van Reuter's murder! And she's one of ours, damn it! She should have known better!"

"Being colony's no guarantee of goodness, Captain." Yolan spoke slowly, as though reprimanding a child. "You've lived out there long enough to know that. Besides, you knew what Betha was about, deep down. That's why you worried about her. But you cut her slack because she was colony. Because she was a dexxie. Maybe if you'd trusted her less, she'd still be alive."

"Not fair, Yolan," Borgie protested. His words came muffled and slurred, spoken as they were through lips now swollen and blistered. "Don't put that on her, too."

"But she wants it that way." Yolan's eyes never left Jani's face. "She wants to be nailed to the cross. She'll even pass out hammers and spikes to all comers, with instructions where to pound." The corporal's head lolled against the back of her chair. Borgie propped it upright with a gentle hand. "Doesn't help, does it, Cap? Won't help till the day you die, and after that, it won't matter." She looked at Betha. "No one deserves to die like she did. Do something about *that*. Take care of what you can."

Jani looked out the window, to the floor, the walls, everywhere but at the three people who stared at her silently. The three dead people. *How far gone are you, when the ghosts are more human than you?* Her right arm itched to the point of pain. Pinkish yellow seepage stained the medcoat sleeve. Her right shoulder felt hot. Breathing had become difficult, as though she wore a clogged respirator. She forced herself to look at Betha. "It was Ridgeway."

Betha nodded slowly, using her hand to stop the movement.

"You'd been working for him. All along."

Another labored nod.

"Ridgeway helped you bugger the docs Lyssa took to Nueva. He had an accomplice at the hospital, a doctor who purposely botched Lyssa's regularly scheduled take-down. Lyssa made it to Chira before hallucinating herself into the rocks, and Ridgeway thought the one person who knew Evan had transmitted the order to bomb my transport was dead." Jani paused to look at Borgie. What did she expect to find on his charring face, an expression of surprise?

"But you had friends at the PM's," she continued. "They told you what Cao and Ulanova suspected. You made friends with Lyssa before she left on that final trip, and she entrusted the proof she had compiled to you. At first, you planned to turn it all over to Ridgeway, in exchange for whatever. Then you got greedy. It never occurred to you he could kill you, too.''

Betha's mouth moved in mute pleading. She managed a sharp squeak when sounds of activity reached them from the anteroom

Jani slipped behind the shelter of a shoulder-high plant. Betha, Borgie, and Yolan remained where they were. Durian Ridgeway burst in, walking through his cowering victim on the way to the desk. He began a frenzied search, opening and slamming drawers until, with a bark of relief, he pulled a grey documents pouch from the bottom drawer and tossed it on his desktop. With Borgie and Yolan as fascinated bookends, he dumped out the contents and flipped through the pages, muttering under his breath.

Jani stepped out from behind the plant, ignoring Borgie's frantic gesturing for her to stay put. "It's not in there, Granny.''

Ridgeway tensed. He looked up slowly. "Risa." His hands dropped below the level of the desktop. "I thought you were in the infirmary.''

"I was." She took a step toward the desk in an attempt to circle around to Ridgeway's side, but he quickly countered, edging away in the opposite direction. "The Consulate com-log. The one that shows the call Evan made to the fuel depot. It's not there." Jani sidled closer to the desk, but stopped as Ridgeway backed away in the direction of the door. "It's in the hands of whoever Ginny Doyle is really working for. Judging from your behavior, that person isn't you.''

"Captain Kilian. Jani. The call recorded on that log does not constitute proof. Our personnel at the depot were in constant communication with Consulate staff. Quite necessary, considering the circumstances. Surely you remember?''

"The way you're acting bitches that argument to hell, Durian. You raised the alarm that Betha was missing. Then you steered Doyle after Steve. When Steve disappeared, you shifted everyone's sights toward me. Anything to deflect attention from Evan. He told me you'll do what you think you have to. You're not stupid. If everything's green, why bother with it? Why clean it if it ain't dirty?'' Jani watched Ridgeway's hands, still below desktop level.

He has a shooter. She glanced at Borgie, who now stood by a sofa on the other side of the room. Betha stood beside him, one hand at her throat, the other over her mouth. Yolan sat on the sofa, her legs propped on the low table in front of her, her arms limp, hands in her lap. ''He's armed, Cap,'' she said.

''I know,'' Jani replied.

Ridgeway stiffened. ''Still talking to yourself, Jani? Who answers? Riky Neumann?''

''Never. Why waste a good hallucination?'' The burning itch in her arm had receded to a dull scratchiness. ''I see Betha. She's over there, by the sofa.'' She raised her arm to point and Ridgeway flinched to one side as though anticipating a blow. He brought the shooter up and pointed it at her chest. Direct line of fire. One shot. Crack the sternum. Stop the heart. Not even augie could fight this one off.

This time, it would take.

Here's the hammer. Jani took another step toward him. *The spikes.* Another. *What are you waiting for?*

Betha's mouth opened in a soundless scream.

The shooter rasped. Jani stumbled to her left as the impact half spun her around. A fleeting pain, in her left shoulder, just above the joint. Then numbness. Her lungs cleared, her breathing eased. She looked down. Her arm jerked uselessly. What remained of it. The exit wound had obliterated the hand. Half the forearm. Rose pink carrier dripped through gaps in the heat-sealed stump, splattering over the synthetic flesh that now soiled the carpet. She looked at Ridgeway, who stared back in stunned silence. ''You missed, you goddamn office boy. Point-blank range, and you fucking *missed*.''

His eyes narrowed. ''Is that your challenge, Jani?'' She could smell the hate as he raised the shooter again.

So slow. He moves. So slow. Jani feinted to her right, then darted close. Right hand raised, fingers straight. Her sudden movement distracted Ridgeway. He discharged the shooter off target—the pulse packet brushed her left cheek just as she thrust at his neck just above the base of the throat. He collapsed to his knees, eyes goggled, grabbing at his throat as his breath wheezed and whistled like air being sucked through a cracked pipe.

"How does it feel, you son of a bitch?" she asked softly as she stepped behind him. The time for ritual had passed. The curve where his neck joined his shoulder whispered, *here.* This time, she listened. Felt augie's strength reinforce her own. Raised her right hand. Brought it down.

"Cap'n?" Borgie drew alongside her. They watched Ridgeway's body until it stopped twitching. Then Jani turned to her sergeant. His face was a crusted mass now. Eyes glazed white. He crackled when he moved. "Wuh be'er go."

Jani edged out into the hall and looked at herself in one of the safety-dome mirrors set in the ceiling. She had folded the empty documents pouch over her ruined forearm. The shooter graze had left a reddened brush burn on her cheek. *I look like a lab accident.* She smiled grimly. *I am a lab accident.*

"See anything, Cap?"

Jani checked the mirror, saw nothing behind her. Then she turned. Yolan smiled up at her, broken body bundled into a wheeled office chair. Betha pushed. Borgie brought up the rear, T-40 raised and ready. Tiny gouts of flame licked from beneath his flak jacket. His face was . . . unrecognizable.

Jani remembered where she was now. *Interior Doc Control.* She led the way, past the offices, toward the elevators. At every junction, she'd look up at a dome mirror and chart her solitary progress. *When I look up and don't see myself, I'll know I'm dead.*

Empty elevators. Deserted hallways. No one to challenge her, to stop her. *Like they're giving me room to maneuver.* Jani and her silent trio bypassed empty offices, entered a large anteroom, stopped before a door. *Like they want me to come here.*

"Once you go through that door, you're on your own, Cap," Yolan said. She'd become spokesman for the trio, seeing as she was the only one who could talk. "We can't help you."

"I know."

"Decision time, Cap."

"I know." Jani gripped the door handle and twisted. Sand shifted beneath her feet. Desert wind brushed her face and riffled her hair.

CHAPTER 32

Evan stood at the bar in his dimly lit office. "Excuse me," he said peevishly when he realized he had company. "I don't recall requesting a med—" He tensed as Jani stepped forward. "Jan." He offered a weak smile. "Glad to see you're up and about."

Jani let the doc pouch fall to the carpet. Tried to let it fall. The nappy material had stuck to the carrier that had crusted on the end of her stump; she wound up having to rip it away. Cloth parted company from synthetic flesh with a keening rasp. Evan moaned and gripped the edge of the bar with both hands. His eyes squinched shut.

"No one even tried to stop me, Evan. Did you ever get the feeling you were being set up?" She walked to the sitting area near his desk. "Have a seat. Bring your bottle. You may need it."

Evan remained in place for a time, breathing slowly, eyes still closed. When he opened them, he looked at Jani sidelong, sighing when he saw her settled into a chair.

"What did you think I was, Ev, a symptom?"

"No." He gathered up a glass and decanter. "That would have implied good luck. Mine ran out long ago." He sat in the chair across from her and deposited his glassware on a side table. "What's this about a setup?"

"I think certain people wanted me to come here. Tie up loose ends, save them the trouble."

"I hope you listened to the message I sent last night. It's true, you know. I do love you."

"You're a liar."

"You think so? You wouldn't say that if you'd heard the fights Durian and I had over you. When we figured out you might be alive, he wanted to send someone to Whalen to kill you. I had to bribe him to leave you alone. I promised to wangle him a spot on the ballot in the next general election. Seems he has dreams of a deputy ministry. For starters." His hand shook. Ice rattled like chattering teeth. "I tried to convince him he operated better behind the scenes, but he insisted. I'm afraid exposure to the voting public is going to prove a shock for old Durian." He looked at Jani, taking care to avoid her mangled arm. "I'm hanging my janitor out to dry. That alone should convince you I'm sincere."

"You may have had a sincere moment or two in your life, Evan. I doubt they involved me." Without warning, Jani's left shoulder jerked. A sharp pain sang down her arm, flicked around her wrist, cramped her fingers. "I was just something to shake in your father's face." She looked down at her left thigh. Her left hand rested there. She could feel its weight, its trembling. She just couldn't see it.

"As I recall, you enjoyed upsetting your colony friends with me, as well."

"It doesn't matter." She watched the hand that wasn't there. Gradually, the shuddering eased to an occasional twitch. "It was a long time ago."

"I didn't think you'd trust me right away. I'm not an idiot, Jan." Evan emptied his glass. "I thought after you settled in, got used to things, realized how I felt, you'd see how good you could have it here." He cast a longing look toward the decanter. "Now, here it is, three days later. Plaster's flaking off the ceiling, and knickknacks are clattering on the shelves. The end is near." His eyes grew liquid as tears brimmed. "How much longer do I have?"

"Not long." Jani poked her left thigh with her invisible hand, felt the tiny impacts against her phantom fingertips. "Doyle's set the wheels in motion. She always suspected your complicity in Lyssa's death. She's working for someone else, by the way. Your Virginia. Service plant, maybe. Or else she's thrown in with one of the other Houses."

The comment fired some life back into Evan's face. His

jaw firmed; his eyes sharpened. "Which one?"

"Your guess is worth more than mine. I'm surprised your janitor hadn't already flushed that out."

"Where is Durian, by the way? We were supposed to meet fifteen minutes ago." Evan waited for Jani to answer, fidgeted with his glass when she didn't. "I didn't kill Lyssa, Jan. She had evidence of my sins hidden all over the city. She told me if anything happened to her, she had someone in place to insure the evidence would be sent to the right people."

"That person was Betha Concannon." Jani etched figures in the air with her invisible fingers. "Bad choice on her part—Betha worked for Durian. Now Betha's dead." Her hand started to ache from the exercise. She stopped flexing.

"And Durian? He always notifies me when he'll be late. This isn't like him."

"I'm sure there's a reasonable explanation."

"If there is, I'd like to hear it, please."

Jani held both her hands out in front of her. The one she could see felt the same as the one she couldn't. "The alliance with Ulanova changed things with regard to Lyssa. With her aunt's backing, she became dangerous, instead of merely embarrassing." She straightened her left leg, shook the pins-and-needles feeling from her left foot. Funny that life should return to it now, when the rest of her felt so dead. "Do you remember that play they ran at the Consulate the night we met?"

"Jani." Evan watched her flex, then reached for the decanter. "*Becket*," he said as he poured. Liquor splashed against the ice and onto the table. "It was *Becket*."

"*Becket*." Sharp sounds. Jani had to concentrate in order to repeat them without softening them into Vynshàrau. *Mbeheth*. "I remember you liked it. I found it stupid. Man hires his friend to do a job, then gets pissed when said friend actually does it. And now look at us." Her chest felt tight. "Life imitates art." She touched her right arm. Even through the medcoat sleeve, it felt hot, swollen.

Evan leaned toward her. "Are you all right, Jan? Your lips are turning blue."

"I'm fine."

"Your eyes don't look right. There's a shooter graze on your cheek."

"I'm fine."

"Where's Durian?"

"I think I know what happened." Jani stared at Evan until he eased back. "You and Durian were talking. You'd just found out Lyssa had made the connection between your com-log entry and my transport crash. With Ulanova's help, she'd bring you down. After all, it was your big sin. No Acton to blame for this one—it was your call. You could have stopped it and you didn't."

"My father—"

"—was three weeks from Shèrá on the fastest ship he had. You could have handled it. Missed messages. Lost records. Lied. But no. You wanted to be the hero. The one who pulled the van Reuter nuts out of the fire." Jani hesitated as her heart skipped a beat. In that instant, her breathing eased.

Hey, augie.

Hey, Cap.

"I didn't know you were on that transport." Evan reached out to her. "Riky told me he'd keep you out of it. He promised me—I made him promise when you left the city with him. Then I didn't hear from him anymore. No answer to the messages I sent him, and the ones from my father started coming in one an hour. Always the same. 'Do something, boy—we're depending on you. Act like a van Reuter for once.' " Evan's own breathing grew ragged. "Jani, I was alone. Scared. I'd acted as go-between for Rik and Dad—that made me culpable. Violating the Bilateral Accord was a treasonous offense. I faced prison. Maybe worse. I didn't know what else to do!"

Jani heard a familiar sound filter in from the anteroom. The sizzling crack of a shooter. "I didn't know what else to do, either." One report. Another. Another. *Twenty-six times. Before the dawn I will have fired twenty-six times.*

"They're all dead, Jan. We're still alive." Evan knelt before her, his hands closing over her visible one. "You said you wanted to remember what happened. You can do that here just as well as in prison. If you feel you have to suffer to make it count, trust me, you will. You'll have to bury yourself somewhere in Chicago. I'll have to resign. But I'll know you're here, and we'll be able to get together eventually. After the dust settles.''

Jani eased out of Evan's grip. "You knew. All of it. About the patients. About Lyssa. Betha. When you left me that message ordering me to stop my investigation—Durian had just told you he'd killed her, hadn't he?''

"Jan, I didn't mean for any of it to happen.''

She caressed the side of his face, ran her thumb over his unshaven cheek. He closed his eyes, rested his head on her knee, didn't even flinch as her hand slipped down around his neck. "I watched a man destroy his face with his bare hands. I helped pull what was left of my corporal from beneath tons of rubble. Evan," she said as he looked up, "there are some things you can't negotiate away.''

"Jan—''

She pushed him away. "What was the name of Becket's friend? The king?''

Evan glanced toward the door. "Henry.''

"Henry.'' Jani could feel the heat generated by too many people pressed into the Consulate auditorium, hear the rustle of evening gowns. "The one scene I remember. Henry's with his friends, his knights. His janitors, like Ridgeway was your janitor—''

"What do you mean, 'was'?''

"—and I'm sure you were drunk, like he was. Henry the king, losing his grip—''

"Jani?''

"—looking for someone to blame—''

"No.''

"—knowing if she were dead, your problems would be over.''

"Please!''

"Will no one rid me of this dam-ned priest.'' Jani's soft voice rang like a shout in her ears. "Lyssa and Betha. Make that dam-ned *priests*.'' Or maybe the reverberation was only in her head. "So Ridgeway maneuvered his mops and buckets and rid you of your priests. Ulanova didn't know about the comlog. You were home free.'' She coughed. Her arm ached again, but it no longer felt hot. Quite the opposite. She shivered.

"Jani?" Evan had slunk back to his chair. "Where is Durian now?"

"I left him in his office."

"Oh. Are you going to leave me in my office, too?"

"No." Jani watched Evan's gaze flick toward the door again. "They want me to kill you, I think. Whoever Ginny works for. Whichever of your colleagues is most fed up with you. But God, I really hate being maneuvered, and I'll be damned if I'll be the tool for another Family bastard." She smiled. "Besides, you knew. And you'll remember, too. That's the one thing we'll always have in common."

Evan swallowed. "We could have more," he said carefully. "We could have everything again—" He shot out of his chair, trying to dart past her to the door. But he moved too slowly, like Ridgeway had. Jani rose, kicked out, caught the side of his knee. The joint cracked with the wet snap of damp wood. He fell to the carpet and lay gasping, thumping the floor with his fist.

She waited until he looked at her with pain-glazed eyes. "I don't want to kill you. I want us both alive when they come. I want you around for a long time. Now I'll have someone to share my ghosts with."

Evan's shallow breathing gradually slowed, deepened. Jani couldn't say the same for her own. Her chest felt heavy. Her left leg cramped. Her right leg was the numb one now. She sat back down, and waited.

"Captain Kilian?"

The voice came from the other side of the door. A man's voice. She didn't recognize it.

"Captain Kilian, I'm going to open the door. I want you to come out here. Please advance slowly and keep your hands where I can see them. That's for your own good as well as mine."

Mine? Did that mean her visitor was alone? Augie tried to rattle Jani's bones in anticipation of a struggle, but she couldn't oblige with the customary battle chill. The only chill she felt left her clammy and numb. Dark patches flecked before her eyes.

"Captain?" The office door hushed open. "Please come out."

She struggled to her feet. With every incremental rise, the dark patches waxed, then waned. As she took her first steps, the room seemed to tilt. She grabbed the chair for support.

"Captain?"

A different voice now. Its source filled the doorway. Tall. Blond. Steel blue uniform wrapped around a steel blue spine. Red tabs on either side of his collar. Matching red wounds on his cheek.

"Lieutenant Pascal," she said.

Pascal fingered his shooter, still encased in the holster at his side. Then he drew to attention and snapped a salute, the sort that made stiff Service polywool crack like a wind-whipped flag on a pole.

Jani touched her forehead in return. "Save it for the A-G, Lieutenant. Allow me what's left of my sideline pride." The floor seemed to shift as though she walked across a deflating pontoon. She turned, found herself within striking distance of another man. Shorter. Stockier. Black hair. Beard trimmed to a sharp point. He offered a courtly bow.

"Dr. Calvin Montoya, Captain." He wore medwhites, carried a large pouch slung over one shoulder, held a large, featureless black cube in his hand. His dark eyes narrowed as he studied her face, then her mangled arm. "I've been charged with seeing you safe."

"Oh." Jani looked from Montoya to the cube, then back. "How is John?"

The point of Montoya's beard twitched. "He's as ever. I'll tell him you inquired. I'm sure he'll be—"

"Surprised?" She looked down at the cube again. "Time for the take-down? Well, Doctor, let's get it over with."

"Yes." Montoya's expression turned relieved. "I think we need to hurry." He held up the cube and fingered one side. Red lights glittered across the face Jani could see. "Watch the lights, Captain. Don't turn away. Concentrate on the sound of my voice and watch the lights." As Montoya continued to murmur directions, a tracery of red, like shooting stars, played across the cube face. Jani found herself tracking the flickering as a flower follows its sun. Her knees weakened.

"Watch the lights, Captain. Don't turn away. Watch—"

Patterns played, each more rapidly. Songs to her brain. Phantom pains shot through limbs destroyed long ago. Around her, flames flashed. Sounds. Yolan's scream as the wall collapsed. Smells. The nose-searing acridity of hyper-acid. The stench of burning flesh.

"Come to the light, Captain," said the voice from the other side of the flashing red. "Don't fight it, or you'll feel—"

"Sicker. Yes, I know, Doctor." Jani took a slow step forward. The odor of berries enveloped her, overwhelming her taste and smell, overpowering the stinging smoke. Her vision tunneled, blocking out the flames, the tumble of falling debris.

Only her hearing remained true. The hardiest sense, John had told her. The last sense to die.

See you soon, Captain, Yolan said.

"Yes, Corporal," the Captain replied, as the last flicker of red winked out.

Patient S-1 remained hospitalized and under close observation for a period of four days. Because of extenuating circumstances and the fact the patient displayed her usual remarkable recuperative abilities, she was then released with the understanding that follow-up visits would take place regularly at a facility to be determined.

It is believed the patient can be expected to recover fully and to resume her normal range of activities, such as they are. However, it cannot be stated too strongly that the long-range effects of her condition are not known at this time.

> *—Internal Communication, Neoclona/Seattle,
> Shroud, J., Parini, V., concerning Patient S-1*

AFTERMATH

CHAPTER 33

Jani opened her eyes. The view was white and brightly lit. The air felt cool and carried the characteristic odor she had long ago dubbed hospital-metallic. She took a deep breath and stretched her arms. Both of them. One was phantom. The real one was encased from wrist to shoulder in a membrane bandage filled with clear allerjel. Jani shook it. The jelly sloshed.

When she tired of that, she sat up, wedged her pillow behind the small of her back for balance, and studied the watercolors hung on the wall opposite her bed. One was a seascape in greys and greens, the other, a gold-and-brown still life. Jani had spent most of the past few days picking out details in the paintings, little nuances she'd missed during previous examinations. If she concentrated hard enough on the exercise, she could almost forget certain things. Why she was in hospital, for example, and what had happened to put her there.

And more immediately, what lay beneath her covers. Or rather, what didn't.

Jani carefully ignored the telltale flatness of her bedspread. As long as she didn't look, she could pretend her left leg was still there. She could feel it, after all, like the missing arm. Funny how its absence bothered her more. *It's the vulnerability,* she thought, in a rare attempt at self-analysis. *You can still run with one arm.*

But run from whom? Calvin Montoya had been her only visitor thus far. He checked in on her five or six times a day, examining her with sure, gentle hands, a joke or a piece of gossip always at the ready.

The details of what had occurred at Interior Main, however, she'd had to pull from him with pliers.

The doctor and nurse from the Interior infirmary were still alive. Their encounter with Jani and the IV rack had netted them two concussions and one skull fracture. And three-month suspensions without pay for not notifying Montoya immediately of their singular patient. *They were arguing about me and looking things up in textbooks.* Her right film must have broken while she was unconscious; they'd probably seen her eye. One glimpse of that pale green orb would certainly be enough to drive any medico to the reference materials.

Her left calf itched. She tried to ignore it.

I did lots of damage that night. Evan's knee would never be the same. After suffering torn ligaments and a dislocated kneecap, his evening went rapidly downhill. The Justice Minister himself placed him under arrest. The warrant was served upon Evan in his well-guarded hospital suite, with Cao and Ulanova serving as the Greek chorus. All the major networks had been invited to record the unprecedented event.

Calvin had brought Jani a copy of the local CapNet broadcast. The wafer still lay atop her holoVee console, its seal unbroken.

She stared at the seascape. Contained by a pewter frame as shiny as summer, sunlight played on gentle waves. How often on Shèrá had Evan told her about his sailing adventures on the Earthbound lakes? His expression had always grown melancholy as he spoke; those were the only times she could recall him appearing at all homesick. *Are they letting you have a drink, Ev? Are they letting you have anything else?* Montoya had seemed worried. He had heard rumors of a suicide watch.

Jani twirled a corner of her blanket and switched her attention to the still life. A tasteful piece, nothing exceptional. Something Ulanova would hang in her dining room.

I can imagine the conversations ringing around that table. The gloating comments, the laughter. *Revenge is a dish best savored cold, to be served with the appetizers and the iced cocktails.* To those with the stomach for it.

Leaves me out—I don't have the stomach for much, any- more. Lucien had tried to visit her several times, but she re- fused to see him and rejected his bouquets of flowers. Ate without appetite when she ate at all. Ignored the holoVee and stacks of magazines and newssheets.

Montoya managed to hide his frustration beneath a cloak of humor and delicate prodding. *He threatened to toss me out into a snowdrift last night.* During this morning's examina- tion, he assured her he'd push the skimchair himself if she'd just agree to a jaunt up and down the hall.

Jani's refusal had plunged him into watchful silence. His examination took a good deal longer than usual. He withheld his usual inquiries, but he also drew more blood and took more swab samples. The only time he spoke was when he announced what he was going to do, inviting her questions. Her response that he should just take it all and get it over with jolted him. As he left, Jani had heard the doorbolt slide into place.

So she'd slept for a few hours, studied the ceiling, slept some more, studied her paintings.

The door eased open, and a cautious Montoya poked his head into the room. "Ah, Jani. You're awake." He entered, pulling a wheeled trolley. A large black plastic bag rested on the trolley's top shelf. "If this doesn't get you out of that bed, I'm going to fill your membrane bandage with detonator gel and whack it with a hammer." He patted the plastic bag like a proud father. "Your new limbs are here."

Jani sat up straighter. "Already?"

"At Neoclona, we aim to please," Montoya said jauntily, emboldened by her interest. "Get ready, milady," he said as he opened the door of an inset wall cabinet. "I intend to have you walking within the hour."

Jani kept her attention focused on the plastic bag. "I've only been here four days."

"Yes?"

"A standard arm takes a week to assemble. A leg takes at least two."

"Under normal conditions, that's certainly true." Montoya

approached her bedside carrying a small metal tray on which instruments rattled. "But in your case, some preparations had already been made."

"How?" Jani swallowed as the doctor placed the tray on her end table. Several long, pointed probes glistened in the light. "Why?"

Montoya activated one of the probes, pulled down the left shoulder of Jani's medgown, and began prodding the smooth, shooter-burned membrane that served as the interface between her animandroid arm and the rest of her. "Once one reaches a certain level in Neoclona, your file becomes required reading." He worked around the outer rim of the junction, searching for dead spots. "The wise facility chief knows to be prepared."

Jani tried in vain to keep from flinching as needling tingles radiated throughout the hypersensitive junction. "What are you telling me?" she asked through gritted teeth. "That every Neo shop in the Commonwealth has a set of left-siders with my name on it sitting in a cold drawer?"

Montoya adjusted the shoulder of her gown and pulled up a corner of the hem. "I'm going to check the thigh junction now."

"You didn't answer my question." Jani grabbed a fistful of sheet and found a riveting light fixture on the wall opposite to focus on.

"The answer should be obvious, Jani," Montoya said as he probed, "to you more than anyone." After eliciting a couple of bearable twinges, he pronounced both junctions functional. Jani rearranged her gown as best she could while maintaining her shaky balance. Meanwhile, Montoya opened another of the room's recessed cabinets and rolled out a tall, silver monolith.

Jani watched him activate touchpads and enter codes. The limb sealer came to life with a characteristic hum. "Why replacements? Why not just fix the old ones?"

"Coming back to ourselves, are we?" The physician smiled absently, his attention focused on the instrument. "So many questions."

"And so few answers." Jani's stomach hadn't ached at all

up to that point. She only noticed it in contrast. Now, it hurt like hell. "Why replace what you can fix?"

As Montoya pushed the limb sealer over to the bed, two disc covers on the instrument face slid open, revealing twin depressions. The upper one was small and green, the lower one large and dark blue. They looked like a pair of misshapen eyes.

"The reason for the new arm should be obvious. As for the leg—" Montoya hesitated. "I believe you'll find your back problems will be a distant memory once it's attached." He bumped the sealer up against the bed. The frame resonated in time to the sealer's vibration. Jani could feel the humming buzz in her teeth. "We'll do the arm first, I think. Then you'll have more leverage when we do the leg. Push your junction against the green."

Jani lowered the shoulder of her gown and pressed her stump into the shallow saucer. Tingling pressure radiated across her upper back as the disc membrane closed around the junction.

"You're implying the leg wasn't balanced. I had no problem with it for over seventeen years. My back just started acting up in the last six months."

Montoya disappeared behind the sealer. Jani heard his footsteps, followed by the whine of a zipper, a *pop*, and a rush of air as he removed the arm from its vacuum casing. "We change as we get older, Jani. Our bone density, muscle mass. Your animandroid limbs were older models in the first place they stood no chance of keeping up the pace. In a more conventional environment, you'd have had them changed out three or four times by now." The sealer vibration ramped. "Press against the saucer," he said, peeking around the unit at Jani. "Hold your breath on three. Ready? One. Two. Three."

Jani pushed, inhaled. She felt a burning as the junction sintered, then split down the middle, exposing her shoulder joint. She felt as well as heard the soft click as new bone met old. Then came warmth as synthon lubricant flowed through the junction and into the joint, followed by the suction smack as tissue met bioadhesive.

"Looks good. Pull out, please."

Jani eased her new arm through the newly opened gap in the saucer. She rolled her shoulder, bent her elbow, counted off on her fingers to check— *"Hey!"*

Montoya poked his head around the sealer, which he appeared to be using as a shield. "Is something wrong?"

Jani winced as she pressed fingernails into fingertips. "I can feel with these."

"Of course."

"I couldn't before."

"An adjustment long overdue, don't you think?" The dark head again disappeared. "I'm going to call in someone to help with the leg." He left the room, returning soon with a burly nurse in tow.

This bout with the sealer proved clumsier, not to mention more painful. Tears blurred Jani's vision as she made a circuit of the room under Montoya's watchful eye. She muttered a prayer of thanks to whoever had had the presence of mind to slip a pair of underpants beneath the gaping medgown. "You're right, Doctor. My back does feel better." She hopped up and down a few times. "I didn't realize people could change so much at the ripe old age of forty-two."

The nurse glanced sidelong at Montoya, then excused himself with a curt nod. Once they were alone, Montoya pulled out a lazor and cut away the allerjel packing from Jani's right arm. As she washed away the gooey remains of the soothing jelly, he scrounged a set of medwhites and a pair of lab shoes.

"Hungry, Jani? Allow me to buy you a very late lunch." He handed her the clothes. "I'm getting you out of this damned room if it's the last thing I do." His dark eyes danced. "As reward, I'll tell you the exciting tale of how you got here in the first place."

"We escaped Interior Main a heartbeat ahead of Ulanova's people." Montoya forked through a tomato-sauced omelet, with occasional stabs at a green salad. "Your blond friend, that lieutenant, knew whom to look out for, which areas to avoid. He and the young red-haired man—"

Jani choked on her soup. "Steve! I told him to stay in Private."

"Well, he obviously didn't listen. He and Pascal bundled

you onto a skimdolly he had purloined from the loading dock. Much bickering went on during this time. I gather Pascal found Steve wandering the Main halls in a furtive manner and set upon him. Steve had a black eye—''

"Why the hell did Lucien hit him!"

"—which went nicely with Pascal's air of 'last one standing.' They declared a truce when they realized your welfare was at stake, but it was shaky at best.'' Montoya dabbed a few beads of sweat from his brow. "I discovered during that time I wasn't cut out for excitement.''

"I couldn't have been too exciting,'' Jani said. "All an augie does after a take-down is sleep and toss around a lot.''

Montoya grimaced. "Your augment was the only thing keeping you alive. After I took you down, you began to slip into anaphylactic shock. Your blood pressure went into the basement—'' He stabbed his fork at her like a fencing foil. "Those two morons knew that goddamn sedative patch was contraindicated in your case, and they used it anyway! Three-month suspensions—if they think it ends there, they're in for a grim surprise. Even *with* your augment, you could have died in that infirmary. The fact that you went on to do what you did . . .'' He faltered and took it out on his salad, stabbing the vegetables into mashed submission.

Jani studied the view over Montoya's shoulder. The small dining hall was empty except for the two of them. Purple in all its shades dominated the color scheme, from tinged white walls to lilac grey floor and nearly black furniture. The funereal surroundings turned the mind to things best forgotten. "I killed Durian Ridgeway,'' she said quietly.

"Did you?'' Montoya's chewing slowed. He set down his fork and pushed aside his half-eaten meal. "Pascal's skimmer was parked outside the docks. It was too small for the four of us. The situation became even more interesting when a hyperactive bundle of winter clothing bounded out to us yelling, 'Steve, Steve,' in a singularly feminine tone. Pascal pulled out his shooter, which caused Steve to spring for his throat like a cat. At that point, your blood pressure took another dive and the bundle started screaming that Exterior Security was hot on her trail.'' Montoya exhaled with a shudder. "Amazing how we suddenly all managed to fit into Pascal's vehicle. He took us as far as the boundary between Exterior and the Shèrá Embassy. I'm still trying to assimilate what happened next. *Tsecha* was waiting for us outside an Exterior guardpost. The idomeni ambassador."

Jani pushed her plate aside. The little she had eaten froze in her stomach. "Tsecha?"

Montoya nodded. "He drove us here. In an Exterior skimmer Pascal took great pleasure in telling us the ambassador had stolen. He wore eyefilms. Makeup. And an evening suit. Pascal treated this like it was the most normal thing in the world. Steve and his bundle, a young woman named Angevin, blinked perhaps twice, then piled you into the backseat of the ambassador's skimmer and shouted for me to, and I quote, 'hurry the fuck up.' " He sighed. "So I did."

He knows I'm alive. Did she ever really doubt he'd discover the fact? What had he told her on the Academy steps, when she handed him back his ring and told him she had every intention of remaining human until she died.

You will never die, nìa.

"Well," she said.

"Indeed." Montoya nodded absently. "Tsecha is a proponent of what he calls evading. He evaded us down side streets and alleys I never knew existed, and I've lived here all my life. We took corners at complete verticals. I yelled that if he didn't slow down, I was going to tear his head off. I couldn't keep you still enough to intubate you. Time was running out. Your throat was swelling shut. The shockpack alarm was blaring."

Jani eyed the entry. *He wouldn't come here, would he?* Risk his Temple's wrath and the Commonwealth's anger by calling upon a murderer. *Of course he would—he thinks killing is just something I do.* Part of the job description. Eyes and Ears . . . destroyer of diplomatic relations . . . toxin. . . .

Montoya rattled on, a captive in his own recollective jet stream. "He just smiled, if you can call what he does a smile, and told me, 'Ah, Doctor, you know my Captain will outlive us all.' I commented that that could be by a grand total of five seconds if we slammed into the side of a building. He then slowed down just long enough for me to reinsert and anchor the endotracheal tube." He bit his well-buffed fingernails one at a time. Just a nip here and there, an old broken habit undergoing spontaneous reassembly.

"So you were getting air. Thank God. We were being pursued, you know, until Tsecha started *evading*. The lieutenant had drawn his shooter, and the ambassador . . . he was armed, as well. A shooter in a chest holster. Knives up both sleeves."

Jani's throat felt dry and tight. "He would have used them, too." She stole a sip of water from Montoya's glass. "Idomeni martial order broke down after Knevçet Shèràa. Self-protection became the order of the day, even for those who had never had to think about it before. Nema always adapted quickly to change."

"Nema?" Montoya's eyebrows arched. "Oh, Tsecha's born name."

"He changed it after the war ended. Then he went into seclusion in his Temple enclave for five of our years." Jani's gaze kept veering toward the cafeteria entry. "And with all they knew about his beliefs, they still let him out of his cage."

Montoya nodded. "I've heard about those beliefs. That someday, the human and idomeni races will be as one." He played with his fork. "Did you feel the same way when you studied with him? Did you buy what he sold the way Hansen Wyle did?"

The sudden sharpening of Calvin Montoya's voice didn't surprise Jani. Anyone who had won John Shroud's confidence couldn't have been as ingenuous as he first appeared. "Hansen believed. But I think he enjoyed the thrill of it all, too. He liked flipping it off in people's faces."

"He died in an air raid a few hours before he was going to try to negotiate you away from my boss." Montoya smoothed away a ragged nail edge. "Seems to me our alien ambassador isn't the only one capable of making associates ignore their better judgment." He eyed her pointedly. "Let's get out of here," he said, gesturing toward a fluted paper cup nestled beside her soup bowl. "Take those. Chew and swallow them."

"Why?" Jani sniffed the dark brown tablets. They smelled like chocolate fudge made with sour cream. "What are they?"

"Enzyme tablets. They'll help you digest your food."

"What's wrong with my digestion?"

"It needs help."

"Why?"

"There's no time, Jani. Just trust that it's for your own good."

"I've heard that before." Jani chewed dutifully, chasing the bitter, gritty mass down with a swallow of water. "John's favorite line. Whatever happened next either hurt like hell or made me sick." The increased sensation in her left leg still jarred her, and she half walked, half hopped as she followed Montoya out of the dining hall.

It didn't surprise her that Lucien Pascal waited for them near the nurses' station, or that he carried her duffel as though he owned it. He looked tired; thin lines of scabs dotted one cheek. He offered her a cool nod, then turned to Montoya. "Think she's up to it?"

Montoya's nails again found their way to his mouth. "No. But it would be no next week as well. No right into next month, but we don't have the time, do we?" Muttering curses in Earthbound Spanish, Montoya ducked behind the nurses' station.

"You're not ready," he said as he emerged carrying a small polyfilm bag. "There's too much that needs to be talked about. Too much left up in the air. But I've been ordered to let you go anyway." He thrust the bag into Jani's hands. "The directions are in with the tablets. When you run out, stop at any facility. You have nothing to worry about, Jani. You're being seen to. If you don't trust anything I've told you, trust that." He squeezed her hand, glared at Lucien, then strode down the hall without a backward glance.

Jani turned to Lucien. "What's going on?"

He pantomimed an explosion. "All hell's broken loose." He gestured for her to follow and walked to a side door labeled, EMERGENCY EXIT ONLY. "We need to get you through as many GateWays as possible as soon as possible," he said as he ushered her though the door. "But before that, there's someone who wants to see you."

CHAPTER 34

"Where are you taking me?" Jani lagged behind Lucien as he led her through the garage. She swore under her breath as she searched for an escape route.

"My skim's charging. I'm just behind that," he said as he pointed to the silver-and-purple ambulance that jutted through a low arch like a metallic tongue. "I hope to hell I can pull around."

"*Where are you taking me!*" Jani's voice bounced off the cement walls. Her eyes teared freely, both junctions ached, the drying skin of her right arm tingled and itched, and Dr. Montoya's enzyme tablets had left a sickening metallic taste in her mouth. Oh, and there was the fear. Fear did wonders in countering take-down malaise. Jani planted in the middle of the garage, her hands curled into fists. "I'm not budging until you tell me where we're going."

Lucien turned back to her, his handsome face a study in angel innocence, his hand resting possessively on her duffel. "We're going over there," he said.

Jani squinted in the direction he pointed, trying to pick out details in the dark. A battered sedan nestled in a charge station, but the flow monitor atop the station's housing shone blue, indicating the vehicle's cell array was already fully charged.

Dark red. The vehicle's color was dark red. An old Exterior skimmer. Jani's stomach roiled as the driver's side gullwing popped up.

"I tried to talk him into stepping up to a better class of

vehicle,'' Lucien said, ''but he seems to have taken a shine to that old wreck, color and all.''

Nema emerged from the vehicle like poured syrup and stepped into the light. He had left his humanish evening suit behind, opting for the Vynshàrau clothing of an elder male of his skein and station. Full-sleeved, off-white shirt tucked into loose, light brown trousers. Dark brown knee-high boots. Wide bands of scarlet hemmed the edges of his cream over-robe. His thin, silver brown hair had been gathered into a single braid and looped like an oversize earring on the right side of his head.

''My Captain,'' he said in English, his High Vynshàrau accent softening the hard sounds. ''I thought I would need Albino John's help to identify you, but to my joy I find you most as yourself. Glories of the day to you.'' He bared his teeth fully, an expression of highest regard. His bony face seemed to split, gold eyes opening wide. Grim Death with a Deal for You.

''NìRau ti nìRau.'' Jani stood up straight despite the stinging pain in her thigh junction and crossed her left arm over her chest, palm twisted outward. She tilted her head to the left. Nodded once. Thank God for the mechanics. If you could concentrate on the mechanics, you could block out everything else. She glanced to the side and saw Lucien watching her like an anthro student on his first field trip. ''Push off,'' she said.

''I don't think so.''

''Go, Lucien,'' Nema said. ''I wish it as well.''

''No, nìRau. I have my orders.''

''Which were to guard. So guard out there.'' He gestured sharply toward the garage's entrance. ''There is no need for guards here.'' He looked Jani in the eye and bared his teeth again. ''My nìa and I are most safe with one another, and together, we win against all.''

Lucien took a step in Nema's direction, ready to argue. But when Nema refused to look at him, he turned on his heel and strode out of the garage.

Jani waited until the echo of his footsteps died away. ''You've hurt his feelings,'' she said in semiformal High Vynshàrau, etching fluid symbols in her air with her right hand. Her gestures accentuated the humiliation of a suborn cruelly mistreated by his dominant. "He is new to the ways of Vynshàrau, and he is not predictable. He might do something to hurt you in return."

"Perhaps," Nema replied, the angle of his head implying tentative agreement, "but then he will find I am not so predictable as well." He shook his head, humanish urgency leaching into his speech and gestures. "There is no time for him. Ulanova searches for you, nìa! She knows you are here in this damned cold city!"

"She wants to see me court-martialed that badly?" Jani glanced toward the garage entrance. She trusted Lucien. In this particular instance. Really. She just wished she'd had the presence of mind to ask him for her duffel.

Nema flicked his left hand in affirmation. "Eventually, I am most sure. My injured Lucien believes she first would force you to testify in Cabinet Court against van Reuter. The trial would be broadcast throughout the Commonwealth. Such a triumph for my Anais." His brow wrinkled in bafflement. "She hates van Reuter so. Lucien tried to explain it to me, but I could not understand. Things to do with business and your ways of marriage, among so many other stupid things. Such ridiculous disorder, inappropriate for dominants of their levels, and truly." He sighed. "So much I do not understand, and no one is to be left to me to explain." He looked Jani in the face and his posture grew somber. "Step closer to me, nìa, so I can see you."

Jani edged nearer, fighting down the urge to bolt back inside the hospital. When Nema grasped her chin and tilted it upward, her eyes stung and her throat ached.

"You have not changed, nìa."

"I look completely different to humanish."

"Humanish only look at the face. I see the gestures and hear the voice of one who is most as she was." Nema's amber eyes glittered like molten metal as he studied her. "I would have spoken with you in your hospital, after your damned transport explosion, but John would not let me. He hid you away, when I could have sheltered you better. He behaved in a most stupid manner."

"He had his reasons, nìRau."

"Yes, stupid humanish reasons. Did you choose him freely?"

"Yes. No." Jani pulled Nema's hand away from her chin. "I thought he'd turn me over to the military police if I didn't. By the time I realized he never would have done that, it was too late. The Haárin had entered the city, the humanish were fleeing—"

"And he, your physician, did not see you safe!"

"I never gave him the chance, nìRau."

Nema took a step back from her, touching the side of his face in a way Jani couldn't interpret. For the first time she could recall, her teacher appeared at a loss for words. "You must go soon," he finally said in English, his speech stripped of gesture. "Lucien has found a ship which will take you as far as Felix. I do not know how he found it. He tried to explain it to me, but I could not understand! It is not as it was with you. My Eyes and Ears. When you saw and heard, it was as if I myself saw and heard."

"You had Hansen."

"Hansen was Hansen. He taught me games—he was not you. And now I have found you after so much time, and you must run again."

Jani took a deep breath. "I killed, nìRau."

"Yes." Nema tucked his hands into his sleeves. "You killed. In that way, as well, you are most as you were."

"I did what I did."

"Yes, nìa. We all do what we do."

She stared into her teacher's eyes, felt adrift in a sea of gold. "I'd do it again."

"Yes. Your own did not know you for what you are. The Laumrau believed your own, and see how they paid." Nema's attitude grew distant, as though he questioned her for an exam. "You have recovered from your injuries most rapidly, I understand?"

Jani nodded, addled by his presence and the abrupt change in subject. "Yes, nìRau?"

"Your Dr. Mon-toy-a, he is confused. Albino John is not so confused, I think."

"I wouldn't know, but—"

"And you, nìa, are not confused at all."

"We're not at Academy anymore, nìRau. We don't have time for philosophies."

Tsecha gestured sadly. "No, you are most right, nìa. The time for philosophies has passed us both." He fell silent, staring at her impassively. Then he pulled his hand from his sleeve. Held the closed fist out to her. Opened it. "Now is the time for realities."

Her Academy ring rested within. The jasperite glinted like the eye of a night creature.

"*Inshah*," Jani said, addressing Nema with the informal High word for teacher, "you're wrong."

"Wrong?" Nema's brow wrinkled as he considered the concept.

"I'm not the one you want. Hansen would have been, maybe, but not me. I'm too disorderly."

Tsecha nodded, gesturing in strong affirmation. "You are toxin, Captain. You bring pain and change. Such is your way. You know no other." He reached for her right hand and placed the ring on her third finger. It was still too small—metal scraped over skin as he forced it into place. "Still some time yet, I think. But soon. Soon."

"I'm not your heir, nìRau. You've made a mistake." Jani sensed motion out of the corner of her eye and turned to find Lucien standing in the garage entry. He tapped his timepiece. "I have to go," she said.

Nema looked at Lucien and sighed. "Yes." He turned back to Jani and stood straighter. "But someday, when you have not killed for a time, you will come back to me. Then we can argue your suitability." His lips curved. It wasn't an idomeni expression of goodwill—he didn't bare his teeth a millimeter, or even cock his head. It was a humanish smile, the smile of someone who knew better. "*a lète onae vèste, Kièrshi-arauta*," he said as he gestured farewell to her, left hand extended, palm facing up. A farewell to an equal. Then he slipped back into his skimmer. The vehicle came to life with a smooth hum, then flitted away from its station and out of the garage like a bedraggled bat.

It took Jani a moment to realize she was shaking.

Lucien drew up beside her and handed her her duffel. "He

drives like a maniac,'' he said, still smarting from his abrupt dismissal. "Not much for good-byes, either.''

"No,'' Jani agreed, "none of the Vynshàrau are. They each live in their own little world. Nema figures if he likes you, you'll come to him again, and if he doesn't, why should he care?'' She tried to fluff her pillow-mashed hair, then tugged at her medwhites in distaste. "Trade ya clothes,'' she said, eyeing Lucien's warm polywools with envy.

"I've got some for you in the skimmer.'' He headed toward his charge slot. "We better get going—your shuttle leaves in an hour.''

Jani fell in quietly behind Lucien, noting with interest that he now drove a stolid blue sedan. "New skim?'' she asked, as they drifted sedately into busy late-afternoon traffic.

"It does what it has to. It's also less conspicuous and loaded with antitracking.'' Lucien frowned at Jani as he maneuvered between lanes. "Yes, I had to give the other one back to Anais. Happy?'' He reached behind her seat. "Here,'' he said, tossing a bundle of clothes in her lap.

"Who sideswiped your face?'' Jani asked as she pulled a heavy shirt over the medwhite top. Service surplus winter-weight fatigues, baggy and dark blue. Her kind of clothes. "Anais or Claire?''

Lucien touched his injured cheek. "None of your business.''

"Be that way. Are we going to O'Hare?''

"No. A private port.'' He unsnapped the top of his shooter holster as he eyed the traffic flowing around them.

Jani tugged on her heavy trousers. "How are Steve and Angevin?''

"Forell was locked up for a day and a half. Unfortunately, they found the code. Ange rousted some of her dad's old Academy chums. Your old chums as well, I suppose. They twisted arms. You could hear the sockets pop all down Cabinet Row.''

"I would liked to have seen them before I left.''

"Not an option. I'll tell them good-bye for you.'' Without warning, Lucien cut across five lanes of traffic and shot down an exit ramp. Jani took a few deep breaths to slow her heart, but kept her comments to herself. She knew the difference between reckless and evasive driving.

"Montoya told me you ignored the news," he said as he maneuvered down a side road. "No mention of Betha. Lyssa's death is still considered an accident." He paused. "Ridgeway's death has been ruled a suicide."

"I broke his neck," Jani said as she pulled off the medshoes. "Wonder how the medical examiner explained that?"

Lucien shrugged. "It's Chicago. Precedent exists." He nodded toward the bag, which he'd tossed on the floor at Jani's feet. "Your boots are in your duffel." He stared at the side of her face until she gave in and looked at him. "I don't know why you should feel bad," he said. "He would have killed you."

"It's just post take-down." Jani stared out the window at the passing scenery. "Look, I do what I have to. It doesn't mean it doesn't affect me." She took a deep breath and opened her duffel. "Ah shit." She picked at the ragged-edged remains of her scanproof compartment.

"Sorry about that," Lucien said. "By the time I got my hands on it, Doyle had already torn it apart. I was able to sweep your room at Private before her people got there, though. Hope I got everything you need."

Jani thumbed through the bag's contents. Her boots. Two sets of coveralls. Underwear. Scanpack. Tools and parts. Her shooter, fully charged and polished. The tiny soldier saluted her from an inside pocket, where he stood guard over a static pouch containing an ID and cashcards.

She probed deeper. Her hand closed around the holocard. She studied it in the half-light of the cabin, tilted it back and forth. The racers swooped and glided, surfing the wind. She looked at Lucien out of the corner of her eye. Lucien the manipulator, who could always be counted on to keep his head. The frosty operator. The beautiful young man with the dead eyes. And a cheek that had been a scratched mess four days before, but was almost healed now. She touched her own shooter graze, mended to barest visibility. "You gave me this card for a reason. For a while, I thought it was your oblique way of telling me Lyssa was an augie. But that wasn't it, was it? You were letting me know. You're an augie, too." She waited until he answered with a scarcely perceptible nod. "When did you have it done?"

He touched the back of his neck, where bottom of skull met top of spine. "About ten years ago. It was my fifteenth birthday present from Anais."

"Is it like mine?"

"Not entirely. It's an improved version of the one Martin had. By then, they'd learned it was better to wait." He turned down a narrower road. In the distance, shuttleport lights blazed against the darkening sky. "I don't know if I'd be any different without it. Like they say, it only augments what's already there. Or in my case, what isn't." He bypassed the small charge lot, parking the skimmer at the edge of the tarmac next to a large baggage trolley. "Let's get a move on."

After a week of frigid cold, a comparative heat wave had settled over the city, making coldsuits and face shields unnecessary. Jani found the double layer of polycotton she wore adequate to keep her warm. She lagged behind Lucien, who broke into a trot as he neared a line of shuttles going through their preflight inspections. A serious-looking older woman in an olive green flight suit, pilot's headset dangling from her neck, walked out to meet him.

Jani circled the woman's ship. Late-model commercial shuttle. Sleek. Well maintained. Even the most suspicious Customs agent would think twice before searching it. It reeked of paid-up docking fees and clean inspection records. Therein lay the problem. *I can't afford to go anyplace you could take me.* Jani reached up to stroke the shuttle's smooth underside. *And anyplace I want to go, you'd stand out like a boil.*

She left Lucien and the pilot as they began the preflight walkaround and set off on her own inspection. She passed along the short line of shuttles, looking for signs of gold striping on the right side of the entry door. Customs' scarlet letter, a sign to all that dockscan had turned up something suspicious and you'd been boarded and searched. Most ships sported at least one such badge of infamy. Law of averages dictated you'd get nailed at least once if you flew long enough. Two or three meant bad luck or a lousy ship's clerk. More than that meant stupidity or bloody-mindedness.

No stripes, however, could mean one of two things. It could mean the ship was brand-new, too young to have a record with Customs. Case in point, Lucien's ship.

Or it could mean the ship had changed hands recently. New owner meant a clean bill of regulatory health for the vessel involved. New owner could mean someone anxious to keep it that way. Someone unfamiliar with the law of averages.

Jani stopped before the first vessel she came to that had no stripe. A few reentry blisters marred the polycoat skin—other than that, it appeared in good shape. A serviceable shuttle. Older model. "Hello," she said to the pilot, who was in the midst of his own walkaround.

The man looked up from his recording board. A serviceable face. Older model. "What do you want?"

"Nothing." Jani smiled. "Just stretching my legs." She sidled up to him, peeking over his shoulder at the board display. Standard preflight checklist. She spotted three coding mistakes in the first four entries. Nothing that would interfere with the actual piloting of the vessel, of course. But Treasury Customs didn't give a rat's furry ass whether a pilot could hit his mark on an ocean float blindfolded. If that pilot could not fill out his forms properly, that pilot would live to regret the oversight.

The man tensed when he realized he was being watched. "Is there a problem, ma'am?"

Jani shrugged, backed off. Kept smiling. "Just checking out your coding."

The man's Adam's apple bobbled. "What's wrong with my coding?"

Jani pointed to the first entry. "You've entered takeoff data on a docking line. When the board tries to calculate your flight stats, you'll get an error message."

"So I'll just erase and reenter."

"If you don't code the deletion, it won't recognize your erasure." She took the board out of his hands. "You need to give it a reason, so that when you download the data to Luna dockscan, it will read 'entry error, deletion because of such and such, reentry.' Otherwise, it just sees an unexplained mistake. Being a Cabinet system, it thinks, sloppiness. Then it thinks, sloppy incompetent or sloppy on purpose? Then it calls a human.'' She activated the stylus and enacted the change. ''A Customs docking inspection is a hell of a way to start the day.''

''It's just a mistake.'' The pilot watched Jani make rapid multistep entries without a hitch. ''You know this stuff, huh?'' He rubbed his chin. ''Have a look at the rest of it, if you don't mind.''

It was so easy, Jani at first suspected a sting, a crackdown on non-Registry clerks. The manifest, however, proved to contain the sorts of convoluted, ingenious errors usually executed by someone who knew just enough to be dangerous. The look on her face must have alarmed the pilot. He started to say something as she handed the board back, but she cut him off with a headshake and an absent ''G'night.'' She turned, started to walk away, counted. *One. Two. Three. Do you want*—?

''Do you want a job?''

Jani stopped, turned back, pretended not to understand.

''Only if you need one, of course. But if you don't, you know, I'd pay for your time. I can get you back here tomorrow. If you need to get back.'' He stuck out his hand. ''My name's Zal.'' He approached gingerly, his face reddening. Obviously not the type to solicit strange women in shuttleports, but honest working-class fear had made him desperate. ''Take you to Luna. Or farther. I'm starting a new transport business with my brother. He's handling the registration up there.'' He waved in the general direction of Earth's only natural moon. ''We sure could use the help, though. Someone who knows how to fill out all these blasted forms.''

The deal was cut quickly. Zal had been too relieved at the thought of handing off clerical duty to ask Jani her name, which was fine with her. It would give her time to think of one.

The stripped-down interior of this shuttle couldn't compare with the one in which she'd arrived a little over a week before. She strapped herself into her seat, stuffed her duffel into the grapple rack beneath, then started plowing through the manifest revisions. As the low powers rumbled to life and the shuttle taxied toward the runway, she twisted in her seat to look out the port. Lucien and his pilot had split up and were darting from vessel to vessel, accosting everyone they saw. Then the shuttle turned, and they disappeared from view. Within minutes, takeoff acceleration drove Jani into her seat.

"Sorry, Lucien. I just don't like being herded." She felt a pang of guilt that she hadn't said a proper good-bye after all he had done for her, but it soon passed. She liked him. Therefore, they would find one another again. She could adopt Nema's attitude, use it to keep her warm tonight.

Her old teacher's gift glinted in the cabin light as she wrote. Jani glanced out the port again as the shuttle banked over Chicago on the way to its exit corridor. It struck her how the ring's glittering red stone mimicked the lights of the city below. And foretold the lights of the cities to come. Wherever they were.

EPILOGUE

The stylus moved across the blank parchment. Beneath the moving tip of the writing instrument, the curves and whorls of High Vynshàrau appeared as though demon-written.

It is only science, Tsecha thought as he read his words, reconsidered, and made changes. Pro-dye impregnation. Ultraviolet light. Delocalization of electrons. So dull, such lucid explanation. He preferred to believe the words appeared on the paper's surface by magic, the work of demons.

His Temple and his Oligarch, if they could have read what he wrote, would no doubt have agreed.

> *. . . for humanish ways are not so different from ours.*
> *A piece of clothing. A color of eye. An intonation. Such*
> *are all that separate us.*

He frowned, stylus poised above the newly inscribed phrases. So obvious, the ideas. Did he really need to explain such?

"Steven is beyond this." He sat back in his favored chair, allowed it to stab him in the usual places, and meditated on the stark simplicity of his room. Yes, his Mr. Forell had come along quite quickly. But then, so eager had he been to learn. He had petitioned Tsecha personally for instruction in Vynshàrau document systems, saying he could not hope to further his Interior career without such specialized knowledge. Of course, Tsecha had not believed him. Not when he pulled

Angevin into the meeting room after him like a reluctant youngish, and demanded Tsecha tell him the story of his Captain.

Yes, Steven had proved most seemly. So open to new thoughts. Almost as though Hansen had fathered *him*, and not Angevin. . . .

"I will not ask." Tsecha contemplated a carved bloom that rested in a wall niche opposite his desk. Humanish were sensitive to questions of parentage, and he did not wish to test his Steven's loyalty so soon. Not to mention his Angevin's temper. Best some things be left between the lines, for now.

This I know as fact, from experience. As always, I only write that which is already known, simply unacknowledged.

Instruction, at times, proved challenging. "Steven accepts as Hansen did, while Angevin fights . . ." Tsecha bared his teeth. "She fights as my Captain does." His Captain, who could read his writings as well as her born tongue, and who understood their meanings all too well. Where was she now? Lucien offered his guesses, of course. Such was his way, to never admit to not knowing. But he had misplaced her at the shuttleport, and his weeks of futile searching had left him morose and prone to sarcasm.

"My Captain is quite skilled at being misplaced, and truly." First by John Shroud, then by Anais Ulanova, and now by the odd lieutenant. How wondrous to be so unknown to so many. To be able to evade so well.

She can never be captured. She will live on, and lead on, into a time so different than this. This, too, is known but unacknowledged, for fear of the future prevents its recognition. This, of all manners, is the one of humanish adopted by idomeni. This is foolish, as I have written before. As I will write again. Until it, as my dead Hansen used to say, "sinks in."

Tsecha continued to trace stylus over parchment. In another room, much as this one, he had written such essays for two other humanish, instructing them how the universe would change. *So it began then.* So would it continue now. Until all would be revealed. One page at a time.